MW01143951

Wicked Initiations

A NOVEL BY

Jennifer Rahn

DRAGON
MOON
PRESS

ACKNOWLEDGEMENTS

Deep thanks for the help and support of my friends and critiquers:

Melanie Smith-Napier, Heidee Stenner, Jean Melax, Nicole Aippersbach, Bean, Tim Reynolds, Sue Allyson Campbell, Dr. Laura Gauthier, Dr. Tom Kim and Dr. Tessa Campbell.

Thanks to Gabrielle Harbowy for keeping me out of trouble.

And always,

JD Williams

&

Gwen Gades

Thank you.

DEDICATION

Für Oma

PROLOGUE

DISRUPTED SLEEP

WHEN ALEKSEI WAS VERY *young, still thin and naïve, he followed his father to the University to view an anthropology display. He hadn't been invited, but his parents always approved of education and no one else had any reason to discourage his participation. Dressed in princely black velvet with gold buttons and chains, he stood very close to the professors and listened as hard as he could, but already knew he'd never be a scholar. No one noticed the dark little boy as he drifted away to lean over the edge of a pool in which white and pink lotus flowers grew. The stones that formed the sides and bottom of the pool were black onyx, and the clear water adopted their colour.*

Bored, the boy fantasized of a woman with blue scales over her skin and delicate fins drifting from her shoulders, slowly writhing towards him through the liquid depths—something from his dreams, a water woman who would come and tell him stories of what it was like to be completely free from all expectations. Daydreaming was much more engaging than the meaningless words of old people.

The mermaid was becoming more and more real, causing the surface of the water to ripple gently from her movements. She swam right up to him and opened her acid-green eyes to stare him in the face. Aleksei was startled into full alertness, and jerked back. When he looked again, she was still there. Had he dreamt her into existence? He glanced about to see if anyone else noticed this newcomer, but before he could call out to his father, the woman spoke to him wordlessly. No sound was made, yet his mind was locked in the overwhelming desire to reach forward and take the small vial of purple drug from her fingers. Try as he might, he could think of nothing else but to take the vial, snap it open and raise it to his lips...

And when the tiny draught was finished, the boy saw that it was not a woman at all, but a black and green nightmare that lay in the water and grinned at him with vicious, orange teeth. He tried to pull himself away from that thing and the dirty grey psychic tentacles it sent into his mind, probing for thoughts to pull at and twist about. Unable to move, desperate to break free, Aleksei finally found something he hadn't known was within himself. His vision went black and he had the sensation of moving through dark aether. He was alone in darkness, except for a metal triangle lit by blue that was rushing up before him. He passed through it, and found himself cast into an endless tumble of voices and powerful emotions.

The dark grey tentacles still clung to his imaginary hands and feet, no matter how hard he flailed.

How do I break free? *his mind screamed into the confusing swarm of brilliant golden auras.*

Free? You?

That's a long wait.

Why does he ask this?

They always want to know.

You, Aleksei, can only continue. You do not break free. It will eventually end, but you can help it along by finding your pure continuance.

Find your pure continuance, and help that break free instead.

Antronos...

Yes. That one.

Not so pure.

By the end of it, no.

Difficult, but it can be done.

So many different levels to consider.

You go, Aleksei. We're sorry for what's happened to you, but there's really not much we can do about it now. You'll just have to find your way.

Yes. Continue.

That's all.

Here's a push!

Aleksei slammed back into his body and sat heavily onto his heels, finally able to lean away from the pool. Feeling sickly, he quickly stood up, wiped his hands on his trousers and moved towards the group of scholars, hoping his father had not noticed. He didn't want to disappoint his parents with his foolishness yet again.

There is no need to wake, just come. I call, you come. It has always been thus since you accepted my poison, and you irritate me by pretending otherwise. A vial of purple venom was snapped open and poured onto the sand, strengthening the summons.

Night had fallen, its reddish darkness resting over the sandy wasteland of the Desert. There was no sound or motion, just a dim glow marking the edge of the horizon of the endless grit that concealed many things in its depths: forgotten cities, forgotten men, and temples that wished to be forgotten. In this barren expanse one could do as one pleased without interference by those who lived in the underground tunnels and feared the Voice of the Desert. Their worries, although convenient, were foolish. Of course the Desert could speak strange things directly to one's mind, but one didn't have to listen.

The Priest muttered to himself, annoyed that his summons still had not been obeyed, and turned to trudge back down a staircase that was disguised to look like nothing more than a hole in the sand. In the heavy gloom of his underground lair, a beast of burden lay curled asleep on its pile of straw. A rope was looped around its neck, and was used to pull the donkey roughly from its caged bed.

The stupid animal, skittish from the smell of its eviscerated brethren that lay around the exit of the cavern, balked annoyingly and pulled against the rope, braying in protest. The Priest had no patience for it, and struck the donkey's rump with a stretch of barbed wire. It jumped forward, suddenly eager to run up the sandy stairs.

Two experiments would be performed tonight: the rather trivial matter of making a beast from a man, then using the observations of the process to attempt the more complicated reverse of making a man from a beast. The Priest led the donkey through the air of the strange, red night to where the rock face of a cliff was cut away horizontally to make room for his temple, and where a long knife lay waiting. Tonight was the Night of the Third Moon, which meant nothing to the Priest, but it was considered by many to be a time of new beginnings, when fortune tellers always pretended to pull the card of Death; a good time to start a business, a good time to marry, a good time to die. The donkey was led through the temple to a mural wall of bronze and black metal, and tied to a post. Its hooves clacked against the marble floor; it seemed frightened of the runes painted in white around its feet. It glanced fearfully at the fire pit and tried to shy away from it, but the rope would only pull so far.

The Priest left the temple. A few hundred metres away, he sat down in the sand and emptied his mind. A few stones that had been painted with runes were taken from his pocket and strewn across the grit in front of him. He meditated for a few moments, then looked up to see that his other subject—the once-small boy who had daydreamt next to a pool of flowers forty years ago—had finally come without being called a third time. Covered in a long black cloak that swung over black armour, lurching as he stumbled forward, the subject approached until the rune stones were directly under his feet, and fell. His human spirit lifted into the aether while his animal body lay in the sand. Streams of purple venom dripped from his black eyes and over his cheeks.

The Priest blew a few dusty grains from his palm into the air. The spirit of the man coalesced around them in a whitish cloud, then solidified into a pebble that dropped into the Priest's hand. He quickly drew on it with ink; a series of runes to ensure that his other subject would never be able to attack his master.

Join with the Desert, the Priest whispered to the man's physical form, then waited. Sand and flesh merged, temporarily allowing his test subject to merge with the larger entity of the Desert, and the Desert to know the directed consciousness of a man. The merged construct lying in the sand smiled, still dripping purple from its face, and pulled itself upright. It suddenly twisted to the side and leaped onto all fours, bounding through the night. Time to hunt or mate, or both. It didn't matter which, to the Priest. All would be interesting, and useful for his understanding of the process. He would collect his data from the body later. A series of syringes and vials were already set up, waiting to hold the biopsies he would take back to his lab.

Why don't you *come be with Us?* the Desert asked him. The Priest ignored it. He preferred to be the only one in control of his brain.

The whitish sandstone that still rested in his hand was carried back to the temple, and the heat from within was welcoming; the Desert had grown cold and lost its red light. The marble floors and ceilings blocked out the noise of the wind, and the yellow glow of the fire pit cast pleasing shadows. Its sooty smell was an agreeable change from the acrid, dusty wind that was rising outside. The donkey had lain down, its eyes blinking slowly.

Water was the element closest in form to the liquid properties of the human spirit, so the Priest crushed the white stone to let the soul of the other unravel from the sand and hover just over a small, rune-inscribed trough filled with its worldly kin, where it would feel the most stable and least likely to seek out the pulsating river of blood that normally anchored it to its host body. He examined the soul closely, looking at its shape, strata, and various levels of awareness. It looked like a pulsating ball of layered golden light, with nuances of pink and orange swirling within it. Hints of the purple venom also stained it, twisting through the layers like dark worms.

When the Priest was fairly certain he knew the basic form of the human soul, he picked up the knife, let his own energies run the length of it, murdered the donkey and pulled its baser auras forward to lock them over a second trough before they could slip away. This would be a satisfying experiment. He had wanted to try such a thing for a long time.

With carefully controlled patience and ignoring the braying, psychic screams, the Priest began to carve the spirit of the donkey into one of human form.

PART I

VLADDIR, THE KING

V LADDIR WAS RUNNING FOR his life. His knees buckled beneath him, sending him sprawling as his feet hit rock at the bottom of the embankment. Clutching his splintered wrist, he fought to keep his grief from erupting out of his mouth with the blood he coughed all over his chest. He heard Taalen scuffling behind him and tried to stand, but his legs collapsed again, leaving him crumpled in the dust like some broken invalid. His ash-grey hair fell into his face, momentarily blinding him until Taalen roughly grabbed his armour by the leather straps crossing his back and jerked him to his feet. The army commander didn't bother with the niceties, dragging Vladdir across the small pit of shale to an outcropping covered with brush and shoving him unceremoniously beneath the prickling branches.

Taalen crept to the other side of the pit, pretending to peer over the edge as if he had no idea where the Aragoths were. It was a ploy to draw the attack from Vladdir, whose shame burned bitterly with the blood welling up from his lungs.

Taalen will live, he told himself. *He was born to this.*

Two Aragoths came silently to the edge of the pit. Their grey rockskin armour covered them to the neck in what looked like jagged pieces of slate, making them seem like the stone dead that sometimes rose out of the Desert sand. Barbed chains swung from the back of their weapons belts as they moved, yet made no sound. Both warriors were dark, their skin mottled around the temples and jaw with the ink of smudged runes, their hair falling like tattered shrouds to their waists, and their eyes nearly consumed with the black irises given to them by their lord, Ilet. Vladdir was sure these creatures and their master had been spewed into existence by the Desert—they had appeared suddenly and begun the war without demands or negotiation. All they seemed to want was to kill everything that moved.

One of the Aragoths gestured towards Taalen like he was an oblivious garden pest; he still pretended not to see them. The other raised his spear and threw it at Taalen's back. Taalen immediately ducked and rolled over the shale, striking one Aragoth in the head with a thrown dagger, and the other in the chest with a crossbow bolt.

The one hit by the dagger howled in pain and ripped the weapon from his skull, still standing. The bolt had ricocheted off the rockskin of the other Aragoth, who arrogantly stepped into the pit, unsheathing his sword. Taalen pulled a pair of duelling knives from his leg sheaths and scuttled into a combat pose. The Aragoth struck at him single-handedly. Taalen barely deflected the blow. One of his knives broke at the hilt, and the Aragoth's blade severed his thumb. Vladdir struggled against the cough building up in his chest and the urge to scream his frustration and fear. He knew if he gave his position away, Taalen would be so enraged he might kill Vladdir himself.

The Aragoth still standing at the edge of the pit threw Taalen's dagger back at him, catching the commander in the ball of his shoulder. Taalen wrenched in pain and missed his parry, both arms now injured. His opponent grabbed the front of his armour, dragging him off balance and forcing him to kneel. The Aragoth lifted his sword and angled the edge against Taalen's neck.

"Where is your king?" he asked.

"In the tunnels," said Taalen.

"We've flushed your tunnels with magma. Vladdir fled. Tell me where he is. Perhaps I will allow you to become bonded to Ilet."

Taalen spat at him. The Aragoth slit his throat.

"Useless," he said, wiping his sword against his leg before sheathing it. "Not worth bonding." He climbed back to his fellow, who was grinding the heel of his hand against his forehead, swearing vilely. "Ilet will heal you."

Vladdir lay silently shaking as they left, terrified that he still might be found, and angry with shame that Taalen had stayed because of him instead of running for dear life. His legs were growing numb and cold as he absorbed the shock. His soldier had been dispatched so quickly. How many more of his men would they hunt down and slaughter—or worse, bond?

The Aragoths couldn't have wandered far. Vladdir attempted to combat his self-loathing by crawling out from his hiding spot and dragging himself towards Taalen until he could brush his hand and weep against the still-warm hair. Half of him was concerned that coming out into the open was a premature and unnecessary risk that could make Taalen's sacrifice pointless, the other argued redemption by exposure to possible danger for the sake of this dead man, who had been one of the last to show him any loyalty. Without him, Vladdir was nothing but empty.

The Desert's heat seeped into his brain as he lay for long minutes, flushed in misery, filling his mind with searing white and fever. Slowly, words coiled out of his discomfort: *Why should you die as well? You can take Taalen's strength. You are entitled, as king.* He raised his head and looked at his trembling fingers, smeared with crimson. The blood was warm. He felt hungry. His mouth was already filled with the cloying flavour of copper and iron. *Why not have a little taste of someone else? See how you like it?*

Shocked, Vladdir tore himself away from such thoughts. Since childhood the Desert had instructed him thus, nearly driving him mad. His nurse had encouraged the madness; his father had tried to beat it out of him. The nurse had been executed. He had learned to hide the cannibalistic desire from others, but it had never left him. He was an unworthy King. Ragged sobs burst from him with a fresh spattering of bright, red blood. Perhaps it didn't matter. He might also be dead in a few moments. He turned his palm downward to hide the blood and stared at his own hand like it was something not attached to his arm. His eyes locked on the tattoo that marked him just past his wrist—the triangle sigil of the House of Dir. He was not the last. How could he lie here, complaining of abandonment, when there was still one last chance for him to correct all that his father had hated about him? *Get up, man. For the sake of your child, get up!*

Vladdir got to his knees, fighting a nauseating swirl of vertigo, and sat down again. He didn't know if his daughter Hailandir was even alive, and he found he didn't want to know if she were dead. And then there was his wife, Arlendan. She had been so cold towards him since the coming of Ilet, more than he could rationalise by telling himself she had just been afraid. Arlen did not want him. Perhaps she never had. The thought of facing her resentment was overwhelming.

You're right, Vlad of the House of Dir. Die, then, and become part of Us.

No! Locking down the part of his mind that craved oblivion, Vladdir pulled the dagger from the commander's shoulder. He had already suffered too much in order to resist the Desert just to lose to it now. Clumsy because of his injured wrist, he cut a small lock of Taalen's hair and tucked it into one of the many small pockets outside his vest. *If ever I have another child, he will bear your name,* he promised silently, and finally struggled to his feet. At the edge of the crusty pit, he paused and gazed around blearily. Several pairs of Aragoths were scouring the surface, as they had the tunnels. He watched them move in tandem with their peculiar stilted march, stopping to lazily poke at brush and turn over stones, as if any of the tunnel-dwellers could have hidden there. The dusty wind of the Desert teased their dark hair, the only blots of colour in the grey of the otherwise barren wasteland. None of the Aragoths had turned back to repeat the sweep in the opposite direction. Not yet, anyway. Keeping low, Vladdir clambered over the edge of the pit and struggled through the sand. If he could make it over the small rise, either he would be out of sight of the searching Aragoths, or in clear view of the next passing group. He supposed he could always pretend to be fully dead if any did see him.

None were there. Trying to feel grateful, Vladdir stooped a little less and broke into a cautious limp, gritting his teeth against the grinding of his cracked ribs. When they had fled the last tunnel stronghold, Taalen had planned for the army to regroup in the Desert Plains. The designated area was seemingly out in the open, but several people could be hidden within the large cracks in the rock that magically shifted position with the Desert's whimsy. While inside the crevices, one did not perceive their motion, but on the surface, the openings writhed with apparent malignancy. It was risky, as no one understood how or why the Desert made the Plains rock change, but better than facing the Aragoths on shifting sand.

The evening clouded into night, bringing with it dust storms and flashes of lighting. Vladdir's shallow breathing was made more difficult by the swirling dust and icy cold Desert wind. The sand heaved beneath his feet in waves, and a ball of electricity shot from the sky, striking the ground several metres in front of him. He dropped to the ground in fear as the brief illumination showed him four or five grey figures stumbling in his direction. A moment later, he heard them begin an eerie, low-pitched wailing and could see their desiccated forms writhing in a slow dance as they came closer. *Just Desert Ghouls. How I hate the surface!*

The presence of Ghouls meant the Plains were near. For whatever reason—perhaps they had died there—the Ghouls always returned to the cliffs surrounding the Plains after going on their stumbling marches. They were pointless creatures that were oblivious to the world, and the world to them. At any rate, if he were lucky, they would distract nearby Aragoths and give him some cover.

A gap in the Earth widened before him, and Vladdir gratefully slid down into one of the many deep, writhing cracks, careful of his injured side and wrist. He sobbed in relief, as the sound of the wind was shut out enough to let him hear the faint echo of voices. As he moved forward, the darkness was interrupted by the flickering of torchlight.

An abrupt hush fell, and he was about to call out that he had arrived when the screaming started. Vladdir lurched toward the sound, only slowing as he drew near enough to peek around the edge of the crack he had run through. Two Aragoths had found the meeting place of the tunnel dwellers. One had been felled by the hail of stones being thrown at him, but the other had already killed three soldiers, and now took hold of a child.

"Stop!" the Aragoth shouted, pulling the child into the air. The tunnel dwellers, some crying, let the rocks slip from their fingers.

"The child will be dead anyway," someone shouted. "Let's take them now!" Vladdir rubbed the grit from his eyes and blinked at the speaker. It was Brin, one of his subcommanders, one of the most ruthless.

"Please, no!" said a tunnel dweller, reaching for Brin's arm. The child's father, Vladdir supposed. Slowly, as quietly as he could, he pulled Taalen's dagger from his boot and rolled it in his uninjured hand until the grip felt sure.

Taking a deep breath, Vladdir lunged forward and thrust the dagger as hard as he could towards the Aragoth's head. The pain of the motion was sudden and overwhelming, threatening to force him to unconsciousness. The fallen one shouted and his opponent turned, just as Vladdir had hoped, giving him a clear path to stab the Aragoth's eye. With the blade buried to its hilt, Vladdir felt the Desert's lust surge within him. *Anger/hatred/desperation.* This time he welcomed it. Using the dagger for leverage, he shoved the Aragoth's head backward and gave in to what the Desert wanted, sinking his teeth into the beautiful, pulsating artery snaking through the other man's neck.

At last! Vladdir! How long have you denied Us? The Desert rejoiced and poured into him as he fed on more than blood, filling himself with Fire. Passion. *Confusion.* The Aragoth's body withered and crumpled beneath his lips, and he felt his ribs start to fuse and heal, absorbing the Aragoth's strength. His vision pulsed red as his first victim fell from his teeth and he turned to the next.

Kill the other! Feed again! the Desert screamed in his head. The second Aragoth had lurched to his feet and was swinging his blade. Vladdir jerked Taalen's dagger free and placed the flat side of it against his other palm, raising it to block the attack. His still-injured wrist gave when the blow fell, and the Aragoth grinned in Vladdir's face as the steel sank deep into his shoulder, cutting off all sensation. For a moment they stood nose to nose, while Vladdir tried to understand why his wrist had stopped hurting, and why his entire left side seemed to be missing. The Aragoth tugged downward on his hilt, trying to force the blade further. The Desert twisted in Vladdir's stomach, making him sick, making him realise that he had succumbed to the failure his father had predicted. *He had swallowed another man's vile, putrid blood.* He vomited it into the Aragoth's face, then stumbled backward and fell, watching in horror as the dark mess of half-congealed substance twisted and stretched into the rough approximation of a headless doll. It flailed its gooey limbs for a moment, then rapidly tore chunks of the Aragoth's flesh from its head until all that was left was a screaming bloodied skull. It fell silent when the blood-creature jumped down its throat, continuing to destroy it from the inside.

It lay still now, the bones glistening shiny-red. Leaning against the rock with his uninjured shoulder, Vladdir shut his eyes tightly and wished the Aragoth corpses would go away. He felt the Desert shift and respond to his thoughts, pulling the remains of both dead Aragoths down into the sand. He opened his eyes and saw his people staring at him, some with awe and some with disgust. None moved forward to help him. Looking down at himself, he was unable to see much other than blood and steel. He tried to force the Aragoth blade upward through the deep wound in his shoulder, and then found it was much easier to simply pull it out. His shoulder still did not hurt, and as he stared at his injured fingers, they would not move. The ends of his severed collar bone ground together as he somehow stood upright, shaking, unable to take a step forward. He wanted something to ease his...*shame.*

"Arlendan?" he asked, trying futilely to focus on the faces before him, to see if his wife had survived the evacuation of the tunnels. He needed a connection with someone, needed a voice of reason to steady his mind, even if she were only to repeat to him the reprimands of his father. Anything to keep this uncertain agony from making him implode. Someone moved, but not toward him. A woman stepped into the arms of—he blinked—Brin?

"Arlen," he whispered. For a moment, she came into focus, her pale hair framing her even paler face, starkly contrasted against the dark blue of her shirt. Brin, swarthy and muscular, looked back at Vladdir like *he* was the one intruding on a private relationship.

"What have you done?" she asked. "Dripping with gore like some surface creature. By the Earth, you *are* of the Desert."

Vladdir tried to shake the murk from his head. Even though he had long felt Arlen's animosity towards him, he couldn't quite believe she would publicly speak to him with such contempt. Her expression was so contorted that she looked like a wax doll about to melt. He had told her of the Desert's whisperings in private, and as much as he knew she despised it, he had thought she was still a worthy queen, stoic to the world, and able to compromise her feelings for the sake of the kingdom. How many had she discussed his secret with? With Brin?

"You are my Queen." She turned her face from him, and a wave of dizziness almost swept him into unconsciousness. Couldn't she understand what he needed from her? He was so empty. If she didn't fill him with something, anything, even derision, the Desert would come and take him again. He could already feel it threatening to push its way into his mind. Would she not save him?

"Queen of what, Vladdir? Of Death? The Desert? I always knew you listened to it, but I never knew you had given yourself to it. You've broken every promise made to me. And now this."

"What...promises?" He struggled to think of any he had broken.

"Look at you. A *thing* that sucks the life out of its victims. Your kingdom was destroyed by your impurities. Your vile nature is what attracted Ilet to us. If I stay here long enough, that which contaminates you will destroy me."

"Then why are you here? You...you stupid woman! Together we are stronger! Look at how you nearly killed an Aragoth by yourselves! You came here to find strength in one another!" *Bloody House of Dan. They are all betrayers!* In irrational anger, Vladdir was glad he had let Arlen defy convention and not change her name to Dir. *As if that matters now.*

"No." Arlendan stepped backwards, pulling the subcommander by the hand. "I came for Brin. That was all." She turned and walked away.

Vladdir grew even angrier. Her condemnation and contrived broken promises were an excuse for Arlen run off with some catamite. "Where is Hailandir?" he shouted after her.

"You're already dead, Vlad. Your nation has collapsed. Accept it."

"Earth's Volcanic Guts, you are not going to keep my daughter from me!"

Hailandir won't redeem you, the Desert commented.

Vladdir shook his head to clear it. "Shut up!"

Hailandir loves Us as much as you do.

"SHUT UP!"

The other tunnel dwellers took a few parting looks, none with sympathy, as they too turned and walked away. Vladdir blacked out.

Sand is in my wounds. Gritty, gritty sand pours into the dried up cracks of my body and soaks up all my blood. I've become stone. So I sink into the Desert and become one of Its stumbling Ghouls. I am a Ghoul. I am rock, I am...I am...

Not dead.

So You tell me.

So you know all by yourself.

How can I not be dead?

It is your right, as King. We have told you this before.

I can't feel my arm.

Well, perhaps part of you is dead. Does it matter?

It matters, because I was once a man.

Too much of you still remains a man.

What would You have me be?

The Desert did not answer. Vladdir gradually became aware that the white, blinding light was the glare of the sun off the grit over which he stumbled, very much like a Ghoul. He stopped and looked at his wounded shoulder, which was indeed crusted over with a grainy layer of sand. The blood on his shirt had hardened to leather. Taalen's dagger hung from the fingers of his good hand. The fingers of his other hand still would not move and were mottled grey. He picked at the wound, and found the flesh had hardened to the point where it might have been stone. That was why he could no longer bleed. He prodded at his once-injured ribs, and found them also hard as rock. There was no pain. No sensation at all. The Desert was making him so very thirsty, and he had no more Aragoth to sup on. But then, why should he even pretend to still be alive, when Arlen had all but finished him off with her few words, disintegrating what was left of his station.

He stood until he nearly fell, and put a foot forward to steady himself, then his other foot. Since now he was walking again, it seemed too much effort to stop. He came across Arlendan, lying in pieces, half-buried in the sparkling dust. Tattered remnants of her blue shirt were sticking out of the sand, still attached to the shredded parts of her torso. *Desert dreams,* he told himself and tried to walk through the hallucination. His foot kicked against her head, and it shifted with realistic weight. Lurching like a monster, he swung his dead arm out of the way and leaned over to pick up the head. The stench convinced him it was real. Vladdir dropped it, too tired and weak to even feel sick or think too much of what she had fallen prey to. Aragoths, most likely. *And where are you now, Brin?* The subcommander was nowhere to be seen. Not even fragments of him. Vladdir pondered whether he should grieve for Arlendan, and concluded that she had probably been lost to him for months before the Aragoths invaded the tunnels. He knew she had not confided in him, but until last night, had not known how far the comfort she'd had from others had gone. *You probably weren't the only one, Brin,* he thought viciously. *Not the first, but certainly the last.* Perhaps the catamite had realised that and abandoned Arlen. Would have served her right.

Vladdir walked through the scattered remains of his wife's body, not caring that they sank into the sand as he passed. *What in Earth ever made me think I deserved to marry? So impure. Unworthy of the love of anything but this damned Desert. Hailandir, will I have corrupted you as well?* He kept walking, wondering where he was, what he was, and where he was going.

Nowhere, nobody, nowhere.

Vladdir gave in. The Desert entered him and didn't leave. It was done now. Vladdir the King had fully surrendered.

The Desert hadn't lied. By the time night had fallen, Vladdir had no choice but to wake up and accept that he wasn't dead, and wasn't going to be any time soon. His thoughts slowed down as the air around him cooled, and he found that it was becoming possible for him to keep up with all the feverish knowledge racing through his mind. He tried to extract his location from some nearby rocks, but grew frustrated when they would only tell him about the geological stratifications they had arisen from and how soon they expected to be ground into dust. He swore at them and tried to hasten their disintegration with his foot, but after a few moments abandoned the activity. Did it even make sense to speak to rocks? What was he trying to do? Damn it. He had known just a moment ago. That was it. He had to ask things so that he would know what he had known just a few seconds before. Vladdir stumbled along, watching the sand shifting beneath his feet, eagerly waiting for an important question to come to his mind so he could ask the sand. He stopped walking so that he could concentrate.

What the hell was he doing?

Oh, right. He was going to die, but he hadn't, and now he didn't know what to do about it. Why was he going to die?

Taalen had died.

The pain of the memory made him lucid for a moment, just long enough for him to realise that he was raging with fever and needed to find water. Earth, he felt rotten.

The sand before him was boiling and growing dark. Was it bleeding? Water sloshed over Vladdir's feet, giving him any icy shock. He fell into it, relishing the sensation of it running along his skin and sinking through his clothes. His mind cooled further, and really began to hurt. His skull felt like it was going to contract to the point where it would crush his brain within. He opened his mouth and drank some of the water. After a few moments, the flow stopped and let him rest. Perhaps he slept, he wasn't sure.

In the morning, the light pierced his eyes when he sat up and tried to see. He swore and wished for something to drink. Water bubbled up all around him, soaking his pants. Was this real? Vladdir scooped some of it up and drank. Tasted real. Maybe he was dead after all, and just didn't realise it. Was that possible? Something tried to answer his question, but his mind spasmed, not accepting the answer.

Still resisting Us, Vlad? Last night you weren't being so difficult.

"Who's there?" Vladdir twisted around, but saw no one. He got up and started walking towards...well, wherever it was he wanted to go. His stone arm swung and bumped painfully against his hip. He wanted to face this person who spoke in his head, always making him angry.

Yes, We have a body. Want to see it? Want to see Ilet? We helped make it with our sand and bones. Had a little water poured on it to give it life.

Vladdir wanted to move faster, and his head spun as his will forced itself through his body until the ground flew past his feet so quickly that it became a white, shining blur. The Desert guided him until he stopped in front of the strangest cave he had seen in his life. Stairwells were cut down through a rocky cliff face that had broken away, revealing two massive, completely straight, horizontal slabs of white marble, one spreading out across the floor of the crevice, and the other forming the ceiling, its farthest edge cut straight and jutting out from under the ragged rock of the surface. Vladdir climbed down to the entryway of the cave and saw that carved pillars held up the ceiling slab. These reached so far into the cliff that he could not tell where they ended. Fascinated, Vladdir approached slowly so that he could absorb all of this miraculous sight. He couldn't imagine how such a thing had been accomplished. None of his engineers or architects had ever made such a cave for him when he had been King.

You still are king, said the Desert. Vladdir ignored this. Where the ground transitioned from dusty sand to white marble, a thin trough of water ran clear and fresh. Vladdir stepped over it and was amazed that the air also changed, becoming instantly cool and silent; he could no longer hear the wind chasing itself around the hoodoos outside. It was as if he had walked through a portal.

The cave seemed to be empty. Vladdir walked for what he thought must have been a kilometre before he found a large box of some sort that had been placed on the floor. Another thin trough of water ran around this box. When he drew nearer, Vladdir was reminded of a tomb. The box was lined with red silk cloths and cushions, and within lay a dark haired man in white robes who sat up in surprise to stare at Vladdir. The man's face was as white as the marble surrounding them, and his blue hair was as dark as his irises, which almost completely filled his eyes.

"Who are you?" he asked.

"Vlad."

You are the king! Tell him so!

The man got out of his strange bed and stood before Vladdir, reaching out a hand to feel the air around him, but not making contact.

"I don't understand what you are," said the man.

"Who are you?" Vladdir asked him.

"Ilet."

"Son of the Desert," said Vlad. Something cold and evil wrapped itself around his heart as he stared at the long, blue hair. He had suffered greatly for the whims of this little poppy, who smelled strangely like a mule.

"I am the Desert," said Ilet.

"I don't think so," said Vlad, and struck Ilet across the face. "You tried to kill me. The Desert forces me to live."

Ilet turned back from the blow, holding his wrist to his bleeding lip. Red embroidered vines and flowers trickled down along the edge of his white tippet sleeve. Vlad stared at the beautiful contrast of the red against Ilet's white skin and felt his mouth watering. Should he? Was there any reason not to? After all, he was already damned.

It is your right, as king, whispered the Desert. *You can have him. We give you Our permission. Now that you're not resisting Us, We'd rather have you.*

Vladdir reached out with his good hand to take Ilet, feeling the Desert's lust building inside him again. Ilet's face contorted with realised betrayal and he recoiled, lashing out with an unseen bolt of energy that flung Vladdir backwards and sent him skidding across the smooth marble floor.

"Vlad?" asked Ilet. "Vladdir, crawled out of the tunnels? You think you can come in here and assault me?"

Vladdir was confused, suddenly unsure of the confidence the Desert had seemed to be feeding him. Was any of that real, or was he just crazy? The Desert never really talked to anyone, did it? That was just a fantasy he had as a child. His father had told him none of that was real.

Ilet had drawn a dagger from somewhere and threw it into Vladdir's chest. He stared at the slim, enamelled handle for a few seconds, musing that it didn't hurt. He pulled it out and saw that his blood welled up grey, then hardened into stone. *Well, perhaps crazy, but certainly not dead.* He stood up, tossing the dagger aside, and began walking towards Ilet.

"What are you?" Ilet backed away and threw another energy blast at Vladdir. This time, it tingled a bit, but that was all. Vladdir sucked it in, like he did the heat of the Desert. Like he had when he'd eaten the Aragoth.

"All right, then," said Vlad. "You be the Desert. I am King of the Desert, so that means you'll kneel to me." Somehow, this struck Vladdir as funny, and he began to laugh so hard his eyes watered and he had difficulty breathing. Oh, if only he could have done this right from the beginning, before the Aragoths had destroyed his home. What a joke.

"You're mad," said Ilet.

"True."

"I'll kill you."

"I would consider that a favour. When you figure out how, I'd like to know what exactly is required. I've already been beaten to the point where my bones have broken, almost chopped in half, starved, dehydrated, burnt by fever, and now struck by you three times. Curious, don't you think? I wasn't like this before. Before I..."

Before you had a drink with Us.

Ilet turned and ran. Vlad thought about appearing in front of him, and the Desert's whimsy came easily, making the floor of the cavern slide past his feet until he curved around Ilet's path and blocked his way. This was a convenient new skill! Perhaps his father had been wrong about consorting with the Desert.

"Where are your Aragoths?" he asked Ilet. "I find it strange that none of them are here to protect you. And why are you suddenly so weak? You were a mighty opponent. You destroyed my kingdom so easily. Something doesn't make sense. Come to think of it, why did you attack me in the first place? Your home is already so nice, why take mine when it was so inferior?"

Ilet did not answer, but dodged around Vladdir and continued to run. Vladdir coasted next to him, unsteady because he could not control his laughter, until they returned to the edge of the marble floor.

"Ah, there are the Aragoths." They stood in a line just behind the trickle of water that edged the cavern. Ilet pressed his fingers along a series of runes inscribed along the sides of one of the pillars and the mysterious air barrier dropped. Vlad could now hear the muttering voices of the Aragoths, feel the heat of the Desert wind blowing on his face, smell the stink of the sweat and blood on the rockskin armour.

The Aragoths ran into the chamber, raising their swords and whirling those hated barbed lariats that hung from their belts. Vladdir thought of Taalen, and feeling the Desert's power surge along the wave of his anger, raised his hands and wished the first line of them cut in half. The torsos of those Aragoths jerked in shock, slid from their legs and thumped to the ground. A second wave of Aragoths rushed in without showing any regard for their fallen comrades.

Vladdir was about to start laughing again. It was ridiculous, the contrast between how he had been unable to defend his forces before and how easy it was to cut down the Aragoths now. He coiled his mind for another strike, and then found his new powers had become stuck. He swung his stone arm upwards to block an Aragoth sword, barely avoiding having his throat slit. Another blade glanced off his temple, making blood flow into one of his eyes.

Now angry, Vladdir shook his mind free of whatever was holding him back (*something black and orange and green*) and flattened the Aragoths standing in front of him. He didn't even bother to see how they fell, but pushed past where they lay to find Ilet. He was stunned to see the self-proclaimed incarnation of the Desert kneeling in front of a strange man dressed in what could have been a professor's robes from a hundred years ago. A brass medallion marked him as some kind of priest. The man gave Vlad a thin glare through narrowed eyes and pressed together his fine lips. His head was shaved smooth and his skin had a yellow, oily sheen to it. One hand rested on the head of Ilet, who leaned against the Priest's leg.

Vladdir took a cautious step forward, all traces of amusement and insanity gone from his mind in the face of this new development. He had never heard of anyone controlling Ilet. The Priest gave a slight smile, and then made some subtle gesture. Ilet charged at him, transformed into a fanged wraith in a swirling mass of dark blue hair. Vladdir struck him aside once with his stone arm, then threw up a mental barrier when the wraith came at him again. Something pierced into his mind and he was forced to defend himself against this new attack, giving Ilet the opportunity to bite into the shoulder that was not stone. Vladdir screamed in pain as Ilet's venom burned into his flesh. His eyes met the Priest's, and he felt the strength of the other man's mind. Vladdir screamed again, this time in rage. Bringing the Desert's heat and whimsy into his body, he made himself dissolve into sand. He was lost and unfocussed in this new shape, unable to concentrate enough to make any sort of strike. He snaked the particles of his dust over to where the Priest stood and reformed his body with fist raised.

The Priest was gone.

Behind him, Ilet stood once more in human appearance. Without his tutor, he seemed unable to transform or attack, so he merely spat at Vladdir's feet. Vladdir tried to reach him with his mind, but the effort exhausted him. He charged forward instead. He would satisfy his urge to kill this spoiled pretender with his hands, and find his Priest-master later. Ilet's clawed hand raked away the skin of his neck, but Vladdir ignored this. Grabbing Ilet by the jaw, he pushed back the false Desert-Son's chin and bit into the alabaster throat. Insane joy filled him as he fed on everything that was Ilet. As he drank, he came to know that the blue-haired man was indeed formed of the Desert. A construct of water, sand, and an artificial consciousness that was made by...something. The empowering sustenance washed away his train of thought as it poured down his throat, expanding his awareness beyond anything he had imagined. He wanted more, and reaching through the Desert, his spirit found other beings—random entities that roamed the surface. The Desert dragged each of them into the temple, their life energies pulled through Ilet's body to be consumed by Vladdir. He didn't care if he drank in the entire world. He needed so badly to be filled, after Arlen and Taalen and Brin and...everyone he had known had gone and left him so empty.

Vladdir choked. He dropped the desiccated blue-haired husk and clutched his throat. Ilet looked sweeter than he tasted. After a moment Vladdir retched, trying to void himself of a strange, unwelcome presence. It wasn't Ilet; there was something else that he had swallowed. Looking around, he saw the scattered remains of shrivelled Aragoths at his feet. He had drawn their life essences into himself, along with that of numerous rodents, lizards and birds. And along with all these, he had absorbed...a tiny knot of grief that had come from somewhere else. Something small and tender. Like his tiny Hailandir. A life energy that had been completely undeserving of his vicious consumption. Arlen's last look of disgust flashed through his mind. Was this what he had promised her he would not do? *By the Earth, am I some insatiable demon now? Have I always been?*

Vladdir ran out of the marble cave and fell on his hands and knees in the dust. The tiny thing he had swallowed was somewhere near his heart now, and he could feel its meagre life essence being pumped away by the flow of his blood. He retched again, trying to bring up the thing he had not meant to eat, but it was too late. It had already been absorbed into himself.

Is my daughter gone?

He struck at his gut and tried to force up his last meal, until he fell asleep, weak and crying.

Vladdir woke when Arlendan shifted beside him and got out of bed. The skylight set into the ceiling of their sleeping cavern let great swaths of light press against the filmy curtains pinned around the frame of the glass, colouring the chamber red and purple. A small tug on a cord by one of the chambermaids released the cloth. A second furled it out of the way. Vladdir sat up and cast an uncertain glance at his wife, wondering how ambivalent her moods would be today. She turned as she stretched, casting him a sleepy smile. He smiled back tentatively. Sometimes her friendliness would only last a few moments—hours, if he was lucky.

"You know, Vlad," she said as she sat back down on the bed. "We should start thinking about having another child. We don't want Hailandir to feel lonely now that she's old enough to start being aware of herself. Being fussed over by Mauvis is one thing, and playing with Brin's daughter is another, but she needs a proper collaborator. One she can trust her entire life. One who would be closer than a friend."

Vladdir felt his heart soar at her words.

"Truly, Arlen?"

She gave him a quizzical look. "Of course. Was this not what you expected?"

Vladdir frowned as he examined the texture of the deep red quilt covering his legs. What had he expected?

"What of..." He didn't dare finish the question.

"The Desert?" Arlen asked softly. Vladdir cautiously met her eyes. She reached over to gently brush his hair back. "Hailan is purity. She is free from all that we are burdened with. She is our redemption. Does it not make sense to allow ourselves the blessing of another such creature? Perhaps a son this time."

Vladdir grinned. Then he felt himself jerk awake for real. He was in the Desert, not at home in bed; his head rested on flat rock, not a raised pillow, and sharp pains needled him around the base of his neck, reaching down through his legs.

I'm getting tired of this. His body felt dried out and encrusted in filth.

Sitting up, he pushed himself to his feet, realising at the last moment that he had used his stone arm. Looking at it in wonder, he clenched the rocky fingers a few times, then probed his shoulder and ribs with his flesh hand. His left side was still heavy rock and there was no pulse, but now he could control it. He swung it around a few times. On the last swing, the sand was blown up from the ground. What was this? There was no wind. Vladdir held out his stone hand again and willed the sand to move. It flew up before him in sandy sheets that rose ten feet in the air before sloughing back to the ground. Interesting. He next tried to move the rock he supposed lay under the sand. If the Desert would allow him to control the movements of large slabs of stone, like on the Plains, it could afford him a tactical advantage when hiding from the Aragoths. *Oh, right. I have no reason to hide anymore.*

Vladdir gave a frustrated sweep of his hand, and several stone skeletons shot out of the sand before him. He yelled in surprise and fell backwards. The stone Ghouls didn't seem to be aware of him, and after making a few half-hearted attempts at their usual howls, stumbled about aimlessly, finally tipping over and sinking back into the sand.

What in Earth? Am I now dead so that I can summon the undead?

I cannot live like this. I am not alive. I am a monster. I have to find a way to die! Things like me shouldn't exist! My father—

Excruciating pain shot through Vladdir's head. He shrieked and curled up on himself in agony.

WE WILL EXIST! screamed the Desert. *You've taken Our body into yourself and now you expect Us to die.* It shot fire into Vladdir's core, shredding every nerve in his body.

"All right," whimpered Vladdir. "All right." He would agree to anything to keep the Desert from striking him that way again. He carefully lifted his hands from his head and rolled onto his knees. The burning pain slowly throbbed away. He took a few cautious breaths and wiped the spittle from his chin, thinking as unobtrusively as he could, lest the Desert disapprove, that he wanted to get underground.

He wanted water, but didn't dare summon it like he had before. What might climb out of the sand now?

The Travellers' Oasis. He could go there. If there were any other survivors of the Aragoths, they might also go there. He could ask about Hailandir. But would the Aragoths have found the stopover spot and be waiting there for any straggling tunnel dwellers? *Were there any Aragoths left?* Maybe Vladdir had eaten them all. Even if he had not, they were no longer worthy opponents.

Walking seemed pointlessly tedious now. Vladdir hesitantly let loose his grip on his mind, and felt a little bit of the Desert's consciousness seep back into his brain. It did not assault him this time, so he cautiously tried using his new abilities again, envisioning the stone rings of the multiple wells of the oasis and deciding that he wanted to go there. The sparkling sand once again slipped beneath his feet, moving him with unnatural speed. He saw sunlight glinting off white rocks as he slid past naturally formed monuments. The air felt almost solid, burning his skin as he shoved through it.

Entering the sudden grey of the oasis cavern, he willed his movement to stop, and had to stumble forward to balance himself against the change of inertia as the Desert's whimsy dropped him onto the sandy rock. The coolness felt strangely uncomfortable, like the verge of a breaking fever. He leaned against one of the wells, and resting both hands against its edge, looked into the water, trying to steady himself.

Whatever forces were shaking the underground rivers, they made the surface of the contained liquid waver and tilt constantly while the ground was completely still. It was nauseating. Vladdir turned away from it and moved towards the tables at the back of the oasis cavern where great metal ladles were left for passing travellers. The sensation of trying to walk on an unsteady raft coursing down the underground Yrati River faded as the damp chill finally sank into him, and he felt slightly saner. A metal tube bearing the Seal of the Royal House sat on the table. Wondering if he hallucinated, Vladdir picked up the cylinder, unsealed the wax on the end and pulled out the paper within. The message was scrawled in Mauvis' nervous hand, and it seemed Vladdir's Chamberlain had been in a great rush, not to mention terrified. His normal eloquence had disintegrated into something overwritten and nearly comical.

My Dear King Vlad, Son of Dir: It is with utmost hope that I plead the Earth send me to meet you again. My King, if you should ever honour me with reading this, please know that I have kept your daughter, My Sweet Princess Hailan, with me. I beg your forgiveness for taking her from My Dearest Queen, but when the Aragoths came, I did not think to unite My Princess with her mother, My Queen. Indeed, when I looked about, the Earth was falling all about me, and there was no time to seek others. I quite simply took the child and ran. What could I do? By the Earth, may you read this and forgive me! I fear Queen Arlen may take me for an evil man who abducts children, and I assure you I am not! I would never harm any of the House of Dir, and pledge my eternal loyalty to you all.

Hailandir was safe! Vladdir tilted his head back and sighed with relief. When he had thought he had swallowed her, sucked her in with Ilet and the Aragoths, he must have been sick with Desert dreams. He must have imagined it. By the Earth, had he eaten anyone at all? Could it be all his impurity had been an illusion? But his arm was still stone. The Desert still coiled in his mind. Mauvis had probably written this before Vladdir had met with Ilet, which meant that maybe he *had* eaten...? Vladdir gave in to the ache in his knees and slid down to sit against one of the wells before continuing to read.

I have eternal faith that you will find this and read it, and when you do, My King, please find me hidden with the Yrati in one of their collection caves, where their medicinal fungi grow. It is a place of unpleasant smells, but I think the Aragoths do not know of it, and as I think I have already cracked my skull, I may need the Yrati's healing arts. Can the Aragoths read our alphabet? I do not know. They seem stupid enough, for all their great strength, so I shall risk leaving this where they might see it, but thus far, they have not molested our Libraries, so I shall comfort myself with the thoughts that if they do find it, they will have no interest in keeping it, and shall discard it where you may come across it.

At this point, the handwriting became almost illegible and Vladdir had to squint, tilting the parchment to the light coming in through the cave entry to read the rest.

I fear I may tarry no longer, Great Vladdir. The Yrati cave is on one of the small rivulets that empty into the ocean, the northernmost one. I have visited it frequently in order to purchase their medicines as freshly made as possible, and to inspect their horticultural husbandry skills, ensuring they never poisoned us by allowing contamination of their crops with something untoward. Thus while I know it well, I hope My King Vladdir should find it without much difficulty. They have a series of floating docks tethered to the rock in the underground portion of the river—about halfway across the Plains, were you on the surface. I shall keep watch for you, day and night, underground and on the surface. May we meet soon. Your Eternal Servant, Mauvis (Lord Chamberlain of the House of Dir).

Vladdir was surprised to realise that he was smiling. Trust constant Mauvis to be able to make everything seem all right, regardless of the crisis. Trust Mauvis to be more concerned with propriety, fungi and titles than with the Aragoths. Dear Mauvis never gave any indication that he doubted Vladdir's survival. With his pathological need to make sure he was clearly understood, would Mauvis not have written a second note and left it here if anything were to have happened to Hailan? With his heart lifted, Vladdir stepped out into the Desert heat and began to walk toward where he thought the underground river split into rivulets—usually they were traced on the surface by small rows of brush, so he was certain that they should be easy enough to find. As he walked, the sand swirled around his feet and up his legs, sometimes forming leering faces that tried to distract him from his good humour. He deliberately ignored them.

See if you can deny this, then.

A wind funnel reached down from the sky, teasing up a pillar of sand that wound its way closer, gradually resolving into the shape of a man with his black robes open and his bare chest glistening in the sun.

The newcomer's clothing fluttered as he strode forward, exposing a broad band of green embroidery lining the edges of the fabric. Vladdir tried to focus on the man's features to see if he was the same Priest that Ilet had leaned against, but his heart began to race, and he found he couldn't breathe. The memory of the sensation of Ilet's life pouring down his throat raised an unwelcome rush of pleasure from the pit of Vladdir's stomach and he began to fear he would be smothered by his own increasing excitement. Why was this strange Priest coming towards him now? Would he taste as good?

Earth! He had to get away before he contaminated himself again.

So you admit that you do want it.

Ignoring the Desert's taunts, Vladdir thought desperately about underground water. He felt an icy cold shock as cool liquid rose up around his feet and soaked through his boots. He forced it away and thought of himself going to the water instead of having it come to him. Immediately, he sank into the sand. The grit filled his mouth, nose and eyes, making him panic and scramble back up onto the surface, where he remained on his hands and knees, gasping for air.

Still not convinced of your kingship? Here. Let Us assist you in softening your mind to it.

A stone Ghoul climbed out of the sand next to Vladdir, and grabbing him by the hair, smashed his face several times against the ground. The Priest was getting closer. Already stunned, confused and in pain, Vladdir could hear him muttering some kind of insinuating incantation that pressed against all thoughts, telling him to sleep. Sleep and submit. Become the next Ilet.

You're going to have to use every last bit of your rightful power to fight this one off.

I will not submit.

That is as We wish.

I will not do as You wish.

Vladdir pictured Mauvis in his mind. He heard the Chamberlain's voice in his thoughts. He imagined Mauvis holding Hailandir in comfort and reading her to sleep.

This time he did not resist when he felt himself being drawn deep into the sand, and then the clay beneath it. He tried to imagine himself as one of the stone Ghouls, an illusion destroyed by the sensation of the Earth ripping at his hair and clothes as he moved forward, until he could feel and smell the water around him. The Earth progressively became more cold and damp and his head pushed upwards into clear running water. After a moment of muted panic, he was surprised that he did not drown. Other beings in the underground rivulet came towards him, swirling against his face as dark mists of black. He beat against them in alarm before realising that the creatures seemed gentle and calm. They gradually moved away after a few exploratory touches against his consciousness, and left him with the impression that they did not trust him.

It was peaceful here, almost as if serenity was radiating out of the rock that encased the water, permeating every part of Vladdir's mind as he wriggled free from the Earth. He felt cool, relaxed. Wouldn't it be nice to stay like this forever? No sooner had the thought entered his head, the water creatures darted towards his feet and pushed him towards the surface in a great bubbling rush. Excited screaming echoed through a cavern as his head broke the surface, and several priests in black robes came running across tethered rafts anchored to one side of the river. The interior was lit by rows of bioluminescent moss that were cultivated in tiers along the upper walls of the cavern, washing everything in pale blue light. Vladdir was pushed farther upward and towards the rafts by the water beings, until he could step from their support and onto the bobbing wood planks.

The Yrati stared at him with open-mouthed awe, then almost as one, knelt at his feet. Mauvis came running, his thin frame encased in the purple velvet he favoured—somewhat tattered but still stylish, with gold buttons flashing. His shoulder-length, curly brown hair was somewhat limp and grimy. The Chamberlain was grinning in delight, and after a moment of confused stumbling through the kneeling Yrati, piles of fish and tangled seaweed, managed to kneel himself without toppling over too many people.

"My King Vladdir," Mauvis gushed. "I knew you'd come! And now... now you've become one of *them!*"

Who?

Vladdir had pulled Mauvis up by the arm and a little apart from the still awe-struck Yrati.

"The Water Ghouls," Mauvis explained, somewhat bewildered by Vladdir's lack of comprehension. "The Yrati revere them. Surely you have heard of this, My King. In Yrati philosophy, water represents life. Unlike the dead Ghouls of the Earth, these ones live. They provide guidance and wisdom. It's because of them that the Yrati were able to repair my head so quickly." He turned about so that Vladdir could see a shaved patch at the back of Mauvis' head, and a few stitches. It seemed the Chamberlain's injury was not that serious, but Vladdir refrained from saying so.

"Please, Mauvis, tell me where Hailandir is."

"Yes! Of course!" The thin man hurriedly led Vladdir across a few of the rafts before stepping onto a narrow ledge of rock along the cavern wall. From there he wedged himself through a fissure in the rock, and disappeared. Vladdir followed him and found himself in a tunnel with a few inches of water along the bottom, lit by lamp bowls set in stands along the length of the corridor. He splashed after Mauvis, coming to an untidy garden of sorts, in a cave with a natural opening to the surface. Rough vines and brambles lined the cave, stretching upwards to the sunlight. Hailandir sat in the middle of the garden, dressed in frilly white, all chubby cheeks and blonde curls. She was playing with a piece of string while a female Yrati sat next to her, trying to wind the string on a bobbin.

Vladdir took a few steps forward, then knelt down. Some Yrati quietly hustled past him to whisper in the ear of the woman tending the child. She turned towards Vladdir with widened eyes, then rose to her feet, made a quick bow and departed. Hailandir looked up as the Yrati left, her brow wrinkling and lower lip starting to curl outward.

"Hailan," Vladdir called softly. She turned her head towards him, blinked in surprise, then got to her feet and tottered towards him uncertainly. He smiled at her and held out his flesh arm. She took another step forward, regarded Vladdir warily with one fist pressed against her mouth, then ran to Mauvis.

"Dear child," whispered Mauvis. "This is your father!" He tried to propel her towards Vladdir, but the girl dug in her heels and started to howl.

"No, Mauvis. It's all right. Let her stay with you."

"My King, I am sorry."

"Don't be. She's right to trust you, and I'm grateful you were the one to take her. It's enough right now to know that she is safe."

"Perhaps when you both have rested..." Mauvis' eyes strayed to Vladdir's stone arm and broken, bloodied armour.

"It's just as well. If you will comfort her, I need to talk to the Yrati."

"Of course—"

Vladdir turned away from Mauvis before he could utter his usual obsequiousness. The Yrati were hovering at one end of the garden, where additional tunnels led somewhere Vladdir hadn't seen yet. He was pleased that they didn't scatter as he strode towards them, or seem to be excessively nervous. One of them stepped forward and politely waited for him to approach, smiling but not fawning. He was of medium height and build, with light brown hair that fell to his waist, clean shaven, and his red and blue embroidered Yrati collar sat slightly askew.

"My Lord Yrati," said Vladdir.

"My King of Dir," he replied. "My name is Rayner."

Vladdir hesitated. "Is that a Temlochti name?"

The Yrati smiled. "No, my mother was a student of medicine, and named me after some famous northern pathologist. I, however, study geology. I also do a bit of the engineering work to make sure these caverns don't completely flood and drown us all."

"I see. You are not a healer then."

"No. But I can see that you need one. Would it please you to come this way?"

Vladdir fell into step next to the priest as they walked into one of the connecting tunnels, finding that he was comforted by this man's mannerisms. He thought he could trust Rayner to speak to him truthfully, and not just tell him things he wanted to hear.

"Are you the High Priest?" he asked. Rayner seemed too young for the role, but appeared to be in charge.

"Unfortunately we lost track of Dagnaum when the Aragoth raid started. Until we get him back, I'm the most senior member of our clan that is here. We know he's all right, we just need to find him."

"How do you know?"

"We can feel him." Rayner tapped his head as he said this.

"I see." Vladdir could feel the Desert coiled inside his own head, and wondered if the priest could sense how corrupt he was. As if to contradict this thought, the wave of gossip about his rising from the water caught up to the other Yrati who stood to one side to watch him pass. They broke into wide grins and knelt. It made a wedge of anxiety push up from Vladdir's stomach. He imagined feasting on them all as they smiled up at him.

"Rayner," Vladdir stopped and gripped the other man's arm. "I need to speak privately with you. I'm...I'm...injured, more than you think."

"Then we should go see the healers at once."

Vladdir shook his head. The other Yrati seemed too impressionable. This one appeared to have a good mind.

"Please just give me a few moments. I need you to understand me, and advise me in regard to whether I should even be here."

Rayner frowned. "Of course," he said simply, and directed Vladdir into a small side cavern with a metal table and set of chairs. The light in here was a washed-out iridescent blue coming from small tanks of bioluminescent fungi set into the walls. Rayner sent one of the younger members of his clan to fetch some tea. Vladdir's stone arm clunked uncomfortably against the metal chair as he sat down. When they were alone, Vladdir took a deep breath and looked up. Rayner was watching him intently, but not in a way that seemed judgemental or impolite. He was also completely unobservant of proper royal protocol, which in this case made Vladdir feel less shamed by the confession he was about to make. Here he could be just a man talking to a priest, not a king about to describe how far he had fallen.

"What do you see when you look at me?" he asked Rayner.

"I see a man deeply troubled."

"I mean my mind. You Yrati are renowned for your intuitive sensitivity. What do you sense there?"

Rayner sniffed and smiled slightly. "I'm afraid, Vladdir, that I don't know you well enough to have a good feel for your mind. Of course I know the minds of my clan very well, and my brothers and sisters who do practice healing can come to know their long-term patients well through repeated touch during treatment. But it takes time and physical contact. Or an extremely agitated mind. We can pick up very intense emotions from a complete stranger. It depends on how strong the feelings are."

Vladdir was silent for a few moments, oddly disappointed that his impurity remained hidden. He would have to speak it after all.

"Are you sure you're not ready to see a healer?" Rayner prompted.

"I need to tell you something. I've changed. My arm is stone."

Rayner frowned slightly, his eyes moving over Vladdir's chest and shoulder, but he remained silent, waiting.

"Your kinsmen seem to think I'm one of your Water Ghouls, but I'm not. I'm changing into an Earth Ghoul, one of the dead ones."

Rayner leaned back a little bit. Old fairy tales described a "stiffening disease" that was contagious. Vladdir hadn't believed it before, but now he was not insulted by Rayner's reaction.

"It gets worse."

Rayner's eyebrows went up.

"I am contaminated by the Desert."

"I take it you're not referring to being sand encrusted and having heat stroke."

Vladdir almost laughed. "I wish that were so." He hesitated again, not quite ready to say what he had done to the Aragoths. Rayner shifted and took a sip of his tea, apparently content to wait for Vladdir to gather himself.

"I...killed Ilet."

"Truly? I had heard he was undefeatable. This means the war is over!"

"No, there is another...man. One who controlled Ilet. I think he was some sort of priest."

"This is most interesting!"

"I...uh...also killed a number of Aragoths."

"By yourself?"

"Yes."

"Amazing! What of this other priest? Do you have any notions of who he might be?"

"I'm afraid not."

"But perhaps you can direct the army to hunt for him."

"That's another problem. I no longer have any soldiers left, or kingdom for that matter. Or a wife. Arlen is dead."

"By the Earth! My King Vladdir, this is extremely bad news." Rayner started to fidget helplessly. "What will you do?"

"Hailandir. I will rebuild around her."

"Of course." Rayner relaxed but still looked concerned.

"But I fear I must finish the Aragoths, and this priest, who I think must be their master."

"This is strange news. Everyone thought the master was Ilet." Rayner chewed thoughtfully on his lip for a few moments. "Is any of this confidential?" he asked.

"No, I intended that you tell this to your clan for me."

"Of course." Rayner started to get up.

"There's one other thing, and it's the worst part."

Rayner sat back down.

"I..." The words still wouldn't come. *I ate the Aragoths. At first they made me sick, but now I find them quite tasty.* Would the Desert strike him again if he told the truth? Vladdir took a deep breath, and decided he would not yet reveal everything.

"I used evil to defeat Ilet. It was an evil force. It came to me and I gladly accepted it in order to win. I think it has poisoned me. I know it has poisoned me. I don't know if this poison will spread, perhaps... perhaps it might cause your clan some hurt."

"Is this what caused your arm to become stone? This is what you need us to heal for you?"

Did Vladdir want to be healed? If he gave up the Desert now, would he be vulnerable to the unknown priest?

"I don't know. I just wanted you to warn your brethren. You must think me strange."

"Not at all. My King Vladdir, we Yrati avoid violence, but we're not so foolish as to think that the world can exist without it. This force has become a weapon for you, and you're not sure if you still have a war to fight. I understand you may not be ready to put it down. We can still try to ease your symptoms, if you'll let us."

"I need some time."

"Of course."

Rayner watched Vladdir's face intently, his head slightly tilted, his palms pressed down against the table with the elbows up, waiting to see if there was more news or if he could leave. Had Vladdir told him enough? His head was hurting so badly that he did not want to continue this conversation. Surely with Rayner's reaction to the mention of Earth Ghouls, the Yrati would keep close watch. So Vladdir smiled and nodded, and Rayner jumped up and went to his curious brethren milling just outside the cavern entryway. Thankfully they did not linger in the passage, and after a few surprised exclamations and a brief argument over whether it would be safe to return to the tunnels to search for Dagnaum, they ran off somewhere to consult some books on Vladdir's condition.

Feeling weary and very self-conscious, Vladdir got up and wandered into the passageway, thinking that perhaps Mauvis would be able to arrange a place for him to sleep, and might have some food. He wanted to impose as little as possible on his Yrati hosts and planned to leave once he was rested, after giving Mauvis clear instructions regarding Hailandir. If he were still going to be king, he had to put his people first and protect them from all things, including himself, while he rebuilt his kingdom. If he had to suffer with this Desert-Infliction then he would use it to—

A soft touch on his back distracted him from his thoughts. He turned and saw a tiny priestess gently prodding his back where the skin was fused to stone. The Yrati were obviously well-bathed people, but somehow always managed to appear dishevelled and untidy. This one had a mess of blonde hair obscuring her from brow to waist, and had to untangle her fingers from her own hair as she reached out to touch Vladdir. He stepped away from her and moved his stone arm out of her reach.

"Did your brother not warn you?" he asked. She unsuccessfully tried to push her hair out of her face and smiled up at him.

"About what?"

"I don't want to contaminate you."

"Oh, we're not afraid of that! Please come here."

Vladdir stepped back again, then found himself dancing away from the small woman as she chased after him and tried to grab his arm.

"My King Vladdir," she said impatiently. "We are *healers*. If we shied away when somebody sick came along, we'd never get any practice done."

"Please don't touch me."

The Yrati managed to catch hold of his flesh hand and in the brief contact, he felt her mind trying to reach out to his, sending *warmth/love/humour* in an attempt to calm him. Vladdir hissed and yanked his hand free. If he could see her thoughts, surely she could see his. The priestess seemed stunned, standing there with hands still outstretched, mouth open, blinking with surprise. She must have touched some of his impurity.

Or maybe she hadn't.

"I am *not* trying to invade your privacy!" she yelled, her expression clouded with indignation.

"Callie, please! This is no way to comfort a patient." Rayner came running at the outburst and cradled the smaller Yrati in his arms, rubbing her shoulders and nuzzling her hair. The little one took a deep breath and attempted to relax, but she still looked furious.

"I'm sorry," she said. "My King has a very strong mind. I wasn't expecting to get pushed off like that. But I really wasn't trying to do anything other than see how you were feeling," Callie explained earnestly. "I have to know in order to make you feel better. Normally I only read emotions and sensations of pain. I only know you were worried for your privacy because you thrust that thought at me."

Vladdir stared at the two Yrati and they stared back, still wrapped in an embrace. Their blatant affection stabbed at Vladdir more deeply than Ilet's dagger had, and a profound, raging grief crashed over him. He felt it slam against his liver, lungs, heart and eyes, making tears well up suddenly.

I am so alone. Arlen never loved me, Hailan doesn't trust me. I can't trust myself. I may kill everyone who comes close. By the Earth, I have to leave.

He was falling. The air had evacuated from his lungs, and black dizziness was enfolding him from all sides. Rayner and Callie were leaning over him, loosening his clothing, trying to help him breathe. The side of his face was being tapped as they yelled words into his ears, but all he could hear was some strange, very loud river that blocked out all other sounds. He tried to gasp for air, but was being strangled by sobs. Mauvis appeared from somewhere. He knelt and cradled Vladdir's face between his hands. The tightness eased somewhat, but didn't leave. He saw another Yrati load a syringe. He didn't feel it pierce his skin. Needing an anchor, he continued to stare at Mauvis, watching his lips move. After a few more moments, he began to hear words. Something comforting. He couldn't pay attention to anything more. His breath was coming more easily now. He leaned over to press his forehead against Mauvis' knees and wept. The release, so impossible before, felt good. Vladdir could feel that the Chamberlain had tensed and was now gingerly patting his back. The words being spoken to him still weren't clear, but Vladdir knew Mauvis was embarrassed. Of course. Why wouldn't he be?

Why don't the Yrati give me enough medicine to make me sleep?

Callie's mind was close by again. This time he did feel the needle.

Mauvis was there when Vladdir woke up. He watched his Chamberlain fussing over the hopelessly crushed nap of his velvet jacket and attempting to straighten his fitted grey leggings, muttering about the Yrati—who could concoct just about any medicine, but were absolutely useless at manufacturing any sort of quality laundry products, which was why they looked so sloppy all the time. They were clean, yes, but the most pustulent vagabonds surpassed them when it came to dressing properly. Mushrooms had better fashion sense. An onion could present itself better than an Yrati. Vladdir huffed with laughter, giving himself away. Mauvis' mid-brown curls bounced as his head came up, his expression vacillating between delight that Vladdir was awake and indignation that anyone could find his plight amusing. He seemed to quickly decide that Vladdir was more important than his clothes and came to kneel next to the thin padding on the ground that had become Vladdir's makeshift bed.

"My King, are you better?"

The simple question ended Vladdir's short moment of pleasure and the heavy grief of the last few days smashed down on him again. It had seemed less painful when he had been out on the surface, unsure of whether he'd even be alive the next few days, unsure if all he saw around himself was even real. Now that old, familiar Mauvis was next to him again, the contrast between what he had been and what he had become was inescapably obvious.

Vladdir didn't realise he was crying until Mauvis gently dabbed at his eyes with a small square of soft cloth.

"Again tears," Mauvis commented quietly. "You have cried several times in your sleep over the last few days."

"Days?" asked Vladdir. "Has it been so long?"

"Three days, yes. Princess Hailandir has been to visit you."

Vladdir tried to sit up and found his shoulder too heavy. Mauvis helped him with considerable effort, until he was shifted so that he leaned against the wall next to his bed. The stone arm was unresponsive to his attempts to move it, but the fingers twitched somewhat. Mauvis was watching him intently. The Chamberlain's mouth was working, like he wished to say something but was hampered by propriety. Vladdir sighed.

"Please, Mauvis. Speak freely. There is no more kingdom. I am not king of anything; merely, I hope, your friend. Can we not be honest with each other?"

Mauvis caught his breath and sat back. Vladdir expected him to retort with some affronted protest, but instead he asked, "Is it true, then?"

Vladdir raised an eyebrow and waited.

"In your sleep, you wept for Queen Arlendan."

"Rayner did not tell you?"

"I have been at your side the entire time. I did not speak with him. Only the healers have been in to see you. We talked of your condition, nothing else. So it's true, then." Mauvis stopped speaking, pressing his fingers to trembling lips.

He would cry for Arlen, she always dressed well.

Vladdir was ashamed of the ungenerous thought. Mauvis grieved more deeply than that, and at least he could grieve for a woman he had actually lost, while Vladdir was left grieving for a woman he never really had. After a moment the Chamberlain regained control of himself and took a deep breath.

"The Yrati tried to heal your arm. Unfortunately they were only able to make it smaller and stiffer. They aren't sure what to do to make it return to flesh. They tell me they have many ancient texts to consult, and it may take some time. This, obviously, is not a modern disease, but something so old that no one is sure how to cure it."

"They treated it? Is that why I cannot move it anymore?"

"You mean you could move it before? How is that possible?"

"I don't know. I feel weak. Perhaps that's why it doesn't respond."

"You haven't eaten in days!" exclaimed Mauvis, brightening. Fussing over Vladdir had always been one of his favourite activities. He seemed energized by the prospect. Within the hour, Vladdir was presented with a remarkably close approximation of what he would have been served in the Royal House before the invasion of the Aragoths. The service pieces were chipped or tarnished, the coffee watery and the meat substituted with some kind of ground fungi, but just having the familiarity of Mauvis' care already gave Vladdir much ease.

After a few bites, the warmth of the food spread through Vladdir's middle, then began to roil uncomfortably. He leaned back against the wall and breathed deeply for a few moments, taking a few sips of coffee. Thankfully, Mauvis had gone to fuss over Hailandir and wasn't around to be insulted or hurt by Vladdir's discomfort. He put the tray aside and quietly shuffled towards the garden cavern which opened to the surface. A female Yrati smiled and nodded at him as he passed her. He returned a faint nod, muttering that he needed some air.

At the far edge of the cavern, Vladdir found that a gentle slope had been dug into the soft Earth along the wall, and rounded stones were embedded to make convenient foot and hand holds. He awkwardly climbed to the surface, the stone arm weighing painfully on his shoulder, and found that the triangular ward stones the Yrati had set along the edge of the opening were rattling in the absence of wind. Apparently the Desert was restless.

Vladdir stumbled through his dizziness until he found a series of obelisks he could hide behind. The pain of his cramping gut had become excruciating, and within moments of crawling into the shade, he vomited his breakfast onto the sand. His stone arm was functioning again, he found, as he wearily shoved a pile of sand over his sick, then slumped against the rock. His head pounded too painfully for him to immediately make the return trip to the Yrati caves, so he let himself rest for a few minutes.

On the surface, the Desert's presence could be felt much more acutely; its heat, its turmoil, its power. Eventually the pain in Vladdir's head subsided and his mind cleared. The stone arm felt like it was part of him now, and he could move it with as much ease as his flesh arm. He thought about standing up, and without any muscular effort on his part, found himself propelled to his feet, his entire body feeling light as air.

Vladdir, King of the Aragoths, has changed, and still doesn't understand how. Silly king, don't you realise you can't eat like you used to? Your food is different now. You are different. See there, on the horizon? Go eat.

Vladdir looked up and saw two stilted figures shuffling towards him. He squinted against the Desert's brightness and saw their long hair, grey rockskin armour, and the runes painting their faces. Barbed chains swayed from their weapons belts. *Oh, Earth! No!*

Why? We thought you were hungry.

Vladdir turned and ran back the way he came, almost falling twice. As he approached the edge of the Yrati cavern, the ward stones were rattling so vigorously they were almost leaping out of their metal sockets. He jumped into the garden, feeling a painful resistance in the air. When he hit the ground, his arm again swung heavily at his side, stiff and unusable. The weakness returned and his breath came with difficulty.

"Aragoths!" he wheezed at the Yrati who were trickling into the cavern to see why the ward stones were shaking. Mauvis and Rayner came running to help him stand.

"Can you fight them off?" asked Rayner.

"No!" exclaimed Vladdir, his fear mounting at what the Yrati might see him do. He stared into Rayner's bewildered expression for a few seconds before the lie came. "I'm too weak." That worked wonderfully. Mauvis immediately warded off all other questions and began an emergency evacuation, herding everyone effectively with boisterous threats of the Aragoths' plans to flood the tunnels with magma in a few moments and warnings that they'd all be baked to a crisp if they didn't move towards cool water fast enough. The Yrati were systematically commanded onto the rafts, which were unanchored from the walls of the river tunnel so that they drifted south towards what would eventually be the sea. All equipment and personal effects were left behind. Within half an hour, the caverns were cleared out.

A few kilometres downstream, they ran into a series of shallows and had to lift the rafts from the water, carrying them over soft puddles of sand until they reached deeper water. The bioluminescent moss did not grow in these caverns, and their few torches sputtered erratically in the damp air. A few of the Yrati carrying the rafts stumbled in the darkness, almost getting crushed as the weight of the sodden wood tilted towards them.

Vladdir stood by helplessly, still unable to move his arm in these tunnels. The smell of the water changed as it became more saline, mixing with the backflow of the sea, indicating that they had passed the normally inhabited areas. The surface plants and sparse fungi that grew in this region tended to be unpalatable, and the fish from the salt water were only good for making poisons. At the next set of shallows they re-anchored the rafts and settled in to wait. Rayner scattered a fistful of ward stones over a red piece of cloth he had spread out on one of the rafts, and was watching them twitch and jump. Vladdir squatted next to him.

"What do they tell you?" he asked Rayner.

"Only that the Desert pushes in on our territory. If an enemy should pass by the wards set out in the caves, these stones will turn black. They've been jumping a lot lately, but not like this."

Vladdir leaned away from the stones, relieved that they had not blackened in his presence, but wondered when they would do so. He shifted over to sit next to Mauvis, who wrapped a shawl around his shoulders. Hailandir was cuddled by a female Yrati next to Mauvis, and was staring at Vladdir with wide, glossy eyes. He reached over and caressed the small fingers that rested on the Yrati's arm until the child curled up her hand and turned away to push her face into the priestess' shoulder.

"My Dear Princess," Mauvis moaned.

"Let her be," Vladdir told him. "She's quiet, which is more important at the moment."

The lapping of the water against the sides of the rafts lulled Vladdir into a stupor as they waited. At one point, Rayner announced that the stones had turned black, and for the next hour all the Yrati sat in tense silence with the torches doused, every sense straining to detect the approach of the Aragoths. When the river tunnel remained silent except for the sloshing of the water for an interminable time, Rayner grew impatient and struck his flint. The stones had returned to their normal sandy grey.

"Do you think they are truly gone?" one of the Yrati asked.

"They should be, unless they destroyed the ward stones," said another. That comment raised a cloud of panicked muttering.

"No, the stones still twitch," said Rayner. "If they had been deactivated, there would be no response at all. Besides, Aragoths generally don't concern themselves with such things. I think we should spend the night here, just in case they make a second inspection, or are waiting outside the caves for us to return. It would have been obvious to them that we left in haste, leaving all our belongings behind."

The Yrati murmured consent and began to set up makeshift beds with the few supplies that had already been on the rafts. Vladdir found himself pillowed on top of a lumpy fishing net and blanketed by a pair of burlap bags that smelled of medicinal fungi. He curled up and let his exhaustion take him.

In his sleep, Vladdir saw the water had turned to pulsating waves of sand that were cascading down from the surface, bumping against the raft he lay on. Something underneath the raft grabbed the wooden slats and jerked them downwards so that the sand could flow onto it, reaching for his feet, turning them to stone, climbing up his legs, turning them to stone, ascending his torso, hardening, hardening everything as it crept along. When his heart solidified and stopped beating, Vladdir tried to call out, and he looked around for the Yrati, who were no longer there. Mauvis and Hailandir were gone, too. His neck and head had solidified into grey, crumbling rock. His paralysis was so complete that he couldn't turn away when a demon wraith came fluttering down the tunnel, its mouth full of rows of bloody fangs that stretched from its lips all the way down its throat. A mass of blue tentacles writhed in place of its hair, slithering around the thick, black chains wrapped around its neck. They contrasted sharply with the red-edged, tattered white robes it wore.

The wraith seemed to drag in its wake a strange aethereal portal that trailed down from the ceiling of the cavern. It was filled with sickly orange light, and a legion of demons sat within, spitting out rhythmic syllables that shot spikes of terror through Vladdir every time they hit his ears. Hovering over Vladdir, the face of the wraith writhed like the Desert Plains, making it difficult to see any features clearly.

Something more powerful sat beyond the wraith and its companions, deep inside the portal and hidden behind the aether. Thin, dark red lips. Thin eyes. Narrow, evil glare.

Vladdir panicked and called the Desert into himself so that he could move his stone body and strike this creature away.

It won't come when you're surrounded by water. Thought you could hide? You've only made yourself vulnerable, like these pathetic Yrati you've put your trust in.

Vladdir struggled against his immobility, feeling like he was being suffocated. This voice was new. It was not the Desert.

You desecrated my beautiful Ilet. Now I'll have you, ugly Vladdir.

The wraith descended onto him and began to sink into his sandy body. It filled his eyes, ears, nose, mouth, lungs, like thick smoke from burning dung, equally corrosive and putrescent. Vladdir tried to twist away from it until he felt his stone body crack, sending excruciating pain through him from sternum to chin. If he could speak, Vladdir would have begged for death, anything to stop this torment. His body cracked again, shooting agony around his rib cage, and again, in a star-like splinter that raced to the tips of his fingers and feet. The fourth crack destroyed his eyes, sending him into profound blackness.

"I think he's breathing again."

Mauvis seemed unreasonably calm, until Vladdir noticed that the Chamberlain's face was grey, tear-streaked, and etched with exhaustion. All the fuss had already come out of him. He sponged Vladdir's face with a sodden rag that was coming away streaked with blood.

"Did I die?" Vladdir asked, but his voice was still cracked and the words didn't form properly.

"Did he bite his tongue during the seizure?" One of the Yrati leaned over Vladdir and prodded at his lips and teeth, apparently trying to see into his mouth. "Damn it, I wish we had brought better medicine with us."

"What caused it?" Mauvis asked.

"I don't know," replied the Yrati. "He made his wishes clear to Callie, about us reading him to find out. It's just guesswork if we can't read him."

The Yrati's words faded out as Vladdir's ears were filled with another sound. At first he thought it was just the blood rushing through his ears, then it seemed that the noise of the river had escalated. A second later his body jerked, and the sound resolved into a rapid repetition of the terrifying chant spoken by the demons in the orange dream-cave he had seen before. He could feel currents of cold air rushing past, and caught his breath as he felt, rather than saw, a black wraith swoop into his body from somewhere underneath the raft, making his back arch. He felt his head slam against the wood of the raft several times, his arms flailing. Pain radiated from the centre of his chest and his consciousness drowned in the presence of the wraith. His anger flared up. Who was this priest to hunt him down like this? If he wanted a fight with Vladdir, King of the Desert, so be it. Vladdir had eaten the beautiful Ilet, and he would use that evil to eat this repugnant Desert Priest as well. Let him come! It was reaching him through the water, this enemy. He had to get away from the water and back to the surface, where the Desert's power would give him an advantage.

As suddenly as it had started, the attack stopped. It felt as if something had yanked the demon out of Vladdir's body and back into the water. He tensed, waiting to see if it would return. Looking up, he saw that Mauvis was holding him by the shoulders, the other man's face white with stunned shock. Their eyes locked and neither one spoke, as if they both knew it wasn't quite over. The raft bucked several times until something struck it from underneath with enough force to splinter the wood upwards. Over the side of the raft, the water was turning dark and bubbling. Vladdir flinched away from the force of several consciousnesses bumping against his own. Disengaging, they sunk back into the depths.

"The Water Ghouls," whispered Mauvis. He turned to stare at Vladdir again. "My King, did they attack you?"

"No," said Vladdir. "I think they fought off whatever was coming after me."

"Something *else* was attacking you?" Mauvis squeaked. "I thought we were just hiding from Aragoths!"

"They don't trust you," said the Yrati, his eyes clouded with concentration. He appeared to be focusing his attention on feeling the minds of the Water Ghouls.

"I have to leave." Vladdir struggled to sit up, but his stone arm weighed him down. His rage built and he jerked the arm onto his lap.

"What do you mean?" demanded Mauvis.

"The Desert Priest and the Aragoths are coming here because of me.

I'll meet them on the surface."

"Vladdir, don't be ridiculous!" Mauvis shouted. Vladdir paused, surprised at Mauvis' tone and lack of fawning. "If the Yrati Ghouls have protected you, then this is where you must stay!"

Vladdir looked around at the Yrati, who were starting to seem worried and distrustful. Was he showing too much of his mind to them? Rayner did say they could pick up on intense emotion. He forced himself to calm down and tried a different tactic. "I must go. My presence is drawing the Aragoths to this hiding place."

"That's absurd!" Mauvis spluttered. "They look for all of us. If they are looking specifically for you, that's all the more reason for you to stay where you are protected. The kingdom. Hailandir. Have to re...build. You...essential...for..." Mauvis was hyperventilating.

"Look, Mauvis, I managed before, I can again. I thank you for letting me rest—"

"Youarenotfullyrecovered—"

"—but I *am* going back to the surface. Now."

Mauvis was sheet white with large, red blotches spreading randomly over his face. It was a startling sight against the purple of his jacket.

"I will come back. I promise."

More blotches.

"Just give me time to finish this. It is my duty, as king."

Eyes starting to bulge.

"Have you lost your faith in me?"

Symptoms receding.

Vladdir acted quickly before Mauvis regained his ability to speak. He turned to the nearest Yrati. "Please take me to where I can reach the surface. I have to end this."

The Yrati looked at him speculatively, but gestured to his comrades to begin poling the raft back upstream.

"It is not time yet for Prince Vladdir to sleep. He must make his wishes known to his Great Servant of Dust. Think of your deepest needs and let them be carried out on your breath as you blow over the sand. That's right,

out the window, into the Desert. Think deeply, Vladdir, this is the way to rule your kingdom."

So Derlan had spoken just before she had been executed. Vladdir had not known that his father had secretly watched the old nurse putting him to bed that night, finally passing judgement and ordering her death. Vladdir had slept through her screams and debasing protests, still under the influence of the medicinal fungi she had fed him to open his mind to the Desert. Derlan had told him she had bribed several officials to become his nurse, because she wanted to feel the power of a true king. He wondered what kind of man he would be if she had stayed with him until he had reached adulthood. Rather frightening, he thought. Entirely too powerful and not in complete control of his mental faculties. Would that make him subject to the control of another, less powerful but more cunning man, such as the Desert Priest who had commanded Ilet?

Determined to retain control, having come into this power as a man, Vladdir sat in the sand with his legs folded beneath him. His mind cleared of all but his desire to find the Desert Priest, who seemed equally eager to find him. As the Desert spoke instructions into his mind, he scooped up the sand and held it to his lips with both hands, flesh and stone. He blew on it and the grains were carried forth on the wind of his thoughts. Vladdir remembered his final attack on Ilet, and how he had allowed the Desert's whimsy to change his mind and body so that they also disintegrated like the tiny mound on his palms, to be carried upwards and ahead. His consciousness flowed over the tunnels where the Yrati hid, and he realised with dismay that their souls shone like bright pinpricks of light and caught at him as he passed by. They weren't hidden at all. Could the Desert Priest have seen the Tunnel Dwellers this way all along? No wonder they hadn't stood much of a chance; no wonder the Aragoths had always seemed to know where to search.

Vladdir didn't know how the Desert Priest would appear to his newly disembodied eyes. He roamed over the area where he had found Ilet in the strange marble-lined cavern, seeing that the emptied husks of the Aragoths still lay there, in a pool of red aura. Several lines of fading residual aura radiated from that spot, most of them Aragoth red, tracing the directions from which Vladdir had drawn them into his last meal. There were other colours as well, some blue, one green, and a few were white, like the Yrati. How many entities had he consumed? It looked like thousands. Vladdir remembered the pleasure of satisfying his deep hunger, he remembered the Aragoths and that one, tiny, child-like dot. Nothing else. Pushing away his shame at that memory, he soared along the lines of red aura that were the closest together, and the longest, to see where they led.

Farther away from Ilet's temple, the lines lost their straight direction. They followed a more wandering pattern, except for a point in the far northwest of the Plains at which many of them intersected. A few red auras, unfaded and still travelling, were in the immediate vicinity. One bright spot of green shone through the sand directly beneath Vladdir's hovering form. He lowered himself and felt his legs, torso, arms and head regenerate from the aether, his grey hair swirling about his face like a halo of sand before coming to rest on his shoulders.

By his natural vision, he saw that he stood in a flat region of the Desert. The sun was bright, the wind was still. Seeing no obvious structures above ground, he took a few steps over the dust-coated white rock, tapping it with his feet as he went along, expecting to find some sort of hidden door concealing the auras he had seen while in the aether. At one point, the sand began to slip from beneath his feet as his weight pressed down on a loose slab of stone. Vladdir knelt and forced the fingers of his stone hand into the crack, then jerked the door open. A staircase twisted downward. From the cut of the stone, Vladdir knew that this was the work of a master craftsman. He had known of such tradesmen within the main civilisation of his own underground tunnels, but had never heard of surface wanderers with such skills.

The moment his feet touched the stairs, he felt echoes of some past life. The man who had made these steps had done so under extreme duress. Cool air washed up around Vladdir's face as he descended, carrying with it the faint scent of butchery. Light also drifted upwards, coming from strange glass tubes inset to the sandy walls, filled with some kind of softly buzzing energy. At first Vladdir thought it was a glowing insect colony within, but these lamps had no living auras trailing them, the way the Aragoths and Yrati did.

He came to the main underground cavern, surprised to find that it was a luxury suite, the low ceiling lined with black, polished onyx, and the floor with pale, green jade. Several oblong jade plinths were covered in white cushions to serve as loungers, some partially enclosed by white hanging curtains. A cage rested in one corner, its bottom covered with clean straw. In the very centre of the chamber was a square box of ornate metal bars, inside of which a hearth could be built. Now it rested cold. No signs of current habitation were in this room.

The cavern exited into a series of tunnels that branched into what could have been a kitchen, several study rooms, bathing rooms, and what appeared to be an abandoned temple. If there had ever been a shrine on the black marble of the altar base, it had long been disassembled, and the bare surface was now covered in dust. Vladdir wandered through the tunnels as far as he could, finally coming to a spot where the floor was no longer tiled and none of the light tubes were inset in the walls. An old tapestry covered the back wall, so dirty and faded that the threads all seemed to be a mottled brown. Looking closely at the woven picture, Vladdir thought he could make out a vague shape of a head, perhaps with horns, and wide, glaring eyes. The tapestry wafted slightly, and cool air brushed against the metal of Vladdir's armoured boots, chilling his ankles where there was chain mail to allow him to bend. Moving cautiously, he lifted aside the tapestry, and found another staircase leading down.

He went forward carefully, his flesh fingers tracing the wall, his toes probing the darkness before taking each step, until he kicked against something that sounded like hollow wood. Reaching out his hand, his fingers closed on a door knob. He twisted it and pushed, greeted by a stronger rush of cold air that carried the scent of a vivarium. Cautious chirps of lizards and squirrels greeted him. As he stepped through the door, more of the strange tubes lit up, showing him a room lined with clear glass cages from floor to ceiling. The inhabitants scurried away from the light, hiding under sparse bedding. Vladdir passed into what looked like a surgical staging area behind the cage room, with several deep sinks, surgeon's gowns hung on pegs along the walls, and several canisters for sterilizing instruments in an oven. Piles of gauze, suture spools and neatly folded towels sat on metal shelves along one wall. The flow of air back towards the animal room was noticeable. The operating theatres were probably through the back exit. Vladdir headed in that direction, feeling himself pass an air curtain coming through a sharp fissure in the rock that must have been cut right to the surface and shielded from the sand somehow. On the other side, the stench was overwhelming.

No semblance of a professional surgery suite was maintained here. The remnants of dismembered limbs from animals were strewn carelessly over several workbenches. Tools were encrusted with dark substances and tossed in a basin of filthy water at the end of one bench. No entrails or decapitated heads were present, and Vladdir wondered what had happened to these. On the last bench of the room, the limbs were distinctly human. Blackened fingers curled upwards from the smooth palm and forearm of a woman. Vladdir turned away, thinking of Arlendan, grateful that he felt nausea rather than hunger.

This chamber led into another long tunnel with what looked like research laboratories all along the left side. At the end of the tunnel he could hear water dripping. Was that a voice? Vladdir crept softly into a circular room with a soft earth floor. A pool rimmed with curving stones was at the far end, and some sort of large, bronze monster idol was placed in a square inset dug into the back wall. The idol's glistening face leered at Vladdir as its pointed fangs dug into the breast of some unfortunate metal man. In front of the pool knelt a woman in dark robes, her head covered by a clinging black hood, her green aura now more acutely visible than it had been from the aether. She was whispering to the water. Vladdir watched her in silence for some moments until she seemed to sense him and turned around, startled. The hood covered much of her face.

"Who are you?" Vladdir demanded, wincing at the way his voice reverberated through the chamber. The woman got up and ran, revealing a red dress beneath the cloak. She fled through a dark tunnel he had not noticed at the side of the chamber. And Vladdir pursued. She ducked and dodged through a maze of tunnels, but did not manage to shake Vladdir from her trail. Finally, he chased her to another wide cavern tiled with grey slate. Her red slippers made flat slapping noises, her shawl slipping to her shoulders to reveal black hair. Pulling himself out of the narrow tunnel and into the cavern, Vladdir felt his hunger rise as he watched the woman run.

No! he told himself. *At least not until I have questioned her.*

"Vladdir!"

He turned to find himself facing a leering, dark-haired female Aragoth whose sword was raised to his neck.

They always attack in pairs!

Vladdir drew the long dagger he carried at his hip and turned, throwing himself backwards with his stone arm raised to block the swing of the Aragoth who had crept up behind him. He knocked over the other man and landed on top of him, his arm thrusting back the Aragoth's chin. Within seconds his blade plunged deeply into the side of his opponent's neck and the man tried to spit blood at him defiantly.

"Who bonds you now?" Vladdir hissed angrily, wanting to know the Desert Priest's name. Had that fleeing woman been the next Ilet? The Aragoth fainted without revealing anything. Vladdir rolled back onto his feet as the other Aragoth swung down with her sword, cleaving the rockskin of her partner. He faced her with his dagger, the whim of the Desert within his stomach making him drool like an insane dog. He wanted her. The Aragoth looked at his dagger with some amusement.

"Are you going to kill me with that?" She struck at his stone arm, creating a spray of sparks and rock chips. Vladdir stumbled backwards, surprised at her strength. "You will not kill me, Vladdir." She came at him again, and he barely parried her blows. She was right; the length of his dagger was not sufficient to strike at her.

The Desert's lust surged within Vladdir, nearly blinding him. He wasn't sure if he ran or flew towards the Aragoth, or if he had reached her, for he was abruptly plunged into cold darkness. Then the agony

started. Somewhere in his gut was a very large tear and it was burning
mercilessly, until it crescendoed with his hunger and his vision
gradually returned. The Aragoth was in his arms. She grinned into his
face, black-inked runes smeared around her mouth, one hand pressed
against his back as she held him, the other gripping the sword she had
run through him. She was now twisting the hilt, apparently enjoying
his pain. Vladdir leaned his head on the Aragoth's shoulder while she
killed him slowly. He wasn't hungry anymore, but knew no other way
to defend himself. Shaking helplessly, he swept back her hair, found
the upper ridge of the rockskin and bit into her neck.

He had no control. Everything was draining out of him. His blood,
his will, his life, his tenuous grasp on the Desert. Out of Vladdir and
into Kyril, for as his mind was drawn into hers, he learned that was
her name. She was absorbing all of him, like the spittle he cast into the
wound on her neck. He felt himself slump to the ground.

Vladdir's will into Kyril, observed the Desert. *Very clever. Well, We
suppose you can't eat all of them. You really are dying, Vlad. Go and eat
the other one, then. Get some strength back. This is very interesting. We
don't want to miss any of this.*

Vladdir released Kyril, who was now lying next to him on the slate
tiles, and pulled her sword from his gut. He could still hear her mind.

No more Lost. Bonded.

"What?" croaked Vladdir. He didn't understand. He tried to think
but his head hurt too badly. He needed to eat. Dragging himself over
the floor, wincing at the sound of the filigree on his boots scraping across
the stone, he bit into the ankle of the other Aragoth and consumed him
completely. Karel, for that had been *his* name, crumbled to dust under
Vladdir's lips. The wound in Vladdir's middle closed somewhat but still
oozed piteously. He had enough strength to pull himself to his knees
and look over at Kyril. She did not seem badly injured at all, and was
sitting cross-legged, one hand covering the bite on her neck as she looked
intently at Vladdir. Her interest was intense as it pressed against his mind.

"You are Ilet!" said Kyril.

That statement shocked Vladdir so much he staggered to his feet in
preparation to run.

"I'm not!"

"You have bonded me. No one can bond me but Ilet. You are My Lord Ilet."

"No! No no no. Ilet is dead. I am Vladdir!"

"My Lord Vladdir!"

"Stop it!"

Kyril was on her knees, bowing her head in obedience and holding up her blackened fingers in a triangle shape to indicate loyalty.

"I unbond you!" Vladdir tried to grasp the presence of Kyril that he felt in his mind and fling it from himself. It didn't work. He realised he didn't know how he had bonded Kyril in the first place, and had no idea how to reverse it. He began to panic, which made the pain in his stomach flare up again as he coughed blood, stumbled and fell. Kyril came to his side and took him up in her arms.

"I will take you home," she said.

"No!" said Vladdir. He squirmed as he felt her mind send a wash of hurt affection over him. By the Earth, she was behaving like Mauvis!

"You just skewered me!"

"I beg your forgiveness."

Vladdir was speechless.

Sitting on a mound of sand, letting the wind cast fistfuls of it over his legs, Vladdir was in a very, very bad mood. When they had stopped to rest and Kyril lay beside him, he did not feel the Desert's hunger, or hear its voice. When she left him to scout, he was nearly blinded with the intense gnawing appetite he felt within, urged on by vulgar suggestions, to the point that he came back to himself to find his will had dragged a multitude of shrubs and small animals into a circle around him, all withered and dead. When Kyril returned, the cravings fell away.

First helpless to resist the Desert for reasons of self-defence, now helpless to avoid the bonding of this stupid Aragoth who quenches my hunger. Earth! Will I next need the Hordes of Hell to help me breathe?

After several hours of such contemplation, never feeling the need to sleep, Vladdir wondered if Ilet had ever needed to eat when surrounded by his Aragoths. He wondered if in time he would need more and more bonded people in order to satiate himself. It was an odd way to be king. *Subject yourself to me or be consumed!*

Now you've got it, said the Desert. Kyril had awoken and was gazing ardently at him. He shifted around so that he could turn his back on her. The gesture didn't help much when their minds were linked. She still radiated love towards him. Well, he *had* been hungry for *that* his entire life—

What in Earth am I thinking?

Could Kyril hear all his thoughts the way he could hear hers?

"Yes," said Kyril.

"Why?" he asked over his shoulder. *Why do you love me?*

"Without you, I have no reason to exist. Your will is now my soul."

"You continued to exist when Ilet died."

"I was meaningless. Nothing. Lost. Empty. Do you understand now, Vladdir, what you had from me when you took Ilet? I was without my soul."

"Then why are you not still angry with me?"

"You've given me a new one."

Vladdir huffed angrily and turned away again. "What were you before you were bonded?"

"Nothing."

Frustrated, Vladdir closed his eyes, rudely probed through her mind and found that Kyril really did believe she had been nothing. It was as if she had actually been created for Ilet.

"You are not to behave as my vassal. Do you understand? You are not part of me. I will not be the Lord of some surface creature."

"Do you want me to leave?"

Can't. Can't go back to the hunger.

"I want you to get that stuff off your face." *She'll have to come with me, at least until I can find a way to stop the cravings. The Yrati may still be able to help.*

Kyril crept around so that she could kneel in front of him. She leaned in close and peered into his face, the wind teasing a few dark

63

strands of hair over her deep violet eyes. Her skin had a light sheen to it, and he could now see that her narrow nose had a light scattering of freckles beneath the rune ink. He was surprised when he felt her mild anger.

"They are not like us, Vladdir. We need the Desert inside us, or we will forever be empty shadows. What were *you* before you were ever bonded? And you question me for not wanting to go back to that?"

Kyril showed Vladdir the painful things that tossed around his mind: Constant loneliness, constant self-doubt, constant awkward wanting. Never getting. The memories swelled up in a hurtful ache that pressed against his innards. They threatened to push out his breath, crush his heart, and squirt his blood out of the wound that still oozed in his middle. He turned away and threw his arms up to cover his face, shamed and angry that she could so easily see all that he had foolishly hoped for in his childhood and marriage and had tried to hide behind decades of mental anguish.

Pressing her mind against his to reveal her certainty and absolute devotion to her new master, Kyril made known the clarity of her own thoughts, her willingness to give him everything. She pulled down his arms, leaned forward and kissed him. Vladdir gasped and pulled away. Even in that single act, she gave him so much that Arlendan couldn't, but his disbelief wouldn't let him release his lifetime of pain. She kissed him again, and this time she didn't let go. The pain was released, and with it, all the Aragoths he had eaten were pushed out. Now Kyril alone filled his soul. In his mind, it seemed like he was standing in the middle of a Desert night, but the wind was warm as it circled him, spiralling upwards, carrying with it red spheres of light that were Aragoth spirits flowing out of his mouth in a rush to be free. One last thing stayed behind and could not leave him. Something small. A bright, tender, tiny knot of grief. Ah, yes. The little one he had accidentally swallowed as he had eaten Ilet.

I should go in alone, just at first. It will be easier if you wait a bit.
All right.

Vladdir let go of Kyril's hand and tried to suppress the doltish grin he knew was stretched across his face. He felt so light and giddy that he thought he might giggle all the way down into the Yrati tunnels. His wound still pained him as he climbed down into the haphazard garden cavern, blood seeping through the fingers he clamped over his stomach. The hurt of it was making him slightly dizzy, but he didn't care. He laughed out loud and wanted to raise his stone arm to embrace Mauvis as the Chamberlain came running, but now that he was below the surface, the cursed thing would no longer move.

"My King! Have you defeated the Desert Priest?" asked Mauvis.

"The what?"

"The Priest!" exclaimed Rayner. "The one you said controlled Ilet."

"Oh." Vladdir stopped in his tracks. "Er—" Well, this made him feel like a right mud-brain. "Not really."

Rayner and Mauvis waited intently for his next words, expecting some utterance that would explain everything.

"I think...I think I found his lair, but he wasn't around at the time."

Rayer looked confused. Mauvis' expression was disappointed.

"I'm going back, it's just that...well..." He gestured hopelessly with his flesh hand, which was covered in blood.

"You're injured!" Mauvis gasped.

"It's all right."

"It's not! What happened? You must have been in a fight."

"Well, I suppose, but—"

"My poor King! When will your suffering end?"

"I'm quite all right, really."

"Yet another wound!"

"But I don't care! Mauvis please don't fuss right now. I need you to listen—"

"Aragoth!" screamed Rayner. At the same time, the other Yrati also cried out. Some ran from the cavern. Others picked up rocks and sticks.

Vladdir whirled around to see Kyril stepping down into the back of the garden cavern.

"My King Vladdir," she said. "You did not instruct me how long to wait."

⟨⟩⋈⟨⟩

"You can't possibly expect me to accept...*this!*" Mauvis waved his arms in the vague direction of Kyril. He was in fine form, but she seemed completely unaffected by his tirade. Limbs flailing, hair standing wildly on end, face white with red splotches, Mauvis had been yelling for the last hour or so, in a conversation that was making very slow progress. Rayner's outrage had gradually faded into resignation as he leaned on his palm to wait for him to run out of steam. He had ceased even opening his mouth to agree with Mauvis or berate Vladdir a good twenty minutes in, having not succeeded in getting a single word in edgewise.

Sitting in a wooden chair heavily padded with cushions and blankets, Vladdir was too happy to care. Perhaps he was feeling the effects of the medicines the Yrati had given him for his pain. Perhaps he was just that relieved to have had the Desert grit rinsed from his body and to have been dressed in fresh clothes. Perhaps he was still knocked head-over-heels by Kyril's kiss. The warm glow in his chest expanded as he watched Kyril sponge away the ink from her face and neck, and then with the help of the female Yrati, from her shoulders and back. The wound on her neck was not questioned, but cleaned and bandaged, much to Vladdir's relief. His eyes followed the fine tracing of runes that remained on her pale skin, but he didn't find it unpleasing. She did not hesitate to remove her armour in front of everyone. Her soft curves were covered by towels and then by feminine robes disappointingly quickly. It was like watching a woman emerge from stone. Or perhaps a flower from decay. Vladdir supposed it was a good thing that Mauvis was too busy yelling at him to notice Kyril's innocent lack of modesty, or he would have had something else to yell about, extending the duration of this noisy session.

Her bath finished, Kyril stepped down from the stone basin and immediately came to kneel in front of Vladdir, leaning forward to touch her forehead to the ground. Her transformation was delightful, and the delicate pink robes the Yrati had supplied her with suited her complexion. Her mind radiated trust, adulation and utter contentment into Vladdir's thoughts. He could feel that Kyril thought herself at home, and although she did register that Mauvis had now turned to yell at her, the Chamberlain's opinion was completely irrelevant, and his shouting was of no consequence.

Rayner took this opportunity to cut in. "Vladdir, will having this woman here increase the risk of other Aragoths finding us?"

"No. But then, you always were at risk. I used Desert magic to find where the many paths of the Aragoths intersected. At the same time, I could see all you Yrati quite easily. I assume that's how Ilet knew where to send the Aragoths in the first place."

"I see." Rayner frowned at the mention of Desert magic, and rubbed his hands together nervously.

"But *I* will not attack you," Vladdir babbled on. "Not with Kyril here, she completely stops me from feeling anything but happiness."

Rayner's brow furrowed even more. "Did you feel like attacking us before?"

"No, not really, but I was worried. All that's gone now." He grinned at the Yrati priest, who didn't seem to share his relief.

"Are you going to bond other Aragoths?" asked Rayner. That made Vladdir pause.

"I hadn't thought about it. I don't particularly want to."

"This one seems quite tame now." Rayner gestured at Kyril, who was now sitting up and letting Hailandir explore the buttons on her sleeve, still completely ignoring Mauvis. "If it could be a peaceful way of converting them, perhaps you should."

Vladdir thought that if Rayner had seen him biting into Aragoths' necks and forcing his will into them, the Yrati would soon change his mind. Was he even strong enough to bond more than one Aragoth? Kyril was in his mind as much as he was in hers. What would happen if he allowed a stronger Aragoth influence into his mind? Would it overwhelm him? There must be a reason why the Desert Priest used Ilet in the first place. Perhaps he needed a filter to protect himself from being overcome. Vladdir frowned and shook his head. That didn't make sense. How could the Desert Priest bond Ilet without himself being subject to all that was in Ilet's mind, including the Aragoths?

Hailandir crawled into Kyril's lap, intent on thoroughly examining the lacy embroidered insects around the collar of the donated robes. Vladdir had not thought it possible, but Mauvis became even more enraged until he was on the point of having a seizure, barely keeping his balance as he reached down to ungently pull the child away. Hailandir showed him that when it came to screaming, she clearly had him outmatched. Vladdir winced and covered one of his ears, feeling dizzy as he made the motion. He felt a huge sense of relief as the female Yrati apparently reached the end of their patience, extracting Hailandir from Mauvis and slapping Rayner aside so that Vladdir could be raised to his feet and led to a sleeping chamber. He was given a second dose of pain medicine. As they eased him onto a sleeping mat and tucked blankets around him, Vladdir thought he felt better than he had in his entire life. He mused that he'd never been surrounded by a multitude of female attendants before, and that even if he had, he wouldn't have enjoyed it this much, being overly concerned with further damaging his constantly tenuous relationship with Arlen. Kyril curled up on a mat next to him and continued to gaze at him ardently. So nice to not have to worry about what she thought. Or even wonder what she thought, for that matter. He let the drug carry him to his dreams.

The cavern was dark. It smelled damp, like stale swamp. When Vladdir reached outward to feel what he could not see, his stone arm clanged against a series of metal bars. He gripped them with his hands and pulled himself forwards.

"Who's there?" someone called out. The voice sounded young. Perhaps a boy on the verge of manhood.

"I am called Vlad."

"Vlad? Vladdir? You *bastard!* Why did you trap me like this? You could have let me escape once you were done with me. You let the others go."

"Who are you?"

"Don't know me? Can't remember you had me for lunch the other day? Earth damn you. Why did you let him keep me? You were stronger than me, surely stronger than him. Why did you take me from him and then hand me right back?"

"Tell me who you are!" Vladdir strained his eyes in the dark, trying to see past the bars that blocked his way. The stone enclosure he was caged into was too small for him to stand. If he pressed himself against the bars at the far end, he could make out a faint light somewhere off to the left. He strained his eyes harder. A stone dais? The youth who had cursed him seemed to be lying there on his side. The boy tried to crawl off the dais and Vladdir heard the rattle of chains as he moved. His long, dark hair brushed against the stone. Something was looming in the dark behind the boy, raising itself like a giant serpent about to strike. The boy began screaming.

"No! Vladdir! Save me! Don't let him take me again!"

The dark thing struck. Vladdir could see the boy's limbs flailing as he screamed and tried to fight off the creature that plunged at his stomach. Vladdir heard a noise like cloth tearing and smelled a combination of blood and sick. He flung himself against the bars, trying to break out. He had to get to the boy, he had to—

"Vladdir. He comes. He will come after you."

The impact of the metal against his shoulder sent Vladdir into numb shock. He twitched, then became aware of a warm hand stroking his brow. Someone gently kissed him. He opened his eyes and saw Kyril by the glow of a small fire bowl placed just past his head.

"You dreamt of Ilet," she said.

"Did you see my dream?"

"Yes."

"Ilet was the monster?"

"No, the boy."

"Do you know what the monster was?"

Kyril shook her head. "Ilet feared things sometimes. But he did not let us see his thoughts, like you let me see yours."

"Kyril, do you know who the Desert Priest is?" Her mind was empty. Vladdir tried to show her in his thoughts the face of the man who had controlled Ilet, but she remained blank. She shook her head again. "What about the woman? The one I was chasing just before I found you."

Vladdir felt Kyril realise she had never spared thought for her before. She had been complete as a warrior, so there had been no need for her to think about anything other than what Ilet commanded.

"Was she Ilet's lover?"

"No. She was nothing. I saw her in our caverns sometimes, but she did nothing. For some reason, though she was useless, she did not leave us. I never bothered to think of her much."

He's coming after you.

Vladdir bolted upright, his skin instantly chilled and crawling.

"Did you hear that?" he asked Kyril.

"I heard nothing."

Vladdir shifted onto his feet and walked into the damp air of the main tunnels. Kyril followed. All was quiet. A few Yrati puttered around, making medicines from the algae and fish they had collected, while most of the others were huddled together in slumber. He found Callie in one of the corridors as he moved towards the garden cavern. She was leaning over a fistful of the ward stones and looked up with a start when Vladdir came close.

"Anything?" he asked her. She shook her head. "Why do you frown?"

"Well, normally the stones jump a bit, even when there is no threat. And you can always feel at least some energy around them. They're usually slightly warm. But now I feel nothing and they don't move at all."

"Have you told Rayner?"

"Not yet. I'm still trying to see if I'm doing something wrong."

"Perhaps if you told him, he could help you."

Callie muttered something that sounded like "he's a big stupid" but collected her stones and shuffled off. Vladdir cautiously ventured to the edge of the garden and looked up into the night sky. The air was cold and silent. After watching for a few moments, he tried to force himself to relax.

"He's coming."

Vladdir whirled to stare at Kyril. Her eyes were glazed over, her long hair cascading down in the darkness like a shroud. He stepped forward and shook her shoulders until she looked at him.

"Who's coming?"

"Ilet."

"He's dead."

"I can feel the thrum of his march through the rock of the Earth."

Vladdir felt all his old insecurities sweep back down on him.

"Will you go to him?" he asked Kyril, his voice trembling. She blinked and the trance-like stare disappeared from her expression.

"I no longer wear his runes," she said, as if that explanation made her answer obvious. "I am bonded to you now."

"Where is he?"

She pointed in the direction opposite to the opening of the garden cavern. "He's coming through the wet tunnels."

Vladdir dashed in that direction and Kyril followed. In the main cave, a swarm of Yrati who were dressed for bed looked up in alarm. Mauvis, who kept his silence now, stood off to one side and glared alternately at Vladdir and Kyril.

"Do we need to arm?" Rayner asked him.

"Yes," said Vladdir.

"Our ward stones no longer work. It's a good thing you can sense them."

"I don't feel anything in the tunnels. I can't even move my arm unless I'm on the surface. It's Kyril who knew they were coming."

"Well, of course. She's in league with them," Mauvis commented sourly. Vladdir frowned at him.

"There's no use hiding, right?" asked Rayner.

"It would be pointless. We should get to the most defensible position. Perhaps I should go to the surface and stop any more from coming into the tunnels."

"Should we flee?"

"You can't," said Kyril. "They come up the river now."

"They've blocked both underground exits?" asked Mauvis, partially coming out of his sulk. Escaping to the surface through the garden was a contradiction in terms, especially at night, when the surface contained more things to escape *from*.

"Let your Water Ghoul friends take care of those in the river. We'll face them on this side."

The Yrati ran into position, gathering whatever could be used as a weapon. Their selections were depressingly poor. One of them even held a pot at the ready. A blunt short sword was pushed into Vladdir's flesh hand and he looked at it miserably, wondering if he should even bother wielding it. It might be easier to just fling his stone arm around. Could he resort to his previous trick of consumption? He examined his feelings to see if there was any hint of the Desert's lust-hunger anywhere within him, but all he felt was Kyril.

"I have to get to the surface."

"Well, you'll have to go through them," Rayner told him. The Aragoths could be heard now, marching in pairs, their feet in matching splashing thuds. From the sounds, there were a lot of them coming.

Vladdir looked around nervously. "Kyril, are they still coming from the river?"

"There are strange men in the water," she said. "I don't know who they are."

"Here they come!"

Vladdir tried to jostle to the front and braced himself for the first swing, his stone arm feeling heavy and off-balance. A curly-haired Aragoth grinned at him through ink runes and stepped into range, landing his back-handed swipe on Vladdir's stone shoulder and knocking him backwards. Two Yrati fell next to him. *They're not even wearing armour!* Blood spattered over his face. As he turned over and tried to stand up, he caught sight of an Yrati woman running towards the river with Hailandir in her arms. An Aragoth caught up to her and struck her across the back, making her fall and lose her grip on the child. Vladdir couldn't see if the Yrati had been killed. He scrambled up and ran towards his daughter. The Aragoth heard him coming and turned away from Hailandir, winding up to strike. Mauvis jumped on his back and was easily plucked off and tossed aside. Vladdir raised his tiny sword to parry and wished he could summon the hunger. He didn't think anything would happen if he bit the Aragoth now. It just wasn't there. The image of Taalen dying flashed through his mind, then Rayner.

The Aragoth struck. Vladdir turned his stone shoulder towards the blow, and was again thrown off his feet. His attacker stepped over him and raised his sword, the tip pointing downward at Vladdir's neck.

A large rock hit the Aragoth squarely in the face. He shook his head and then took a step back, this time raising his sword in defence. Kyril stepped over Vladdir's body, her feet gliding like a dancer's. She had gotten hold of an Aragoth sword, which she swung in an arc at her opponent's head, forcing him to lean backwards. In the same movement, her sword came down and she cut his legs out from under him, rockskin and all. While he twisted and flailed, sliding off his severed legs to fall forward, she took off his head. Vladdir lurched to his feet and ran shoulder first into another Aragoth, knocking her over and breaking his tiny sword with his first blow against the rockskin armour. He had to content himself with picking up a stone and smashing it into the Aragoth's face.

"The river is cleared!" Rayner was yelling. The Yrati were picking up their fallen comrades and running to the back of the cavern. Vladdir searched for Hailandir and saw her wailing in Mauvis' arms. The Chamberlain was looking back at Vladdir, positioned to run, but it was clear that he was waiting to move until Vladdir stood up and came with him.

"Go!" Vladdir shouted. "I will follow!"

The Aragoth underneath him was moving again, forcing Vladdir to strike her a second time. Mauvis still hadn't moved.

"Kyril!" Vladdir shouted, looking around to see where she had gone. At that, Mauvis' expression became devastated, and he turned to jog after the Yrati. Vladdir swore. If only Mauvis would let go of deciding what was best for his king, just this once. Usually his attentive concern was appreciated. Now it was not.

Kyril had moved farther into the Aragoths' midst, attracting most of their attention away from the Yrati. Vladdir had to pause and blink a few times before he could believe what he was seeing. Unburdened by armour or an Aragoth fighting partner, Kyril was dancing through them like a blood-spattered lotus on the wind. When they struck at her, it was as if the force of their blows pushed her unharmed out of the way. When she struck back, it was deadly. She knew exactly where to strike to weaken or find the chinks in the rockskin. The Aragoths seemed like clumsy, flailing dolts, stumbling towards certain slaughter as they clawed their way over fallen comrades to reach Kyril, only to join their fellows in a spray of blood once they entered her range. Kyril was vengeance. She was light. She was death. When she finished, only Vladdir was left standing.

PART II

MAUVIS, THE CHAMBERLAIN

SEN KAI HURRIEDLY SHUFFLED his bulk down the tiled corridors of the Royal House with the small, wriggling bundle clutched tightly in his arms. He was still shaking with the revelation he'd just had and dreaded reporting it to his king, but didn't know what else to do. Alekseidir was a terrifying man when he was calm, never mind when he was enraged.

The old Sen paused when he passed the shallow fish pools embedded alongside one of the king's sitting rooms. He could drown the baby, have the remains burnt. Gleddys would fire up the ovens if he asked, and was cynical enough to not bother asking questions. Did he have the mettle to do the drowning? He took one step towards the water, hesitated, then took another. A heavy stride sounded behind him. It was too late. Aleksei could move with absolute silence when he wished. He intended for Kai to hear him coming. The Chamberlain turned to face his king and knelt, bowing his head. Alekseidir approached unhurriedly, black cloak swishing over black armour. He had a calculating half-smile on his face as he reached out one black-gloved hand to pull back the blanket. He already knew. Thank the Earth that

Kai hadn't drowned the child.

"She brought it to you?" Alekseidir asked.

"The Guard summoned me when she came to the tunnels. They tried to keep her silent. I think they were successful. Regardless, she could have been lying," said Kai.

"She wasn't," said Aleksei.

Kai was speechless. He could not disbelieve the word of his king, especially when spoken so plainly, even though he wanted to. His hands shook so badly the child began to slip in his grasp.

"You're surprised I go to the surface, Kai?"

That hadn't been it at all. He knew his king liked to roam the sands at night. It was not his place as Chamberlain to question such things.

"The Desert calls me. Eats at me."

Kai dared to look up to meet Alekseidir's black eyes.

"Sometimes I do strange things."

Kai wished Aleksei would not tell him this. Obviously one of these strange things was lying with surface women and begetting bastards.

"What should I do?" he asked. He tried to hold out the child, hoping the king would take it and kill it himself. Alekseidir eyed him speculatively.

"You keep it."

"My King?"

"You have no way with women, Kai. This may be your only chance for a child."

"Where shall I say it came from?"

Alekseidir shrugged. "I'm sure you'll come up with some tale."

"Should I hide it? Keep it away from young Prince Vladdir?"

Aleksei shrugged again and smiled over his shoulder as he turned to leave. "It's up to you, Kai..." The king turned back, tapping his lips with one finger. "Just give it a name of one of your ancestors. One who was distinguished."

Kai bowed as much as he could over the baby in his arms and his own protruding stomach. "As My King wishes. I am honoured." Kai ran to his chambers as soon as Alekseidir had turned away, his flat sandals slapping annoyingly against the marbled floors. The last thing he wanted was to be stopped and asked questions by the other servants before he was properly prepared. With pounding heart and trembling fingers, he ripped open the door to his private chambers, slammed it shut behind himself and twisted the key in its lock. By the time he had plopped down in his favourite chair by the hearth, he was already in love; already thought of the warm, squirming child as his.

Amidst his relief and happiness, Aleksei's words still burned at him. *You have no way with women, Kai.* So what? If one could not find a woman of quality that was worth courting, what was the point of wasting time with inferior ones? Just to beget bastards? He immediately chastised himself for the thought. He was no handsome brute worth chasing, himself, and Aleksei's pursuits had given him this little one, still twisting in its blankets, turning its tiny, soft face upwards to blink blindly at Kai.

"Well, there's no point in *me* running after women, hey?" he asked the baby. "I have different pursuits. I pursue things of the mind, as I shall teach you." He sat in a moment of stunned contentment, trying to think of something important to do. After all, he was a father now. Oh, yes. He checked, and the baby was well diapered with lots of absorbent moss. Good. He sat back and let his eyes roam over his precious book collection. Inspired, he stood up with the baby and began to scan through the books until he found his favourite one, a thin tome of well-illustrated architecture, written by one of his great-grand uncles; a well-learned man, also childless, who had left behind this immortal masterpiece. He ran his fingers over the author's embossed name plate as he read the inscription.

Mauvis. The baby's name was Mauvis.

It was happening again. Tiny Mauvis could feel the vulgar thrill race down his spine then spread through his bowels, making him feel sick and tremble with fear. The smell of blood and decay came in through the opened skylight with the darkness of the night and Aleikseidir's blackened form as the king tumbled from the surface and into Kai's chambers with a rush of sand. The skinny child untangled himself from his blankets and ran for a wash basin of hot water and towels as his father leapt from his bed to help Alekseidir to his feet. The king's night sickness was becoming more intense and striking him with higher frequency. This was the third time in a month he had come to Kai like this. Mauvis' father dragged the king to his study chair and shoved him into it, then turned to wave Mauvis forward, reaching out to take the hot water. Alekseidir was strewing Desert sand and gobs of black something all over the floor tapestries as he waved his arms blindly, reaching for Kai. His eyes were coated with dark purple that spilled over his cheeks when he blinked.

"Kai," Aleksei rasped. "I can't let them see me like this. Oh, Earth! I still hunger!"

"No one will see you," said Kai as he roughly sponged gore off his king's face. "Mauvis, bring more towels, then run to fetch some clean robes. Get night robes. We'll say the king could not sleep and came to have some tea, and it spilled on his clothes."

The child nodded solemnly and dashed to the closet for the towels. He returned with them cautiously, approached as near as he dared, trying not to gag at the smell. The king's eyes cleared and his head snapped towards Mauvis, his hand shooting out to grab the child's night shirt and drag the boy near. Mauvis dropped the towels in fright and tore at the king's black gauntlet as he looked into Alekseidir's maw, lined with fangs all the way down his throat.

"No!" shouted Kai, using his arm and body to force the king to let go. "Enough, Aleksei! You must resist this evil! Mauvis! Go!"

Mauvis ran to the door, turning just before he left to make sure his father was all right. Kai was forcing something down Alekseidir's gorge. Kai never told Mauvis what it was, but whenever Alekseidir had come to them like this, it had calmed him enough to sleep.

Mauvis ran through the red-carpeted corridors of the Royal House, dodging the legs of courtiers and guests who never seemed to sleep, knowing that Kai's words of discretion had been unneeded. None of these people ever gave any attention to one such as himself. The ceremonial guards placed at the vaulted doorway of the king's chambers also paid him no mind as he dashed past them, skipping over the white marble tiles. Nor did the chamber servants question him when he wrenched open the great wooden doors that lead to the king's wardrobe and took what he pleased. After all, he was the Chamberlain's son. Before returning to Kai, he slipped past other guards and into the sleeping chamber of the youngest prince, Vladdir. He was three years younger than the prince, but felt that Vlad was his only real friend, and often pretended that they were brothers when they played together. The last time he had come here after one of the king's night time wanderings, he had done so seeking comfort from Vladdir, only to find that he could not wake his friend, who seemed to be breathing with difficulty, twitching in his sleep. He knew that Alekseidir's demons had found their way into Vlad's dreams; when he had once childishly tried to peel the prince's eyes open, he had seen the same purple venom seeping from beneath the lids.

Mauvis pushed aside the heavy blue curtains that hung around the bed. The prince seemed at peace now. No sign of the curse that befell Aleksei was showing. Mauvis didn't want to wake Vlad or call any type of attention to him. He wished he could find out what Kai used to calm the king, so that he could steal some of it for when the evil seized the young prince. He didn't dare ask his father in case Kai wanted to know the reason for his curiosity. Mauvis had seen what Alekseidir had done to the eldest prince, Vasha, when he found the same hunger also grew in him. The memory of the deep welts on the prince's back and how they had oozed when Kai had silently cleaned them still burned in Mauvis' mind. Vasha had lived in Kai's chambers for a month while he healed.

Mauvis put his hand on Vlad's shoulder for a few seconds, glad that it felt warm, then turned and ran.

The next morning, Mauvis was woken by the sunlight filtering in through the closed skylight and the sand that the wind had kicked over it. He peered over the edge of his wooden box by the hearth and regarded his father carefully to see what kind of mood he was in before calling out any sort of greeting. Kai's face was rigid and lined with tears as he tidied the table, setting out their breakfast. This was bad.

"Do you see what the Desert does, Mauvis?" asked Kai without turning to look at him. "It makes you eat until you are eaten yourself. It's a dangerous thing." Kai did turn then, and came to gently lift Mauvis out of his box and set him on his feet. "Tell me, boy. Do you feel anything at all from the Desert?"

Mauvis shook his head emphatically, feeling no guilt at his lie. He felt it, all right. He always knew when Alekseidir was coming home. But the sensation repulsed him. He knew the hunger, but was able to fully reject it. It would never take him. Like his father, he was strong, able to reject all of the indulgent weaknesses that afflicted the king. No fermented drink, no rich foods, no visitations from women, no roaming in the Desert. Evil would never take him.

Kai stroked his hair fondly before wiping away his own tears.

"If anyone asks, Mauvis, say that the king was here the entire evening. Do you understand? There has been some misfortune, but...we must repair it the best we can. No point in ripping the whole thing open and making it all worse. Do you understand?"

No. But Mauvis nodded anyway. Sunlight always made him feel safer, and there was plenty of it now. He shovelled down his breakfast, looking forward to going to the Royal Chambers as they did every morning, to inspect the servants' housekeeping and give the princes Vessek and Vlad their early day lessons. Vasha was training with the soldiers now, and wouldn't join them. Kai helped him into his formal jacket and leggings and slipped on his boots. As they walked through the white-tiled hallways, now glistening with the morning light, Mauvis had already decided which pens and tablets he'd select for Vladdir this morning, and which games he'd suggest they'd play in the afternoon—

Kai was pulling him in a different direction. Mauvis looked up at his father curiously and was startled to see that he had begun crying again. Very bad indeed. Feeling his blood run cold, Mauvis also felt his tongue and throat freeze. He knew he wouldn't be able to talk, so there was no point in trying to ask what had happened. Not that Kai was ever in the habit of giving straight answers.

The feeling came again. This time it went straight to Mauvis' bowels, making him fear he might shame himself and his father. Seconds later he was stunned into immobility as the sound of Alekseidir's howl slammed against his body. He felt rather than heard the mix of anger, shame, grief and anguish carried by the noise, and his eyes were flooded by light that seemed to knock something loose in his head. He didn't realise Kai was tugging on his hand until his father picked him up and carried him farther down the corridor, towards the overwhelming illumination that filled the chamber beyond.

Mauvis closed his eyes against the strange brightness, burying his face into Kai's shoulder. Everyone around them was rushing about, their bodies giving off vast oceans of light. Even with his lids squeezed shut, he could see them in his mind. Alekseidir's form was dark red light, Queen Sulandor was dark pink. The other people were bright white, hurrying to the king, trying to raise him from where he had fallen, still screaming out his pain. Why was everyone suddenly glaring like the sun? Everyone except...Vasha lay silently on a carved slab of sandstone in the middle of the room, hands folded over his chest, completely lightless.

Mauvis carefully peeked from Kai's shoulder, to make sure his mind had gotten it right. Yes, Vasha's light had gone. The soft glow surrounding him came from the flowers stuffed around his body. Flowers were also packed under Vasha's chin, but failed to completely cover the purple bruising at his throat. Mauvis lifted his head completely and scanned the room for Vladdir, finally seeing him glowing pale blue, slowly growing colder. The prince was staring at his lightless brother, one of his uncles holding him upright by his shoulders. Mauvis wriggled free from Kai's grip, ignoring his father's admonitions to remain still, and ran to Vlad.

The prince looked down at him for a moment before whispering, "Vasha died last night. Mama is so angry she won't speak to Papa." Vladdir's cheek was tapped by his uncle's finger, shushing him. Mauvis grasped Vladdir's hand tightly, feeling his friend tremble through the contact.

Three months later, Vlad's other brother Vessek was also dead. The courtiers in the hallways whispered of Aleksei and the Desert. There was talk of unnatural hungers. Queen Sulandor left the Royal House, returning to her family in the North.

Six months later, Alekseidir attacked Kai in his chambers, nearly gutting him. The sedatives were no longer working. In the morning, Kai died. That was when Mauvis stopped seeing light around people. He just didn't want to know.

Mauvis dressed carefully, as his father had taught him. Almost five years old, he couldn't get his leggings straight without Kai's help, but he'd have to do it himself from now on. He felt like crying, still remembering the troubling conversation he'd had with Vladdir the night before. The prince had told him that he wanted to go live with his mother, since his father was no longer any good. If Vladdir left, who would bother speaking to Mauvis? For the first time, Mauvis wondered if *he* had a mother to go live with. What had happened to his mother, anyway? Didn't most people have one?

Knowing he'd be early but not having anything else to do, Mauvis made his way to the king's chambers. Alekseidir had summoned him to come this morning. It was astonishing to Mauvis that the king would even bother thinking of him. There was only one reason why he would, and Mauvis hoped he would be able to speak if Alekseidir should ask him *that* question.

What do you know of Vladdir's communication with Desert, Mauvis?

To his surprise, Mauvis was led inside the king's chambers the moment he arrived. Alekseidir was pale against the ruby of his bedclothes and a doctor was leaving his bedside with a great basin of blood. Vladdir had told Mauvis that his father insisted on these treatments, though they made him so weak he could barely sit up. Alekseidir beckoned Mauvis to climb onto the bed, which he obediently did. The king tightly gripped his fingers and pulled him closer, making the thought of being eaten flash through Mauvis' mind, but it left quickly. He could feel that this was not what the king wanted.

"Do you know how to be Chamberlain, boy?" Aleksei rasped. Mauvis nodded. Of course he knew, but—

"I don't know about medicines," he said.

"Ah," Alekseidir responded. "Kai hadn't begun to teach you yet." Tears appeared in the king's eyes. "I did love him." Mauvis nodded. "He protected me. He never judged me for my stupidity...for being so foolish as to take that vial." Mauvis nodded again. "That's why I gave you to him." Mauvis blinked in confusion. "I'm glad I did. You are proof I could father a pure son, and this arrangement allowed me to see you." Mauvis had no idea what the king was talking about, but he nodded obediently.

"I want you to remain here, and become Chamberlain when you are older. As for medicines," Aleksei paused. "I suppose I can have...the Yrati tutor you." The king's expression was halfway between a smile and grimace. What was wrong with the Yrati? Mauvis rather liked them.

"They see too much." Mauvis' eyes widened as he realised the king could hear his thoughts. "Pay attention now, boy." Mauvis leaned closer.

"I need you to purify Vladdir, do you understand? Don't cover up for him like Kai did for me. I need you to keep him safe. Tell me you understand." Mauvis nodded until he thought his head might come loose. Joy was spilling into his heart. That meant that even if Vladdir left, Mauvis would be able to go with him.

"Vladdir isn't leaving. I know he is angry with me, as well he should be. But he is now the Crown Prince. He can never leave."

Aleksei smiled then, and put a hand to Mauvis' chin to stop his head bobbing. "Noble Mauvis. I am ever so glad you were born."

That day Mauvis stopped fearing and started to love Alekseidir without hesitation, Desert demons and all.

Alekseidir's tomb had been plundered. Mauvis, fully grown and Chamberlain of the House of Dir for decades, cursed the Aragoths as he stumbled into the piles of rubble that had fallen from the knocked-in ceiling. The shards of glass from the vaulted skylight now lay haphazardly on the broken, black marble tiles, where they shredded the bottoms of his boots. His hands groped the air as he moved towards Aleksei's casket. It had been smashed open, the back of it still standing against the wall. He couldn't accept that it was completely empty. Every time his eyes returned to the place where Aleksei had been propped up in eternal rest for so many years, his mind had to re-register that the silver-inscribed, black stone lid was no longer intact, instead lying in pieces scattered over the ground. There were definite footprints in the dust around the casket. This was no accident—the king's bones had been carried off. The man had been *dead*. Did the Aragoths recognise *nothing* as sacred? Was there any purpose to desecrating his remains thus? For an instant he was glad—*glad* that Kyril had stayed with the tunnel dwellers and turned against her own kind.

Rayner was calling his name and pulling at his arm, but Mauvis was incapable of answering him because he could not breathe. He thought that Rayner must have caught him, just barely, before he lost consciousness and fell to the ground.

How many different ways were there to lose a father?

I have a lot of work to do.

Mauvis sat up, realising first that he had been put to bed fully clothed, then that his left temple was throbbing painfully, and finally that his head had been wrapped in bandages. He *tsked* as he brushed away the dust that his boots had left on the bed sheets, wondering not for the first time how in Earth the Yrati managed to live in such squalor and not get sick themselves.

He slowly stood up and regarded the simple bronze triangle placed at the foot of his bed. The Yrati insisted it represented a balanced Earth, though try as he might, Mauvis could not see how. Still, he would pray in front of that thing. He muttered a few passages to it now. As always, Vladdir was first in his prayers. Mauvis loved Vlad until his heart hurt. Only as an adult had he come to understand that unspeakable secret of his own true parentage, whispered to him when Alekseidir had lain on his sickbed. It had only made Mauvis love Vlad more. Sometimes, when he thought he could no longer bear the silence, Mauvis wished desperately to voice the secret, but the cold realisation of how he would sound made him suppress the words once again. Vladdir would think him some kind of pretender, would not believe him. It would separate them irrevocably.

Well, first things first. He would have to tour the remains of the underground tunnels, determine which were repairable and which would have to be sealed off for safety. The main livestock caverns were unusable, all half-filled with magma that was still soft and steaming, having been released from the Earth's core by the Aragoths' drills and explosives. He doubted any of the floors that had been destroyed where one set of tunnels lay over top a second set could be reinstated without a great number of supporting metal bars. That meant he'd have to send out prospectors to find a plentiful vein of iron. And he'd have to get rid of all this damned rubble. He resisted the urge to kick some of it aside, knowing that doing so would hurt his foot rather than the rock. And when he had the time, the tomb of his father would have to be repaired. Both of them.

The main river tunnel that had underlain the agricultural caverns was no longer intact, and most of the connecting piping had been torn out, so plumbing and hygiene would be a problem until that was repaired. So much damage had been done by the Aragoth invasion that the river lay exposed all the way up to the surface, and the tunnels that had wound through the Earth above it appeared as nothing more than gutted shelves, protruding like ribs into a massive, emptied body cavity. Mauvis heaved a weary sigh. His inclination was to close off this section as well, but this stretch of the river was the most easily accessible, and the people did need water. But what in Earth was he to do with that great, gaping hole several tiers above his head? If he didn't have that covered up somehow, the dust would be blown in, and the water would be evaporated out—

He put a hand over his eyes and tilted his head downward until the throbbing ache receded a bit.

He would quite simply have to design a massive skylight that would allow expansion and contraction as the Desert heated by day and cooled by night, that could withstand the frequent dust storms and the sudden pressure changes in the cavern that would occur as the river either sped up or slowed down depending on the tide of the ocean it connected to far in the south. Right. Simple. He chuckled to himself. Well, wasn't he the namesake of a famous architect?

A skylight would give a lot of light here. A lot of light, a lot of water. He began to imagine the gutted tunnels as tiers of a massive garden, with imported fruit-bearing vines spilling over their edges; children laughing as they collected multi-coloured bounty to deliver to their parents, who could have market stalls lined along the waterfront, which could have docks built in all along the edges, so that their produce could be transported along the length of the river. *Hmmm.* Some definite possibilities were there. He would have to talk to Rayner about how strong those broken shelves of the former tunnels were. Perhaps he could have the edges reinforced with some metal and stone pillars.

By the end of the week, Mauvis had completed his sketches of what he had tentatively dubbed the "Market Caverns", as well as his plans to rebuild the Royal House and repair the front end of the University, which had received most of the damage. The Library had been rifled through, but at least they hadn't set fire to it.

Vladdir was still recovering from some of his injuries, and his stone arm had caused a few new ones, particularly great muscle strain along the side of his neck and shoulder. Regardless, he sat relaxed and happy, smiling as Mauvis presented him with the drawings. Vladdir was smiling a lot lately, more than he had even at his wedding to Queen Arlendan. It somewhat distressed Mauvis, especially when those smiles were directed at Kyril. At least Vladdir's relationship with Hailandir had improved with his more peaceful demeanour. She sat on her father's lap now, sucking on a few of her fingers while shaking some rattle thing Callie had given her.

By the end of the month, most of the rubble had been removed, or at least piled out of the way. Old Dagnaum, the Yrati High Priest, was recovered after the former mercantile block had been cleared. Apparently he had been "trapped" in the larder of a gourmet restaurant with a rather buxom trader from Raulen, and the two of them had been ensuring their survival by happily cooking up a storm and drinking the wine. When they were "freed" by the construction workers, Rayner set upon them. He slapped Dagnaum's arm and head repeatedly, while complaining that the sounds of munching and farting that had been coming from under the rock had been louder than the workmen's hammers and drills, frightening all the old folk and children.

A few more rescues were made as the work progressed. With each façade, carved pillar or tapestry the craftsmen put in place, Mauvis could feel the morale of the tunnel dwellers increasing, and many seemed happy to indulge his wish that the tiling be laid out even more precisely than before, since they were at it. The colour schemes were limited to white, grey and red, as those were the colours of the stone materials that were plentiful. The blue, green and brass accents would have to come later, after the import agreements had been re-established with surrounding nations.

The Yrati were wonderfully helpful, setting a fine example by taking off their scholars' robes and working with the tradesmen as hard as their spindly limbs would allow. Their efforts to regain moss farming and herded fish stocks were greatly appreciated—most of the workmen were growing tired of constant fungi. Some of the nobles were following suit, although their priorities were to work on the new river docks and other facilitators of commerce. Thankfully, the need for a police force was not apparent. The army remained thin, and were most often deployed along the perimeter of the new city-state. The Yrati didn't know yet, but Mauvis had planned an entire series of caverns to be inhabited exclusively by their clan, complete with laboratory and living space. He had selected the design for the front entryway from a book of Yrati mysticism, which had crisscrossing troughs of water, knotty stone tree-fountains, haphazard moss beds, and made absolutely no sense to Mauvis...a fact which made him feel even more assured that the Yrati were going to love it.

By the end of the year, Hailandir had six teeth, was saying a few words, and could hold a pen correctly. The Royal House, while incomplete, was inhabited, and the structural base of the Market Cavern was finished. It gave Mauvis great satisfaction to see the tiers and railings among what had been the greatest mark of the Aragoth-inflicted devastation. One of the student architects had designed an interesting pumping system that was powered by nothing more than the flow of the river, to carry water up the curving support struts and deliver irrigation to all the creeping vines grown along the struts and railings. The skylight was made entirely of uncoloured glass. However, by controlling the content of the sand used to make the panes, or by frosting certain sections with the injection of bubbles, the natural colours of the Desert were let through to varying degrees, seeming to bathe the cavern in silver and golden hued light.

Vladdir made no effort to hide his relationship with Kyril. He would walk hand in hand with her in public, and took her with him into his chambers every night. Mauvis watched Vladdir's movements like a hawk, but could find no evidence of night time ramblings, purple eye venom or the blood-thirsty hunger that Alekseidir had suffered from. Still, it pained him that Hailandir's siblings might be gotten on some surface creature. He feared it might increase the probability that those children—his own nieces and nephews—would also be called by the Desert.

Early one morning, Mauvis jerked awake. He had fallen asleep in his chair without having made his usual check on Vladdir after the king had gone to bed—just to make sure he had stayed there. He yawned and stretched, moving carefully in case sleeping in the odd position had given him a crick in his neck. Lately he had been wondering if there was any point to his constant vigil over Vladdir. He knew that the Yrati assumed the constant checks were solely because of Kyril, because Rayner would smile and shake his head knowingly at Mauvis before walking away.

Kyril was proving to be nothing more than a dim-witted nuisance. Mauvis could not fathom why Vladdir found her so interesting. She never seemed to know what was going on, and it was a rare occasion that she seemed able to piece together enough words to actually have a conversation with someone. All she did was moon over Vladdir, which he supposed could flatter a man for a while, but six straight months of it should have grown tiresome. It was suspicious that not a single Aragoth had been sighted since that final battle in the Yrati caves, and was very unlikely that Kyril had gotten them all, but it was growing increasingly difficult to build a case that she was in league with them and sent to poison Vlad's mind with Desert dreams. Indeed, for the first time in Mauvis' memory, the king was content to sit and be an administrator, showing absolutely no sign of midnight restlessness. Maybe things really had settled down. Perhaps the Aragoths had disbanded. Perhaps it had been their chantings and magics out in the Desert that had cursed the House of Dir in the first place.

Or perhaps it was because every last trace of Alekseidir and his purple venom had been removed from the underground. Well, whatever it was, Mauvis supposed he should be content that the Royal House was now a more appropriate place to raise Hailandir. He got up and straightened his rumpled clothing. He would take a walk through the parts of the House that were under reconstruction, check the progress of the tiling, then come back and change his clothes before attending the morning planning sessions.

He wandered past the shrine that was being built in Alekseidir's honour and felt satisfied that it was going well. Kai's tomb hadn't been as badly damaged and repairs had been completed some time ago. Rayner may think what he liked, but the main reason why Mauvis kept to his vigil was because he had promised his fathers he would protect Vladdir in every way he could. It seemed to be his last connection to either of them. Although, he mused, as he stopped to trace a triangle pattern in water over Kai's catacomb plate, there was some jealousy involved. Kyril had replaced him as Vladdir's "saviour." Perhaps it was time. Hailandir's formal education would have to start in a year or two, which was exactly when he planned to have completed rebuilding the underground. His focus would shift from father to daughter.

From the corner of his eye, Mauvis caught the movement of a lithe figure in a swath of pink, moving gracefully past a connecting hallway. Kyril. What in Earth was she doing about at this hour? It wasn't like she had any interest in tiling. And king's mistress or not, she had no business walking about in her flimsy nightdress. She could at least conduct herself with some dignity and dress properly before allowing herself to be seen. Mauvis schooled himself to be patient and started after her. He would speak to her slowly and gently, in the way that always seemed to lessen her confused twitching, and explain to her that she had to get dressed first before leaving the bedchambers.

She was at the end of the hallway by the time he had passed through the connecting tunnel. There weren't any skylights in this section and the lamps hadn't been relit, so it was still quite dim, but he could see her clearly enough.

"Kyril!" he called out to her. She either didn't hear him, or hadn't figured out yet that she was supposed to answer when called. She continued on her way. Mauvis jogged after her. She had gone to the water reservoir, and was sitting on the edge of the glass cover, staring down into the swirling pool. Had she decided to pray like the Yrati? Now that he thought of it, where were the Yrati? There were usually a few of them sitting at the reservoir at all hours, mesmerised by the churning of the water. It just made Mauvis nauseous, but then it took all types.

He was about to speak her name again when she suddenly moved in that cat-like way of hers, scooped up an empty bucket and with a deft twist of a faucet, filled it with water before disappearing down one of the recessed tunnels. How did she always make mundane things seem like a painstakingly choreographed dance when she was so mentally challenged? And what did she need a bucket of water for? Maybe she was going to bathe in public again.

"Kyril!" He stepped up onto the wall of the pool to see which corridor she had gone through. He hoped she wasn't headed towards the breakfast hall dressed like that. A cold breeze came down through one of the tunnels off to the side. Mauvis leaned over, careful to not slip onto the weak part of the glass water cover, and peered into the side corridor. There was pale morning light at the end of it, which opened to the surface. That old warning feeling suddenly hit him in the gut, and then it was gone. Had he imagined it? He jumped down and strode into the tunnel, beginning to worry. Vladdir hadn't been afflicted in his sleep by the purple venom since the end of the war with the Aragoths. Was Kyril touched by it? Would she re-poison Vladdir with the Desert's hunger? But why now, in the morning, when Alekseidir had always been drawn to the surface at night?

The sandy colour of the Desert light was as warm as the wind was cold. Mauvis pushed his brown curls out of his face as he stepped out onto the surface, looking around for Kyril. A trail of shallow-pitted footsteps indicated her path. He followed it over a dune and saw that her steps had continued down in front of a small cliff, perhaps four or five metres below where Mauvis stood. The ground there was flat plains rock, pushed into slabs along one edge of the depression, forming a natural staircase.

Kyril was kneeling with the bucket in front of her. She was muttering something about water coming. Mauvis shook his head and squatted at the top of the cliff, trying to hear her more clearly. She was making no sense. After a few moments she started picking up the bucket and tapping the bottom of it against the rock. Then she began to slam it down so that the water splashed out of it. Was she trying to break it?

"Water come!"

The wind rose suddenly, forcing Mauvis to blink against the grit carried with it, and he rubbed his eyes in disbelief as water came. The bucket bubbled and overflowed with clear waves, rapidly spilling over the rock and filling the depression where Kyril sat so that it became a small pool. She tilted her head back and raised her arms to the sky, smiling with what looked like immense relief. A small hurricane seemed to be building around her, whipping dark hair across her face and arms. She began singing some strange, wordless song, perhaps more howling than singing. The veins in her arms turned dark green beneath her skin, as though some dark liquid was suddenly flowing through them.

Oh Earth! This was magic. Mauvis got up and ran down the rock steps until he teetered at the edge of the pool in front of Kyril.

"Kyril! Come out of there at once!"

The air immediately fell still. She lowered her chin to look at him, and he saw that her eyes were swimming with green venom. Her mouth was also filled with it.

"Why are you here, Mauvis?" she asked, green spilling from her lips. She moved to the edge of the pool, retreating when he tried to grab her arm.

"Get out of there!"

"Why?"

"Just *what* do you think you're doing?"

"I..." She tilted her head in that way of hers which indicated confusion. She looked at him expectantly like she had fully explained herself and was waiting for his response.

"Look, if you're going to stay with Vladdir, there are certain boundaries of acceptable behaviour that you're just going to have to observe. You can...bathe properly *underground!* Like everyone else."

"I eat."

"What?"

"Here water, and Earth, and light. Eating."

Mauvis crouched down and let himself flop into a sitting position as the realisation hit him. Kyril did put food in her mouth to please Vladdir, but she really didn't take much. Maybe Aragoths weren't human, but were some sort of Desert construct. Maybe Vladdir had fallen in love with some paper woman who could disintegrate at any moment. She was only meant to live long enough to finish the war—she had no other purpose.

"Why are you upset?" she asked. "Usually you are only angry about blood ritual. Water is..." Again the confusion. "Purifying."

"How often do you do this?"

"I don't know."

"How can you not know? Did you do it yesterday? Are you going to do this tomorrow? Next week?"

"Your question has to do with...time?"

"It seems my question is pointless."

"You are frustrated with me because I do not think."

Despite himself, Mauvis laughed.

"Vladdir fills my mind." She paused for a long moment. "That's all."

"What exactly are you, Kyril?"

The question apparently caused extreme confusion and agitation. Kyril's head jerked as she tried to think. Her eyes cleared and she stood up from the water, moving to sit at the edge of the pool. Mauvis sighed with exasperation at the way her wet nightshift clung to her. He took off his jacket, regretting that the lining would get wet, and wrapped it around Kyril's shoulders. The water began to drain away.

"Why do you have to 'purify' yourself?"

"Wash out the Desert. Fill my space with light and wind."

"And if you don't?"

"I'll have to leave."

"What do you mean? Why are you leaving?"

"No one stays forever."

"When are you going?"

"Time?"

"Never mind. Where are you going?"

"To dust and the Desert."

"Are you dying?"

"No. I have water."

"So you're just leaving."

She didn't seem to think this needed a response.

"What of Vladdir?"

"He is of the Desert."

"Meaning what, exactly?"

"He will also leave for the Desert."

"Is that what all this is about? The Aragoths were unable to defeat Vladdir in battle so they sent you along to lure him away from the underground?"

"You wish him to stay with you?"

"Of course!"

"Have you bonded him?"

Mauvis felt his face turn numb with shock. "*How dare you!* I would never—"

"Then why are you trying to control him?"

"Look, you...sludge-brain. I am Vladdir's *servant*. I'm not some sort of Desert witch who goes around taking people—"

"Then you are bonded to him."

"What? *Earth*, no!"

Kyril stood and began walking back up the rock stairs.

"Wait!" Mauvis called. "You answer my question. Are you here to take Vladdir back into the Desert, or harm him in any way? Because

I warn you—"

"I do not control Vladdir."

"But you poison his mind."

Kyril paused, looking back over her shoulder. She showed none of her confusion quirks, and her expression seemed mildly angry. She pushed Mauvis' jacket off her shoulders, letting it drop to the sand, and continued on alone.

"Is this water magic or something else?"

Rayner shrugged elaborately.

"I thought you Yrati communed with water."

"Well, you said she turned green. Maybe she's a plant or something. Then it would be vegetable magic." Some of the Yrati working nearby snickered. He grinned.

"Sometimes I think you're as dense as she is."

"Mauvis, what are you all worried about? You obviously aren't afraid of all magic or you wouldn't be here bothering me now. I practise water magic. Why don't you consider me evil?"

"Perhaps I need to rethink that."

"Honestly, as far as I can tell, she calms Vladdir down. Makes him happy. Everyone I know who knows him well has commented on it. He's the most relaxed he's ever been in his entire life. How is any of this bad?"

"She is an *Aragoth*. And Vladdir is not himself. He's all dreamy and floating in the weeds all the time. As you say, he was never like that before. His mind is going to mush."

"You're exaggerating. He resoundingly slaughtered Dagnaum at stones this afternoon."

"This isn't a game."

Rayner sighed. "The war's over, Mauvis."

"Is it? We haven't seen an Aragoth legion in several months, but this priest who controlled Ilet was never found. How do you know they aren't regrouping?"

"Well, go raise an army, then. I'm sure you could easily justify the need for added security. I'll have some designs for you after dinner." Rayner picked up a roll of parchments and walked off, apparently weary of the conversation.

Was he making too much of it? Vladdir wasn't exactly a normal man. Perhaps it was appropriate that he be with an abnormal woman. Mauvis just wished he understood it all better so that he'd know when to help and when to step back. With all due respect, the Yrati were accustomed to fixing things after they had gone wrong, while Mauvis felt he was trying to avert a disaster that no one would be able to fix.

Well, if he couldn't count on Rayner for help, could he ask Dagnaum? He'd probably get many of the same answers. The Yrati High Priest was even more insouciant and relaxed than Rayner. As with all things, he supposed he'd have to get the answers himself.

When Kai had died, Alekseidir had confiscated a certain trunk of books but had never disclosed what he had done with them. He certainly wouldn't have told Vladdir where they were, and he may well have destroyed them, but Mauvis was fairly certain this same trunk had shown up in the rubble of the destroyed Royal Bedchamber and had been put aside when the suite had been rebuilt and decorated. It now sat in storage with the archives.

Not much attention had been given to this part of the Royal House, the archives being a place where no one would spend a considerable amount of time. A cylindrical room had been hewn deep into the rock, with shelves lining the wall from the ground to the windowless ceiling, about five storeys in all. The light was provided by lanterns, not a very safe option considering the amount of paper in the room, and ladders stretched between ring-shaped scaffolds that provided a place for clerks to stand when they searched for a particular file. Mauvis mused that he should get some railings put in and replace the ladders with staircases. It was only a matter of time before someone broke their neck in here.

He found the trunk at the lowest level of the archive chamber, jammed against the supports of one of the scaffolds to help keep it upright. Tugging it forward so that he would be able to open the hinged lid, he kept one eye on the struts and hoped the platforms wouldn't come crashing down on his head. It was extremely heavy. It was only when he touched it that he realised that it was made of black stone, rather than the dark wood he had assumed as a child. He rubbed off some sooty dust as he ran his hands over the surface, finding that there were silver runes etched into the case. His fingers recoiled from touching them when he tried again to open the lid. Strange. It was almost the same as the repulsive force he felt when toying with magnets. Perhaps it was some minor trick Kai had used to protect Mauvis as a child.

The trunk turned out to be locked, which was no problem for a Chamberlain. A few moments with his set of universal keys opened it quickly enough. The inside was lined with cream broadcloth, and the books and folio pamphlets were arranged by the colour of their covers—red, blue, black, green, white. After a moment's hesitation, Mauvis pulled out a green one. It was about the wind, or an unseen force. Completely pointless. He set it on the sandy floor and picked out a red one. This spoke of blood. Disgusting. Blue was water. Black was the Earth. White was fire. Interesting. In the text, fire was synonymous with light. His eyes strayed back to the green books. Was there something else represented by the wind that Kyril had called upon?

The language in the books was either archaic or just grammatically horrifying, and the script was difficult to read. After flipping through four or five of them, a pattern was starting to appear. The unseen wind-force, apparently, could move or carry things, like water and Earth. When caught together in an immovable basin, usually described as stone, they could create life, usually represented as some sort of vegetation, which also needed fire, or light. Logical enough, although Mauvis would have written that they could support life generated from some sort of seed, not create it. Since the authors were not present to argue with, that was neither here nor there. Kyril, basin, water, Earth, light. Green flowing through her veins.

So where had Kyril's seed come from?

In the red books, blood also meant life. Was this describing some sort of seed? Who had written all these books anyway? A few of the blue and red ones were actually penned by old Dagnaum, probably when he was much younger. Some of the green and black ones were written by the surreptitious "Dark Lady of the Wind Caverns." Were these the same wind caverns lining the southern edge of the Plains? Mauvis supposed it was possible that someone could be living there. He had heard that these caverns—large crevasses, they actually were—had been hollowed out by the wind and resembled a sort of natural network of catacombs.

For a moment he considered taking a walk through the wind caverns to investigate this further. But his common sense jumped in and reminded him that a complete non-warrior such as himself had absolutely no business traipsing about the surface on his own, where there were all sorts of surface creatures, predators and natural disasters, just waiting to pounce on some naïve tunnel dweller. He sighed as he collected the books and began stacking them back into the trunk. Rayner's approach was starting to have more appeal. He paused before closing the lid. Were these books really all that he had left of Alekseidir? Without warning, the enormity of the theft of his previous king's remains crushed him again. He leaned his brow against the edge of the trunk and sobbed, letting his grief rush freely since he was alone.

So terribly alone.

The Chamberlain dabbed his face with a kerchief, closed the lid and returned to his chambers so that he could go to bed early. He didn't bother checking on Vladdir.

Mauvis bolted upright. The night wind was rattling his skylight latch, but that was all. His heart was pounding not with fear, but with excitement that someone might be trying to get in. After a few moments, nothing more happened and he lay down again, tugging the russet-coloured, floral scented covers up to his chin and listening to the sounds of the night. This was Kai's bed. Kai's room. Kai's books. Kai's exotic, imported carpeting. Who was Mauvis anyway? The realisation dawned on him that he had put his real self aside his whole life. His identity, his personal interests, his due acclaim. And for what?

Money didn't interest him. He loved Vladdir, but the king didn't really need him. Not the way Aleksei had needed Kai. He felt tolerated in return, rather than esteemed. Damn it, even his name was borrowed. Too upset to sleep, he got out of bed, pulled a grey shawl over his nightshirt and unrolled his drawings over Kai's table in the center of Kai's room. He corrected the designs for a few minutes, and then listlessly let the pencil fall out of his hand. The wind rattled the glass panes again. He gazed out through the skylight wistfully, envying the stars their freedom to roam the entire heavens. On impulse, he dressed himself in his favourite lace shirt and a dignified charcoal crushed velvet suit, pulled on a stout pair of boots, slung a journey sack over his shoulder and climbed out into the Desert.

The coolness of the air felt good. It blew his curls back from his face. Mauvis marched along in the darkness, feeling his spirits lift as strange lights chased each other far above in the atmosphere. He had no idea where he was going, and at the moment he really didn't care if something were to come along and kill him. Out here, he could speak his secrets without fear.

"I am the unacknowledged son of Alekseidir!" he announced loudly. "And that, my friends, makes me the Bastard Prince. Yes, I am the Bastard Prince of the Desert!" He made a mock bow to his non-existent audience. Something in the sand moaned and turned over. Mauvis couldn't see what it was, but he skirted around it, enjoying the chill it sent up his spine. "Good evening, sir! Lovely to meet you. Hope you enjoy tonight's entertainment!" The thing didn't respond and Mauvis continued on his way, singing loudly about a warrior king of the past, changing the lyrics as it suited him.

By morning Mauvis wasn't feeling well at all, but it hurt less to keep moving forward than to turn around and go back, so he kept walking. By now, Rayner was probably wondering if Mauvis had fallen sick. Perhaps he was sending his healer brethren to inquire after him. Or, they were so immersed in their own lives that no one would notice until tomorrow afternoon. Or, everyone was so relieved that he wasn't around to nag at them, that they thought they might enjoy it for a few hours more before going to see what had become of annoying, fussy Mauvis.

He stopped and crouched in the shade of a slab of rock protruding from the sand, hoping that for the next few minutes the damned thing wouldn't slip into the ground with the ever-changing Desert's whimsy. It was getting too warm to wear his jacket, so he slipped it off, slung it over his shoulder bag and rolled up his sleeves. Perhaps he should have brought some cream to soothe his skin from the harsh light. He drank a little bit from his water skin and wondered if he were anywhere near the oasis. He hadn't bothered to keep track of which direction he was going. He was on holiday; why should he worry about such things? If he died of dehydration, perhaps he would experience some form of delirium first, and maybe inscribe some weighty prophecy in blood on the rocks surrounding him to inspire future generations. He got to his feet again and surveyed the horizon for something interesting to go visit. There were some hoodoos on the horizon. Perhaps they would stay put long enough for him to go have a look at their rock striations. He might collect some pretty stones; while there was no real point in his doing so, it was his holiday and he would do as he pleased.

He started off in the direction of the rock pillars, and the Desert, as was its wont, moved them somewhere else. Mauvis stopped in exasperation.

"You could at least show me a little courtesy," he said to the Desert. "After all, I am your guest."

As if in response, a gaping hole opened up in the sand in front of Mauvis' feet. A large pocket of slipsand, and he had almost walked right into it. He'd want something much more interesting than *that* to happen before he died! Feeling aggravated, he marched around the hole determinedly, and was irritated when another of the pockets opened up into nowhere by his side. And another. One opened up right where he had placed his foot, and yet, what he stood upon felt relatively solid. And level, now that he tested his weight against it. Cautiously, he kicked aside some of the sand and was surprised to see a flat, white surface underneath. Looking closer, he saw that this was no mere sinkhole. It was angled, and there appeared to be a dim, waffling light coming from somewhere deep within.

"Is that an invitation?" Mauvis asked no one. Swinging his travel bag around to his back, he took a step downward and found that another solid, flat surface met his foot. He continued downward, mystified to be traversing some sort of staircase in the middle of the Desert and mildly worried that the sand was going to collapse in over his head once he reached the bottom. Hardly an interesting or pleasant death.

The tunnel that he entered at the bottom of the stairs seemed to be in a constant state of flux. The sand coating the walls looked like it was crawling upward in waves, making a steady scratching sound as it moved. At the end of the hallway, a dark space stretched backwards. It emanated a shimmering blue light, almost like a reflection off water. Mauvis entered cautiously, feeling relief at the coolness of the air. Out of the corner of his eye, the shifting sand seemed to be rumbling in behind him to close off his exit. When he turned to look, he could have sworn the dusty grains and small pebbles stopped in their tracks and turned about with feigned innocence. He turned back to the cavern and moved farther in. A dark pool of water, apparently naturally formed, lapped against an uneven shoreline several metres in front of him. The waves seemed purple. Blinking in the darkness, he eventually made out what appeared to be a curving table farther along the edge of the water, and four or five crooked pillars of rock built up from the drip of mineral water from the ceiling. The light had grown annoyingly dim. Mauvis turned in exasperation and was shocked to see that the entrance was nowhere to be found. He raised his hands and let them fall against his sides.

"I didn't think to bring a globe of light moss," he said. "How in Earth is anyone supposed to get out?"

"But you just got here."

He twisted in the direction of the voice, his eyes scanning the darkness and seeing nothing but the rock pillars. A woman had spoken.

"Hello?"

"Hello. Vladdir's servant, aren't you?"

"Yes. And to whom do I have the pleasure of speaking?"

A purple shadow shifted at the back of the cavern and shuffled towards the dark pool. The woman appeared to be wearing a dark cloak. Why she would need such a covering in this sunless place, which really wasn't that cold, was a mystery. Mauvis squinted at her and took a few steps forward. She paused and seemed to tense, like she might move away.

"I am Mauvis," he offered.

"I know who you are, Son of Aleksei."

Mauvis froze. How in Earth could anyone else possibly have known that? Unless...

"Did you know my father?"

"The Desert knows him."

"That's an uninformative answer."

"My, you're a very direct gentleman."

"You have me at a disadvantage. May I ask how you know me, Madam?"

She chuckled and began to move around the water, towards him. He could see the shape of the cloak better now, and surmised that she was a small woman, quite slender, with the clinging hood of her garment hanging down over her face.

"Can you see like that?" he asked her.

"I see everything," she murmured.

"How lucky for you."

"Mauvis, why are you so angry?" She edged closer to him, cautiously staying out of arm's reach.

"I'm not angry, just a little annoyed. I would like a straight answer."

"I doubt you would accept my answers. You would scoff. Disparage. Call me a liar."

Mauvis squinted in the dark, trying to manoeuvre so that more of the reflected light from the water would fall somewhere near the woman's face. He supposed she had a point.

"Are you the Dark Lady of the Wind Caverns?"

"No. There is no wind here. I am Saanae."

"Are you an Aragoth?"

"No, all the Aragoths are dead." Her voice sounded tight, as though she was very upset. "All except *Kyril*."

Now *this* was interesting. Mauvis pressed his fingertips together and tapped his lips thoughtfully. He chose his next words with care.

"Thank you, Saanae, for telling me your name. If I promise that I will not react, will you tell me how you know me and my father?"

"All right, Mauvis, Bastard Prince of the Desert. I see all in the water." She drifted to the edge of the pool and seemed to walk out onto it. Mauvis blinked and strained his eyes. Was she standing at the edge of the water or in it? Her height hadn't changed and the water lapped past her feet. She must be standing on a rock.

Mauvis twisted his mouth in embarrassment. "I suppose you must have been watching me for some time."

"I heard you sing."

"Dreadful, wasn't it?"

Her head turned away from the water and back towards him. "You sounded angry." She hopped back onto the shore and came right up to him. Mauvis instinctively took a step back and wished he had some sort of light. Her head moved in front of his chest, as if she were intently looking him over.

"Why did you come here?"

Good question, thought Mauvis. He decided not to broach the subject of water magic just yet. "Uh, I don't actually know. Just needed to get away, I suppose."

"Get away from what?"

"Well...Kyril, for one."

"*Kyril*," spat Saanae.

"You don't seem to like her, either. Look, this is very difficult for me. I don't suppose you might have some candles or something around here?"

Saanae reached out an arm and made some gesture that resulted in several blue flames flaring up in sconces set around the cavern. The space was larger than Mauvis had presumed, and the water was only a small pool, perhaps five metres across. Saanae looked like some little crocheted ghoul, wrapped in a woollen shroud. He looked around for an exit and saw none.

"Erm. How exactly does one come and go from this place?" he asked.

"Why? Does Mauvis want to leave so soon?" Saanae flitted up to him again and reached up to twirl a lock of his hair around her finger. He pulled back and was shocked to see a large chunk of his hair had come away in her hand. She held it up to a split in the sandy wall and the bit of hair jumped into the small crevice. Mauvis gasped in surprise and clamped a hand to his head, bewildered that his own hair could betray him thus.

"What did you do that for?"

"Sometimes I get lonely."

"Don't you have your *own* hair?"

In answer, Saanae flipped her hood back and regarded him with a sardonic curve to her lips. She was pale, but that was to be expected, living in a dark cave like this. Her lips were painted a deep purple-red, and her eyes were dark. And she did indeed seem to have a large quantity of dark hair resting on her shoulders and down her back. Fine lines tracing her narrow features suggested she was not a young girl.

"Uh. Hello." He offered his hand to her, as if they were just now being properly introduced. Saanae raised her eyebrows at this, and her smile grew a bit wider. She barely touched the tips of her fingers to his palm and drew them away immediately, giving a bit of a curtsey as she did so. The motion seemed rather cynical to Mauvis, but it would be rude of him to comment on it. "I have..." He rummaged through his sack. "...some biscuits here." Saanae's eyebrows lifted even more. "Perhaps we could sit and talk for a bit." Mauvis gestured towards the low bench next to the curving table he had seen earlier.

"Yes, I would like that." She led the way, and Mauvis noted that under her black cloak, she wore a dark red dress of a rather good cut, judging from the way it ruffled at her feet as she moved. Where in Earth would anybody find such a high-quality tailor this far out in the Desert?

"I'm a little surprised that the Lord Chamberlain of King Vladdir's court would stoop to socializing with a Desert creature like me," Saanae commented as she sat.

Mauvis spluttered in indignation. He was completely taken aback. And she said *he* was direct.

"Madam, you are clearly nothing like...as if I would...how could you think..."

"Are you going to share your biscuits with me?"

"Oh. Yes." Mauvis wiggled the lid off the tin and offered it to her distractedly. She took one and delicately bit into it, seeming to enjoy his discomfort. Had he done something to make her think he looked down on her? He *had* been rather terse when he first arrived, and he *had* come into her home, expecting to be answered immediately. "Please be assured that I do not think you are anything like...well..."

"Kyril?"

"Well, yes. May I ask how you know her?"

"She is the betrayer of the Aragoths. She's legendary now. How could anyone not know her? Are you worried she'll betray your king?"

"Ah, you *have* been watching me closely."

Saanae did not answer that, but instead seemed to glance off into the distance at nothing.

"Did she betray you?" Mauvis asked softly.

"Of course," said Saanae.

"What happened?"

"I was there when she tried to kill your Vladdir. Ran him through with her sword. Smiled in his face as she twisted it."

"And despite that, he brought her back with him."

"Yes."

"This is something I will never understand. But, Madam, what did she do to you? And why were you there?"

Saanae shifted on the bench and peered into his tin with interest. "May I have another biscuit?"

"Yes, of course." He held it out to her, disappointed. He told himself to be patient—what he asked must be related to a rather painful memory. He would have to build up her trust before asking again. Perhaps if he offered her information first, she would reciprocate. "I think it's just a matter of time before something disastrous happens. I don't know why Vladdir can't see it. Just the other day I caught her in the act of some strange magic. It involved water, but the Yrati seemed to know nothing of it. Whatever it was filled her eyes with green venom, and she said she ate. I knew it was just a matter of time before some mark of her evil became apparent. Madam, do you know much about water..."

Saanae was watching him with her dark eyes, biscuit forgotten and chocolate melting over her thumb.

"Mark of her evil?" she asked.

Mauvis was puzzled. She seemed offended.

"You mean like this?" She pushed her foot towards him, and then pulled up the hem of her skirt so that a runic tattoo showed on the pale skin of her ankle, just above the edge of a dainty red slipper. Mauvis gasped as his embarrassment gave way to something much more pleasant, and then blushed until he thought his face was the temperature of the core of the Earth. He tried to regain his composure and ended up smiling at her like an idiot.

Now Saanae looked amazed as she saw his reaction. A smile spread across her face as the realisation dawned on her. She looked down, still smiling, and retracted her foot, letting her skirts fall again.

"I guess it wasn't like that."

"No, Madam. Nothing like that at all."

Mauvis wanted to ask her what the tattoo meant, and to see it again. And finish his question about water magic. He had so many questions, but for the next few moments, he needed to just sit quietly. He stared at his hands where they rested on his knees. The fingers of his right hand wouldn't stop tapping.

"You're not what I expected, Lord Chamberlain."

Mauvis shrugged helplessly. "I always thought I was rather predictable." He glanced up to see her eyeing him speculatively.

"Perhaps I can help you answer your questions about Kyril, but I will need to know more of her actions first." Saanae rose from her seat and moved to the edge of the pool. She lifted a plain-looking goblet from the water and brought it over to hand to Mauvis. Fishing out a clear seal from the sleeve of her cloak, she deftly pressed it over the rim of the cup, capturing the water within. Mauvis tipped the goblet experimentally, tapping his finger against the covering.

"Is this glass?" he asked.

"Something like that. Listen to me. Take this scry cup back with you. You can speak to me through it. Just lean over the water and tell me what you see each day."

"Must I remove this cover first?"

"Yes, but be careful not to lose the water. It's special."

"I see. Wait! You have an entire pool here, why must I speak to you through this cup?"

"Kyril is too far away from here. Sometimes seeing her is difficult."

"But this is such a small bit of water. Surely your pool is much more powerful."

"Do you not wish to speak to me?"

"Of course I do, but—"

"This will make it much easier."

"Oh. Say, this is water magic, like that which the Yrati use. Perhaps I should ask them if—"

"Please don't."

"Why?"

"Well, if you want the Yrati to help you, then perhaps you should just ask them!" Saanae turned her back to him.

"I'm sorry, Saanae. I just don't understand why—"

She whirled around again. "I am a Desert creature. The Yrati do not approve of one such as me. If you already had their help, then there was no point in your coming here."

Mauvis' shoulders sagged. He hadn't meant to come here in the first place. And as for Rayner, well, he really wasn't much help at all.

"I really didn't mean to offend you. Please, explain to me how this works. Just to make sure I use it right."

Saanae softened and sat next to him again, her fingertips resting on his hands around the cup. The touch sent a warm thrill up his arms and deep into his chest.

"Just gaze into it, so you can see your reflection," she said softly. "Then speak to me. The vibrations of your voice on the water will be transmitted to my pool. I will hear you."

"Will I be able to hear you?"

"No. The flow of the magic will not go that way."

"Why?"

Saanae sat back and stared at him, that sardonic curl back around her mouth. "If you must know, the influence of your precious Yrati will interfere with it."

"Oh."

"So do you still want to take it?"

"Well, yes."

"Very well." Saanae stood up again and retrieved something else from the water. "Perhaps you should take this, too." Mauvis accepted a small red vial from her fingers.

"What is it?"

"So many questions."

Mauvis blinked in confusion. Had it not been a reasonable query?

"Why don't you just take it, and if it seems that you need it, I'll tell you what it is."

"Oh. All...right." Mauvis looked uncertainly at the two items in his hands, wondering how he was going to fit them in his sack—or for that matter, how he was going to find his way home. He stood up and handed his tin of biscuits to Saanae, who accepted them with a smile, and he tucked the goblet and vial in the place of the tin. He shook the sack experimentally and the goblet did not leak.

A wind started up and blew away part of a wall so that the staircase reappeared.

"That is truly amazing," said Mauvis.

"So," said Saanae, taking his elbow. "There you are. Thank you so much for your visit and the biscuits, Lord Chamberlain."

"I—I will speak to you," Mauvis promised as he stepped onto the lower stairs. "And I won't leave it too long, you know. I might say a few things, even if Kyril hasn't done anything remarkable that day." Saanae smiled and nodded, waving him toward the surface. "And, oh! My hair! Perhaps I should take it with me. You know, that bit that jumped into your hand."

"But I need it to help me hear you," said Saanae, pouting prettily.

"Oh. Right. Well. Farewell, then. Thanks for the, uh..." He waved his hands in the air, finally pointing at his travel sack. Saanae waved goodbye as the sand wall closed in again, forcing Mauvis to climb to the top of the stairs.

He stood on the surface for a few moments, as the wind blew grit through his hair. By the Earth! What a strange day! He had forgotten to ask how Saanae would contact him to tell him what to do with the vial, but he supposed they would have to meet again. That was preferable, anyway. He'd have to make sure he had some biscuits ready, since she seemed to like them.

Mauvis shuffled along a white expanse of rock, dragging his sack behind him. His jacket was long lost, and his skin was peeling off his face and arms. He expected that it must be burnt beyond recognition on his ears and scalp as well, judging by the intense pain he felt. He did have a goblet of water with him, but...just a few more steps. He might not need to drink it. Not just yet, anyway. He fell over.

Mauvis' burnt face was pressed uncomfortably against someone's shoulder. It smelled pleasantly of shaving soap and shook with uncontrollable sobs. Someone tried to pry Mauvis free of the sobbing man and he found himself suddenly pulled into a fierce hug. His lips, already scorched, were crushed between his own teeth and something made of stone.

"Ow," said Mauvis.

Vladdir loosened his grip a bit, allowing Mauvis' mouth to come away from that horrid stone arm. He looked up into the king's tear-streaked face and his curtain of grey hair.

"Earth, Mauvis!" gasped Vladdir. "I thought we'd never find you. How the hell did you end up on the surface?"

PART III

SAANAE, THE SORCERESS

SAANAE COULD NO LONGER suppress her trembling as the rock walls of her domain closed against the Desert light. Vladdir's servant, here? She was too afraid to feel rage, remembering the terror she had felt when the monstrous tunnel king had chased after her in the Desert Priest's home, feeling the hunger in his mind as he came ever closer to her and seeing what he had done to Karel...and then Kyril, false Kyril who had not finished her duty.

The metal biscuit canister fell from her hand and thudded dully on the sandy rock ground. She brushed her fingers against the heavy folds of her robes to dislodge the crumbs and tried to swallow the caked dryness in her mouth. He was very good, this Mauvis. Almost believable. It was impossible to gauge how many of her half-truths he had accepted, and how many he had discerned as lies. Had she made a mistake, giving him that goblet and allowing him a connection to herself? Was her magic strong enough to keep the flow of thoughts in a single direction, as she had intended? She knew she was no match for the collective strength of the Yrati, but would they even be involved?

It didn't matter. She already knew full well the brutal force of

Vladdir's power. The king had shown limited ability to move the Earth, but he could move well enough through it. She could always run, if he came after her. She would shift her caves daily through the Desert. Perhaps they thought she had been fooled by Mauvis' expert manipulations. That might give her time to get some information, at least, while they toyed with her. And if Mauvis continued his act, pretending to go along with what she told him, she might actually trick him into using the vial of red venom she had given him. Assuming he wouldn't immediately have it tested, and dispose of it as soon as he knew what it was.

Earth damn it, there was no use trying to convince herself that she had any confidence about this at all. She had stepped into sand that was too deep, but what more was there to lose? When Vladdir had killed Ilet, he hadn't been satisfied and had sucked away and swallowed everything around him, and that still hadn't been enough. He'd only stopped after pulling away and eating the tiny, tender part of her soul that she had separated from herself for moulding. Then he had flown past in the aether, then chased her, then sent his scout all the way back—it just proved that he was out to get the rest of her. He wouldn't get an easy surrender.

She began to worry intensely about having let Mauvis into her home. She had done it defiantly, to let him know she wasn't afraid that he had somehow managed to find her. He hadn't attacked her outright, even though he had had ample opportunity. It only occurred to her now to wonder why. Had he left some tracking device behind? Some cursed item? Vladdir must want to use her for something. But what? She crouched and swept her hands over the sandy floor, feeling the vibrations of the Earth, hunting for anything that might have been obscured from view. She also had the pebbles hunt for her, and they reported nothing. Of course, it wouldn't be so obvious.

Saanae felt cold in this upper chamber and stepped out onto the water, pushing it aside with her mind and telling the pebbles to open the bottom of the pool so that she could pass into the lower catacombs. Green light from the clumped bioluminescent algae that lived below pulsated in waves through her own aura as she descended into the glassy under-cavern, releasing the Earth and water so that they re-closed over her head. She moved to her work bench, soothed by the extra layer of privacy surrounding her, and the constant, quiet drip from the stalactites. White blindfish and eels struggled through the thin layer of water that covered the entire floor. White frogs queried her with chirps from the scattered lily pads around which the algae grew. She wished they were her creations, but the little creatures had emerged on their own, from some unknown route they had found through the Desert's harshness. Resting on the stone work bench of almost clear quartz, the tips of her fingers touched her only attempt at creation, the construct of hair, clay and beads that was now so devoid of life. She remembered the warmth that had coursed through it when she had placed a bit of her soul in this false body. Then Vladdir had sucked it away. Now it was undeniably nothing more than a doll.

Crushing grief slammed over her again and she curled up against the table. Unbearably alone, her desire for vengeance turned to misery as she shook with helpless sobs. She held the construct in her hands, feeling its floppy little limbs drape loosely over her fingers, and stroked the hair on the small head made of clotted sand—hair that had come from a dead man she had found in the Desert. He had worn armour, had probably been one of Vladdir's soldiers, but what did that matter? Had she offended the underground king by taking that tiny bit of nothing? It was of no use to anyone but her, and Vladdir had ripped away a lot more in revenge.

Perhaps she should forget about reclaiming anything from the king. Let him keep what he had taken, and she would try to raise her child again. This time she would be careful to hide its tiny life aura from the bloodthirsty Vladdir and keep it safe. She rose and stepped out into the middle of the cavern, lightly tapping the wet floor with her mind so that the liquid rippled softly. Droplets rose in a fine mist all around her. *Water.* The little doll in her hand was made of rope and clay beads. *Earth.* One more thing was needed—*Light.* Saanae sang softly to it, reciting the lilting aria that she had used before, when she had taken a piece of her soul and made it separate; a tiny, tender, glowing clot of life that had wound its way around the child she tried to form. The pain was threatening her consciousness, and the thread-like wraith that she tried to pull from her soul snapped free from her hold and dissipated back into her body. There was no more of herself that she was able to give. The little doll she held remained inanimate, and Saanae remained wounded.

As her body floated in her dark pool, Saanae's mind drifted in the dark world of sleep. *Try, try again,* the pebbles encouraged her. *Give us all a child,* sang the Water. *We are as lonely as you are, Saanae. Why should some of us not become alive by your hand? Vladdir does not eat now.*

Only because there is nothing for him to eat, Saanae replied.

Still, think about it.

Saanae thought, in the strange, incoherent way of sleep. Random thoughts sorted through like puzzle pieces. Her mind split into several lithe figures that darted down through the black water, dark fins flipping rapidly, hunting through the pebbles at the bottom, picking them up, spitting them out, until she came across some that were of interest.

Mauvis' hair. Could he track her through that? No. She had removed it properly.

Mauvis' hair. Could she drain energy from him through it and use it to form the life of the child? Perhaps. But then it would have no part of her. Besides, that hair was reserved for vengeance. She planned to make a black torture doll with it when she was done with the Lord Chamberlain.

Mauvis' deep blush. His smile. A nice smile and a man strong enough to brave the Desert. Form a child half of him, half of Saanae. Make it of real flesh. Easy to do the natural way if he came back here and smiled at her again like—

She awoke, and sat up in the gently bobbing water, irritated. What in Earth kind of stupid thought was that? She shifted to the edge of her pool, wringing the water out of her hair and refusing to dwell on that last idea any further. There was another way. She had to find the one who knew the deeper, darker magic that had been used to make Ilet, and learn it from him.

The wind and light on the surface quickly dried her clothes as she slid her feet rapidly over the sand, passing several kilometres with each step. She stopped when she felt the *black/green, brown/green* presence of the one she sought. In the distance, she could see his shiny, yellow skin glistening, the image distorted in waves of heat. He turned to look at her. She was sure he was smirking over the thought that she had come to him at all. Even though she knew he could have covered the ground between them in an instant, he took his time coming, making her wait. She would not approach him. It would be improper.

When he drew near enough that she could see the detail of his medallion, the evil smile on his thin lips, the glint in his narrow eyes, she fell to her knees and bowed her head.

"My Lord Murdek—"

A small chunk of skin was ripped from her thigh. Saanae gasped and bit her lip. She had not seen his hand move, and didn't know how he had taken it from her. Warm blood stained her gown from within, but she did not complain. There was always a price for an audience. He said nothing, waiting for her to plead. In the past, he had always already known what she wanted. Saanae endured this game and spoke for almost an hour, not bothering to remember what she said. At length, the Priest gave a wave of his hand and used the Desert's power to move them from the surface to one of his many underground caves. This cavern seemed endless, another in his apparently favoured style, with slab marble lining the floor and ceiling, brass pillars and walls to the left and right. The orange hue of the brass was enhanced by the fire from intermittent coal pits that lit the room. Saanae wondered with irritation why he always wanted to waste so much time with her when it was clearly unnecessary. She controlled her fatigue and anger and rose to her feet, outwardly showing humility as she followed the Priest.

"Ilet," he said, as he cast his hand out over a rectangular trough of water. The sides of the trough were encrusted with red and white enamel, separated by a thin filigree of gold. A tiny blue-black fireball of aura rose up from the water, wailing in distress. Saanae caught her breath and clutched her chest in agony, recognising the similarities between this separated life force and the one she had made herself.

"I had to retrieve him, after he was released from the cage within greedy Vladdir's soul."

Saanae shot the Priest a look of worried despair. "Could you not have made another?"

He shrugged. "I suppose. But I like this one. He's beautiful."

"What would I have to do to make another?" She shivered as she felt the Priest touch her forehead and make a shallow pass through her mind.

He gave a nasty laugh. "You'd have to eat souls like Vladdir does. It seems you haven't got enough in you, my darling."

Did that mean the Priest ate souls? Saanae shuddered inwardly, but didn't dare voice the question. Instead she asked, "How would I retrieve my child from Vladdir?"

The Priest placed his entire hand on her head and drew his thumb across her brow, sending a chill through Saanae's body as he did so. He made his annoying laugh again.

"Little Saanae has already been laying the foundation. Why don't you just pull it out through this Mauvis-connection you've made?"

"Master, I am not strong enough."

"Hmm. And you fear Vladdir. Well, I have a proposal for you, small one. Vladdir has plenty of power. Enough to raise the bodies of both my Ilet, and your little—what have you called it?"

"Nothing, Lord."

"Very well, my Ilet and your little Nothing. I will reach through you, and you will reach through Mauvis, and we will pull away enough of Vladdir to form the flesh. If he tries to follow us back, all he will find is his own man, Mauvis. We will not be caught."

And if he does follow past Mauvis, thought Saanae, it will be me he sees first. But she accepted this and said nothing. It was the Priest's prerogative, and she presumed that it was also why he had made Ilet in the first place, as a shield between himself and his controlled Aragoths.

As skilled a sorcerer as he was, the Priest was a lousy teacher. However Saanae supposed that was intentional, to prevent her from learning his more powerful secrets. For several days she watched the Priest with forced patience as he prepared himself, trying to read the vibrations of the Earth as he meditated, to feel and perhaps understand how he collected his power. But the marble slabs absorbed most of the Priest's intentions, leaving her very little to interpret. He did not explain the incantations he muttered incessantly as he knelt on the cool floor of his cave, alternately rubbing himself with coloured soils and probably blood. From time to time, she could feel his presence in her mind so strongly that it was as if he had walked into her skull and was ransacking her thoughts as he pleased. His arms were caked with grit when he finally came out of his preparations and roughly forced Saanae into a kneeling position in front of a Murdek shrine. In this cavern, it was a brass wall etched with black depictions of strange beasts feeding on men. White paint had been splashed over the metallic victims, as if to represent blood. The Priest stood behind her, and she could watch his warped reflection in the wall.

He stretched out his arm, palm down, and something red shot out of his fingertips. Whatever it was hit Saanae squarely at the back of the neck and wrapped itself around her throat. She panicked, trying to rip it away with her hands before the squeezing pressure suffocated her, but her fingers felt nothing but her own skin. Her vision turned starry black and closed in until all was dark. After a moment, she no longer felt the urgent need to breathe.

She was floating through the night sky, the sparkling atmospheric dust dancing just past her toes, and the glowing stars filling her eyes when she looked up. If she turned to look over her shoulder, she could see the red stick that was still attached to the back of her neck, pushing her along. From her stomach, a rippling cord of liquid stretched forward into the night. If she strained her eyes, she could see it pouring from its source: the scrying goblet she had given Mauvis. Despite herself, Saanae was amazed. She hadn't known this type of projection was possible. All she had done with her water before was watch for images, or listen to the hushed sounds carried by the waves.

Saanae felt herself start to change as she was pushed along and the Priest began to enfold her with layers of the Desert's whimsy. Her head bent forward into the rush of wind. Her face narrowed and her mouth stretched wide to let fangs grow down. Her knuckles folded into paws and clawed at the night air as she lurched into a run.

There was a second force pulling on her now, leaching her attention away from the flow of water from the goblet; a small, tender, green dot of light that had once been a piece of herself. Finding her rhythm, she raced through the sparkling darkness towards the Royal House and the multi-coloured mass of shimmering light that was Vladdir, who had eaten her child.

Thought was no longer possible. Saanae's consciousness melted into boiling rage as she lunged at Vladdir and plunged her fire-form deep into his abdomen to take back what had been hers. She felt him yell in surprise and fall back, sending unknown objects scattering. Cups? Chairs? They were blurry images without form. They didn't matter. She reached deeply into Vladdir's self, and there she touched it; felt the warmth and intact entity of her little child-soul as it charged her with joy and determination. The king managed to hurl her spirit from his body with an awkward swipe of his mind, but this did not discourage her. It was truly possible to get it back. She gathered her demon form to spring into a second attack, when green light with ripples of red stepped in front of her and blocked her way.

Kyril! You who didn't kill Vladdir properly and force the release of all the souls he has eaten! You left some behind, and then you became his helper!

Saanae tried furiously to rip the green light apart with her teeth.

Rip out her throat!

There was heat where she bit, and the taste of ripe blood as she shook her head violently to render her prey further. She saw Vladdir raise his arm to strike from the corner of her vision, but she was too busy with Kyril to pay attention to him now. His blow knocked her out of her senses and into an empty void. She spun helplessly. Perhaps she felt pain. It was difficult to discern.

No, not an empty void. There was a dripping sound. Something hard pressed against her back. One leg was uncomfortably jammed up against the brass Murdek mural. After a moment, she noticed that her head was turned to the side and her arm was bent around her face so that she was looking at her hand.

"Feh!" said the Priest. "You're not subtle at all." He pulled some cloths out of a satchel by his side.

"I told you to go through Mauvis, not rush in and attack directly. I suppose it doesn't matter. When you do attack as you were supposed to, it will be different enough to confuse him. Might actually be to our advantage."

Saanae was confused. Hadn't the Priest been controlling her? Hadn't he deliberately turned her into that mindless beast? She hadn't been aware that she had acted on her own. He wiped her face and around her eyes, the cloth coming away yellow and green. She tried to sit up and found that her limbs were too rubbery, while the Priest seemed to have lost none of his own strength.

"You'll have to stay put for a while. When you do get up, make sure you eat. We've used up all your power. I'll have to re-do all of my preparations and won't be able to tend to you." He looked down at her for a moment, and then smiled. "You have some unique talents, my dear. I've never seen someone so able to manipulate the physical world like that while in astral form. I honestly wondered how you would cope without using Mauvis' hand for your own."

Saanae lay still for what felt like an eternity after the Desert Priest had left, until she regained sufficient interest in the world around her to flip over onto her stomach. As she faced the floor, trying to get her arms to push against it, thick, green fluid fell from her eyes, leaving gooey droplets on the marble for her fingers to smear. Finally on her knees, Saanae managed to get into a wobbly stance after a few tries, and carefully made her way towards a small pot strung over one of the fire pits. Whatever was in it smelled tremendously good, and she mused that the Priest couldn't have been that angry if he had provided her with a meal. Perhaps she had generated him some interesting "data" for one of his "experiments."

Next to the pit sat a plate of bread and a folded sheet of paper. Saanae ate with her fingers, not caring that the food was too hot. When she was full, she sat back and wondered why she still felt strangely empty, and realised it was intense disappointment that she felt.

Tiny, warm. The memory of touching her would-be child was difficult to replay in her mind; it brought with it a knotting agony that threatened her too-full stomach. Needing to distract herself, she picked up the paper that had been under the plate and read it. It was a surprisingly gently-worded note from the Priest, telling her to go home and rest. When he was ready next, he would summon her. Saanae shivered and pulled her cloak more tightly around her shoulders. She looked around the cavern hoping to see someone, anyone else, but it remained deserted.

Like me.

Going home would also place her in a desolate cavern.

It was easier to magically travel through the Desert after her strange projection experience. It felt almost effortless, her mind only needing to indicate direction without guiding the motion of her limbs. As she set her feet down on the sand over her caves, the whitish grains flew to the sides until the stones of the stairwell came up under her red slippers and supported her weight. Once inside her cavern, she saw that the pool was shimmering with a pale light. She stroked its surface and saw several images of Mauvis' face, appearing at many different depths. He must have spoken into the goblet and sent her messages almost every day while she had been waiting for the Priest to finish his preparations.

Just as he had said he would.

Saanae was surprised. Despite the aching tiredness that now suffused her body, her curiosity got the better of her and she filtered the messages so that the oldest one floated to the surface first.

Uhh. My greetings to you, Saanae.

His face was shadowed by his hair, which had fallen forward as he leaned over the goblet, but she could still see that his lips were burnt and cracked, and some skin was peeling from his nose, cheeks and forehead. Mauvis paused and looked around, apparently feeling foolish to be speaking into a cup, even in privacy.

Well, it was my deep pleasure to meet you. He smiled when he said that.

I'm sorry I haven't tried this before now. I fell sick on my way home. But don't worry, I'm much better now. A bit of heat exhaustion, that's all. They were actually worried about me here. Imagine that! I wasn't sure anyone would even miss me. Um. Well, that's all for now. Just wanted to let you know I've reached home safely and to say hello. And, uh, well, now goodbye. Oh, and I hope you enjoyed the rest of the biscuits.

Saanae leaned back against a stone pillar and chewed on a fingernail thoughtfully. What an idiotic message to get from one's enemy! And the range of emotions that he had let run across his face as he spoke. This Mauvis. So convincing. She was duly impressed. She carefully checked the ebb and flow of energies through her caves. Once satisfied that the message had truly been one way and that the security of her home had not been injured, she filtered through to the next message.

Hello again, Saanae. Mauvis was wearing a white shirt this time, open at the neck, and his curly hair was bound back except for a few strands around the temple. He was going a bit grey. She could see his thumbs at the sides of the image, absentmindedly gliding over the edge of the goblet. His face seemed pensive.

I suppose I should have expected this, but their concern for me didn't last long. Things have pretty much gone back to the way they were before. Should I be burdening you with all this? It seems very ill-mannered of me. But you're the only person who has shown any interest in having me talk to you. And, well, you already know about Kyril. I feel like you're the only person I can be truly honest with.

His eyes started to redden. How realistic! He sat back a bit and sniffed before continuing.

The repairs are going well enough. You know, we've been rebuilding since the Aragoths attacked us and destroyed everything. I wish I could show it to you. I'm very pleased with the way the new Market Caverns are developing. And the Yrati are extremely pleased with my design for their new home. Some of them actually danced about and jumped so much that they tripped over their robes. You'd think certain members of their clan would treat me a little better, considering. Ah, there I go again, feeling sorry for myself. I apologise. Unfortunately, I have nothing of interest to tell you about Kyril. She does nothing. Just sits around staring at Vladdir like he's both the Sun and Moon. She hasn't done any more of that green water magic. Or vegetable magic. Whatever that was.

Saanae threw back her head and laughed. How did he get vegetables from wind? And water magic was based in blue, not green.

I wish I could see you again. Perhaps, when a little bit more of the work is done, I will have time to venture out into the Desert and we can meet again.

Not likely. There was no way she'd risk meeting Vladdir's servant after what she had done this night. She wouldn't give him a chance to smell it on her.

Well, I will talk to you again tomorrow. Good night.

Chewing more vigorously on her fingernail, Saanae pulled up the next message. This was proving more interesting, not to mention entertaining, than she had imagined.

Hello, Saanae.

Mauvis was resplendent in a jacket of rust-coloured crushed velvet with a gold jabot. His hair was loose, but tucked behind his ears. He seemed sad.

I wish you could also talk to me. Let me know how you are. I'm afraid I'm starting to miss you. Our last, well, only visit, was the most delightful thing that has happened to me in years. I wish you were here. I suppose you must be wondering why I'm being such a miserable wretch today. I wish I could give you happier news. It's just...well, I fought again with Rayner today. He's my friend. An Yrati, but we disagree heavily where Kyril is concerned. I had the staff stop feeding her, to try and force her back to the surface sooner. She didn't seem to mind. Vladdir didn't notice, but when Rayner found out...well, as I said, we disagreed. Kyril hasn't done anything yet. I will let you know as soon as she does. I will try to be happier next time. It's just...I feel so...

Alone, thought Saanae.

Well, never mind. He smiled. *Good night. I hope you are well.*

Saanae stopped her chewing. The quick of her finger was getting raw. Was this servant of Vladdir genuine? He had to be faking. How else had he found her, if not by Vladdir's instruction?

But, Saanae thought, if he *had* been looking for her, making all those bold statements about being her guest and how she should show him more courtesy when he was out on the surface, then why suddenly start playing the fool after he had entered her caverns, pretending he didn't know who she was? Was it possible that he actually hadn't known about her, and his comments had been mere coincidence? But why would he have said such things while rambling about on the surface? To whom had he been speaking? The Desert? Though, if she were to brutally put things in perspective, she was insignificant. It was pompous of her to assume Vladdir would even have mentioned her to his man, never mind sending him after her, wasn't it?

Saanae watched the remainder of the messages, helplessly indulging in pretending the intimacy of them was genuine—*but what if it was?* Still, Kyril had done nothing of importance. Her head spinning, her body stiff, Saanae stood up, awkwardly stretching her limbs after having sat in one spot for so long. She shuffled over to the can of biscuits she had discarded so many days ago and picked it up. The contents were stale, but she found them oddly satisfying, and finally felt sated. Another message shimmered to the surface of the pool.

Saanae looked at the pulsating light rather fearfully, knowing that whatever Mauvis said this time would ruin the warmth that had been building inside of her. This message would be about the attack. She wondered if he knew it had been her. She put down the canister and went to lean over the image waiting in her pool. It wouldn't tell her anything she didn't already know, or it would tell her what she didn't want to know. Unable to leave it alone, she reached out to brush her hand over the water.

I dreamt of you tonight, Saanae. It was a wonderful dream that you were running towards me, and just as I reached out my hand to catch yours, you were snatched away by some fierce man in black robes. I couldn't see his face, but his very presence made me afraid. Are you all right, Saanae? If you can, please send me some indication that you're well. You see, something else has happened. I know you don't like Kyril, although you haven't told me exactly why. You know I don't trust her either, but... Vladdir was attacked tonight. I woke up to the guards' alarm. When I saw him, they were trying to hold him down, and were unable to protect him from whatever had entered the room. I had seen this kind of attack on Vladdir once before, when we were hiding from the Aragoths in the Yrati river tunnels, but this was much worse. His body started to thrash, and we were unable to see what was wrong.

Kyril could see the malevolent force that had entered our home, and she drew the attack from him and took it herself, but it was more than just thrashing. This time the attack was able to draw blood. I wish I could be happy for her actions, but she was nearly torn to shreds. I did feel sorry that I had wished her ill before. This isn't the first time she's saved Vladdir. They're both going to be all right, by the way. I just wish I could cut her off from that green, whatever it is. I think I could tolerate her if she were free from that thing which ties her to the Desert. There are so many things in the Desert that are dangerous. I know you are a strong, independent woman, Saanae, and you don't need me. But if you wished to come here, and stay with me, you'd be more than welcome. Then I'd know for sure that you were safe.

Saanae's legs gave out and she plopped down hard. She didn't know what to think anymore. Was she being too gullible? She got up again and paced the room, her mind reeling with doubt. Should she go to Mauvis? If she did, she might more quickly gather information that would allow her to retrieve her child. Or, she might be recognised. But she had already asked the Desert Priest for help. How would he react to this proposal? Certainly if he did agree to such a plan, then she would become disposable, and once he had what he needed to reform his Ilet, he would most likely abandon her to Vladdir. No, that would be getting too close.

Saanae sighed in frustration and flopped backwards into the water. She floated into its warmth and wondered what was real. Of course, the best option was to remain as isolated and independent as possible. This small connection had already muddied her mind. She would go back to the Priest. At least they were both clear that theirs was nothing more than an association of convenience, and once they both had what they wished, it would be over.

Another message flickered into the water and its light shifted right through her head.

Saanae, come.

So soon? Last time it had taken the Desert Priest days to prepare. Saanae sat up in the water, sluggish with aching hunger, and realised she had been asleep. How much time had passed? There were three more messages from Mauvis floating around her. Had it been three days? She sloshed out of her pool and ran a sodden hand over her face. Wishing she had time to find something satisfying to eat, she found herself filled with a strange urgency to make it back to the Murdek caves as quickly as possible. Night-dust whipped around her as she slipped her feet over the darkened sands. The Priest had lit the entrance of his home for her, sending orange light out into the Desert to guide her way. Her feet touched his marble floors with a light patter, and she ran across the smooth stone, toward the bronze mural.

The Priest was kneeling motionless next to a brazier, his arms stretched forwards. Patterns had been drawn in brown- and black-caked substances all along his arms and chest. He did not turn towards or speak to Saanae, but she felt the flow of his energy from the tips of his fingers, towards the top point of a diamond that had been sloppily painted in white over the etching of the mural. She let her cloak slip from her shoulders and knelt in her red dress and slippers in front of the Priest so that her neck was in front of his arms.

She was not surprised this time when the bolt of energy hit her from behind and cast her out of her body. The ascent was much slower than before, and she rose past the layer of silty dust that blocked the stars from the surface. She glided along the night, seeing lines of aura tracing the world as the living forms made movements, innocently going about their business. Despite this calm approach, the feeling of urgency returned. Her excitement grew as she drew near the tunnel dwellers' caverns.

Feeling as neither wolf nor wraith, she was aware of keeping human form as her spirit pretended to walk along the corridors of the newly rebuilt Royal House. She could "see" more than just the vague, approximate forms this time. The details and colours of the objects around her were well defined, and she could easily resolve the features of the servants and night guards. She felt their vibrations as they passed by—or through—her without noting her presence. She flitted towards the servants' chambers, delighted by the tastefully set tiles along the light grey floors and walls, and the gauzy curtain panels that hung from the ceiling at random intervals to partially block the night breeze coming in through the vents of the ceiling and keep it from making the underground too chill. The supporting pillars set at intervals along the walls were cut into rounded columns, etched with straight lines from top to bottom.

She stepped onto a series of circular stairs that rose up towards a door. She could feel Mauvis behind it; the energy of his mind had become familiar from his messages. Her own mind was racing with anticipation. First her outstretched hand, then her arm, then her body passed through the solid nothingness of the door, and she saw the comfortable yellow light of the room reflected off the worn but elegant russet carpets and bedding, the deep brown of the bookshelves lining one entire wall, the stone hearth where a fire had been built, and the slightly tilted, wide surface of the architect's table, at which Mauvis sat. He was wearing a night shirt covered by a grey knitted shawl, his head bent in concentration as he madly sketched some building façade. What an odd way to hold a pencil, Saanae thought. She reached out and passed her non-hand through the brown curls hanging down his back.

Mauvis sat up and twisted around, his eyes searching the air where her head should be.

"Saanae?"

Oh Earth! Saanae pulled back and flitted from the room as fast as she could. Somewhere across the Desert, the Priest's grip twisted her around and tightened, trying to force her back to the Chamberlain. She would not go, and ran instead towards Vladdir's light.

I will go myself! She couldn't use Mauvis in that way, not now. In the end, the Priest really did not care, and he let her run. Carefully, now, so as not to attract Kyril's attention, she flowed towards Vladdir's bedchambers. White marble. Soft blue light from bioluminescent moss tanks. Red bed linens. Kyril was there, but she slept. An angry bruise spread outside the bandages across her throat, her limbs twisted in the sheets and Vladdir's arms. Saanae paused and collected herself. This would have to be accurate; she would most likely only have one attack. She lightly ran her non-hands over Vladdir's body, assessing his energy *and that which was not his!* She could feel the Priest outlining what he wanted and left him to it, while she searched for her tiny piece of self that should have been her child. It was difficult. There were not as many eaten souls as she would have expected. She was sure she had seen Vladdir consume far more than Kyril had made him release, but the few that were left were swarming together and becoming part of him. She touched deeper—it had to be here, somewhere. Vladdir shifted in his sleep. *Oh!* She could sense it now, just over—

Her hand shot out and, with the force of the Priest's strike, tore most of the flesh from Vladdir's side. It smacked into Saanae's spirit, making her corporeal, a bloodied demon of ripped flesh floating in midair.

Saanae, come!

She and Vladdir screamed together in outrage and betrayal. The Priest was supposed to let her get back the child-energy, and now the chance was gone! Kyril leapt forward, sword in hand, and cut Saanae's new form in two. Bewildered, Saanae spun wildly for a moment, before the Priest forced her to scoop up the portion of Vladdir's meat that had fallen to the floor and fly up through the ceiling. She passed through with a wet, sticky splat that left a good quantity of blood behind on the white marble tile.

No longer only a spiritual entity, Saanae's chunky form hurtled through the night, across the Desert and into the Murdek caverns. The meat hit Saanae's actual body as she was flung back into it, and she immediately fell forward and threw up.

When the retching subsided enough for her to start to control her sobs, Saanae did not immediately turn towards the Priest to confront him with his treachery. Her anger had stolen her words. What could she say that would even begin to make him understand what he had done to her? As she lifted her head, she saw that the Priest did not care. He had already raised the dark bluish glow of his Ilet from the small pool, and was reconstructing the body with vigor. Limbs and head were forced into messy approximations and suffused with black-green light before the blue of Ilet was embedded within. If Saanae had not seen the final thing move, she would not have believed such a process would work.

"That's ugly," she said, surprising herself that what came out of her mouth was so banal.

The Priest was only mildly annoyed as he finally turned to her.

"It will take time," was all he answered.

"You could have waited."

He regarded her with marginal interest.

"If you had given me one more second, I would have freed my child."

"That will come later."

"What do you mean?"

"The next time, we will get your child."

"The *next* time? How is that possible? After what you did? Vladdir will be guarded more strictly, probably by the Yrati. How do you propose I get past them?"

The Priest gave her one of his annoying, smug half-smiles and turned to gaze into his stupid rectangle pool. "You forget, now we have Ilet."

Saanae wasn't sure what that meant.

"Did you really think your little Nothing could parallel the strength of this entity?"

"It seems Vladdir defeated him easily enough last time."

"That was last time. Now it wears the flesh of our enemy. You must learn to trust me, Saanae. I can do more than you think. I need to learn about my opponent. However, with that done, our next attack will surely free your little Nothing, because Vladdir will be dead."

Saanae chewed on her lip and tried to wipe from the side of her face the smeared blood that had been left there by the impact of Vladdir's flesh. Her eyes burned and she was starting to feel sick again.

"Go home," said the Priest. "You anger me. I do keep my promises, regardless of what you may think right now."

Saanae picked up her cloak and ran.

Sleep had been elusive, and when Saanae finally awoke she was still exhausted. She had ended up out of her pool and curled in the sand. The pebbles were shifting and twisting around her, muttering their concern. They had collected under her head in an attempt to push her into a more comfortable position, but her neck felt sore and strained anyway. Her red dress was in desperate need of cleaning, but the blood had been washed from her skin. She stood shakily and saw that there were seven more messages from Mauvis. Had she slept that long? No, only two days had passed. The pebbles, relieved that she had finally risen, brought her some tubers they had found hiding underneath the Desert sand. She took them sadly and didn't listen to the messages: she would feel profoundly unworthy if they were friendly, and she did not want to feel the anguish that a hostile message would bring her. Mauvis must have figured it out by now. He had seen her the last time, or at least had felt her presence. As she knelt by her pool scrubbing the tubers, she felt someone calling her name and it wasn't the Priest. She waved her hand over the water so she could see outside.

Oh Earth! It was Mauvis. He was struggling through knee deep sand, at least 20 kilometres off course, one arm up ineffectively to keep the wind from blowing sand into his face. Without thinking, Saanae commanded the sand to bring him to her caves. She saw Mauvis struggle frantically against the pull of the Desert as it sucked him into its depths, and Saanae cringed. He would not have been expecting it, and must have been terrified. A few moments later, he fell from the roof of her cavern and onto the ground in front of her. She took a fearful step towards him, both hands pressed to her lips, then paused. She remembered she had no idea of his current feelings for her.

Mauvis floundered, scattering sand from his hair. He stopped, blinked a few times, and stared at Saanae in disbelief.

"Saanae!" He bounded to his feet and made an abortive motion as if he had intended to embrace her. "Oh." His hands went to the satchel slung over his shoulder. "I'm sorry. I know I had promised you more biscuits. I completely forgot. I was in such a desperate rush."

A laughing sob burst out of Saanae and she couldn't stop her eyes from filling with tears. "You are so stupid!" she yelled at him. Mauvis stared at her in bewilderment.

"What have I done?"

Saanae ran forward and threw her arms around his waist, unable to stop the sobs that were wrenching her entire body.

"Oh, I see," he said. He gently returned the embrace. He smelled faintly of laundry soap, perspiration and Desert dust. "Here I am, nattering about biscuits, when you're clearly not well. I did come here to make sure you were all right. You're covered in sand. Were you sleeping on the ground?" She felt his nose and lips press against the top of her head. "At least you don't seem too badly hurt, although it seems you must have had a great fright. Vladdir was attacked again, and this time I also dreamt of you, right before it happened."

He didn't speak again for a few moments, waiting for her to regain control of herself. When she was calmed, Saanae stepped back, feeling like an idiot. She couldn't look Mauvis in the eyes, so she stared at his boots, awkwardly trying to straighten her hair. Mauvis took her hands, led her over to one of the benches and sat by her side. "That thing did come after you as well, didn't it? Were you able to run away? You must have fended it off at least, since you're more or less intact. After what it did to Vladdir, I was so afraid for you."

Saanae hung her head in shame and felt the tears coming again. Was Mauvis for real? If he were trying to lure her into captivity, he wouldn't have to play such an elaborate mind game. All he'd have to do would be to strike her unconscious now, or drug her with some biscuits, which he'd forgotten. He'd already had ample chance.

"Is Vladdir all right?" she asked thickly. Mauvis' expression twitched.

"The Yrati are doing what they can. He wouldn't be able to walk again, if not for the Desert magic that seems to rebuild him. Unfortunately the parts of him that It replaces are always made of stone. The beast bit most of his upper leg from him, and took a great deal from his side. But he will live. This is the curse of the Desert he inherited from his father."

"What?" Inherited curse? Did Mauvis have any idea of what was really going on here?

Mauvis looked at her curiously. "I would have thought you'd have known about Alekseidir's curse, since you watch those who roam the Desert."

"W-well, yes. But I don't see what it has to do with Vladdir." *Or me.* Saanae took a deep breath and told herself to speak carefully. It was coming out now: they would talk of Vladdir's consumption of souls. She wondered how Mauvis perceived it.

"Sometimes, when we were children, Vladdir would also feel the pull to go to the surface. His father tried to beat it out of his two brothers. It didn't work. With Vladdir...I don't know. He is touched by it, but doesn't seem controlled by it, at least not yet. I can't quite tell. That's why I'm so worried about Kyril being near him, in case she increases the Desert's influence over him. But so far, that doesn't seem to be the case."

"Controlled by it?" Saanae was confused. Did Mauvis not know how Vladdir had defeated Ilet and the Aragoths? The question burned inside of her.

"Saanae." Mauvis leaned towards her earnestly. "Did the black wraith-demon thing, or whatever it was, also come after you?"

She didn't know how to answer that. Her mouth opened, but no sound would come out. Apparently that was more than enough answer for Mauvis to come to his own conclusions.

"Well that settles it," he said, and stood up resolutely. "You must come back with me. I've been worrying myself sick wondering if you're all right out here by yourself. Are there things you need to pack?"

"I can't go with you!"

"Of course you can. What do you mean you can't? Is there something holding you here? It wouldn't have to be permanent. Just until we know it's safe."

"I wouldn't be accepted. It's impossible. So you see—" The tears were coming again, and Saanae furiously fought them. She was giving away too much.

"Not accepted? My dear lady! If Kyril is accepted, and by the Yrati at that, what makes you think you wouldn't be?"

"Why aren't you afraid of me contaminating Vladdir?"

Mauvis sat down again, looking sympathetic and exasperated.

"There's that cynicism again," he said. "I know you're of the Desert, but you're clearly in control, and it's not impossible to have a conversation with you that makes sense. You're not addled, like she is, which I think makes her largely unpredictable, and therefore a threat."

"I'm sorry. Thank you for asking. I can't."

Mauvis was silent for a while. "Are you afraid?"

Saanae dared to look up at him. He was getting close.

"More afraid of the tunnels than what roams out here?"

It was too late to pretend otherwise. Perhaps she could convince him to accept some other arrangement.

"I'm safe here. I could give you a second goblet, one that would let you hear my messages. That way we could talk to each other. I could just tell you if I needed something."

"And by the time I got out here, it would be too late. I was completely lost just now. We both know it."

She gave him a searching look, and wondered why he didn't ask if she knew what had attacked Vladdir. He returned the gaze steadily, and somehow, perhaps through an inexplicably deepened connection, she knew he was not asking to avoid having her retreat further.

If she did go with him, and Vladdir or Kyril knew what she had done, then what? Might she be executed? Would Mauvis protect her or wield the axe himself? If she did go with him, it might bring her closer to releasing her child. Could she do it so gently that Vladdir wouldn't notice?

"Maybe—"

"Yes?"

"I have to ask you something."

"Go on."

"How did Vladdir say he defeated the Aragoths?"

"Oh. I don't know. I assume he fought them with that stone arm of his. It must have made him stronger. Actually, come to think of it, he never really said."

Getting dangerous. One step further and she might end up telling him what she really wanted. "Never mind. Tell me, is...is he a cruel man?"

"Vladdir? No. He's never been cruel. Abused, perhaps, but never cruel in return. I've known him my whole life. Certainly tormented and miserable. Although now, well, he's happy."

Mauvis became introspective. Saanae imagined he must be again struggling with accepting the reason for Vladdir's happiness.

"Would you know if he had been cruel?"

"Well if he has, I doubt it was intentional. Or it was done out of necessity. What is it you want to know, exactly?"

Vladdir's consumption of her child had been unintentional? Well, after all, if Saanae were unimportant, so was her little Nothing. Maybe Vladdir hadn't even noticed what he had swallowed up in the rage of battle. But then, why had he come to the Murdek caves and chased after her, the smell of his hunger oozing from him on the night he had fought Kyril? Had he intended that she just be another random victim?

"Do you think if he were asked...he might..." She gulped down her rising terror.

"It's Vladdir you're afraid of? Do you want me to ask permission before bringing you back? Really it isn't necessary, but if that would make you feel more assured, I suppose I could do it."

That hadn't been the question, but it was easier than explaining about her swallowed child, so Saanae mutely nodded.

"All right. I don't like to leave you, but then, this means you will come." Mauvis' tense expression broke into a wide grin. Saanae weakly smiled back, then caught her breath as Mauvis leaned forward and kissed her hands.

"I'll be back in no longer than three days. Come hell or sandstorms, I will be back."

Saanae, come.

She no longer had any reason. She stayed asleep.

Saanae, come!

Whatever for? Her mind drifted back down into her pleasant dream. She dreamt of being unnoticed but happy, collecting mushrooms, shopping for clothes, sitting with Mauvis for a private lunch. Having a child.

A savage jerk on her ankle dragged her halfway out of her pool and forced her to wake up. She pushed herself up on her elbows and blearily glared at the Desert Priest who had somehow come into her home.

"What are you doing here?"

"I called. When I call, you come."

Saanae groaned. "You've gotten your Ilet, and I no longer want to bother with Nothing, so why are you here?"

"You don't want to *bother*? We had an agreement."

"I think I've more than fulfilled my end of the bargain, and I release you from yours." Saanae's pebbles were nowhere in sight, and it began to worry her. They should have warned her before the Priest had come this close.

"We are *not* finished."

"I *am* finished. You have what you wanted."

"I do not. You are not finished until Vladdir is dead."

"That's not what I agreed to."

The Priest splashed into the water, grabbed her by the hair and shoved her face towards the pool. At his touch she understood that the Priest had anchored himself within her mind during their previous sessions, and she could do nothing to force him out. He pushed against her power and the water surface of her pool snapped, forming an image of Mauvis and Vladdir that radiated out from the centre, spreading across the ripples, clearer than any she had ever been able to summon. Vladdir sat bandaged in bed with Mauvis next to him. They were smiling and clasping hands. No sound came, but Vladdir's lips shaped the words, "Yes, of course she can come." The Priest gave her head a rough shake and she could determine no more.

"Did you think I couldn't find out what you were up to?"

"You don't need me. You have Ilet. Use him."

"And let you run off and tell Vladdir everything? I don't think so. I don't see why I should use my precious Ilet and have Vladdir kill him again, when I have you."

The Priest released her hair, but before she could turn around, she was struck square in the back of the head by the red light and flung out of her body.

No! Saanae drew up the water and stones from her pool and coalesced them around her spirit. Using rocks as fists, she turned on the surprised Priest and struck him twice across the face. He retreated, disappearing in a swirl of dust. Saanae dropped back into her body and fought against the sluggishness she felt. She had to move, now! Her home was no longer safe. Struggling to her feet, she stumbled to the crevice in the wall where she had hidden the lock of Mauvis' hair. Once it was safely in her palm, she raced up her stairs, straining at the effort it took to push aside the sand overhead without the help of her pebbles.

On the surface, the wind was calm and the early morning light was clear. Saanae wasn't sure if it was safe to use the whimsy of the Desert to travel more quickly, as it would most likely enhance the Priest's ability to find her. Conversely, she had to reach Mauvis before he came too far into the Desert, looking for her. The Priest's knowledge of him put him in danger. If what she had seen in the pool had happened at the same time as her seeing it, then it was probable that Mauvis was still underground. She hoped the fool was busy packing his biscuits and hadn't left yet.

She didn't use the goblet to trace Mauvis, in case he had left it behind. Instead she used the lock of hair to focus on his location. For what seemed like hours, she slid across the Desert's grit, heart pounding more from fear than exertion, and finally she stood still when she reached a half-buried trapdoor in the sand. She knew this was one of the maintenance access doors used by the tunnel dwellers responsible for cleaning the skylights. Mauvis' presence was clearly beyond this door. Spreading her fingers over the lock, she used the force of the Desert sand to make the door buckle and crack open, and her hands to pry the splintered panels completely apart.

The underground was dark, and it took a few moments for her eyes to adjust to the dimness of the pale and neglected tanks of bioluminescent moss that would light the way for the maintenance workers. She had to go slowly—this tunnel was not yet tiled, and the ground was uneven with plant roots and stones.

"There she is. Do you recognise her?"

"Yes."

Saanae strained her eyes in the dark. A lamp was uncovered, showing her the smug, oily countenance of the Desert Priest as he stepped aside to let Kyril pass. The former Aragoth had returned to her origins, and was armoured in full rockskin, sword drawn.

"She is the one who ripped Vladdir apart."

"You liar!" Saanae shouted at the Priest. He grinned at her and continued to fill Kyril's ears with poison.

"She came here to finish him off. You should stop her before she does."

Kyril stepped towards Saanae with her sword levelled. "You tried to kill Vladdir."

Saanae stepped backwards as carefully and quickly as she could.

"I recognise how your spirit feels now. You also attacked me."

"Kyril, he is using you! Don't you remember Ilet? He's the one who used you through Ilet. If you live for Vladdir, don't let this man command you! He's lying!"

"I don't need to ask who the liar is," said Kyril. "I still heal from your teeth." She swung at Saanae, who fell over backwards. A warm rush of blood flowed from the cut.

Pebbles! Saanae had finally found them, surfacing under her fingertips. She threw a fistful in Kyril's face, then ordered the Earth to open so that she could rapidly sink into the ground. It was more difficult to trace Mauvis this way, her thoughts made blurry by the intense concentration she needed to focus on moving through the sticky clay. After half a kilometre, she resurfaced into a tiled hallway, not bothering to worry about the startled servants who shrieked and dropped their loads of washing or food to run off and sound the alarm.

No point in being discreet now.

"Mauvis!" Saanae shouted as she ran in the direction she thought she felt him. She stopped, suddenly feeling the pain of the cut across her chest, and put her hand up to the wound. Only now did she realise how serious it was. It was wide and deep, but nothing that wouldn't heal. She forced herself to keep moving.

Kyril stepped into the hallway in front of her. Saanae skidded to a stop and ran down a different hallway.

"Mauvis!"

Kyril blocked her way again. Now there were fewer halls for her to turn down, as the guard had been alerted and were also coming after her. Should she run into them? If she were to ask for Mauvis, were they more likely to listen to her than to Kyril?

There! Mauvis' presence flared in her mind, and the lock of hair itched on her palm. He was somewhere behind Kyril. Of course, the Aragoth would intentionally place herself between Saanae and her goal. She sunk back into the Earth and forced her way through the mud and rocks, guessing how far she had to go. This time she emerged in a cavern, staring at Mauvis' retreating back. He had one arm outstretched, as though he had just been leaning against the doorway, craning his neck to see what all the fuss was about. She was about to call his name when she realised he was not alone in the room. She was face to face with Vladdir, staring into his great, violet eyes.

Saanae dropped to her knees, intending to beg his forgiveness, when Kyril caught up with her. Vladdir's eyes flicked to Kyril and some unspoken communication passed between them. Recognition flooded the king's expression, and Saanae knew she had lost her chance. She felt the king's spirit reaching out to her, coursing through the aether, until it touched the edges of her being. She became aware of a great, spiralling vortex at his very centre—the seat of the curse set upon him by the purple venom, which she could see now was very similar to a technique that the Priest had once taught her. As his anger rose, so did the power of the vortex, drawing in energy from every living creature nearby. The feeling it created was the same as Saanae felt when she had first seen the king eat in the Murdek temple, drawing Karel's soul into his mouth. He was drawing her own life energy out, and to prevent herself from dying right there, she dragged the heat and coiling malice of the Desert down from the surface, through her body and fed it to him instead.

It was a mistake. Vladdir took this sustenance from her and used it to loosen the cooling effect of the Yrati water magic that stabilized the underground. Its presence had been so subtle as to escape Saanae's notice until the flow of its energy had been disrupted. The king rose from his daybed, his eyes filling with purple venom and his body taking on a sinuous demon form. He rushed at Saanae, forcing her to retreat back into the Earth. He followed her easily, confirming all her fears of how skilled he was at attack. And now he had seen her face, knew the enemy he wished to hunt. Saanae cursed bitterly as she fled, almost getting caught by Vladdir as she fought against the pull of the Earth. It was too difficult. She rose from the underground and pushed herself onto the surface in the Desert.

She only had a few seconds to sputter and gasp before Vladdir shot up through the sand next to her. His eyes and face were blurred with purple darkness that swirled around him, but his fangs were utterly clear, as was the rage that formed the claws of his hands. The side of him that had been torn away was encrusted with black stone that did nothing to hamper his movements. Saanae realised she would have to retreat all the way back to her caverns if she were to have the remotest chance of protecting herself, and she began to weep. She hesitated a moment too long before trying to run. Vladdir's stone arm, made electric by the power of the Desert, cut through her—body and soul.

It was an incredible, painful shock. There was nothing but infinite time and silence now.

Her upper body spun with the momentum of the strike, so that she could see her legs and hips, severed from the rest of her, tumble down towards the sand in a splash of blood. She noted that the dark arterial fluid was a very close match to the colour of her dress. As her head also hit the sand, she wondered pointlessly if she still had her womb, or if that part of her had been lost with her legs. What did it matter, she laughed at herself, this was all over anyway. No more life. No more child. No more Saanae.

It was transiently interesting, being dead; nothing like she had ever expected. Saanae had always thought she would become a part of the Desert, but instead she had become light. After a while it became rather boring, floating about with no direction. An endless sea of white, where she herself—also endlessly white—buffeted the aether with little fins to no effect.

Gradually, she became aware of coolness and water somewhere around her, but she couldn't tell the exact source. A tugging sensation grew where she had previously thought the middle of her body to be and the feeling grew into hot, burning pain as the sound of rough stitching became obvious. Sight slowly came back to her. The white became black, with intermittent flashes of the inside of her home cavern. A tall, dark man was walking towards her. All she could see of his face was that it dripped with purple venom, but he was otherwise as black as the armour he wore and the heavy cloak spread over his shoulders. If she had any sense of direction Saanae would have pulled away, but she couldn't see how, or where, to move.

What do you want? she demanded.

I want an end to that Earth-damned priest. Taking things from me. Taking my skin, my blood, my family. Now he thinks he can take my last two sons: my tainted one, and my pure one, who I intended to be my redemption and my continuance. I'll have him. I'll make sure he's born, Saanae. You have stepped into the flow that would ensure the continuation of my pure son. This will ultimately result in my vengeance. Then I will rest in peaceful longevity. I release you now to finish your work.

Who are you?

There was a hesitation, then a laugh.

Who was I, or who am I? I'll be the Undertaker, the Custodian of Death. It's my prerogative that you will leave here, but when the time comes I will see you again.

Why?

Do you think this extra time will not cost me? Giving this to you means I have to stay here longer. Now I can't leave here until you do. Not to worry... With me, you'll be treated fairly, and will eventually cycle again.

What will happen to me?

We all return to the Desert. I've left my tomb to wander thus. So shall you, as my servant, when the time comes, until we've burnt away enough of our sins to let ourselves swim free.

When she could hear again, she became aware of the pebbles shuffling about her, muttering disgustedly at the state of things. They were not pleased that they had been called upon to deal with so much trouble. Saanae was supposed to take care of them, not the other way around.

Who called you? Saanae asked.

Oh, the Desert. The Desert. And that old Dir. Thought he had been bound by silver and stone, but looks like we are mistaken. He's broken free somehow. That's not supposed to happen, but the pull of the purple is strong, and he's a very angry man.

Why did the Desert call you?

Who knows? It wants something from you. Not clear what, exactly.

Saanae could no longer focus her thoughts against the pain she was experiencing, and contented herself to lie still while the pebbles completed their work.

Tsh! It's that bothersome fellow again. None of this would have happened if not for him.

Saanae grit her teeth as the pain intensified and didn't bother trying to understand what the pebbles were complaining about now. Besides, other thoughts were pressing into her mind, like why she wasn't dead anymore. Or perhaps she was dead, but in the process of being transformed into one of those undead skeletons that the Desert was so fond of harbouring? Stiffened, as the legend went, so that her soul was forever trapped within her hardened body.

No. Not you, said the Desert. *You are being lent extra time.*

Do I have any say in this?

None whatsoever. And your son will give Us his eyes.

WHAT?

Oh, not to worry. We shall give him his father's old ones, fully restored, of course. We'll be able to see what he does. We need such a one, as we also want to witness the destruction of the power that harnesses Ilet. It was interesting for a time, but We grow weary of the constant arrogance.

What in Earth are you talking about?

Hee hee. What in Earth indeed. We are in Earth. That's really funny.

You're talking rots. Such nonsense!

You have a visitor, Saanae.

Saanae angrily discarded what the Desert had told her, and finally managed to lapse into unconsciousness.

Soft and fluid like music, the warmth and scent of comfort wrapped itself around Saanae as she slept. She was embraced to the very bosom of ardour while healing dreams wafted gently through her being. Gradually, she came back into the world. She found herself in her caverns, but wrapped in soft white linens instead of floating in her pool. She pushed the fabric away, a little unnerved that she had no idea where it had come from, and then equally unnerved by the odd realisation that she couldn't feel her legs. When she moved, stabs of burning numbness shot up her arms and neck, right to her face. Her fingers scrambled over her body, trying to find where she remembered being cut in two. Instead of encountering the rough, ugly stitches that she imagined, she felt gauzy bandages. Confused, she tried to turn her head so that she could see more of her body. The linens she was wrapped in were actually a large ruffled shirt.

"Saanae?" Mauvis leaned into her view. "Thank the Earth! I thought you were going to die."

Saanae began to cry. She wanted Mauvis to scoop her up and murmur to her soothingly, but instead he merely looked pained and reserved. It was to be expected, now. He must know what she had done.

"Why are you here?" she finally asked.

"The same reason I came the first time. Feeling out of place, looking for answers. I saw Vladdir attack you in his chambers. It was the first time I had seen him in his full Desert form. I had seen Alekseidir like that before, but over the years I had forgotten how terrible it was." He paused, seeming to need to collect himself before continuing.

"I understand now that you were more afraid of Vladdir than you let on originally, and it seems clear to me that the two of you had met before. Yet when I mentioned to him your name, he did not react badly. I would very much like an explanation, Saanae."

"From me?" she sniffled. "Did Vladdir not tell you?"

Mauvis shook his head. "I left. It has been about a week. I don't know why, exactly. It was much like the first time, when I just felt I had to go. Like there wasn't any reason for me to stay underground any longer. And I couldn't face Vladdir again, not after he had given in to the Desert so completely, especially after I had tried so hard...I was just so angry. He seemed too comfortable in that form, so controlled, more so than Alekseidir ever had. When I saw him like that, I was so sure he must have done it himself, and Kyril couldn't have had anything to do with it."

He paused again and licked his lips. When he spoke again, his voice sounded a bit breathless. "And now, I have to ask, Saanae...please explain to me what happened, in a way I can understand."

His expression was a mixture of despair and suppressed hope. Saanae thought that regardless of what the pebbles and the Undertaker had done, there wasn't much of her left for this world, and there was no reason to hold anything in secret.

"You've always been truthful with me, haven't you Mauvis? To be honest, in the beginning I doubted you."

She sighed and let herself relax, no longer caring what had become of her lower body.

"He ate my child. That was how he defeated Ilet and the Aragoths in the first place. He ate them, and my child along with them. I did attack him in spirit form, at first because I was angry, but then all I wanted back was my child's soul, so that I could raise it again. That was what I truly wanted to ask, if Vladdir would willingly release the spirits he had eaten, not if I could live underground with you."

Mauvis' face was contorted in hurt and confusion.

"Oh, I did want to go with you. But now, well, I see I've hurt you as much as I've hurt Vladdir, so that's lost."

"He...ate...? And after that, *he* attacked *you*? Why?"

The conversation was making Saanae feel dizzy and breathless. She forced out her answer. "He attacked me because Kyril told him I was the one who had struck at him with the Desert Priest. He never knew *why* I had attacked him. At least I don't think he did. He couldn't have known, not if what you told me is true—if he is not intentionally cruel. I was going to tell him all I wanted was my child back, and then we could leave each other alone, but I never got the chance! I wanted to tell him it was the Priest who used me to rip him like that. I would have told him, if not for Kyril!"

"Did he...chew...how...could you get the child back after that?"

"He ate the soul, Mauvis. That's what he does in that form. He eats life energy." She pointed at the little construct lying half-buried in grit, and Mauvis picked it up. "I made it, you see." Tears began to run down her face as she remembered the initial joy as seeing her tiny creature move. "And then...I took a little piece of my spirit, severed it from me...and gave it to my child. And then Vladdir sucked it away from us and swallowed it."

"Intentionally?"

"I'm not sure. I don't think so, not now. I think that's why he didn't know who I was, until Kyril told him her half-truths. I was so close. I could have made it work if the Desert Priest hadn't told her poison about me."

"*Earth!*"

Silence stretched between them for an interminable time. Perhaps Saanae slept. When she could focus her mind again, Mauvis was still sitting next to her with his elbows on his knees and his hands supporting his head.

"What will you do?" she asked him. Mauvis contemplated for a moment, then began tapping the air with a finger as he spoke.

"I can straighten this out. Where Vladdir is concerned, it's very simple. I made a promise to protect him from the Desert, so I must go back and tend to him as best I can, regardless of how disappointed I am at his lapse. I shall be blunt with both him and Kyril, and let them know for their own safety, that I will be strictly enforcing limitations on their behaviour."

Can he do that? wondered Saanae, but she was too fascinated to interrupt.

"I will leave you here for now, for your safety, until I have made the situation plain to Vladdir. Then, you will return with me."

"And then what?" Saanae couldn't help asking. Her hand strayed restlessly to her abdomen.

Mauvis suddenly seemed less sure. He turned to look at her and smiled in a self-deprecating way. "This is difficult to say out loud."

"I have finally become honest with *you*."

He wrapped his arms around his knees and tapped his feet a few times before answering. "I thought you would live with me. As my wife. If you consent."

Saanae's hand clutched spasmodically at the bandages around her middle and her very core felt like ice. All her blood seemed to drain from her skin.

"How badly damaged am I?"

"What do you mean?"

"Vladdir cut me right through the middle. I don't know if I can still be a mother."

Mauvis lost all his hesitancy and finally reached out to touch her, stroking her hair back and taking her hand in his.

"I don't care about that. I was adopted by Kai, the former Chamberlain. I couldn't have asked for a better father. We don't have to worry about having a birth-child."

"But it would have been nice," said Saanae, beginning to cry.

"Yes, it would."

"What name would you give a child, if it were a boy?"

Mauvis grinned through the tears that were welling up in his own eyes.

"A boy? Hmm. I think I would combine a few names of authors and illustrators I've always admired in my father's library. If I were to do that, well the name would be Antronos."

"And a girl?"

"Well that's easy, Phanthea, for the healing flower."

"I..." Saanae wanted to voice a declaration of her feelings for Mauvis, but what came out of her mouth was, "I really like those names."

Mauvis smiled and stretched out on the sand next to her, keeping her hand enfolded in his. Feeling exhausted, sad, relieved, and slightly hopeful, Saanae turned her head so that Mauvis' curls were touching her cheek and let all her consciousness drain away.

PART IV

ILET, THE DONKEY

I WOULD SCREAM, BUT *he hasn't given me a mouth.*

Ilet visualised his existence as a prison made of stone, his soul held in place by heavy shackles that wouldn't let him fly free. When Kyril had satisfied Vladdir's hunger and allowed the other souls to be released from the deep, black vortex that was hidden in Vladdir's soul, he had seen them race up into the sky, shining like stars in the heavens, far out of reach of all mankind. But when Ilet had tried to follow the others as they jumbled towards their freedom, he had only been able to taste the fresh Desert wind for a few seconds. His old master had cast a magical net about him, reclaiming what he had no rights to. Why couldn't stupid Vladdir have opened his stupid gorge just a little sooner? Why had he resisted Kyril so much and wasted so many precious seconds? In his agony, Ilet dreamt of Vladdir, and shouted accusations at him.

Much later—Ilet didn't know how long, since he could not watch the days pass—the Desert Priest opened the prison of runes and brass triangles to slap Ilet into yet another cage—this one made of flesh. As his eyes formed out of the meat Saanae had ripped from

Vladdir's side, he began to perceive his prison more accurately. The process would have been fascinating if it hadn't felt like every nerve in the gooey encasement of muscle and skin was about to explode with every sensory impulse it received. He blinked away slimy redness and found himself looking upwards through water. He was in a tank, the sides of which were stone. The surface of the water was covered with a transparent, hardened shield, against which his bloody little stump-limbs could bump futilely, but he could not break it. He stopped attempting to escape when the trails of blood left in the water from his stumps sickened him. It wouldn't have been so disgusting if he had not remembered anything from before—what it was like to be clean and whole.

He saw the Desert Priest lean over the tank, his features distorted by the slight movements of the encased water. Ilet recoiled and bumped against the bottom of his tank, knowing that the next session was about to begin. Purple was dripping into the water from above.

His hands were being shaped, and it was excruciating. Ilet hoped he would forget this scintillating pain once he was fully formed. His limbs were pushed into the stone and drawn back out, and each time the bloody tips of his fingers were stretched a little farther as the Desert caught at him and tried to hold him in. Now he was a lump of torn flesh with spindly arms flapping at his sides.

My mother said I was ugly when I was newly ripped from my father's side, but what would she say now? thought Ilet. *Would she see any improvement? I wonder if my father would accept me. I'm backwards, having been ripped from my father, instead of my mother. I would laugh, but he hasn't given me a mouth.*

A little more, and a little more. The Priest paused and glared at his work with narrowed eyes as he decided what to change next. He was a sculptor unsatisfied with his clay. Finally, he took Ilet from the tank and wrapped him in white gauze, allowing him to rest. The peace did not last.

After a short time—unfairly short, Ilet thought—he was unwrapped. As the bandages were peeled away, he found that he could scream. Itchy little lightning ants ate at each part of his exposed flesh.

The Priest was holding a little vial of blue venom, which he forced through Ilet's skin where the mouth should have been. He picked up a knife and carved sections of Ilet away, then wrapped him up again. Later, he peeled him again, until Ilet finally screamed himself into black silence. With some relief, he thought he must have died.

When he woke, he found himself back in his tank, and this time he had to blink away blueness. He reached toward his face to brush away the hair that had grown from his head. Now when he pressed his limbs against the hardened surface of the water, he saw the small-fingered hands of a child, and no trails of blood to trace their movements. The pain had completely left him, but Ilet still wondered if there might be more torment to come, so he pulled what he thought should be his feet towards his face and was greatly relieved to see small, rounded toes protruding from each foot, complete with tiny toenails. He touched his face, found lips. The absence of hurt left him filled with glee. His mind was different, as was his body. Things that had bothered him before now seemed like trivialities that he could deal with quite easily if he were interested enough in doing so. Everything seemed newly simple, easy and interesting. Perhaps, he mused, he had inherited some of his father's power with this new flesh.

When the Priest came again, he touched the surface of the water and it dissolved, allowing him to lift Ilet out of the tank. Ilet pulled his legs up into a ball and eyed his master warily.

"I am your father," said the Priest. "You will obey me."

You aren't and I won't, thought Ilet, but he did not say this aloud. The Priest's words made him wonder if his master realised that he remembered everything, including the fact that obeying the Priest last time had not brought him any satisfaction.

He was lathered and rinsed, then dressed in a soft white gown and slippers. The Priest set him on his feet and stood back to assess his work.

"It'll do," he said. "Will you go to Vladdir, Ilet?"

"Yes." *Truth.*

"Will you kill him?"

"Yes." *More like a 'maybe.'*

"And you won't die? You will come back to me. You're a lovely creature, and I'd hate to remake you again. It might not turn out so nicely."

"I won't die." *Truth again.* Ilet omitted commenting on whether or not he'd return.

"Of course not. Go, then."

Ilet was quite happy in his new body, skipping through some tunnels he'd found below the surface.

I want to meet my mother, my mother, my mother, he thought as he danced about the labyrinth. He knew she would love any child that came her way. He knew what love was because he had felt it from the kiss Kyril had given Vladdir to make the old swine release the souls he had eaten. Having had more than his share of pain, he had decided that now he wanted to feel nothing but love. Saanae had plenty in her, he had felt it from the resonance left when she had carried his body through the Desert on the night he had been torn. He just had to find her first, and tell her that she was to love him.

The underground tunnels were cool after the heat on the surface, and Ilet was happy to just *be* for a few days. He found small muddy streams to drink from, and the occasional meal of fungi. He was slightly disappointed that his clothes had become dirty, but after seeing that wiping at the mud with his small hands only made things worse, he decided there was nothing he could do about it and worried no further. A few days more, and he began to grow impatient. Why was it so hard to find his mother's lair? He began to voice his complaints to the roots and beetles surrounding him, feeling himself growing upset when no answer came. He was about to indulge in tears when a mass of little voices reached toward his mind.

Who are you? Why do you look for Saanae?

"She's my mother," said Ilet.

Can this be? It isn't possible.

"It is. She tore me from my father's side. She made me."

Hmm. It seems Saanae has been doing some strange things lately. But we don't believe you. If she had a child, she would have told us. She tells us everything. Besides, you're the wrong colour, all aglow with blue and orange. We'd expect green from Saanae.

"Please tell me where she is."

No.

Ilet let his anger rise. He didn't speak any more, but stepped forward until he could sense the little entities that had spoken to him resting under his feet. The stupid little pebbles believed he couldn't discern them from the rest of the Desert. He squatted and picked up several of them, feeling delight as they squawked in alarm. Closed in his fist, they twisted about but couldn't roll away. The pebbles remaining in the mud twisted into its depths, but now he could trace where they went from the communication they foolishly continued with their captive brothers. He climbed the roots of a dead tree, pushed through underneath its twisted brambles and finally stood up in the vast openness of the surface. It was fun running in his new body, as tottering and slow as it was, along the Desert's sandy rock-ground in the cool morning light. Ilet laughed, not even minding when one of his slippers fell off and he had to stop to clumsily shove it back onto his muddy foot with only one hand; the other still firmly entrapped the pebbles.

At the entryway to Saanae's lair, the free pebbles sank down to warn their mistress, and they commanded the sand to not open the stone stairway for Ilet. Sand had a fleeting memory, however, and it shortly obeyed Ilet's command to shift aside and show him where the stairwell hid. He went down carefully, one inexperienced foot at a time, through a small tunnel that formed over the white stone steps.

He wasn't the first one there.

Ilet crouched down in surprise as he watched a second master, a skinny one with brown, curling hair, leaning over and working his magic on Saanae. The man's aura leached purple venom into the sand around him, despite his best efforts to keep it hidden. Who was this? Ilet ground both fists against his mouth to stop any sounds he might make as tears ran down his cheeks. Just seeing the white gauze being wrapped around Saanae's middle made his innards tighten up and his skin crawl with the anticipation of pain. The master picked up a pair of shears and Ilet almost shouted at him, but the man only cut the bandages before tucking their ends neatly beneath the wraps. Saanae's body was laid back down on some blankets spread over the sandy rock, and she did not move. Her eyes had remained shut through the entire wrapping, and Ilet thought that she must have screamed during the peeling, and now had fallen unconscious.

"I must return to the Royal House," the man said to Saanae, even though she was asleep. "We need fresh bandages and supplies. I'll be avoiding Vladdir, so you don't need to worry about that. We'll sort him out later, after you've recovered."

The master stood, and Ilet quickly curled himself into a ball, commanding the sand to cover him before he was discovered. The bastardly little pebbles twisted about and bounced at the master's feet as he walked towards the stairwell, trying to give Ilet away, but thankfully the man's arrogance was too great to allow him to listen. He strode past in ignorance, apparently in a hurry to reach the surface. As he swept by, Ilet felt the ferocious, coiling power of the master brush over his body, and was deeply worried that there was no way he could remain hidden from someone so dangerously formidable. The curly-haired man did not stop for Ilet either, and did not turn around when Ilet cautiously let the sand drop from his body.

Saanae still lay silently, her dark hair providing glorious contrast to her too-pale face. Ilet thought she was the most beautiful person he had ever seen. He put out one dirty hand to touch her face, then hesitated, thinking that he should rinse off his mud in the pool first. As he tried to reach for the water it pulled away from him, and lapped just behind a ring of stones that had previously been hidden beneath its surface. He leaned over the stones and stretched out for the water, almost touching it, and then fell in.

The rock floor of the pool opened wide and swallowed him whole, sending him tumbling into a pale green stomach that was filled with jade stalactite pillars and little white fish and frogs that darted out of the way. From here, he was drained into the deeper bowels of the Desert where an underground river caught him up and tossed him along the rocky riverbed, until he fell into a deep, dark pool that seemed to have no surface and no bottom. Far distant, somewhere deep in the water, was a dim purple glow. Its regal aura pulsated towards him and made Ilet afraid. This was the same power as the second master who had wrapped Saanae, but much, much stronger.

Stones were moving around in the water, making it wash against his small body as these new entities spiralled up and around him. They brought with them a faint light which emanated from strange, eyeless bubble fish that swam with long tentacles trailing in their wake. One of the grey stone beings reached out a bony hand and took Ilet by the arm, gently propelling him towards the purple light. As they drew nearer, Ilet saw that the light was actually venomous aura leaking from a dead man's soul. The man was enormous, wearing black armour, and his chin rested on his fists that were crossed over his chest. When the moving water lifted the man's hair from his brow, Ilet could see that small, white rock inscribed with runes was embedded in his forehead. A sword that glinted with inlaid jewels hung scabbardless from his belt. He seemed to be asleep.

Do you know what you are, Ilet?

Not really.

Beast of burden. You don't seem to remember, but we were once captive together. On the night you were first made, I was the model for your animal soul to be carved out as human.

Ilet had no response to this. He was rather offended by the thought. Had this been anyone else, he imagined he would have answered rudely, but he was aware that the person he faced now was incredibly dangerous and must be shown respect. He wondered what was wanted of him.

You will give your power to ensure the continuation of my pure son. That continuance will let me have my revenge. Your priest thinks he can command me? Let him call me now, and I will again come. I will break him and this damned stone that binds me here.

Give my power? What power?

Come here, child.

Ilet had no intention of approaching something so frightening, but he was pushed by the stone men from behind and had no choice.

The glowing bubble fish hovered by the dead man's face, giving Ilet brief glimpses of sunken and empty eye sockets, rotten teeth displayed in the grimace of mortis, and naked, browned finger bones tucked under the withered chin. The man never moved, but still Ilet felt him reach out and touch his mind, forcing change over both his thoughts and his body. The transformation was unbelievably gentle after what he had experienced from the Desert Priest. Bones, sand and seaweed were flowing upwards from the depths of the water, pouring themselves into his body through the soles of his feet. Involuntarily, his back arched in the water as his form lengthened and filled with energy. The white gown he wore ripped apart and fell away. He saw his hair becoming longer as his body flung itself the other way, and the blue strands floated in front of his face. His fingers elongated, at first translucent so that he could see the bones, then they became opaque and coloured like the palest flesh. His heart fluttered as it too changed, compensating for this sudden growth. His mind grew larger and opened wider, enabling so many new thought patterns that raced through him with electric potential.

Do not betray me, Ilet, and you will be rewarded with your freedom. I cannot give you anything now, not since I've just contaminated you with the Desert. It will take two cycles for you to be purified, but then, you will be allowed to swim free with the light. Just remember, when the water comes to take you, do not resist.

Ilet realised that he couldn't breathe. It suddenly, urgently, began to matter. Lungs burning, head throbbing, he kicked as hard as he could in the direction he imagined was up. He was growing desperate, and was imminently grateful when he felt the round, head-like protrusions of the stone beings press against his feet and force him upwards more rapidly, until his head smashed against a wall of soil. His body crumpled with the impact before he was pushed through and onto the banks of an underground tunnel. He coughed uncontrollably until all the water had been spewed from his lungs and only a trickle of blood dribbled from his lips. He was shaking as he pushed himself up onto unsteady adult-length legs he had never before used. It took him a few moments to gain his balance, then, leaning heavily on the rock wall, he slowly made his way back to Saanae's caverns.

She knew him immediately. Despite his changed form, despite the fact that half his body was now made of water and Desert, she still knew him as the child she had carried from Vladdir's flesh. Saanae stared at him wordlessly, her expression a mixture of wonderment and horror, until he shakily made his way over to where she sat, the bedding cloths fallen around her waist, and rested his head in her lap. When she finally touched his face, pushing back his hair, she read his mind as he had left it open for her, and understood that he had left his master and was now here for her love. He felt her withdraw both her hands and her mind, reeling with uncertainty. She lay back down and they both slept.

When Ilet awoke again, Saanae had risen, and he had been covered with a sheet. He listened to her pace in the darkness, and imagined she must be adjusting to finding herself with a new son, one she had awaited for so long. Ilet got up.

"Please wear the sheet." Her voice was soft, barely discernable over the quiet lap of the water in the pool.

Ilet opened his mouth to tell Saanae all he wanted her to know, but she stopped him with quiet words.

"I know who you are."

"You tore me from—"

"I know."

Ilet began to feel uncertain, now that he had not automatically gained Saanae's acceptance as he had imagined. Everyone else seemed to want him, but this confused unhappiness that he sensed from his mother did certainly seem to be directed at him.

Tell me what to do, his mind begged her.

"I don't think you're what the dark man in the Desert promised me," she finally said. "You came from the Priest. Why have you left him?"

"He sent me out."

"To do what?"

"Kill Vladdir."

"Ah." Saanae sat unmoving and watched him with her dark eyes, and Ilet suppressed his impatient urge to demand that she embrace and comfort him. After a moment, another thought formed in his mind.

"Oh! Then there was the other master. The third one."

One of Saanae's eyebrows rose and her head turned slightly. Ilet thought she looked beautiful. When he said nothing, Saanae asked, "And who was this...master?"

"I don't know. Met him in the water. I didn't understand what he told me to do."

"So he was of the water, and not the Desert?"

Ilet had never needed to think this hard before. "Nn...no. I think he was Desert."

"Do you remember what he said?"

"Continuance."

Saanae's expression darkened. "Do you remember what he looked like?"

"Dark and purple. Dead." Why was this important? Ilet felt his irritation and impatience rise. He wanted Saanae to refocus her thoughts on accepting him. He knelt and hung his head, blue hair spilling onto his lap, and felt the tears leaving his eyes trace burning tracks down his cheeks.

After a long moment, when Ilet had begun to think that there was nothing for him here; that it must be time to fall asleep and not bother to wake up again, he again heard Saanae's soft voice.

"What do you want, Ilet? For yourself, I mean. Not what others have told you to want."

This was a complicated question which became more complicated as he tried to answer it. His simple answer of "love" no longer seemed to describe what he thought he wanted from Saanae. He anticipated that whatever answer he gave, Saanae's next question would be to ask him why he wanted such things. Delving into that realm of thought left him feeling empty, wondering if he really wanted anything at all. The dark master in the water had promised him freedom, but was that what he wanted? Hadn't he come here seeking to be bound to Saanae?

"I don't know," he finally said. "I think I just want to feel . . . warm. Sleepy. Not needing anything. What do you want?"

Saanae was sitting on a low bench and now reached to pick up something off the floor. It looked like a limp, little doll. Ilet didn't need to ask what it was, and yet, it confused him. What was the difference between the doll and himself? Why couldn't Saanae accept one as the other? Ilet took a deep breath, opened his mouth, and realised that words would not serve him. Not any that he had, at least. He shuffled forward and pushed his head under her hand, resting his cheek against her knee, and let the drowsiness come. Perhaps this was what he wanted, after all.

As he dozed, he was peripherally aware that Saanae was browsing through his thoughts, finding him a simple creature. He didn't mind this, as he felt her finally coming to accept him. She rearranged a few thought patterns, tidied a couple mental connections, and cautiously backed away when she came across the chains that bound him to the Desert Priest. Ilet didn't want those, and sleepily tried to tell Saanae to clear them away. However, when he fully awoke, much later, he found himself very much alone with the chains still intact. Not knowing what else to do, Ilet curled up and went back to sleep.

"You haven't done a single thing I've asked."

Ilet blinked in pain, raising a hand to shield his eyes from the bright glare of the sunlight bouncing off the Desert sand. Hadn't he been safely hidden underground in Saanae's caverns? His new skin was unadjusted to the harsh light and wind of the surface, and already felt crusty as he moved. One of his ankles was shackled and chained to a post.

"You're greatly changed, Ilet. I trace through your mind, but can't see where you've been. You were with Saanae, I know, but parts of what I see are unintelligible. It would seem there are many forces wanting to use you, and if we had the time, I might bother to find out which. But right now, I would prefer you serve the purpose I made you for."

Ilet tugged futilely on the chain, then glared warily at the Priest. First Vladdir had given him back, now Saanae. Was this stupid Priest the only one who wanted to keep him? His first master held up a vial of blue venom and snapped it open. He very deliberately tipped it out onto the sand in front of Ilet's face.

"I thought having a construct like you would eliminate the need for such crude measures, but it seems you're a willful little ass, just like the rest of them. Do you honestly think you can be human? *When I call, you come. It has always been thus."*

Ilet squealed and brayed, sounding very much like a donkey, and felt his insides start to slither out from his body. The Desert Priest was kneeling with his eyes shut, muttering an incantation that forced Ilet to move away from his corporeal self. He was free floating in the aether, then felt the tug of his master's energy chains force him downwards. He resisted and kicked, but felt himself losing form, becoming liquid that flowed through an underground channel according to his master's will.

Saanae should know that if she uses tricks she has learned from me, it won't take much on my part to turn them against her.

Ilet was completely helpless now, unable to distinguish himself from the Priest's command. He tried to focus on Saanae's final question to him: what did he want for himself, aside from what others had told him? *I do want freedom! Freedom to choose who I am with, who I might serve.* But as his form became more intermixed with the aether, it became next to impossible to hold onto anything that had been his own.

He was surfacing now, up into a tiny bowl of water perched on a stem. Up into a small column of water, like a fountain flowing back on itself, a little waterfall of blue in Saanae's magic cup. Up to stare into the eyes of the second master who had wrapped Saanae, and was now frozen in amazement as he gazed back at Ilet. One hand was full of bandages and cloths, the other clutched a travelling sack. Ilet's small blue arm raised and pointed at the vial given to the second master so long ago, droplets of water dripping from his fingers to splash against the rolls of paper drawings that rested under the goblet he rose out of, to tell the master it was time to drink the vial of red potion. *Drink the red venom. It's the only thing you can do.*

The second master, his eyes wide with fear and completely unable to resist the magical delivery of this simple command, picked up the tiny vial from his desk. Using his finger and thumb, he snapped it open.

PART V

CALLIE, THE HEALER

IND MY OWN BUSINESS, *indeed. It is my business to not mind my own business. How can I get anything done if I'm expected to work blind?*

Rayner could stumble around in the dark if he wished, but Callie had had enough of feeling threatened in her own home. As Yrati, they were supposed to *fix* things, not stumble around hiding behind other people, waiting for someone else to step up to deal with the problem. Not a single Aragoth had been seen for months, and most of the tunnel dwellers seemed to think the war with the Aragoths was long over. Despite this, the strange attacks that had afflicted Vladdir during the war still continued. It was this Desert Priest, she was sure of it. Rayner knew how to build stupid buildings, but he didn't have any idea how to heal. And just because *Rayner* knew about rocks and stones most certainly *did not* make him any sort of authority on how Vladdir's stone arm should be treated. And neither, for that matter, was *Vladdir*.

The interior of the new Yrati home was still not completed, yet the deepest sanctuaries had already been well buried in the most secure caverns. Callie didn't have enough rank to be allowed this deep within the archives, the official position being that Priests without the proper training could hurt themselves if they tried to use the heavier magics, but she was only going to look. What harm was there in looking? If anything seemed beyond her capabilities, she simply wouldn't do it. Besides, the area was still under construction, so *technically*, it wasn't *really* a Deep Yrati Shrine. Not *yet*.

The entryway to the archives was marked off only with a thin strip of warning tape. There was never any concern that the boundary would not be respected. Callie ducked underneath it and began running lightly through empty bookshelves and half-assembled study carrels, her leather slippers making soft taps as she went. This cavern was full of grey dust, as some of the walls were still in the process of being hewn straight, and the wide opening for the intended skylight was still being roughed out. A mild dust storm was raging in the night outside, pushing some of the surface silt in through the hole, making the room even colder and dingier. It seemed there was no colour at all. She saw a lantern approaching and heard Rayner's voice discussing something technical with one of the engineers, so she quickly ducked into the bottom of a shelving unit, curled into a ball and held her sneezes until they walked by. They were probably the last to leave for the evening meal, so once they were gone, there would be no one to avoid.

It wasn't difficult to decide which direction to go. She kept moving forward as long as there was another cavern to move into. The last cavern was extremely large and seemed to stretch the full length of the Shrine, from left to right. The air carried a chill and the mineral scent of underground water. Very little light penetrated the room. Callie rubbed her eyes and strained to see into the darkness, cautiously stretching out her feet, toes first, feeling her way across the floor. A lot of energy was coursing through this room, making her fingertips tingle, and if she concentrated on her peripheral vision it was almost as if she could see lines of pulsating blue running along some sort of cross grid. She wondered for a few moments if the location for this room was selected because the area already had energy, or if the energy was built into the room, or if the energy had come because of what the cavern was intended for. During her ordination studies, she had always assumed that the power—the vibrations that only the Yrati seemed attuned to—built up in a Shrine after years of prayer.

It was probably safe to pull out her light globe now, so she wrestled it from a too-small pocket within her inner robes, relieved to have the bioluminescent moss to give her a bit more to go by. A line of round pools ringed with stone bricks opened onto the floor—the sort of pools that the Ghouls could be summoned into through mediation. Callie passed them carefully, feeling heat rise to her face. She would not remain undetected here if the red Water Ghouls should come. She wondered if they would find her disrespect of the archives worth reporting to the other Yrati. The surface of the water in each pool rippled with concentric circles, as if some unheard tremor shook them from within. Despite that, they seemed empty. Perhaps the Ghouls were sleeping.

After the pools, Callie ran into a wall. That was it? Would she have to go back to the last chamber of books? They hadn't been unpacked yet, still boxed up in crates, so she had assumed they weren't that important. She put one hand out to the wall and walked along it, looking for some other passage that wasn't immediately visible. Her fingertips left the stone surface and felt cool air brushing against them. The globe of moss was actually obscuring her vision here, and when she tucked it behind her back, she saw a narrow passageway through the wall. Something within was faintly glowing blue. As she moved forward, she saw that the pale light was coming from the inside of an empty brass triangle sitting on a narrow stone plinth. What was this? She had never seen anything like it. Why was this thing sitting here all by itself? How could it glow like that? It sort of looked like a prayer triangle, but was much bigger, had rounded points, and was missing the centrepiece, which usually carried some engraving. This was nothing more than a three-sided outline of metal. Overcome with curiosity, Callie leaned close to it. She thought she heard a soft, intermittent murmuring, but she wasn't certain if it was actually sound or if she was just imagining it. It was mesmerising.

She bent her head again, concentrating hard, until she slipped partway into a trance, resting her chin on the cold stone base. It was...an information stream...a connection to knowledge of...everything/body. Before she realised what she was doing, her fingers had crept around the edge of the metal, then reached through it in her attempts to hear better. She felt an electric rush flood through her arm and up her scalp, along with a thousand voices all talking inside her head at once. She ripped her hand away and jumped back, deciding to leave the triangle alone. Her fingers felt numb, but she could still flex them, so the feeling should return soon. Had she disturbed anything? For a moment, nothing. Then the world pulsed blue, showing her straight lines and square angles in intricate patterns. Another moment of blackness, then a second pulse, and this time the lines glowed red. Isolated sections of the lines moved in a quarter turn, leaving motion blurs sweeping across her retinas. She squeezed her eyes shut tightly and rubbed them. The pulsing stopped, and when she looked around nothing else seemed to be moving, so she continued her sweep of the room.

Several metres past the triangle, the glow of her moss globe showed her a wooden wall or divider of some sort, just standing in the middle of the room. She stepped around it and saw that it was deep like a book shelf, with the other side covered by a hanging cloth. Lifting the fabric aside, she thought, *Aha! I've found them.* Several very old tomes were placed reverently on flat cushions within. Not knowing which one to pick, Callie decided to start with the first. She pulled on a pair of soft gloves she had carried in her pocket so that the oils of her fingers would not damage the old papers, and carefully lifted the book and placed it on the floor, settling her little moss globe off to the side.

The script within was annoyingly difficult to read. Who in Earth made their letters like that? *Styffeneg*? Was that stiffening? *He who hathe styffend ith he whoe seeke the deepe place of hys souls*...what did that say? *Ne'er to tell whatever he cannot rymembyr...*

Right. This was not going to be easy. But Vladdir's arm had indeed stiffened, so this might be what she was looking for, if she could just read it. She flipped ahead a few pages to look for illustrations, and found some rather horrific depictions of Yrati priests recoiling in apparent fear from their own limbs that had taken on a skeletal appearance. A few pages more, and these priests were being dragged against their will into pools of water by what could have been Red Ghouls—if these plates had been in colour.

"Well, that's disturbing," Callie muttered. She had always been taught that the Ghouls, no matter how frightening they looked, were protectors and guides. These appeared to be kidnappers. She tried to read the text on the facing page: *styfent and stykt en bodie, to became bodhisattvae and reemaen to the benefice of the otter mane.* She skimmed through to the end of the book, hoping irrationally to catch on to something describing how to reverse the stiffening. Perhaps in another text...

The next three volumes were completely useless, inspiring her to make a silent vow to rewrite these books in much less annoying format as soon as she got the seniority to do so. Stiffening this, stiffening that, running around the Desert and through the Earth, something about choosing yogurt instead of rock formations, something about fish and light underwater, swimming free—oh, there it was. The Ghouls could apparently become unstiffened by turning into fish that turned into light that swam up into the sky. Great! That knowledge made everything completely unclear.

Something wet fell onto the back of her hand and bounced to the floor. Callie picked it up and held it to her moss globe. It looked like a curved fragment of...well...perhaps a partially mummified lower mandible. A red one. A few drops of water fell onto the top of her head. She slowly turned and looked upward.

"You're a young one to be coming here."

Forgetting about the book, Callie accidentally crushed the pages with her legs as she whirled around on her knees and fell prostrate in front of the Red Ghoul. She had never seen one like this, with clear, blue eyes fully round in his wide, red sockets, and a complete set of senior Yrati robes hanging from his skeletal shoulders. And *never* had she heard one speak so clearly.

"So young. And so tiny. Normally they only sacrifice the older ones, when they can no longer serve without taking the next step."

Callie was afraid to ask, yet the question spilled from her lips: "What do you mean?" She lifted her head and blinked up at the Ghoul.

"Oh, dear dear dear dear. Look at your hand, little missy. You've gone and touched the other side in your search for deeper magic. Have you not had the training? Were you not told of the cost? You should have attempted to continue yourself first, for now you've lost your chance. You and I are now 'We,' and We go to prepare the way for others. We stay between worlds, while others are permitted to leave. You're trapped here now, I'm afraid."

Callie looked down at the hand she had extended into the triangle, realising only now that the nagging itch she had been ignoring was turning into a painful burn. She pulled off the soft gloves and saw red welts forming along her fingers and at the edge of her wrist.

"You're quite determined. The transformation is proceeding more quickly than usual. Perhaps you have a week. I'd advise you to return to your Humani friends for the little time you have left." The Ghoul turned and shuffled off into the darkness.

"Wait!" Callie stumbled to her feet and ran after him. "Sir? I know I wasn't supposed to come here, but all I wanted to do was heal My King Vladdir. No one seems to know how."

"Vladdir." If Ghouls could snort without all the required nasal tissue, this one did. The puff of air he produced smelled of wet dust. "He's gone and found other solutions to his problems. Leave him alone. He doesn't want us. Didn't he tell you?"

"Well, I guess."

"Stop guessing, little one. Start Seeing. You've got a difficult job ahead of you. It's Vladdir's brother you should concern yourself with."

"I *can* See!" Callie protested. She meant that she had learnt to interpret the images that Ghouls sent to the Yrati through the water, but now, even as she spoke the words, her natural vision was starting to darken around the edges with blue. Her fingers involuntarily curled up, and the globe dropped to the floor with a loud smack to roll off beyond her reach. She rubbed at her eyes.

You can See? Not like this, little one. We guarantee you.

Callie screamed in frustration and fear as her head began to fill with light. Red and blue bursts of colour were entering and leaving her mind as the thoughts of the Ghouls passed through her soul. There were so many of them, in this world and not in this world. All of them constantly talking, Seeing, telling each other what they Saw. It abruptly stopped. She opened her eyes, no longer seeing blue. Red bony fingers of a second Ghoul were reaching up from the rock at her feet to press a small, triangular charm into her hand. The Ghoul chittered, then sank back through the floor. The blue-eyed one had already left. Callie flipped the charm over in her palms a few times, feeling inexplicably angry and emptied. Different runes were scrawled on either side of the triangle, and depending on how she held it, she could either hear or not hear the information being constantly rattled out by the Ghouls. After a moment, it didn't matter how she held it, she could control the information flow by just what she thought, so the oddly shaped pebble was slipped into her pocket along with the now-cracked moss globe. Feeling overwhelmed, afraid, ashamed and disappointed, she carefully replaced the book on its shelf and decided to leave the chamber.

"Forgive me, Dearest Father, for I have erred."

Callie felt hot tears run down her face as she spoke the words, kneeling just inside the door of My Lord and High Priest Dagnaum's private study. She deliberately shoved her hair back from her face, giving herself no chance to hide her shame.

"My Dear Earth! It must have been a boulder of an error for *you* of all people to suddenly become so formal!" Dagnaum tossed his stylus onto his desk and swivelled on his stool so that he could face Callie with his hands leaning on his knees. Seeing that Callie was going to adhere strictly to protocol, he sighed and pushed back the heavy hood of his robes, revealing his bald head and the massive scars along the side of his face. He normally kept his old wounds covered because they had become very sensitive to cold. "Child, I used to swap the napkins on your bottom. Do you really think it's necessary to keep your feelings hidden from me? We all err. How does this make you special?"

At that, Callie let the sobs burst from her mouth and ran into Dagnaum's arms. As they embraced, she could feel him reading her aura. One of his hands passed gently over her head.

"You've begun the Change," he said quietly. "What did you do?"

"I crushed the pages of the book. One that was sacred. I don't know which one it was."

"You've done more than that."

"I put my hand through a triangle. I heard voices. I met a Ghoul with blue eyes. They gave me a stone. Now I can hear them loudly all the time. They don't like My King Vladdir."

Dagnaum was silent for a long moment. "Why have you done this?" he asked.

"I just wanted to know if there was any way to reverse the stiffening of Vladdir's arm. That's all. The Ghoul said something about training. What training?" She pulled back so that she could see the old priest's face.

"It's not just training, Callie. It's an enormous choice. You've gone and done what only the most carefully selected Yrati are chosen to do."

"But I wasn't selected. I just went into that chamber anyway."

"You are selected now. Look at your hands."

"They're red. They itch."

"You've begun the initiation to become one of the Red Ghouls. Do you have any understanding of what you've done?"

She hung her head, hiding her face as the tears started again. "I'm sorry. I only wanted to help. I should be punished now, right?"

"I suppose you will be, but not by any of us."

"Because I've become selfish, proud and mean."

Dagnaum gave her a strangely unhappy smile. "Quite the opposite. You've become Holy. By giving up your right to die, you are transforming into one who walks the 'in between.' Neither dead nor alive, or perhaps both, you will be able to guide the living and the dead by what you See in both worlds. You'll help them pass through safely. The term of servitude is unending, from what I hear."

"But...can't I become...a fish, afterwards?"

Dagnaum smiled again. "If only we really knew what that meant. It seems you will find out before I do."

Callie sniffled and rubbed her face with both sleeves. "The others will be upset with me."

"I think 'furious' is the correct term. You're going to be leaving us, you know."

"Really?"

"I don't see that any of us has any choice in the matter."

"No choice? Dagnaum, please! I swear I won't ever be disobedient again."

"Callie, there is no point in pleading to me. I can't change anything. I'm sure you've already figured that out."

"*Please don't send me away!*"

"Haalom, I'm not going to do anything of the sort. It's just that the Ghouls do not live among us. They never have."

"What should I do now?"

Dagnaum pulled Callie back into an embrace. "Don't waste the sacrifice you've made," he whispered in her ear. The finality of his words made the tears explode from her again, and she wept uncontrollably in his arms until she eventually became so tired that she curled up under his table to hide from the world, like she had when she was a child. She couldn't think about how things were changing, or she might run screaming through the tunnels, climb out onto the surface, find a cliff and commit the unthinkable.

Several hours later, Callie woke and found Dagnaum's chambers empty. A blanket had been tucked around her, but the lamps were cold and none of the High Priest's writing implements were left on the desk. The itching red patches on her hand were spreading up her arm, and her forehead was also starting to feel funny, so she tried to return to her own chambers through the tunnels that were less frequently used. She needed to see how bad it was, and if she could use powder to cover it up before anyone saw her. As she neared the residential area, she heard someone gasping and moaning in the tunnel ahead. She froze and crouched, peering into the dimness, then cautiously began to edge closer.

"*I will not, I will not, I will not,*" came the words, over and over. *Who is this?* she wondered, and the little Ghoul-stone flipped over in her imagination. Red, blue, pink and purple lines pulsated in her field of view, snaking outwards from whoever was in the tunnel ahead.

Vladdir's brother, the Red Ones told her.

I thought both his brothers were dead.

He has three. This one is not dead.

And I am to help him?

Hmm. Well, perhaps you should. From this man will spring someone who is a bit of a moron, but capable enough when it comes to setting things right.

I have no idea what you're all talking about.

The damned Ghouls actually laughed.

"*Your* lack of communication skills is hardly reason to laugh at *me*," she muttered irritably, and strode down the corridor boldly, no longer caring who was up ahead. The lines of light flickered in what she imagined was distress. "*Mauvis?* By the Earth!"

Mauvis was crouched against the wall. He looked damp and dishevelled, some of his clothes torn and his arms tucked loosely around his knees. His head came up, and he gawped blindly in her direction, red fluid dripping from his eyes and running down his face. "I will *not*," he insisted. A small vial slipped from his bony fingers and plinked quietly against the floor. "By the strength given to me by my father Kai, by the honour given to me by my father Aleksei, *I will not!*"

Callie rushed to his side and knelt. She blinked and forced herself to see things normally, then began searching her pockets for gauze. Was he bleeding? "What happened to you?"

"I can't...I can't believe I actually drank the potion, no matter what the Desert and its little messengers whispered to me, no matter how my mind was twisted and pulled. I had resisted for so long, it had always been so easy, and now I have succumbed to this."

Callie began dabbing at his face. The stuff that came away was too red to be blood, and had no smell. Mauvis' eyes were filled with the stuff. Perhaps he couldn't even see.

"It's venom, you know." His head dropped again. "It's obvious why Saanae had given it to me. I was a threat who had entered her home. I do wish, that she had remembered to take it back, or at least warn me to have it destroyed."

"You're making as much sense as the Ghouls. Can you see, Mauvis?

Does it hurt?" Unable to curb her fear and annoyance, Callie grabbed his head and rubbed at his eyes vigorously, trying to make the red go away.

"It was warm, flowery-tasting. It awoke the senses I had shut down so long ago. Now the living auras surrounding me are forcing my eyes to acknowledge their presence. I feel the tugs, the angry shouts of the Desert Priest trying to command me, but such tactics won't work here. Discipline and determination were two gifts given to me by my father Kai, and the purple venom given to me by my father Aleksei, although diluted in my blood as I am the fourth son, has given me ample opportunity to train against such an attack."

Callie sat back and stared at Mauvis for a moment, giving herself the space to consider the notion that this gentle, slightly awkward man she had known for most of her life was actually the king's brother. Why had no one ever said? Ah. Queen Sulandor had not been pregnant again. That was why. But did Vladdir know?

Nope, said the Ghouls. *He's a self-righteous prick anyway. Gonna take a few cycles to straighten him out. Doesn't know a thing about self-sacrifice. Takes, takes, takes. Never gives. Mauvis here knows a thing or two about giving. Like he says, his father Kai gave him a proper upbringing, and that will go a long way in helping him resist. Vladdir was spoiled, spoiled, spoiled. That's why* he *thinks* he can't resist. *Total lack of mental discipline. Total arse-head.*

Callie did a double-take at the Ghouls' language.

You heard us, they said. *He is* king, *blah blah blah, let us all kneel and give thanks.*

Surely he can't be that bad!

Oh, no one ever is. Some people are complicated, *like that justifies everything and makes it all right. Let's all be* complicated, *shall we? Mess up the entire Earth! Lack of manners and consideration for others, if you ask us. Big dummy never figured out that reversing the flow and giving energy instead of absorbing it also lends him great power. The one time he did think to give little Kyril something, see all what happened? But does he think to repeat it and let himself heal completely? No. Of course not, because taking and holding has become a habit with him, no matter how much damage he does to himself in the process.*

Mauvis reached out to caress the air around her face. "I can see your light, Callie. So many colours. So delightful."

Callie felt her face wrench sceptically. "How many mushrooms have you been eating?" she asked. But Mauvis just kept pawing at the air, a look of wonderment on his face. At least he was calmer now. The red was still dripping from his cheeks. Callie looked down at her fingers and sniffed the substance again. Then she licked the tip of one finger. It was indeed warm and flowery tasting. Mauvis' head snapped towards her, and his blind eyes seemed to bore right through her skull and into her brain. The venom did try to influence her thoughts, but its strength was perhaps a thousandth of Rayner's nagging, which had absolutely no effect on her at all. As the redness seeped through her being, a cord of energy formed between her mind and Mauvis' so that she could hear his thoughts and feel everything he did. She was suddenly aware of the blood pulsing through his legs, the stiffness of his shoulder pressed against the wall, the pain of his rattling breathing, the ache of his hip that didn't want to bend. There was also energy transfer pulsating along this red. She could follow it in lines moving in concentric circles away from his body, but unlike the energy-lines associated with the Ghouls, she couldn't read what it said.

The mixed venom writhed inside him again, somewhere next to his heart, pulling, calling, commanding. Callie picked up the red string of light they could now both see stretching out from Mauvis. He plucked it from her fingers, staring at it in wonder and tried to break it, to no avail. The more he struggled against it, the more the thread lengthened and tangled, until he was lost in knotted snarls of light and struggling for breath. The little stone began flipping over in Callie's pocket as she reached out to help him, tearing away the light with reddened fingers that were becoming more skeletal by the minute. She felt her forehead crusting over as she drew on the Ghouls' power through her ever-growing connections to them—it was more than enough to release Mauvis from the trap he was in. The final red strand snapped, but instead of the venom leaving Mauvis completely, half of the strange energy gradually pulled into his body and congealed around his heart, which solidified into a lump of stone. The Chamberlain gasped and clutched his chest, his entire face turning grey and cold. The whites of his eyes also dulled. Callie clutched at his hands—they were like ice, but somehow, he was still alive. She could feel his solid determination and fed it with her own life energy. The connection between them deepened, and their minds further mingled.

In amazement, she watched Mauvis' thoughts shift through her own, surprised at how natural it felt. As his emotions were contained in his frozen heart, his logic flared dominant. He was about to shut down his aura-vision, then hesitated. *Perhaps this is useful,* he thought. *I can use this sight to find Vladdir's connection to the Desert, and sever it. It's about time I straightened my brother out.* Now anger seeped from his lumpy heart and he was ready to do whatever needed to be done without worrying about the reactions of Vladdir, or Rayner, or anyone else. *I am the Chamberlain, and ensuring that this House runs properly is my prerogative.*

"Uh..." Callie stretched out her hands to Mavis as he stood and turned back towards the rebuilt Royal House. She stumbled to her feet and ran after him. "The Ghouls, they don't think Vladdir should be, uh, tampered with. They said you were more important. You're the one who needs help."

"Did they?" said Mauvis sharply. "They've never liked Vladdir, but I don't really care why. I made a promise to my father. If you're to help me, then this is what I'll have your help for, or you can keep it to yourself."

"Wow." Callie stopped short for a moment, absorbing this information, then ran after the Chamberlain again. At least someone had made a decision about something, and if Mauvis "straightened out" Vladdir, then maybe the Ghouls would be less testy about him. Then perhaps the world might make more sense.

As they strode through the rebuilt Royal House, Callie found she could see several trails of coloured light lying across the halls, tracing the paths of the many souls who had walked through. Some of the lines pulsated, and the nauseating quarter turns were again happening where lines intersected with other lines. Now she could see that whenever one of the turns occurred, a surge of energy was emitted along a perpendicular vector. These surges appeared as a cylinder of concentric circles that seemed to move along a peristaltic wave. More transmission of condensed information. Ahead of her, Mauvis' light was dark purple with the angry blot of red around his heart, vibrating with outraged commands that the Chamberlain chose to ignore. They continued forward. White, blue, yellow, pink. These auras were of little consequence. They came across one of deep violet.

"This must be Vladdir's," said Mauvis, and began to follow where it led. "This is the strand that connects him to that damned venom, and the one who would control him." They ended up in Hailandir's chambers, watching the princess slumber contentedly, her thumb tucked in her mouth, slivers of purple venom seeping from under her closed eyelids. The chambermaids looked at Mauvis' and Callie's faces, then scuttled out of the room in fear, presumably gone to call the nurse.

Mauvis picked up the trail of purple light and forcibly severed it.

Hailandir bolted upright in her crib and stared at him for a few moments, all colour draining from her aura—first the purple, then the dark pink, then a blackness and red taint. She exploded into an aura of bright yellow and a scream of pain and loss that reverberated sharply off the stone walls of the cavern. Any magic she may have inherited from her forebears or the Desert was resoundingly gone.

Seeming satisfied, Mauvis turned and his jaw dropped slightly. Callie followed his gaze and saw that it wasn't the nurse that the chambermaids had fetched, but the king himself. Vladdir wore an expression of shocked disappointment as his eyes raked from Mauvis' face to Hailandir's burning aura. Callie knew Vladdir could see it too, the changes in his daughter's magic.

"Mauvis. What have you done?"

"As you can see, the purple venom is gone. I've set the descendant of Aleksei free, exactly as our father wished. I'm sorry I've let this go on for so long. These measures should have been taken much earlier, before you ever gained the ability to reach your full demon state. I see now that I was weak, and should have taken a much firmer hand.

Well, better late than never—"

Ooh, too much too fast, thought Callie. *Slow it down. Let him be convinced of one thing before launching into the next!*

But either Mauvis could not hear her thoughts, or he was too determined to hurtle forward. He was about to launch into an explanation that would make Vladdir see with clarity how they had all been played, but the king was not listening, staring with intensity at the red venom that continued to spill from Mauvis' eyes.

"I don't know who you are, or what you've done to my people. But either you release my Chamberlain now, and undo what you've done to Hailandir, or I will rip your soul to shreds!"

Callie felt Mauvis think that this was about to get stupid. He very deliberately snapped a handkerchief out of his pocket and wiped away the red from his eyes.

"I have no doubt that you could, Vladdir. Please stop jumping to conclusions, it's just making things worse."

You two really do need help, thought Callie.

The purple venom swirled through Vladdir's aura, building in intensity.

"Oh, for Earth's sake, stop that! If you just give me a moment I'll explain everything. Alekseidir gave me very specific instructions regarding you and that purple stuff—"

Mauvis was staring down Vladdir's widened maw, which was lined all the way down his throat with vicious looking fangs. He speculated that all Kai had ever shoved down Aleksei's gorge was nothing but dusty cotton batting, to make him wish he'd never opened his mouth in the first place. (*What in Earth?* Callie wondered.)

"I can see it's going to be easier getting through to Kyril," Mauvis commented dryly. He shoved Vladdir, making sure he toppled into a padded chair. A sudden pulse rippled through his red heart-energy. At first it only distracted him, then Callie felt it build up into blistering pain. Mauvis winced and rubbed his chest, raising a hand to point at Vladdir, who was coiling himself to spring back.

"I'll be back as soon as I rid myself of this red venom. You calm down and make sure you don't eat Hailandir. Aleksei used to lose control when he was like that." And then, Mauvis turned and walked through the wall, dragging Callie by her wrist. She heard him think to himself that passing through solid objects shouldn't be a natural thing to do, but only after he'd done it did it occur to him to be surprised.

This is turning out to be a most vexing day, he thought.

Mauvis' aura-vision was proving to be useful, after all. Callie trotted after him through the blazing white of the Desert as he retraced the residual aura of the footprints of someone called Saanae. She was no longer in her caverns and now he tracked where she had gone. Callie whimpered quietly. She was unable to focus on lines of energy now—or on anything else, for that matter. The bendability of her knees was lost, and as her fingers dried out, the tips dropped off into the sand. She doggedly scooped up the little red lumps of bone, desperately hoping that she would somehow be able to put them back on the ends of her phalanges. She'd *glue* them on if she had to. At least her hair hadn't fallen out yet. Most of the Ghouls she had seen were bald. But that one Ghoul still had eyes in his sockets. Did that mean that maybe she could keep her hair? Was it seniority related? It was hard not to wail in regret. Turning into a Ghoul had to be a good thing, right? It was the centre of her faith. Distress at her transformation *must* be illogical.

Her arm fell off at the elbow.

Mauvis was acting exhausted and irritable, so she kept her worries to herself. When she looked up to see how far behind she'd fallen, she saw Mauvis striding all twisty-stepped over shifting dunes towards a dark haired woman kneeling in the sand. The woman rested one hand on the back of a blue-haired person who lay sprawled face down in the grit. Callie roughly shoved her arm back together and ran over to them. The blue-haired one was a boy who was naked and chained by his ankle to a post. Mauvis was checking over the woman. She seemed strained but otherwise all right, even though she was surrounded by an odd, dark blue/black aura that didn't appear to be her own. Mauvis turned his attention to the boy, who was breathing shallowly and seemed feverish. Gently, Mauvis rolled the youth onto his side and tried to rouse him enough to take a few sips from a water skin. The boy's mind seemed to be injured, as far as Callie could tell.

"Saanae, who is this?" he asked.

"Ilet."

Mauvis raised his brows and Callie felt her jaw drop in surprise. The woman picked up the mandible and gave it back to her, apparently unfazed by her appearance. Saanae offered no further explanation and only continued to look sadly at the boy, so Mauvis set himself to wrenching free the chain. He tried several alternate methods, including attempts to smash the links between rocks, but the chain wouldn't budge. Finally, he managed to pry the end hook of the chain out of the wooden stake, using a second piece of wood that the Desert had conveniently decided to spit up. It was nearly dusk by the time he finished. They wrapped the boy in Saanae's shawl and Mauvis carried him back to her caverns.

Several days passed, and Ilet slowly recovered. Callie found immense pleasure swimming in Saanae's pool. For some reason, if she went around in circles really fast, she could make the lines of energy align in a way that allowed her to hear conversations on other worlds. The level of clarity was variable. Sometimes other Ghouls would pop up in the water, and they'd giggle senselessly for hours, simply because they were so delighted with each other. Ghouls were happy creatures. Sometimes she would exit the pool and stumble over to Ilet, passing some of her energy to him so that he would heal faster. She did this mainly out of curiosity, since she'd never seen a donkey-man before and wanted to know what sorts of stories he'd tell. She tried to also give Saanae some energy, but the woman was oddly resistant to accepting it. The wound that Callie sensed somewhere along her middle had a resonance that was very much like Vladdir's stone arm. But what did that matter? Things that she'd thought were so important before, she no longer cared about—things like time, food, death, and the opinions of others. Perhaps she would very much like living as a Ghoul.

After a while, Callie no longer bothered to walk out of the pool.

She just wiggled through the Earth, popping her head up through the floor of the cavern when she wanted to peek at Ilet. He didn't seem to pay much attention to her, but he watched Mauvis fearfully. He would let himself be tended by the Chamberlain, although he was clearly in awe of him; Mauvis seemed rather annoyed by Ilet's fear.

Saanae didn't do much but mope. Finally, one evening, Mauvis quietly asked her to remove the red venom curse, and she immediately roused herself to do so, as if the matter had completely slipped her mind. Callie watched her carefully, noting the motions of her hands and the muttered words that fell from her lips. Mauvis seemed to struggle with his release from the curse. His crusty bronchioles and aorta threatened to rupture as his heart again started its rhythm. Callie poked a bony red finger against his knee and transferred some energy to him, as well. When he finished thrashing and making unpleasant sounds, he quietly pushed himself to a sitting position and reached for Saanae's hands, gazing into her palms. Callie's eyes goggled in anticipation. Drama was coming.

"Why won't you talk to me?" he asked.

"Because then it will be over," Saanae said in a tiny voice. "You will leave and never forgive me."

"I've already stayed thus far," Mauvis said gently. "Why don't you give me a chance?"

"I never told you what became of the piece I ripped from Vladdir." She turned her head to look at Ilet. Mauvis turned to follow her gaze.

What's this? squealed Callie. The other Ghouls popped up around her and quickly filled her in.

Well! This has been quite the tragic love story!

Indeed! It was love at first sight, this. But Mauvis is from Vladdir's camp—

And Saanae is the enemy of Vladdir, because he ate her child—

What child? And I thought you didn't like Vladdir.

Do you want the story or not?

Yes, please!

Shut it, you! They're about to speak!

I'll tell you later, then.

The Ghouls fell silent so none of them would miss the next bit.

"Ilet was your child?"

"No. The Desert Priest wanted him. My child remains inside Vladdir."

Ilet shifted at this, and looked as if he might protest, but said nothing. Mauvis looked over the pair of them and sighed.

"And do you want to keep this one?" He nodded at Ilet, who now sat up fully and looked like he might start to cry.

A sad energy bubble of joy burst inside of Saanae as she reached out to caress Ilet's cheek, and a sob escaped her. The Ghouls jostled for position to get a better look at this strange emotional phenomenon. Callie resisted the urge to smack some of them apart when they blocked her view.

"When has what I wanted ever mattered? When have I ever been able to keep anything? The Desert Priest will come back and take Ilet again."

"So you do want him, then." Mauvis had plucked a twisted cord of blue/red/purple light from Ilet's stomach and began twisting it around his index finger. Ilet panicked and clawed at Mauvis' fingers. The Chamberlain ignored him, and with finality, grasped the cord with his other hand and snapped it.

The power attributed to Ilet by the blue venom died inside him, and he screamed. His soul filled with ash and started to crumble. His hair faded to black. Perhaps this abrupt strand-breaking wasn't such a good idea, Callie tried to say, and then she tried to tell Ilet that what he had lost wasn't good energy, so he shouldn't fret about losing it. But her words came out funny and didn't make much sense, and no one was paying attention to her anyway. She pushed through the Earth until she was underneath Ilet and tried to help his suffering. He would be rather ordinary now, and really, it didn't matter. Certain things would be easier. But he just couldn't understand. Only when Saanae pulled him partly into her lap and folded herself over him did he start to calm. A natural gold, touched with blue, slowly filled him from within as a new balance established itself.

"I'm beginning to understand now, how all this works. I can see more of the connections," said Mauvis. The Desert and Earth were starting to shift in circles around where he sat. Pebbles screamed and Saanae looked up in alarm as the churning ground pulled her along with it. "Yes. I can reach it now."

Uh oh, thought Callie. The other Ghouls quickly shifted the pattern of the Earth to triangles, which would not turn so easily. Mauvis was starting to change things the wrong way. All the energy lines in the Earth were about to be severed! Did he not understand that some connections were absolutely essential? When did he get to be such a sorcerer?

Mauvis reached into the Earth and grabbed Callie by the skull, pulling her out onto the surface. She noticed that her hair hadn't fallen out after all and was getting caught and yanked by the sticky clay in the ground. Perhaps one had to just really not want to lose hair or eyes in order for that particular aberration to occur. She wondered if she still had eyes.

"What exactly do you lot think you're doing?" Mauvis asked.

"What?"

"Yes, what?"

"Fish swim along the light that you want to make all drown."

"Typical Ghoul talk. You don't ever say anything non-cryptic, do you?"

Callie's mind swirled in confusion. Had she not just clearly said that he would end up destroying all life in Earth if he continued on severing every single energy line he found? The other Ghouls around her chittered in assent. They had understood perfectly. What was cryptic about it? Mauvis sighed and began to shove her back down, then hesitated. "Tell me how to free Saanae's child from Vladdir, and try to keep it simple. No allegories, please."

"Reverse the flow."

"Of what?"

"Energy."

Mauvis contemplated that for a few seconds. "This energy is the light that I see around people?"

"No, not that one. String, string, string." Callie stopped herself and tried again, straining to remember how thoughts and information used to flow through her mind and out of her mouth. "Um. Lines. Life lines light."

"I see."

She reached out bony fingers to touch the knees of both Mauvis and Saanae so that their energy could be read. Both of them did indeed seem to understand what she had told them. An idea was hidden in Mauvis' mind that she didn't quite trust, some angry determination and rigid control that made her think the Chamberlain still hadn't quite let go of something he wasn't willing to let the others see.

They dressed Ilet in some extra robes and Callie followed the three Humani out into the Desert. Saanae carried a funny little doll in her sleeve. The other Ghouls did not wish to follow, so they admonished her to not keep what she learned to herself—after all, *they* had shared. She twisted through the Earth at Mauvis' feet, stopping only when she hit an intersection of the energy lines, unable to pass it until she had absorbed enough of the energy/information flowing through that she could jerk free. The first time this happened it startled her, as the process made her tremble uncontrollably. Some sections of the Earth only contained lines flowing in one direction, and these were much easier to pass through, provided she and the energy were not moving in cross directions.

When they finally moved into tunnel-dweller territory, the route through which Mauvis took them was one that Callie had not known. She indignantly gave him a mental poke, to which he thought at her, *Of course I know of such things. I am the caretaker of this place. And why would I tell the Yrati about every single secret of the Royal House?*

Because we were helping you rebuild it!

The narrow passageways appeared to be hidden behind false walls that lined corridors with heavier traffic. At certain intervals, view ports into adjacent tunnels were disguised in elaborately carved motifs which had bits of embedded glass in them.

Perfect for spying on politicians thinking they are having a private conversation.

"Or escaping Aragoths," said Mauvis in response to her thoughts. Saanae and Ilet looked up at him, but did not ask for clarification.

The walls were thin, making it not the best place for a discussion. The Chamberlain still exuded irritation and seemed like he was ready to explode at any moment. No one seemed to want to risk pestering him further.

The wooden false walls ended behind a heavy shelving unit in the larders. Mauvis peered through yet another view port before releasing a few latches and shoving the entire structure aside. Some canned goods fell off the shelves, making a racket. He didn't seem to care, muttering something about wanting to know who had done such a sloppy stocking job in the first place. A few of the cans bumped against Callie's head as she zig zagged through the floor, barely breaking the surface.

The kitchens were bustling with activity, yet it was still relatively easy to move through the busy servants who were occupied with receiving deliveries from grocers, yelling at busboys and preparing food. A few of them did show alarm at seeing the Lord Chamberlain, and Callie felt their intent as they ran off to inform their superiors. Clearly Mauvis was now a wanted man. It was inevitable. Mauvis was also aware of it, but completely unconcerned. He took his time picking out livery that would fit Ilet, and Callie noticed with some satisfaction that the Chamberlain seemed to be developing nascent affection for the once blue-haired one. She ran a circle around Ilet, absorbing the energy he gave off, and found that he was regenerating nicely. The gold energy was becoming more and more light blue, which she supposed was his own version of how his soul should be, now that it was allowed to grow undisturbed for the first time ever. There had been bidirectional flow of information between him and Saanae for some time, expressed more intensely for brief spurts whenever the two touched hands or leant against each other. The more this occurred, the faster each one seemed to regenerate their energy and regain equilibrium. Mauvis, too, was beginning to tap into this amplification of his own power through similar exchanges with his companions. Callie popped her head out of the ground for a moment to confirm what she read from the irradiated information in the Earth. Yes, all seemed as she thought. Some of her teeth, now red, fell out and rolled across the floor tiles. *Damn!*

From the servants' chambers, they again slipped into another hidden passageway, this time with a low ceiling that forced the Humani to crouch and shuffle along in an almost squatting position. They passed some strangely shaped caverns full of books which were so stuffed with information that Callie jittered. She thought she might be permanently stuck at that spot or end up completely disintegrated, until a huge wash of energy knocked her free. Vladdir had walked past in a parallel corridor.

The low tunnel ended in a square wall panel that Mauvis kicked out of the way with his foot before crawling out into the chamber beyond. The room was decorated with white textured tiles, deep red wall hangings, and a raised portion of the floor where a large canopied bed rested. Filtered vents brought in dust-free air from the surface. Callie rose out of the ground to let her bony feet tap against the tiles, and a couple metatarsals rolled away from her. Overall, she found the patterns made with the bits of ceramic pleasing and wonderfully straight and calming. She could see how meditating on them could allow extreme clarity and efficient energy flow. Who had designed them? Perhaps Rayner was not as stupid as he seemed.

Mauvis pulled a large cushioned chair into the middle of the room, turned it so that it faced the door and settled himself into it elegantly, while Ilet and Saanae remained huddled near the opening of the hidden tunnel. Saanae had removed the floppy little doll from her sleeve and laid it out on the floor so that she could sprinkle Desert sand around it in a triangle and pour energy into it. Her hair fell to the tiles in a tangled mess, threatening to sweep away her construct, but she seemed to know what she wanted to do. The energy wasn't able to stay within the doll, and kept diffusing into the aether, eventually returning to Saanae, but the repeated flow of information was beginning to form channels around the doll. Interesting.

Thunder was approaching. It grew louder and louder in purple colour as it drew near and Callie gulped nervously as the door was flung open. Every last free spec of energy in the room was drawn towards the black void that oscillated menacingly in the centre of Vladdir's physical entity. He already knew they were here. Callie hadn't really Looked at him carefully since she had Transformed, but now that she did, she found the king unreadable. Unlike other Humani, his energy was almost all drawn into that void, glowing purple around his being, constantly churning wave after wave into the darkness. How could he walk around like that for so long and not die? Was this why he was turning into stone? There was one ropy, thin strand of green light flowing into Vladdir from another source. Kyril. That alone was causing a slight rift in the flow of purple light, preventing it from imploding on itself completely. As long as something external could provide outside information, the half-dead king would live. Yet, no energy was being released in exchange for the green light. Normally, in order to maintain equilibrium, energy in had to be equivalent to energy out. Vladdir was completely unbalanced. No wonder the other Ghouls didn't like to be around him. One little disturbance and he'd take everyone nearby down into that black pit.

Vladdir stared at Callie with an expression of confused anger as she tottered towards him. Pushing her hair out of her face, she lifted a hand to his chest and carefully tested the strength of the green light. Following the information stream, she read that Kyril was out on the surface, absorbing power from water and wind to continue fuelling Vladdir's need. There had been an initial bolus of energy given to Vladdir, which had filled him to the point where some of the random outside life forces he had absorbed were pushed out, but it hadn't been enough to seal this dark rift within him, or establish an equilibrium that would allow the king to give as much as he took, stabilizing himself and those around him through an information exchange scaffolding on which networks could be built. Even now he was draining energy from Mauvis, who was cognizant of the transfer, and willing.

Vladdir pushed aside the Yrati water influence that normally protected the underground and sucked in energy from the Desert, widening the rift further. He swiped at Callie with his stone arm, shattering her body and sending bits of her in all directions. *Now, that was completely uncalled for!*

"Did that give you satisfaction, Vlad?" Mauvis asked him. "It was pointless, you know. You can't kill her like that."

Vladdir seethed in Mauvis' direction. "Who are you?" he demanded.

"You know perfectly well, you just refuse to accept the manner in which things have changed. I'm no longer just your servant, and you seem to have a problem with that." Mauvis stood up, coiling around his hand the strand of purple light that stretched from Vladdir to the Desert, connecting him to the venom and the curse that fuelled his hunger. Vladdir clutched at his chest and looked down at himself, trying to perceive what he could not see. Mauvis tried to rip the trails of energy apart, but despite the added influence of the Yrati water trying to keep out the Desert, this light was resilient and would not break. Vladdir screamed in rage and rushed at Mauvis, his mouth stretching unnaturally wide, the blackness reaching out through his lips. Callie pulled herself together through sheer force of will and stood up, her bones rattling noisily as they tumbled over the tiles to snap back into place. She shot a bolus of pure golden light into Vladdir's emptiness. *She* had endless energy.

Vladdir was overwhelmed by the sudden light filling his mind, his anger lost. He looked unaware of anything outside of himself, and like he was about to throw up. Kyril's energy was flung back to her. On it, she could feel the former Aragoth's concern, and knew that she was running towards them, axe in hand. Callie poked at Mauvis to hurry up. He was still struggling with the purple cords of light. Saanae's little doll still failed to move, and she began to cry out in frustration, her tears jolting Mauvis' attention away from his task. Vladdir lurched towards him, rejecting the golden light that was beginning to seal the rift inside his spirit and trying to re-establish the negative flow of energy to which he was so accustomed. Mauvis' head jerked back towards the king, and he shot a second bolt of his own life force against Callie's golden energy, shoving it back into Vladdir and jerking madly on the purple strands at the same time. Vladdir spasmed, belched, and something tiny and glowing green popped out of his mouth. He fell to the floor, convulsing as if he were in extreme pain. Tears were running down his face, dripping on the white tiles.

The little thing was made out of fuzzy energy. It wailed, floating about with no direction. Callie put out her hand and called to it, watching in amazement as it calmed down and came to her palm. It didn't know what it was. It wanted her to tell it. So small. So...tender.

"My..." Saanae was reaching out towards the light. This was the little thing she'd been after all this time? Callie stumbled over as quickly as she could, holding it out to her. Saanae laughed with incredulous relief as the energy coalesced around her doll, which twitched feebly. She cut herself and dripped her blood over the doll, using the drops as anchors for the tiny blot of light.

Ecch! Callie turned away in disgust. That was not the way to do things. Although...Ilet did seem to be turning out all right. Still, why reinvent the wheel when there was already a perfectly good way of making people without all this hassle? There was Saanae, there was Mauvis—what was the problem? If they needed a little help here and there, Callie could provide that. She *still was* a healer.

Mauvis started swearing, and it immediately became apparent that he had no real feel for how to use such words. Callie sighed and sank back into the Earth. It was getting tedious moving around on the tiles, and easier to wiggle underneath where Mauvis was. She reached upwards to wrap her fingers around the strands of light Mauvis twisted, and began to gently reverse the flow of energy, at the same time trying to coax shut the wound in Vladdir's spirit. The king did not resist, instead lapsing into a deep sadness. Vladdir thought of people called Arlen and Taalen, and thought that it didn't matter if he died. *Earth's Sake! You're not dying, stupid!* But he didn't seem to be able to hear Callie's thoughts like Mauvis did.

The energy flow halted. Something nudged it back the other way. *What?* It was shoved again, deliberately, and Callie felt her anger surge. *Who in Earth thinks he has the right to do such things?* she demanded, and wiggled through the Earth, trying to feel along the energy lines. She began to sense something black, yet not a void; it was filled with an eerie, translucent green. It was cloying, noxious. She backed off, unsure if her golden Ghoul energy would have any effect against such a thing, or if it might be tainted by it. The black/green thing didn't seem to have detected her, but was inching its way along the purple energy path, every now and then giving it a thrust, trying to re-establish the original direction of flow. Kyril's footsteps thundered past, leaving pale green imprints in her wake. Her agitation and fear for Vladdir's well being were clearly apparent. Callie zipped back to Mauvis and considered resurfacing to confront Kyril, then thought, *I'm not getting smashed apart again!* She instead reached upwards, intending to pull Mauvis to safety.

A backwards surge of the purple energy riding on a wave of gold and blue blasted Callie's hand to bits. Since she was underground, her finger bones ended up embedded in clay, several centimetres apart. She swore viciously, then thought, *Right, I'm a Ghoul and here I am cursing. I guess it's not so strange.* She popped her head up past the tiles to see what was going on. A second pulse came as Ilet brought his foot down on the purple light stretched between Mauvis' hands, and this time he succeeded in severing the energy. Like a rubber cord stretched too tight, the ends of the lines snapped back in opposite directions, one end hitting Vladdir in the chest and flinging him right off the ground. It wasn't too hard to imagine that the other end was also snapping at the black/green energy that lurked somewhere in the distance.

Vladdir pushed himself up. His eyes and mouth were black gaping holes, and he was gasping as if for air. He had turned the flow of energy back inwards, and the pit within him again started to widen. What was this with him, a bad habit? *Turn it the other way, you dummy!* Kyril ran in, and was momentarily halted as Vladdir pulled on her life force, feeding from it. With the energy line severed, there was no way for Callie to reverse the direction. Particles of light drifted from Mauvis, Ilet, Saanae, and the little doll, back towards the king. Callie pushed her entire head above ground.

"RUN!" she yelled, this time her meaning coming out clearly. Saanae dove towards the hidden tunnel with her doll, and Ilet half-dragged Mauvis after her. Callie just managed to shove the square wall panel back in place and sink out of reach before Kyril's axe came smashing down on the tiles.

The owner of the black/green energy knew exactly where they were—hiding in Saanae's caverns—yet it did not approach. It would send out little tendrils to dance around them, never lingering long enough to be clearly viewed. It was waiting for something, but Callie didn't know what, and it was making her nervous. Saanae said it was coming from the priest who had been her mentor. Mauvis seemed to be watching it, perhaps studying his opponent for weaknesses. Vladdir had gone repeatedly to the surface to drink in any life force that came within range of him, including Kyril's. He seemed to be controlling himself, recovering, yet when Callie went back to the Royal House to check on him, he'd eye her with hatred and a look that said, *just you wait*. Attempts to speak to him were futile. The gash in his spirit was still inexorably moving inwards on itself, stabilized somewhat by the heat of the Desert but still gradually eating him alive.

The other Ghouls visited Saanae's pool a few times, but they were unwilling to stay for very long, uncomfortable with the energy surrounding the place. They didn't mind the little doll, as unnatural as it was. *Sometimes one fights fire with fire.* Callie protested that it didn't make sense, as that would only make more fire. Her brethren replied, *yes, but then it competes with itself for fuel.* The little one would help draw out the black/green infection later, so they would let it be. *What do you want to do?* they asked her. *Kill it?* No. Of course not. Still, Callie was discomfited by the strange thing, by how it would lift its little clay-bead head try to look about without eyes, and then start wailing even though it had no mouth.

From time to time, Ilet would pick it up and look at it curiously.

"Why does it look like this," he asked Saanae.

"It isn't finished yet. It still needs several essential components of a human, but I haven't the energy to make these things for it. It will take me some time."

"How long?"

"Depends on my health. With what I have now, perhaps decades."

"So long? Can I give you energy for it? Some skin?"

Saanae smiled and took the little doll from his fingers. "No, you are his brother. That energy should come from his father."

They both turned to look at Mauvis, their smiles fading. Mauvis was not ready to make any such contribution, nor had he shown any interest in becoming the little doll's father.

"*They move.*"

Saanae and Ilet both started. Mauvis suddenly stood from where he had been crouched for several days. He turned to look at them, his eyes blazing. Callie felt it too. The Desert Priest and the Desert King were both shifting their accumulated power through the Earth.

Part VI

Aleksei, the Undertaker

ALEKSEI HADN'T INTENDED TO die when he did. That morning, the child Mauvis had done a sloppy job of mopping his brow. The king had enjoyed it greatly, as it gave him the opportunity to gaze at the boy's rosy little cheeks and pout of concentration as the new chamberlain-in-training reached across the bed with the sponge. The child was wearing his little white shirt, and his little brown curls stuck out over his funny little ears, and all the while he showed absolutely no signs of temptation by the purple venom.

The contentment didn't last. Less than an hour after Mauvis had left him, the venom began to tug at his own body again. Aleksei felt it like a pulse, and resisted the throb of energy that tried to push his spirit out of his corporeal self and into that agonizing state of mental paralysis where he seemed to lie flat in the air over the bed, unable to turn his head to see what his body did beneath him. But he could hear the sounds. And he had seen what had been left of Vasha and Vessek after his body had finished with them.

Aleksei whimpered, disgusted by his weakness. The venom tried to make him think that he had enjoyed what he had done to his sons.

Every last bit of his strength was not going to be enough to keep himself sane.

"SEN BYRNAE!" he roared, trying to funnel his anger against the building lust. "BYRNAE! I NEED YOU NOW!" He sat up and took in a great breath of air to yell again, and his vision faded out. Not to black, as it usually did, but this time everything washed out to white. Objects seemed to slant and bend at strange angles. He tried to climb out of bed and fell, smashing his head against the floor. "SEN!"

The attendants came running and picked him up, trying to put him back into the bed, but he struggled too much, pleased that he could generate enough strength to give them at least that much difficulty.

"My Dear. King. Alekseidir." Sen Byrnae had finally entered, clapping in mock appreciation. "Look at you. This time you've managed to fall out of bed."

Aleksei realised how pathetic he looked. Wearing a white nightshirt stained with sweat, half his hair falling out of his braid, unshaven, he stood on one foot while suspended between two servants who held his arms and a third who had one of his legs. In contrast, Byrnae was neatly dressed in a gold and black robe made of stiff fabric with pleats around his waist that barely moved as he walked, a starched white shirt, grey gloves and matching boots. His grizzled hair was shorn to half an inch all over his head, and he never wore a beard. The deep creases around his eyes and mouth only made him seem more dignified.

"You insolent pig. I'll have you whipped."

"Certainly, My King. If you can muster the ability to give the order. And then, I wish you the best of luck finding another doctor who will tolerate your tantrums. Put him back in bed, will you? And change the sheets. It smells in here."

Aleksei gasped and wrenched against the hold of the servants, who released him as soon as he was over the bed. He felt another of the energy pulses surging within him and turned his face into the pillows, hiding the changes that would be crossing his features.

"I can give you more laudanum," said Byrnae.

"No," Aleksei rasped through the pillow. "It's the blood. Take the blood."

"Why the blood? And what blood? You hardly have any."

"It's the blood that curses me! Take it, I tell you!"

"Will you at least try the laudanum?

"It takes me faster when I lose my mind! I've told you this, damn you! Why won't you listen to me?"

"*When*...you lose your mind?"

"You *pig*!"

"Well if you won't take the laudanum, then there is nothing I can do for you." Byrnae turned on his heel and left the room, pausing only to speak to the servants. "Keep it dark and quiet in here. Earth knows that doesn't do much to keep him from being over-stimulated, but do it anyway."

Aleksei got off the bed and crouched in a corner, waiting for the servants to change the linens. He shuddered against the increasing intensity of the energy pulses, first trying to shut them out, then to let them pass through his being harmlessly. Neither approach was working. He tried, *tried* to resist, but the pressure was building. He could feel his mind drifting upwards from where he felt it should be, and he could smell a woman's flesh somewhere nearby.

His eyes snapped open to see that one of the chambermaids had knelt in front of him, holding out a small, metal cup of Byrnae's laudanum. The attendants had gone. The girl was clearly terrified, yet had that same resolute set to her mouth that Mauvis wore when he was determined to serve, no matter what.

What have I done to deserve such loyalty? Aleksei wondered. For her sake, he took the cup while he still had the control to do so, tipped the contents into his mouth and forced himself to swallow it. The purple venom was going to take him anyway. At least if he did this, the girl would leave peacefully, thinking she had done her duty. He wouldn't have to yell to make her go.

His mind loosened with the drug, slipping more easily into that strange paralysed state in which it felt as though he floated blindly above himself. His body twitched as it picked up the scent of its next prey. *The girl!* Oh *Earth*, was it going to hunt down here? Why did it not go to the surface? Aleksei struggled to his feet, trying to climb onto the furniture and out through the skylight before it was too late. The

Beast within him was rapidly gaining control, and jumped back to the floor, landing on all fours. He could feel his body beginning to morph into the hunter's shape—his heels stretching up into knees, haunches tightening, shoulders becoming ridged, back humped, fingers folding into paws, mouth stretching wide.

The memory of Kai's death and the look of abject misery on Mauvis' face when it had happened flashed through what was left of his mind and brought him back to his senses. Aleksei summoned the pain of that moment and used the hazy control it lent him to creep slowly across the room until he found a knife, which he drew across his ankles to let the blood flow out and weaken the Beast. It really was the only thing that worked. Pleased that he finally felt the power of the Beast fading, Aleksei contentedly sat in the middle of the white tiled floor, watching the red pool spread out underneath him. He felt so very tired, and was so relieved to have managed to avert disaster, that even though he knew he should bind his wounds to stop the bleeding, he thought he could just let himself rest for a moment. He fell asleep, then died.

For a short time, Aleksei did know peace. But, even devoid of blood, he could not completely pass over into death. His spirit had been left accursed by the ravages of the venom and the actions it had forced him to. He floated some distance from his body, unable to detach himself completely. Trapped, but utterly satisfied that the energy pulses could no longer control his physical self.

The funeral was grand, and he was well pleased with its splendour. The music had been specially composed for the event. For over an hour it played, serene and ponderous. The odd colour scheme of white and black was strangely appealing. Unexpectedly, Sulandor and her father came from the North to pay their respects, their entourage bringing fine gifts for the Royal House and decorations for his tomb. Aleksei's only regret was that the child Mauvis threw himself to the ground in rage and cried bitterly the entire time, with no consideration for the musicians' efforts. It was the first he had ever seen Mauvis not behave like the young gentleman he always seemed, and Aleksei wished he could pick up the small form from the ground and quiet him with caresses. Vladdir knelt next to Mauvis and covered the child's body with his own to prevent him from being removed, but it still did not stop the little one's howling.

When the processions were over and Aleksei was sealed in his casket, he still couldn't leave. It was like lying in bed unable to fall asleep, but he accepted this. It would be enough, and he was content.

Thirty years later, the old king was forced to end his contemplation of the peaceful runes inscribed on the inside of his casket lid, and again think about the outside world. His House had been laid to ruin, his tomb had been plundered, and the heavy rings and other ornaments of death had been removed from his corpse—all because of the black/green man from the Desert whose purple venom had already caused him so much grief.

Aleksei stumbled from his broken tomb in search for a new resting place where he could again lie undisturbed. It was difficult for him to move, so he searched for fluid, yet all he could find was still not enough to soak into his deadened limbs and restore his body. He finally found some measure of peace in an underground tributary of the Yrati River and nestled himself amongst tree roots that cradled him gently against the soft tugging of the water. At least now he had some privacy from the marauding Aragoths. It was quiet, and despite evidence to the contrary, he still thought of himself as fully dead and didn't want to engage in any sort of activity.

The problem with running water was that its form was similar to flowing blood. Lost spirits trying to find their way to the afterlife were constantly being attracted to and diving into it; some of them were idiots, unable to figure out that it was an energy stream, not a liquid stream, in which they needed to swim. Those entities found it necessary to disturb other things in the water to ask for directions. Sometimes Aleksei could just ignore them, and they would go bother the tree roots or the snails. Some were more persistent, even rude, and they demanded to know what made Aleksei think he was so special that he need not answer, despite his former rank. He was more or less as dead as everyone else.

To alleviate his irritation, the old king would drag himself out of the water, find the physical remains of whatever spirit was bothering him, and destroy it, so that the entity would finally find its fins and dart away into the aether like it was supposed to. Some would thank him as they left; others were too stupid. While this practise would often buy Aleksei some immediate peace, he eventually became known as one who could break connections with the living world. When things in the Desert were asked for directions, they would tell various entities *to seek him out.* At least his reputation for being cantankerous ensured that he would be approached with respect, and sometimes with gifts.

Over the last few weeks, there had been several unnatural shifts in the Earth, the vibrations of which were more pronounced in the water. Aleksei eventually realised that it was his sons who were causing the disturbances, and gradually his mind became aroused enough to feel concern.

Now he heard an unnatural call from Vladdir, summoning him from his watery grave. No—it didn't call to him. It summoned anything that was dead and buried in the ground. How troubling. Aleksei still felt responsibility towards Vlad in this strange afterlife, so he again shifted himself out of the tree roots. Angry nonetheless, he let the underground water push and swell, sending his form bobbing just under the surface of the waves. Others answered the call alongside him, crashing into him with complete lack of dignity as they struggled awake and flailed at the water. Such creatures should have been granted eternal rest. Why were there so many? And what business did Vladdir have with the dead? After a moment, he realised that they were all Aragoths.

Finding himself wedged beneath the Travellers' Oasis cavern, Aleksei gathered the will to move against the water. His stone-encrusted bones rose up from one of the wells, a few of the Aragoths rising with him. A gurgled chuckle escaped him as he imagined the reaction of some traveller finding so many dead things in the drinking water. His black armour fell from him as he stepped heavily onto the ground, so that only his black hair and the tattered remnants of his burial clothes dripped across his shrivelled frame. His knees did not bend easily, yet he would not crawl beneath the Earth like an insect. He lumbered across the surface as the Desert wind thieved every last bit of moisture he had vainly tried to bind. He could no longer move, paralysed like a grim signpost between the lands of the living and the dead.

When the call strengthened, Aleksei was no longer able to respond through movement. Instead he slid as a statue across the dusty rock towards a broken cliff. Atop it stood his second last son, arms raised, rigid against the forceful wind, his mouth opened with voiceless sound. He looked very much like a Desert King with his blouse and silver chestplate sculpted to fit around his stone arm, his hair the colour of the writhing grey dust-ridden sky, and the coarse filigree of the armour wrapped around his leather boots and lower legs clearly visible even at a distance.

Aleksei was dragged as far as the flat sand reached, then his legs knocked and ground against the base of the rocky cliff. He and the others could go no farther. Vladdir's anger still pulled at him, the venom at his core still drawing spirits into its void. He experienced a fleeting memory of asking Mauvis to protect Vladdir from the venom, and wondered if he should be angry that he had not been obeyed. Yet Mauvis had been his favourite, so he let the moment pass, deciding to believe that he had set a very difficult, if not impossible task for his youngest son. Since the solid things around Vladdir would no longer move forward, the atmosphere itself seemed to give way, and eventually it drew what little water the Desert had into thick clouds that darkened the sky into deep azure.

Still, Aleksei could move no farther, even with the coaxing of the wind. It churned the sky into funnels that reached down to tug at his hair. Finally came the rain, softening the Earth to muck and loosening the limbs of his comrades that lay half-buried in the ground. The others at Aleksei's feet jerked and twisted their grey and brown bony forms free from the Earth, turning their heads up to howl their misery at Vladdir. The dead Aragoths began a stilted, awkward climb to the top of the cliff. Some still had tattered hair and rune-inscribed skin stuck to their skulls. Made from the detritus of the Desert, they had returned to it, perhaps not understanding that they were not meant to stay. As the rain continued to fall, they became more limber and began to ascend the cliff in jumps, but Aleksei could not. He remained at the bottom of the cliff, looking up at his son in despair as Vladdir called up armour of stone to cover his new soldiers. The Aragoth army was being reassembled.

Father.

The barely whispered word crashed like thunder in Aleksei's ears. He turned to face his other, most beloved son standing a few metres away, his hair and red crushed velvet suit streaming with the rain. The Chamberlain came to kneel before him and kiss the remainders of his hand, before looking upwards to where Vladdir stood. Some of the Aragoths stopped to howl at him, but since the only commandment given to them was to continue moving upwards, none of them attacked the newcomer.

Noble Mauvis. I am ever so glad you were born.

I regret that I have been unable to protect Vladdir from the venom, as you charged me. I continue to work towards correcting this.

Hmm. Of course you still try. Now when I am called, it is to collect the dead after destroying their physical remains. The dead themselves call me. This time, Vladdir has called me, and although he does not wish the service I offer, the pattern is set, and I must follow my normal course of duty.

You mean to kill him?

I mean to settle unrest and make things quiet. Vladdir is stirring up what is meant to be still.

He raises the Aragoths to hunt down Saanae and her sons, and means to make an end of me.

And why is that?

He thinks he controls the venom, rather than the other way around. I tried to free him from it, but he only saw me trying to take away his power.

He still cannot see it for what it is. Aleksei sighed. *I suppose I should have been as truthful to him as I was to you, but I was too vain to admit my mistake to him. Too proud to tell him that it had been my sin all along.* He lifted a finger to briefly touch Mauvis' cheek. *But you, you had the benefit of Kai's patience and attention. You understood it well right from the beginning.*

Let me try again, Father. I am newly understanding even more of the energy tracks that can manipulate life. Perhaps I can free him yet, and you may rest without carrying out your purpose.

Very well. I will give you time.

As Aleksei waited, Mauvis' sodden brown curls eventually emerged from the crevices of rock that snaked up to the top of the cliff. Vladdir turned towards Mauvis without surprise, and the half-brothers faced each other. No appeals were made. The king showed his contempt by turning his back on Mauvis and beginning to summon his army once again. Mauvis firmly planted one foot in front of himself and the wind fell suddenly, as did several loose bits of shale and debris that had been dragged halfway up the cliff. Mauvis began to shift the energies of the Earth in a circular pattern that thoroughly disrupted the venomous call to the dead. Aleksei felt a second shift, this time a reversal in the direction of natural energy flow. His own body began to disintegrate with this forced return to its more natural state, and he opened his mind to it with great welcome and anticipation of oblivion. He could also feel the void inside of Vladdir begin to close, along with his consciousness. The dead Aragoths shuddered and struggled weakly against the muck that spread upwards to reclaim them.

Something wicked this way comes, whispered the gleeful Desert.

Aleksei felt an immense green/black entity slithering towards the base of the cliff, disguised by orange mist as dust on the wind. The attempt at concealment was deliberate, and the thing was collecting itself to strike. It intended to kill one son while irrevocably crippling the other, turning him into a slave. It wanted to once again control the Aragoth army, no matter if it were undead, and meant for Vladdir to be the new puppet to rule them. Aleksei fought against his dissolution, drawing on the collapsing identities of the Aragoth corpses to fuel his efforts. The slithering one also latched onto the energy from the Aragoths and tore them from Aleksei with glee. As the old king tumbled into a pile of bones, the presence let him feel its satisfaction. It then advanced rapidly up the cliff, now and again showing the form of a human arm inscribed with lacy blood runes along the sinewy muscle, reaching out to take hold of the rock.

Discarding the remnants of his body, Aleksei remoulded himself as pure energy and shot himself into the body of his youngest son. *Run!*

The Wickedness comes!

Mauvis shuddered from the force of Aleksei's spirit crashing into his own. For a moment, his concentration faltered and he let go of his control over the energy direction. Vladdir took advantage of the break to hurl his dagger at Mauvis. Aleksei barely twisted his son out of the weapon's path in time, then lunged at Vladdir and knocked him away from the orange mist that had been reaching for his leg.

"Look at what comes for us!" Aleksei shouted at Vladdir. The voice came out of Mauvis' mouth deep and garbled. After a moment of bewilderment, Vladdir tore his eyes from the Chamberlain's face to look at the dust demon that was forming from the orange mist.

"You." Vladdir got to his feet, flexing his stone arm. The demon grinned and let itself coalesce into human form. As its feet touched the ground, black and green robes seemed to settle around it out of nothing, and there stood the Desert Priest, the skin of his chest and bald head gleaming with the rain.

"My dear King Vladdir. I see you've recovered nicely from little Saanae's bite. However will you fare from mine?"

"Yours? You haven't dared face me before, I doubt—"

"I can assure you, it wasn't lack of daring."

The Priest stretched out his arm, his fingers trembling slightly as his energy adjusted the harmonics of the power that flowed through Mauvis. Aleksei tried to help his son resist, but was not prepared when a burst of white energy struck Mauvis through the back of the neck. It felt like a sword-blow, forcing his spirit out of him and into the aether. It hurtled towards Vladdir, but his brother struck Mauvis' spirit form aside and it snapped back into Mauvis' body. Vladdir rushed forward, his second strike with the clawed fingers of his stone arm cutting deeply into Mauvis' chest. Aleksei forced rock to encrust over the wound, but the pain of it was great and Mauvis fell to his knees. Vladdir coiled to attack again, and the Priest, seeing an opportunity, began feeding power into Vladdir, again widening the spiritual rift and causing the vortex within him to churn more vigorously. As Vladdir stumbled against the shift in equilibrium, Aleksei got Mauvis to his feet, pretended to charge at Vladdir, then dodged his outstretched arm, diving towards the Priest's legs and knocking him over. Aleksei coaxed his younger son to pick up a shard of rock and slashed with it at the Priest's throat. Infuriated, the Desert man clasped one hand against his neck to quell the splurting blood. He twisted and kicked against Mauvis.

Aleksei had miscalculated. The Priest's leg lifted Mauvis into the air and continued to push against his ribcage, lofting him over the edge of the cliff. The Chamberlain caught hold of the Priest's robes, dragging him toward the edge, but the Priest turned himself into vapour and dissipated. Mauvis fell, soundlessly, until he shattered his back and skull on the rocks below.

The shock of Mauvis' spirit being cast out of his body with such finality sent Aleksei's spirit also reeling off into the aether. He felt his son's confusion, his desperation to continue his relationship with Saanae and Ilet, and his distraction by the awareness of the life energies around him, swimming towards the after world. Mauvis became lost in the tide and was easily swept away. Aleksei did not call to him. As deeply as he felt grief at the departure of his youngest son, it was not his wish that his little chamberlain should also become undead like him.

Despite his best intentions, resuming his previous form was very difficult. It took long moments for him to recognise that he was back in his body, and not merely aligned with the physical structure of a tree root, or the curve of the cliff base. Once he was sure of it, remembering how to move was also challenging. He started slowly, grateful for the drizzle of rain that made his eyes soft enough to work, so that he could see the blackened tips of his finger bones scrape along the ground and by sight know that they moved, since he could feel nothing. Next he moved his toes, digging them into the Earth until he could finally lever his body upwards. Carefully, slowly—he had time and plenty of it—Aleksei tottered over to where his son lay smashed on the rocks, and picked him up.

Mauvis' body was heavy, perhaps made heavier by the weight of grief. How strange it was, Aleksei mused, to have been dead for so long, yet be more alive than his newly dead son. He carried the body back towards Saanae. He remembered only that she was important, but not why. His rotted mind raced to piece together something that didn't quite make sense just yet. He had given Saanae extra life so that she could continue his son, who was now dead. Mauvis was dead, Aleksei was dead, Saanae still walked around, but in truth she was also dead, since he had only loaned her life. Ilet? Ilet was a donkey. Saanae was alive to continue his now-dead son...before she had died, Saanae had designated a bit of her life to her little doll, which was not yet quite alive. *Hmm. Perhaps Saanae will know what to make of this.*

When she saw Mauvis' broken form, Saanae wept bitterly for hours, and Ilet was unable to console her. She lay on the ground, her face and hands pressed against one of Mauvis' dead palms, refusing to lift her head in response to any distraction. Aleksei dried out in her cave, and stood motionless, unable to move or think, until the energies of the Earth shifted below his feet and revived him. He tottered over to Saanae to remind her of the agreement he assumed they had made.

You were given my extra energy, Saanae, taken from the Desert to make life. I will need to claim it back from you later so that we can pass from this world. But first, make my pure continuance.

"I don't know what you mean," she replied, finally allowing Ilet to pull her up from the ground.

My son! My son, Mauvis! Take your little doll and finish it. Continue my son Mauvis!

Saanae looked up then in wonderment, and Ilet ran to fetch the empty biscuit tin which held the little doll. It was still only capable of feeble movements. She took it up in her hands and ran her fingers over the little bead head, and again began to weep, this time with the breaking of the dam that she had built up against hope. She shifted herself closer to Mauvis' body and sprinkled Desert sand over its chest, singing an incantation as she did so. Aleksei watched closely, not satisfied with the formation of the construct's spirit, and picked up the residual strands of energy that were left behind after the passing of Mauvis' soul. He wound them around Saanae's fingers as she worked, so that small aspects of Mauvis' essence were also woven into the nascent entity she formed. The little doll was placed on top of the sand, and water was summoned to bubble up around Mauvis' form to soften the sand, rock and flesh, making it supple enough to rope around the little construct, forming little red bud-limbs that twitched and wriggled. And the small thing began to cry. Saanae picked it up and pulled it to her chest, ignoring the bloody shreds of flesh that still attached the two bodies.

"It's ugly," said Ilet. "But you shouldn't worry. I know that things like us can grow."

Saanae didn't answer him, rocking the little creature in her arms, her hair covering her face and her new child. Aleksei stumbled over to retrieve the remnants of Mauvis' body, slicing away the ribbons of skin and sinew still attached to the doll, and dragged the rest away by the foot, since it was now his job to go and bury dead things in the Desert. All back to ashes and dust. He looked forward to when he could also dissolve, but he'd have to hold out long enough for Saanae to do a reasonably good job. With what was to happen, and her current lack of energy, that might take a very long time. Best to not tell her how strongly he had felt Vladdir's determination. He would let himself dry out in the Desert for now, and return to claim his portion of life from Saanae when her work was done.

PART VII

KYRIL, THE BEAUTIFUL

VLADDIR LAY WITH HIS head in Kyril's lap, moaning in restless fever. He had come back to her from the cliffs, hardly able to breathe through his grief. He wanted to call for the Chamberlain, who had always been able to give him ease, but he could not. Kyril did not know what to do. The vortex that resided inside her master and king was strangely sated, and thus she did not know what part of herself to give. Vladdir had smashed several bottles and ceramics before drinking too many spirits and falling sick. The Yrati looked into the king's chambers, but were unusually reticent, seeming repulsed by the strange energies that clung to Vladdir. They certainly did not like the dead Aragoths that occasionally surfaced into the room. Neither did Kyril, but without her Lord commanding her to dispatch them, and because they obviously had come to serve the king, she had no choice but to leave them alone.

A strange little Ghoul with red bones and yellow hair had come to visit, and Kyril had tried to speak with her, sensing an intention to heal from the energies she exuded, but nothing either of them said made sense to the other, so the little one had sadly left.

Kyril placed a cool washcloth over Vladdir's brow and her hands rested near his face as she let herself into his mind. She could see that Vladdir reviewed the Chamberlain falling to the bottom of the cliff over and over; his head bouncing once, the brown curls splashing blood and tissue; the back and legs acquiring extra bend points as they finally lay still; the grey eyes staring upwards, unseeing; lips slack, completely at peace. At that moment, Vladdir had seen something in the Chamberlain's face that he had been blind to for far too long, and it had left him devastated. When drained of expression and relaxed in the repose of death, it was obvious that the curve of Mauvis' cheek was Vessek's. His brow and chin were the same as Vasha's. He remembered how Aleksei had liked to touch the child Mauvis' cheek tenderly, and had always wondered why his father would care so deeply for the boy of a servant. And old Kai—when had he ever married? The realisation made Vladdir want to either tear his own heart out, or jump to the bottom of the cliff to join his brother. Indecision had left him doing neither. He wanted to kill Aleksei for having hidden the truth from him. So much he'd had, but had never known to fully enjoy.

Kyril pulled back into her own head so that she could attempt thinking with greater ease. Was it the lack of full bonding with Mauvis that made Vladdir ill now? She leaned down and gently kissed him all over his face. He woke briefly and stared up at her, momentarily lucid.

"How could they take him away from me, Kyril? How could they be so cruel? Were my body and power not enough for them? How could they do this, and not kill me?"

Kyril's eyes spilled over with tears. The intensity of Vladdir's pain was near unbearable, and she felt more helpless, still at a loss for what to say or do. Was there someone she could ask? *Mauvis*, said her mind, but of course, he was gone.

"They changed him. He wasn't himself at the end. I could...*feel* others in his mind. And before that, I could sense in him strange energies that had not been there before. They must have been controlling him. I'm sure of that now. How could I not have seen? *I should have rescued him.* Instead I tried to fight him, like he was an enemy. First Taalen, then Arlen, now Mauvis. Oh, Kyril. Will I next cause Hailan to die? Or you?"

Kyril shook her head against Vladdir's words, still unable to speak. Even if she were to die to feed his power, she would experience it as exquisite sweetness. Such use was what she had been made for. Even though Vladdir had brought her farther along the path of human experience than she could ever have expected, to once again become merely something to be consumed for his purpose would still be completion and fulfillment. She leaned over Vladdir again and wept.

"What reason is there for me to live now, Kyril?"

For me, she thought desperately, *if you have no desire to blot out my existence*. But Vladdir was in too much turmoil to hear her mind, and it was not her place to press her own wishes more forcefully. He became feverish again and returned to his fitful sleep, purple venom seeping from beneath his eyelids. Kyril also rested, although she did so sitting up, rousing herself to move only when the chambermaids came to change the purple-stained linens. It was difficult for her to understand Vladdir's lack of contentment, when she herself had nothing more to wish for than what was around her right now. She needed to comprehend his agitation if she were to serve him better.

If she were separated forcefully from Vladdir, what would she do? It had happened once before, when she was severed from Ilet, and then all she had wanted was to kill those who had made her so worthless and empty. In her quest for vengeance, she had attempted to kill Vladdir, and instead had found herself fulfilled in ways Ilet had never made known to her. Her emotional depth had expanded unimaginably, and she had become immersed in love and contentment, two things she had never known existed. Considering that, perhaps severance was also the path her king should take, since it might lead him to deeper fulfillment. But if he were to be fulfilled by another, would he no longer turn to her? Maybe she would be consumed in the process, and it would not matter. She would have to ensure that she fought viciously. She would have to enable the most energetic death possible, thus generating the maximum amount of power to support Vladdir's cause.

When he woke again, Kyril steeled herself and then spoke the word to his mind: *vengeance*.

It was all the king needed to raise himself from the sickbed. He stared up at her for a few moments, his mind finally acknowledging her and opening up to once more express love. Kyril sobbed in both relief and regret, knowing that it was all coming to an end. Still Vladdir was not able, or did not bother, to fully read her thoughts, and he got up from the bed to put on his armour, never pausing to confirm that she was following him. Of course she was.

They proceeded slowly through the underground, leaving the newly constructed Royal House to walk through the adjacent tunnels, past the new Yrati residence and finally through the emerging eminence of the Market Caverns. This last was the most magnificent in Kyril's estimation, and she felt the influence of Mauvis' creative thoughts resonate through every structure. Although she knew the Chamberlain had distrusted her, she fully enjoyed his handiwork, especially the way it transformed the chaos that had surrounded them after the Aragoth invasions into ordered structures that also regulated the forces around them, effectively keeping the Desert above them calm.

The Market Caverns were the ones in which she always felt the most comfortable and refreshed. The rushing water of the now exposed Yrati River polarised the energy within the central cavern and spread a cylindrical force outwards to the curving walls. The light flooding in from the skylights touched almost every surface of the tiers being constructed out of the broken tunnels, which now looked like opened hands presenting the slowly appearing gardens towards warmth and security. Already the cultivated herbs and flowers, with which she felt a great kinship, were flourishing and spilling over their troughs placed along the walkways. The solidity of the Earth was strengthened by the metal beams and girders reinforcing the struts that supported the tiers, which again ordered the magnetic forces within the cavern. Here was everything she would ever need, all in great abundance. Kyril stopped and tipped her head back, wanting to summon the winds generated by the rush of the water so that she could feed, or perhaps just commune with the elements one last time.

It is beautiful, isn't it? she thought she heard Vladdir speak within her mind, but when she turned to him, clearly that had been her imagination. Vladdir was still greatly confused by Mauvis' death, and his thoughts no longer held the familiar anchors she was so accustomed to. King and Aragoth ascended to the surface through one of the temporary stairwells erected to facilitate construction. They traversed the Desert, searching for those who had led Mauvis to his end.

The journey continued for days. More than once, they sat in the sand for hours as Vladdir traced his fingers through the white grains, trying to feel the lines of energy and determine which he wished to follow. Kyril leaned against him quietly, savouring the contentment she felt in those moments while they lasted, and suppressing her disappointment when they again stood and resumed travel.

Vladdir paused at a spot where the sand seemed confused. It was moving erratically, stopping to turn about as if searching for something beneath the surface. He squatted and brushed his hand over it, and Kyril saw there were actually pebbles under the sand that were moving about. She blinked in surprise and leaned closer—she thought she might have heard them squeak in alarm before they burrowed deeper into the Desert. Vladdir crouched with one hand resting flat against the ground, sending test pulses of energy into the Earth. Reading his returning vibrations, Kyril brushed away some of the sand where the pulses were outlining a solid structure. White stone slabs were revealed. She paused, realising with a stab of sadness that she and Vladdir were functioning in paired format, as was typical for Aragoths. *Wouldn't this be enough, Vladdir? Must you be filled otherwise?*

Once again, her king failed to read her emotions. He summoned wind, water—any element to move the sand away and open the hidden staircase. They descended into a damp cavern with a strange green-lit pool off to one side, churning its water in a great vortex. Kyril walked the perimeter of the room, trailing her fingers along the walls. At one point, she stopped, reading energy that had clearly been Mauvis'. She pushed her fingers into a small crack in the wall and pulled out a few frayed hairs that had been caught on the rough edges of the rock. Vladdir came to her side and cupped her fingers in his own, breathing deeply to inhale the residual essences from the curled strands. Their eyes met.

"Taken for witchery," he said. His head jerked upwards, his eyes searching blindly as he read the energy lines around them. "I can feel more. They've taken more of him and made a golem from his corpse." Now he turned towards the green vortex of water. "They run from us."

The king strode up to the water and splashed in, Kyril following obediently. They were swept into an underground cavern where the water kept running up the walls, not filling the room. White toads jumped off pale lily pads as Vladdir rushed past them. He fumbled through the instruments on two work tables, finding nothing of interest, then moved towards a smaller vortex in the corner of the room. It looked like it drained into an underground tributary.

"I think they went here," he said, and let the water suck him under. Kyril did not want to go into a water-filled tunnel without knowing how long it would be, but she still followed her king unquestioningly.

The water turned much colder in the small tunnel. Kyril kicked and stroked past tree roots and partial sets of bones that had settled at the bottom, struggling to reach the dim light at the end. As she got closer, she could see that the surface of the water was lit by the white light of a bioluminescent species of water lily. She emerged gasping, and had to quickly clamber up onto the muddy shore to run after Vladdir, who had already picked up the trail. His radiated aura was so strong that she could also see the lines of energy ahead of them. They were growing brighter, indicating that he was closing in on his quarry.

They ran through the tunnels for what seemed like an eternity, Kyril's sorrow growing ever deeper as the end of the chase drew surely near. Vladdir finally stopped, raising a hand to signal her to caution. Kyril dropped into a fighting stance and pulled her sword out of the sheath on her back. An answering slither of metal came from the darkness ahead. She stepped forward, firmly placing an arm across Vladdir's chest and pushing him backwards, making it clear that she would take the first fight.

As she crept along the blackness, she could hear the change in the shape of the tunnel from the echoes of dripping water. It had widened. A blue light flared up in the cavern, and she gasped at the sudden beauty of Ilet, standing before her. Had he not died? She felt him push against her mind, searching for the old bond that had once been there, only finding a new one that made her Vladdir's. Ilet's smile did not fade as he tested the bond's strength, but it perhaps grew more sardonic. He looked different. His face seemed longer, eyes narrower, hair darker, and the light surrounding him had more gold in it. He did not lift the blade from his shoulder as he stepped forward, barefoot, dressed in his long hair, and for some odd reason, servant's livery.

"Kyril, who is Desert dust cast in an impression of me," he said. It felt like bells of joy rang in her mind at the sound of his voice. Her eyes were sliding shut in ecstasy and the sword was slipping from her fingers. "Did you ever realise that's what you were? I can see you've become more than that now, but I have no resentment of your transformation. I have also chosen my own wants over meaningless duty. Don't you see, Kyril? Our fight is meaningless and will change nothing, achieve nothing other than to give satisfaction to a few old men. Stand down, Aragoth. There will be no more of your kind. This war is over. Go home with your king."

"*It shall not be!*" Vladdir rushed forward to strike and Kyril awoke, quickly raising her sword to block him. Ilet merely raised an eyebrow, watching as Kyril turned to look at Vladdir. She could see his will crumble with doubt; could see thoughts of betrayal seep into his mind.

"No," she said to him softly. "It shall not be." Silly man. He didn't realise that she was not about to turn against him, she only meant that her king should not have to engage in such a lowly fight. Besides, there was not enough room in the tunnel for both of them to attack at the same time. She turned and struck at Ilet, who finally lost his smile. He parried and struck back, almost knocking Kyril's sword from her hand. She had never fought against her former master before and did not know his strength, but she had always assumed him to be physically weak. Her mind reached out to him and found strange things. He was very young, younger than he should have been, yet somehow fully a man. He had been charged with fighting skill and strength from a very great, dark king...Kyril tried to reach deeper to seek out this king, but all she could see was blackness and blinding purple venom that had not come from its original source. Behind her, she could feel Vladdir also gathering himself into a massive charge of purple energy.

She cried out as Ilet's blade came out of a fog of purple, nearly striking her in the face. She parried, and he struck at her again, and again. She couldn't mount an offensive—Ilet was too quick, and his blows were too strong. Her arms ached as they had never before, her hands numb from absorbing the impacts and the black energy fuelling them. She could only keep up her defence for so long, and then Ilet's strikes began to draw blood. He dodged past her guard, cut the tendon along the side of her knee, and Kyril stumbled and fell in surprise at her failure. She rose to one knee, her other leg bent out awkwardly to one side, and twisted her sword into a double handed grip. She was prepared to *throw* it at Ilet if she had to. Her former master closed the distance to tower over her and drew back his arm. There was no expression on his face, and she knew there was no animosity between them. How could there be, when each was only protecting their respective masters?

As Ilet's arm swung down, Vladdir stepped in close behind her. He caught the blade with his stone hand and knocked Ilet off balance with a psychic intrusion. The younger man's back arched and he rose onto his toes, his eyes wide with pain. He dropped his sword and grabbed his head with both hands. It took a few seconds before his screams started, and then his fingers curled, tearing at his own face, trying to get Vladdir out. When the king was finished with him, Ilet dropped to the muddy ground in a ragged heap. Dark purple leaked from his eyes, ears and mouth. His breath blew out bloody saliva in a small bubble.

"Did you ever stop to think *why*, Vladdir? *Why* all of this is happening? Could have saved us all much difficulty if you had. We were both pawns at the beginning, but now we fight by our own choice. I only wanted to stop you from eating...my brother again," said Ilet. "You could have just left us. I already said the war was over. I hope your greedy appetite will be satisfied with me. Antronos is so small, you would hardly notice if you swallowed him. And besides, he is meant to rescue your line. Best to let him be." He smiled, and then he died. The golden blue light faded with him, leaving only the dim glow of the lilies and patchy growth of moss along the edges of the tunnel.

Vladdir lifted Kyril to her feet and cradled her against his chest like she was the most precious thing in the world to him, even though she knew it was not true. He kissed her, and transferred his energy to her so that her knee could mend. As soon as the kiss ended, the energy slowly began to trickle back towards its source, and Kyril knew her leg would again become weak.

There was a shifting of the shadows, and something pulled away from the walls to run further into the tunnels. Vladdir illuminated the tunnel by his will, and Kyril saw that a small form in a knitted shawl was running away from them. Small red slippers flashed from under the shawl as she fled.

"*WITCH!*" howled Vladdir. He turned into his demon form and shot through the tunnel after her. "*Return to me the flesh you stole from my brother!*" Kyril snatched up her sword and followed. A bolt of red light erupted from the end of the tunnel and caught Vladdir in the face. It momentarily confused him, but it had no power behind it and did no harm. When he finally swept the light out of his eyes, he let his legs reform and set his feet back on the ground. The tunnels were empty.

"Where did she go?" he snarled. The little witch had been clever, and had cast several lines of light across their path. Some were from people, but others were Desert animals, and even insects. Vladdir closed his eyes and breathed deeply.

"Mauvis," he said, "show yourself to me." One strand was faintly entwined with green and gold, illuminated with pulsating light. Vladdir picked it up and let the energy dance over his fingertips for a few moments, tasting the direction of flow and finally returning to his demon form so that he could shoot through the Earth to the surface. Kyril wailed in distress and did her best to follow, stumbling along in the dark, stabbing at the ceiling with her sword until she found a weak spot and the damp soil above collapsed over her head. She ducked and shook dirt out of her hair, spitting it out of her mouth. She clambered out onto the surface, favouring her weak knee, and limped as fast as she could in the direction Vladdir had gone. Her king swooped back and took her up into the air with him. Below, the landscape zoomed past. The little sorceress had gone back to Ilet's temple. It was a good place for her to either hide or make a last stand—the energy there was so thick that she would be next to impossible to trace. Kyril tried to communicate this to Vladdir, who still did not listen, intent only on retrieving Mauvis' remains.

Vladdir's feet set back on the ground just outside the small trough of water that demarcated the barrier between the temple and the Desert. He stepped over it, still carrying Kyril, into the unnatural quiet and coolness that filled the marble entryway. He let her slide to her feet, then ran lightly around the perimeter of the first room, peering into all adjoining passageways and any nooks in the floor or ceiling. He moved on, deeper into the main cavern. Hefting the weight in her heart, Kyril did her best to assist him, even though she knew this place would be dead and empty; there was no resonance of other Aragoths, and the memory of being connected to all of them made her ache. Her own breathing became laboured as she felt Vladdir's anxiety. The energy here was structured into what she perceived as a triangular tunnel, and its sides pressed Vladdir's mind into difficulty as he struggled against it, trying to force it away so that he could sense the energy of the Desert as he was accustomed. Her other senses broke through the distractions and she froze, then crouched, the pain in her knee forgotten as battle instinct took over. Vladdir picked up on her alertness, and his head moved back and forth as he tested the aura of the place. They caught the scent of blood at the same time.

"This place is familiar," said Vladdir.

"Yes, we've both been here before," she replied.

"That's not it. I mean, I was brought through another plane that resides here."

Vladdir moved quickly towards the interior of the cavern, letting his guard drop completely. He broke into a run, Kyril following, until they reached a room with an engraved brass wall that had been splashed over with something white and brown. A brazier and a rectangular black trough half full of water bisected the room, and the floor was dirtied with black and green spilled liquid, along with blood. Vladdir fell to his knees next to the trough and swept his hands through the water as if searching through it, a confused expression on his face.

"I was in here," he said. "I think…"

Kyril also reached down to touch the water, and felt the residual orange and blue essence of it.

"Ilet," she said. "The part of you that was torn away rested here, and became Ilet." Vladdir gave her a strange look, then moved away to examine the other objects in the room. He rummaged through some discarded chains and manacles and some odd metal cylinders, finally picking up and looking more closely at a burnished triangle. He held it with two of the points pressed against the fingers of either hand, and let it swing around. The energy in the room whooshed around with it, making Kyril dizzy. He spun it again experimentally, feeling the change of the energy flow as he did it, altering the direction he swung it each time. He finally let his own radiations lift the triangle into the air over his hand, where it rotated on its own, and Kyril began to see that it was forming a portal. Through it, she could see a funny little doll made out of rope, beads, blood and skin that was slowly morphing into something else.

Vladdir's mouth set in a twist of malicious anger. He let the triangle come to rest in his palm, so that he could reach through it with his will and bend his intent around the image of the little doll's head.

"For this, you defiled Mauvis," he breathed, and started to unwork the magic that had been cast to make the thing. Kyril's own breath caught as she felt the doll writhe in agony. She heard the screams of the small witch, struggling against Vladdir in whatever distant hiding place she had found. A wall of green energy swept forward from the brass wall and knocked both of them to the floor. The air that came in its wake carried vibrations heavy with sorrow and rage, and it contained a message: *Why must you keep eating my child's soul, Vladdir? Is it not enough that you've killed my son, Ilet, twice? Now you must come and reclaim the spirit of my little one again? Why can't you leave us alone?*

"Your child?" he whispered. He raised his hands and waved them through the dissipating green, watching it waft through his fingers. Kyril also reached out towards the light, unable to sense Vladdir's thoughts clearly. His mind was racing through a memory of facing

Ilet for the first time, consuming all that was around him, taking up something small and tender, quite by accident. "That green light. I think I remember it now. That small thing I hadn't meant to eat."

Hadn't meant to? Let's leave it then, Kyril thought desperately. For a moment, it seemed that the king was about to relax, let himself become open to Kyril again, but the whitewashed images on the brass wall seemed to shift, and an unseen dark green essence began to leak out of it to fill the room. Kyril took a step back and dropped into a fighting stance, not knowing what to attack. Someone or something lay hidden behind the essence, trying to influence Vladdir's thoughts. One pulse. Two. The vibrations were forming a pattern in the air, like a wordless chant. Vladdir clutched at his chest and purple fluid seeped up around his eyes. He leaned against the brass wall, his face ragged and wild.

"This small entity of light, encased in Mauvis' flesh. This child. I must have it. I will take it and rename it *Taalen*!" His thoughts rapidly developed from idle fancy to obsession, and then to insanity, as the vortex within him extended again for victims to drag into its maw. His eyes rolled toward the little witch's hiding place—*she's in the next room underneath the altar trust me trust me trust me.* Kyril's brow wrinkled, and she wondered where this new voice was coming from. Perhaps something orange, or was it black and green? Vladdir did not wonder, but seized the information being fed to him. His mouth widened into an unnaturally tooth-filled grin as he pushed up from the wall and started after his prey. *Now, Vladdir, you know the shape and texture of the little doll's mind. You can follow it anywhere.*

He walked slowly through the door, muscles rippling like a surface predator's. His armour was not silent, and the way the sound bounced from these strange walls made him seem more frightening. Kyril imagined that the little woman would be able to hear his inevitable approach, but not be able to determine from which direction he would come. *Now she's moved,* said the strange voice. *Crawled out from underneath and into the back tunnels. Hurry, hurry, or she'll slip away.*

Vladdir was in full demon form now. He sprang into a loping run on all fours, bursting through a soft spot in the clay portion of one of the walls. Kyril followed, again seeing the light trailing from the small woman as she neared the king and shared in his vision. The little one was agile, and could command the stones quite easily. Her first attempt to block them with a cave-in failed—Vladdir could pass through the Earth, and Kyril managed to dodge through before the tunnel collapsed. The witch sprayed Kyril in the face with pebbles, slowing her down, but it did not slow Vladdir. At the end of a tunnel, the witch finally turned and faced them in a crouching position, only her nose and mouth visible underneath the hood of the clinging wrap she wore. The squirming construct was clutched to her chest; one of its arms was still rope and bead, the other showed the grasping fingers of a child.

Kyril paused, feeling pity for the thing, thinking that it would not survive without the witch to nurture it. But Vladdir had decided he wanted it, so she let her sword swing around in her hand, gathering energy to strike as she cautiously approached. The little woman looked poised to suddenly dart away, and it was very likely she'd hurl more stones.

Vladdir let his human form reappear next to Kyril with one arm outstretched. He began muttering an incantation, and Kyril turned to him in surprise. When had he started using such things? It wasn't his. His mind was being influenced by the green vapour that seemed to be emanating from his hair, and his eyes were dark. She turned back to the small woman and saw tears streaming down her face. Her mouth opened, wrenched by a sob that wasn't sounding. She held desperately to the legs of the construct, resisting Vladdir's efforts to draw it toward himself. Through her connection with the king, Kyril could feel that he had latched his newly gifted power around the creature's nascent consciousness. She let her sword arm drop. This would soon be over and there was no need to kill the witch.

"*It's mine!*" the small one screamed. "*You won't take it from me again!*" Her head snapped back suddenly and she struck not at Vladdir, whom she could not reach, but at the child-thing, shattering its mind. Vladdir shouted in pain as the shards of the construct's thoughts pierced through his psychic barriers and cut him within.

Kyril also felt like her brains had been sliced to ribbons, but she resisted the agony and rushed forward to catch Vladdir before his face hit the rock. He wrenched his arm free from Kyril's embrace and reached out blindly towards the child's light, which he could no longer touch without injury.

"No," he gasped, "Mauvis!"

The small witch scuttled back against the wall, chest heaving with desperation. The wall began to shimmer as if a pool of dark purple water had appeared on its horizontal surface, and something reached out of the wall to pull the woman into its depths. It looked like one of the stone undead, except for its long, black hair. She seemed to be familiar with the creature and went with it willingly. This time, there was no way to tell where she had gone. The trails of light had disappeared.

Kyril tried to resist feeling annoyed. It didn't matter what she thought or felt, since she would sit obediently and silently by her king until he was ready to leave. That was always the way it had been, and so she should expect that was the way it would remain. They had been on the surface for a week, ever since the little witch had escaped, and Vladdir had moped the entire time, bemoaning "his" lost child. Despite all she had learned to endure before, Kyril was tired of the Desert. She wanted to return to the underground, and for the first time since she had ceased to be an Aragoth, she thought of speaking to Vladdir waspishly. He *had* a child, waiting for him in the Royal House, and Hailan was nobody's but his. Why could they not go there, if a child was what he wanted so badly? Certainly, she had been the one to speak vengeance into his mind, but that had been only to rouse him. Could he not shift from it now?

She came out of her meditation, feeling the wind let her hair fall back down to her shoulders, and the water recede from her waist and legs. She had taken extra from the elements to also supply Vladdir with the energy he needed, which was not difficult now while the deep vortex within him seemed stable.

The king was staggering around in the sand, looking lost. "My child," he said. "Kyril, my child...made of my brother...Mauvis..." She couldn't stand it anymore.

"Hailandir," she said.

"What?" Vladdir looked at her, confused.

"Your child's name is Hailandir." She wanted to say more, of how he had never wanted Mauvis as a brother until he was lost, and probably would not want Kyril herself until she was lost, but she held her tongue. She had already spoken above her station. Vladdir stared at her for a few moments longer, seeming to awaken into realisation for the first time in weeks. At first he seemed bewildered by what he found there. Then, as understanding slowly formed in his mind, she felt him experience a flash of shame followed by the determination to do better. He came to drop next to her in the sand.

"Yes," he said, nodding. "Yes, you're right. Hailandir is my daughter. Of course she is. Have you waited long to say this, Kyril?" She merely raised her eyebrows at him, but said nothing. He chuckled and put an arm around her. "And you, Kyril, you wish to return to my daughter. You would be her mother, is that it? I suppose the two of you always did like each other."

"Her mother?" Was this an empty promise, or could she allow herself to believe what she thought Vladdir was saying?

"And would you, perhaps...give me another?"

"Another? Yes. I would. Both sons and daughters!" Kyril scrambled onto her knees in excitement as she spoke, and clutched Vladdir by the front of his shirt. He laughed even more. *We don't need to take children from elsewhere! We can make our own!* The sensation of hope and release was so strong that despite her eagerness to return to the Royal House, it was difficult for Kyril to stand. It was made even more awkward with Vladdir half-draped over her shoulders, laughing with complete abandon. They fell over in the sand a few times before finally managing a few wobbly steps and starting their trek back home.

Their first night together after their return to the Royal House was tender, passionate and more open than ever before. Kyril felt so completely mixed with Vladdir's soul that at times, though she was still aware of his touch, she was unable to distinguish the edges of herself. Afterwards, while Vladdir slept, Kyril cautiously tested the vortex within him and found it strangely cold. It hadn't disappeared, but was still and grey, like his stone arm. Why was it still there? Would it remain inactive? She didn't want to disturb it lest it reawaken, so she left it and carefully checked the rest of his mind and spirit, hunting for the purple venom or any hints of the green, black or purple aura that had seemed to invade him whenever he had been unable to control his temper. All she found was Vladdir. Was it now safe to hope for the best?

They didn't get up until late the next afternoon, and Vladdir was so cheerful that after a few hesitant moments, Rayner seemed to release whatever lingering suspicions he had. The Yrati began to relax and joke around the king. Vladdir pushed aside the new construction drawings being presented to him and called tailors, cosmeticians, papermakers and jewelsmiths to his audience chambers to discuss Kyril's bridal arrangements. The artisans were delighted at the prospect of a wedding and immediately began draping unravelled bolts of fabric over Kyril's shoulders. Some of them brushed coloured powders over her cheeks and pinned up her hair, only to remove everything and start over again with other colours and combs. By the end, it was declared that pale green fabric best suited her complexion and light peach-coloured powder best suited her cheeks. White flowers would decorate her hair, and the combs and jewellery would be encrusted with white gemstones. Kyril didn't really care, but was happy that Vladdir hadn't stopped beaming the entire time. She was also asked to select stationery patterns and table decorations. She chose them at random, and was praised for every choice. By early evening, she had been presented with a delicate coronet that would be replaced by a crown when she properly became Queen, and a beautiful white jewel to wear on her finger.

After a late meal, Vladdir finally surrendered to the craftsmen responsible for reconstructing the underground. They had patiently waited through the fuss of the wedding planners, and could not wait any longer for the king to approve their plans without delaying their work yet another day.

Exhausted and satisfied, Kyril carefully stowed her coronet in a padded box and found a small flask of water, then quietly slipped away. She wound her way through the Royal House until she came to Mauvis' shrine. The morticians had been unable to retrieve his body, so a plinth and bust of the late Chamberlain had been mounted next to the tomb of Sen Kai. She knelt before it, resting her brow against the cool stone, and poured the water around its base. Even though Mauvis had never come to trust her and she had not really liked him, she respected that he was also part of Vladdir's family and she was saddened that his funeral had passed by while Vladdir had been in the throes of temper and fever. She was also upset that Vladdir seemed to have forgotten his brother after all the fuss he had made; it made her determined to have the keeping of Mauvis' memory as her duty. Wherever Vladdir was incomplete, Kyril would make sure she filled the void.

Over the next week, dresses and more coloured powers and perfumes appeared. Everyone in her presence seemed to rejoice, and while she was perplexed that she appeared to be the focal point of the new morale, she was glad that such positive energy had entered the caverns. When she walked with Vladdir to inspect the buildings, she could see that while the tunnels and Market Cavern were becoming more beautiful and complete, the people were becoming thinner and more haggard. Their numbers were small, seeming unequal to the task of rebuilding an entire city-state, and at the same time crop farming and animal husbandry had become a second priority. Whenever Vladdir stopped to speak a few words of encouragement, the tradesmen would pay just enough attention to him to be courteous, then turn to beam at Kyril. Mothers would bring their children to show her; at least these small people seemed fat and content. Many of the parents expressed wishes that Kyril would also soon be blessed with children. This pleased Kyril, as it made her think of Hailandir, who would spend many hours sitting in her lap and babbling nonsense. Occasionally, the princess would say a word clearly, usually related to food. The joy-filled days were a happy blur.

Early one morning, Kyril returned to the surface to eat. The strengthening of her bond with Vladdir was making her sense of time become much clearer. She remembered her last conversation about this with Mauvis with a sharp stab of emotional pain, and quickly swept it away, lest Vladdir also feel it through their connection.

She found a comfortable spot and sat in the sand, letting her awareness of the elements rise. Wind and sand began to swirl around her and the water bubbled up from the depths of the Earth. The energy of the elements flowed into her form, bringing her comfort and re-establishing the parts of her being that had become weakened and stiff. It was as enjoyable and refreshing as always, until a stale taste came along with the wind. The Earth took on the flavour of swamp, and the water seemed sour. Kyril slowed her consumption of these things without dropping the lines of conductance. Instead, she extended her awareness along them, feeling for whatever was spoiling the experience. The unusual flavours were coming from Hailandir—which didn't make any sense.

Kyril rose to return. Because her time with the elements had been cut short, she had failed to completely regenerate her injured knee and she moved with a limping gait, toward her awareness of the princess. The sourness was increasing in intensity, so she fell into a loping run, clambering as quickly as she could down the nearest staircase into the underground. In Hailan's nursery, the maids were fussing and trying to calm the child, who was crying and retching with alarming vigour. Kyril ran her hands over the princess, trying to get a sense of her sickness, but it was nothing she could identify. Not knowing what else to do, she tried releasing some of her stored energy into the child. She saw a faint haze of orange and black lift from Hailan's body to swirl in a mini-vortex before dissipating. This was something she knew—a familiar, hateful thing she could now sense waiting in the back tunnels.

Regretting having been caught without her sword, Kyril ripped a near useless half-sword out of the hands of a ceremonial guard before heading into the back tunnels behind the gardens. Where the tiled path stopped and the walls were nothing more than damp Earth, she paused long enough to lift a small torch from its sconce, then continued on. A strange sound led her deep into some rough hewn passages that had been excavated in search of water, and as she grew nearer, she could recognise braying, but such as she'd never heard before. Something...was moving towards her in the dark tunnel. At first she thought it might be human: the long, dark hair swept the ground as it came forward, and the features partly concealed behind it seemed to form a blunt nose and full-lipped mouth. But then she saw that it stumbled forward on four hooves, leaning heavily on the wall as it did so.

Its head came up and a thick shackle attached to a heavy chain was now visible around its neck.

"Left me again, left me again," came a blurbled voice. "Thought it was over for sure this time, damn you, Vladdir, but you just handed me back. Left me there and let him just come along and take me, you awful bastard. I hope you rot in hell, forever being teased about being set free, only to find what a disgusting sense of humour you have. Thought I'd walked out the door and into Nirvana, only to find out it was all a joke. You're really a nasty piece of work, you king, you are."

Kyril took another few cautious steps forward, sword out and ready, the torch held out as far as her arm would stretch.

The thing had no eyes. The entire top half of its face was missing. She gradually realised that it was the destroyed leftovers of Ilet, which Vladdir had discarded in the tunnels. It had somehow been recomposed, reanimated, and was now moving towards her in the darkness.

The creature stopped and pushed up onto its hind legs. The front hooves scraped at the wall until white fingers began to form out of the cloven toes, and a naked boy appeared before her. He lifted his dead face to her. "Won't you save me this time? Please? Just make it end."

It took a second or two to sink in, but Kyril found she was happy to oblige. She stepped forward with the habitual circling motion of a warrior and moved in close. She jabbed the blunt sword upward sharply under the creature's arm, trying to reach the ribcage and plunge into its heart. The useless weapon scraped up the side of Ilet's body and he jerked. Then a green light filled his head where the top half of his face should have been. He clamped his arm down over hers. Now his mouth over-spilled with purple/green/black. As his body twisted around in a counter-attack, fangs ripped through the gums of his normal teeth to snap at her. She jerked back to protect her neck, but he immediately redirected his strike towards her arm, his teeth sinking in deeply.

It felt like the molten core of the Earth was being pumped up through her veins. Ilet snarled and his entire body shook as his fangs sank in deeper. The green haze surrounding his head seemed to be wrapping itself around her arm and creeping up the side of her bicep, so tangible that it felt like cold fingers touching her, reaching under her clothing to find their way to the core of her body. She cried out in rage and pain, unable to twist free. She kneed him several times and tried pushing against his face, all to no effect. Transferring the sword into her other hand, she finally tried to *cut* him off of her, sawing against his mouth, just above the teeth.

Ilet finally spat her out and lunged, trying for a better hold point. She smashed him against the side of the head. How was she going to kill an embodiment that was already dead? Destroy it with fire? Immobilize it somehow? If she tried to force out this unnatural energy as she had with Hailandir, it might not dissipate as a normal person's would—

Ah. She must do as Vladdir had done to defeat the Aragoths. Remove this energy by drawing it out and swallowing it.

It seemed such an unsavoury task, especially to Kyril, who did not much enjoy regular eating in the first place. But there seemed to be no other way. She steeled her mind, pulled Ilet forward and swung around so that they both fell. She pinned him underneath herself, then inhaled deeply and snapped her head forward, biting into his neck with all the force she could muster.

He actually didn't taste that bad. A bit fermented, perhaps, but tolerable. She felt a vortex open deep inside her spirit, and the drawing in of energy began.

When it was finished, all that was left of Ilet was a desiccated husk. It didn't sink into the Earth as most dead things did out in the Desert—even those things twice dead—and Kyril wasn't sure what she should do with it. She was feeling tired, hurt, and quite sick. She decided to leave it alone, and not try to bury it.

It was hard to keep the negative energy in, but if she released it, where would it go? Ilet had made his feelings clear about being "given back," which apparently was what happened when he was left to roam the aether. There would not be much she could do to ensure where the energy would go if she released it, so it had to remain within her. She stumbled back towards the main tunnels of the Royal House, wishing Mauvis could tell her what to do. With each step she took, she staggered into the wall. The thing she had swallowed had actually been two entities, and she could now feel the dark green/black one building up force within her, shuddering inside as it moved to escape. Every muscle in her body was quivering with the effort of keeping it in. She could no longer continue forward, yet could not slide to the ground.

Vladdir was near. She could feel him, but not see him. She was dimly aware that he had touched her, wrapped his arms around her, and was trying to carry her to safety. He was yelling something, she couldn't discern what. Unable to stop it, Kyril's entire body wrenched in an enormous spasm, and the demon inside her came flying out of her mouth, nose, ears and eyes all at once. It felt like her face had exploded. And then, it was quiet. The green demon had fled. Perhaps it would not come back, but she very much doubted that. Putting a hand up to her face, she understood why she could no longer see. Vladdir was crying, softly whispering her name against her hair. As she faded, the pain also dissolved, and everything around her became white.

She was moving backwards. The energy flow had completely reversed. First with Vladdir, then alone in the Desert, then bonded to Ilet, then...how strange. Her body was made of wind, water and Earth. It unravelled from her consciousness, which was then punched backward through the spirit of Ilet—the template for what she had known as her spiritual form while existing as Kyril—and split into three entities. She had been in cages underground. And before that, carried by the wind on thin, white wings. Or scrambling with scaly toes over the hot Desert sand. Or basking her dried branches in the sun and waiting for the rain. A different king stood before her selves now. There were two of him, overlapping each other strangely. One looked like a dead body, while the other was strong and proud, with dark hair spilling over dark armour. He smiled faintly through the purple vapour surrounding him and pointed at the rolling, white sand dunes she was meant to walk through. A pinpoint of light shone far away on the horizon. In this place, the Desert glimmered and sloshed like water.

Must We go now? she asked. *Vladdir will need Us.*

You go. I'll make sure he follows you shortly. He's done as much as he can to break the curse that keeps us here. Where you're going, there won't be the pull and push of energy to send you astray. Swim free. If you went back into that damaged body now, you'd be little more than a golem anyway.

As she stepped forward, Kyril wondered if Ilet had also finally made it to the other side.

EPILOGUE

PURE CONTINUANCE

SLEEP NOW, LITTLE CHILD. *Your soul is soft. Your mind is mild.* *Sleep now, dearest mine. Sweet shall be these dreams of thine.*
  Did you make that up?
  Yes. I want to sing to him. He's becoming so beautiful. I love him.

The little thing in Saanae's arms was not growing or developing further, but it was halfway alive. It would take time for her to garner the energy needed to complete its body, but the parts of it that were covered in flesh were natural-looking and warm. It filled her with such joy, even having that much of it finished. Her joy was also painful; it smelled like Mauvis, who was no longer here to share it with her. The hair that was coming in had much sharper curls than its father's, perhaps it would even be frizzy, and it was much lighter in colour. Saanae wondered at that, but didn't care really, so long as it lived. The pebbles shifted around her feet in curiosity.

  Perhaps we could form part of the body. Make it grow faster.
  Saanae chuckled. *Then he'd be like Vladdir.*
  Hmph. Almost made the blue one out of Vladdir and stone and kept it, too. Vladdir didn't have a problem with stone. Why are you so elitist?

Saanae found the pebbles too adorable to be insulting, and smiled as she continued to hum to her little doll-child. A lump of Earth shifted around the cavern in a funny zig zag pattern, sometimes trembling for a few seconds before continuing on its route. Some red phalanges sprouted out of the ground next to Saanae's slipper, then a little yellow-haired Ghoul popped out from the soil.

Greetings!

Hello, Little Yrati.

Ooh! So cute! He has my hair!

Yours?

I've been trying to give him some energy. Guess he got my hair along with it. He's to make sure the fish won't die permanently, which is what the old Dir's been on about. Keep the Water in the Earth, don't you know.

I suppose.

Hee. You don't care, do you? But you're happy. That's good. Happy helps Water.

The little bony fingers reached up to tap Saanae's ankle, making her feel a bit stronger, then an entire red arm reached up (minus a thumb, which had dropped off) and gently caressed the doll's bead head. Some more golden energy was passed to the doll, but there wasn't enough real flesh to hold it, and it merely spilled off onto Saanae's lap.

Hmm, this will take some time, mused the little Ghoul. She seemed to grow distracted after a while, and eventually sank away to tend to someone else.

Saanae no longer dared live in her cave, since Vladdir occasionally swept the surface looking for her. Although his efforts were weak and she expected he would die soon, she still did not wish to engage in a fight with him. Once, when he had fallen to the Earth and could no longer hold his demon form, Saanae had approached to ask him to end his vendetta. The vortex within him had shrivelled his lower body almost to a complete husk, and only his upper self was recognisable as anything remotely human. He had looked up at her, his eyes dimly shining in the Desert night, and had hurled accusations at her, even after she had knelt before him and pleaded for him to listen to what she was actually saying. She supposed his pain was too great. When the little Ghoul came to help him—she seemed to be the only one of her kind that would—Saanae had to leave before Vladdir gained enough strength to stand again. He had already been taking feeble swipes at her with his stone arm.

She now lived in a rickety little shack she had lashed together from bits of things she'd found in the Desert. It was enchanted to move with the Desert's whimsy, since she also did not want the Desert Priest to find her again. He had been keeping a low profile lately. Saanae had actually dared to sneak into his old haunts to see what he was up to now, but the temple was half-filled with sand and heat now that the air barrier was no longer maintained, and all the creatures in his laboratory were dead; abandoned. She supposed perhaps Alekseidir and Vladdir were chasing after old Vernus as well. Once the king was dead, she expected the Priest would come out of hiding and resume his old tricks. She found she didn't care so long as he left her to her child and caused no further havoc in her life.

Don't worry too much about Aleksei and Vlad, Callie had once told her. *Your little construct will help bring about the destruction of the blocks that keep them here. They will be able to swim off into the light, one following the other. It's why the old Dir saved you, you know, so that you could finish your work and continue his line without the purple. I know he's already got one, but we can see that the green will be the one to keep it all going in the end.* Saanae didn't know what that meant and didn't want to encourage anything that involved her little construct having anything more to do with the Dir family. She knew she'd have to pay back her extension of life to the old king someday, but that seemed a long ways off. A stray emotion of pity for the Princess Hailandir passed through her mind, but she forgot it when the thing in her lap twitched and gurgled, making her feel nothing but love.

Yes, my Antronos.

Be sure not to miss the next adventures of
all your favorite characters in

THE LONGEVITY THESIS

by Jennifer Rahn

Turn now for a preview, and pick up a copy today.
Available now.
ISBN 978-1-896944-37-1

I

Awakening

ANTRONOS WAS BEING SWALLOWED by the Desert. He stood petrified, watching a great wall of sand heave upwards and seethe past him overhead, covering his world in red gloom. Turning to look back towards his mother's hovel, praying it hadn't disappeared, he found he was somewhere else entirely—in an instant, all had changed. The sky churned and a vortex of wind stretched down from the red, sooty clouds to touch the ground and tease the sand into a great column that tipped sideways, and slowly writhed towards him, like a great, opened maw. At his feet, stones were sliding towards that opening, becoming caught up in the spiralling wind and tumbling out of sight. He called out to his mother, his trembling, skinny hands clutching the few dried brambles he had found, as he continued to turn in a circle looking for what he knew would not be there. Hell had returned.

Sand was beginning to boil around him, sending up small spumes as the Desert's dementia cast up buried rubble and bones that had lain hidden under its surface. Collecting together in the crude shapes of headless torsos with legs, the unearthed debris stood up and marched resolutely towards the darkness at the end of the wind tunnel. The very Earth was flowing towards that gaping orifice, forcing Antronos to run in the opposite direction, or risk being dragged in himself. It began to rain. At first it was a light drizzle of grit, then small pebbles began to pelt Antronos in the face. He dropped his bundle of kindling and screamed, both arms held up to cover his eyes. His feet were sinking ever deeper into the ground as he ran, until he was struggling to pull his legs free from the sand that had engulfed him up to his knees. Something grabbed his ankles from below and dragged him down. After a few agonizing moments of breathless torment, he felt himself being ripped free from the grip of the Earth.

"*Mea Haalom, mea Haalom.*"

Antronos stopped struggling and collapsed into a sobbing heap as he recognized his mother's voice. She was nearly smothering him in her arms, forcing him against her shoulder as she rocked back and forth, not letting him look at her face. He knew the Desert must be changing her again. After a few moments, he quieted. The magnetic whimsy of the Desert still raged outside, but his mother's magic ensured the moaning debris creatures would not enter their home; neither would the Earth reach into the hovel to sweep him into its gullet.

"*Lea Chaakan bestt inalan takat, mea Haalom.*" *The Desert has turned to fire, my child,* she began, telling him the story that always calmed him during these storms. Antronos relaxed in her arms, feeling her hands gently roam over his back and pull his crinky, yellow hair out of his face. *But the fire is not all-powerful. It is held at bay by water, which has the magic to conquer its flames. There is a river called Yrati, which flows underneath the Earth and forms an impenetrable barrier that the Desert cannot cross. In time, you will learn to summon the river that protects us, as it does the people who live underground. The water is within us, and it is that which the Desert cannot conquer. You are safe.*

Antronos no longer believed her as he had when he was younger. He could reason now that he was not safe, and the only people who were underground were already dead.

His mother chuckled as she read his thoughts. "These people don't lie buried in sand. They roam about in tunnels."

"Then why can we not go live underground?" he asked. He pushed away from his mother, and saw that this time the Desert had rendered half her face into a mass of writhing tissue that snaked down her neck and wriggled beneath the shoulder of her tattered, red robes. Through her tangled, dark hair, he could see her remaining violet eye watching him compassionately.

"There are two kinds of magic, *Haalom*. The water magic, which protects humanity . . ." She spread her fingers, palm down, over the floor of the hut and a small amount of water bubbled to the surface. ". . . and the surface magic, which is also necessary for life." Antronos reached out to touch the water, fascinated, although he had heard and seen this story many times before. "The Desert must be mixed with water before life springs from it. But the Desert is wild, and its magic can deliberately mislead people to their death. It mixes you with other things, and gives you a death that lets you live forever." She moved her hand over another patch of ground, and a broken skull that had petrified into stone twisted upwards to leer at them. The thing snapped its jaws, then twitched and pulled back downwards. "I have already been touched by this magic. It has made me part of the surface, and I cannot go underground. Perhaps you can, but I wish that you would not leave me yet."

Antronos pressed his face against her neck. "I won't leave," he promised.

"You will leave, *Haalom*. Just not yet."

This troubled Antronos. His mother had never spoken of their separation before and he knew he couldn't cope with the Desert's mad rages on his own. "There's nowhere for me to go." He sat up again to search her face, but she was gazing over his shoulder, the skin over her left eye now settled into what looked like a hideous melted scar.

"The Desert has come for me. It told me It would."

"What?" Antronos turned and saw that one of the stone skeletons from outside had entered the hut. "Make it leave!" he said to his mother. Sand crept upwards to wrap the fossilized bones in an approximation of flesh, and a rotted shroud pulled free from the Earth to clothe the figure. It turned its empty sockets towards Antronos and seemed to grin at him. "*Itya*, make it go!"

His mother stood up and shook her head sadly, saying, "Not this time."

The sand creature was horrible. He slept with *Itya* in her bed, broke Antronos' clay pots, and burned everything he could get his hands on, including Antronos' only other tunic. Antronos had tried to dissolve him with precious water, but the thing had howled his psychic laughter as he sopped up his muddied flesh from the ground, and packed it back against his bones. Sometimes he would stand silent for hours, only to crush all hope that he had died by springing back to life when Antronos tried to bury him. What made it worse was that *Itya* seemed to accept this sandy monster into her life even though it appeared to sap her strength, bleeding a little more of her away with every passing moment. When Antronos raged at her, she would only answer, "If you live long enough, *Haalom*, you will see me again."

"Please stop saying that! I'm not going to leave!" But his mother grew more and more distant, spoke to him less, and never reassured him satisfactorily.

The sand creature grew ever more presumptuous, and began issuing orders. He had acquired a thick staff from somewhere, probably regurgitated by the Earth, which he refused to burn in lieu of Antronos' possessions, and which he beat Antronos with when his commands were not obeyed.

Out into the Desert, boy. Find me wood.

Antronos glared at the sand creature. "What for?"

I am the undertaker, and I need to build a funeral pyre.

"Are you dying then?"

The creature laughed at him. *I am already part of the Desert.*

Antronos scuttled away from the raised staff, seething with resentment.

The sandy dunes were not willing to relinquish the sparse scrub, dead and twisted as it was. Antronos tugged hard on a particularly stubborn tangle of brush, partially pulling the gnarled root to the surface, and thinking he could wrench it up a bit further before chopping it off from whatever it clung to. He heaved on it again, and felt something flat and hard shift beneath his foot. He froze, his heart thudding as he waited to see in which direction whatever he had disturbed was going to leap. Nothing moved. Carefully, he lifted his foot away and peered down at the sand. Something black with a straight edge was poking upwards. He brushed the sand away gently, and found that the black substance was soft, slightly sticky, and formed a completely straight line around a square-shaped panel of clear stone. He felt around the edges of this strange object, found another one exactly like it, and another. Many of them were stuck together, with the black stuff all around the edges. Sweeping away more of the sand, Antronos marvelled at the clear stones, as he began to see tiny people moving around inside them.

A few of them glanced up at him, but didn't seem bothered by his presence. He pried up the one he had loosened, intending to take it home as a gift for his mother, and was disappointed to see it empty of people as it came free in his hands. But there were sounds now, coming from the gap he had made in the pattern, and the distinct, metallic tang of water. He looked down at the hole and saw sand falling through it, and realized that the people were down inside a massive cavern, not inside the clear stones at all. Was this . . . a tunnel? Was his mother's story real?

A few of the people were suddenly swiping at their necks as they passed beneath him, then looking up to where the sand was trickling through. Some pointed, then moved away. Others merely stood, staring back up at him.

Excited by his discovery, Antronos moved to another section of the panels and swept away the sand. He pressed his forehead against the clear stones, trying to make out more of what was beneath the surface. If his eyes did not deceive him, there was indeed a massive river coursing through the bottom of the cavern, without any mages constantly summoning the water.

"The Yrati River," he breathed in fascination. Bright spots of light were coming from somewhere around the edges of the water, but they were white-blue, so they couldn't be fires. Antronos took one of the twigs he had collected, and began to pry up another of the panels so that he could see better.

A sharp bang startled him so badly that he jerked to the side, painfully twisting back his fingernails caught at the edge of the clear stone. He gaped at the man coming up through a door that had been slammed open from the ground. He had never seen anyone with hair so short when he obviously had not been burned, or with so much cloth to wrap around his body. This man wore magic cloth that encased him almost like skin, without having to tie the edges in knots over his shoulders.

"Get away!" he shouted at Antronos. "Go on!" He picked up a stone and threw it, nearly striking Antronos' head. "I said, go, *Pachu!*"—*filthy creature.* Antronos got to his feet and stumbled back a few steps. "Your kind's not welcome here!" The man pulled out a series of metallic links from his sleeve and walked forward threateningly. Antronos had never seen so much metal in his life. The man must be incredibly rich.

His amazement was halted when the man swung the links over his shoulder and hit Antronos across the face with them.

"Get away!"

Antronos finally turned and ran.

Flames were teasing the sky without any shifting of the Desert. The fire was real. Antronos squinted as he approached, trying to make out what he was seeing more clearly. Why had he bothered to collect kindling if the undertaker could summon enough wood from the Earth to generate such a blaze on his own? And why did he choose to place this funeral pyre so close to *Itya's* hovel? The bruise on Antronos' cheek throbbed as the realization hit him.

He wouldn't have dared . . . she wasn't that sick. Just tired. It was someone else.

Antronos dropped his bundle and began running, his feet sliding in the dusty grains. He was almost at the pyre when he hit a pocket of slipsand. His hands flailed out desperately, trying to catch hold of something, anything, as the sand beneath him gave way and his body was sucked into an immobilizing swathe of grit. *Itya* was clearly visible now, just beyond his reach, steadily burning out of existence. He stopped struggling and tilted his head upward as far as possible, straining to watch her these last few minutes as he slowly sunk deeper. He squeezed his eyes shut to force away the tears blurring his vision, and focused again on his mother's scorched face; it would have to be enough.

As if marking an ending, the sun dropped to the horizon, sparkling through the dust coating the sky. The Desert moaned in protest, shifting sand and rocks around Antronos' head and launching plumes of grit into whatever forms suited its magnetic whimsy. Incomprehensible pillars of sand shot out of the ground and collapsed; far away boulders drew closer, then grumbled as they burrowed back into the dust. An entire stone building surfaced in a thunder of unearthed debris, only to tip sideways and crumble a few moments later. For once, the prospect of being swallowed whole by the Desert's writhing didn't terrify him.

Rage swelled up inside Antronos. The sand creature could have waited. He could have allowed Antronos the chance to say goodbye. Somewhere behind him, he could hear the unreal man shuffling towards the fire.

This wasteland eats all comfort. Takes it for itself. It doesn't care anything for you. Pointless to cry and waste your fluids.

Antronos shoved the words out of his head, twisting his face away from the undertaker's proffered staff as much as he could. What made the disgusting thing think he'd want to live after this? Being alone in the Desert would slowly drive him insane.

Your defiance is meaningless. You're willing to die out of anger against me? After this moment, I won't even think of it, and you will lose your chance for whatever misguided vengeance you want to take.

The staff fell away, and the creature's grey, skeletal ankles came into view from under a frayed robe, as he tottered towards the fire. His feet barely sank into the sand.

I will tell the Desert to release you anyway.

A buried pillar of sand pushed up against Antronos' feet as it forced its way to the surface, sending him sprawling. It collapsed behind him in a torrent of dry granules. What was the point of setting him free? What would he do now without his mother? She had been the only unchanging thing in this fearsome existence, holding him close, and anchoring his sanity whenever the terrifying Desert storms struck and until they had passed. Hatred for the sand creature surged up inside him. He opened his mouth to tell the despicable being that he'd find a way to—

You don't need to tell me things I already know, Antronos. I don't bother hating you, because it isn't worth the effort. Almost gone now. Where's she gone? All back to the Desert and dust.

Antronos felt his mouth twist in futile anguish. Still covered in chalky grit, he crept as close as he dared to the pyre, trying to decide which emotion held him more strongly—his wish to follow his mother, or his wish to find a way to kill what was already dead. He pulled out of his waistband one of the three thin, precious books he had hidden from being burned, the nap of the soft vellum cover catching on his rough fingertips.

"*Itya,*" he whispered. "Do you remember reading this to me? All these old water prayers?" He scrubbed away his tears, then carefully flipped open the crumbling pages to one of his favourite hymns: a sinuous lyric about the circle of life, describing how it always started again. As he read, the wind raged at his back, tugging angrily at his hair and the flames, as if trying to extinguish his voice along with the light and heat of the fire that ruined its perfection. The bed of the pyre split with a great crack, startling Antronos into silence and sending his mother's bones tumbling deep into the brambles. He caught his breath, unthinkingly reaching towards the flames.

His mother's charred corpse sat up and screamed at him. Antronos yelled and fell backwards. When he looked again, the pyre was nothing but a pile of bones and coals. No movement, but his mother's skull now rested at the top of the burning refuse, where it had not been before. The sand creature did not react, and continued standing motionless and vacant off to one side. Antronos cautiously crept back towards the pyre. Maybe, he thought, if the Desert was choosing now to exercise its power, its next shift might awaken his mother, lifting her out of the flames and back into the world.

"*Itya?*" he prodded. He searched the pyre for any sign of movement for several minutes.

The oblivious force of the Desert ignored him and continued to work change only within itself. Unnoticed by the magnetic fury around them, bones turned to cinder. Cinder crumbled to ash.

Faith splintered inside of Antronos as he scanned the dying fire through blurring tears, and still saw no movement. The book of water hymns was still in his hand. *The circle of life? Had this made Itya move?* He began to read again, this time raising his voice bravely over the moaning protest of the Desert as it responded to his call. The shifting of the sand intensified as he continued giving sound to the hymn. Pointed rocks shot up around where he knelt, yet he wouldn't stop.

But the Desert did.

Antronos looked around, scanning the pyre and the wasteland, now washed in thin, evening light. Nothing moved. Not even the undertaker. Determined, he began the hymn again. His voice slowly faded as he realized that the Desert hadn't responded to the lyrics at all; its motions had been coincidental.

His mother was truly gone this time. She wasn't lost in a sandstorm or mystically transported over the next dune. Waiting for her to come to him again would be futile. He swallowed his grief enough to pause, stubbornly searching for her return one last time, and cried out as he saw her ashes wriggling out of the coal pit in tiny streams. He shoved his hands into the ground, trying to scoop her away from the Desert, succeeding only in mixing her more thoroughly with the dusty grains.

"Don't leave me," he moaned through his teeth. The blue ash coalesced into a set of fingertips that reached out of the sand. Antronos caught his breath, staring at the unmoving fingers. Cautiously, his hands trembling, he reached out to touch them, feeling their solidity, their reality. The sand just above the fingers shifted, rose up in a mound, then fell away in a pattern which formed his mother's face, mouth stretched open in a silent scream.

"What . . . what's wrong?" he asked. All around him mounds of sand were rising. Antronos half stood, watching them uncertainly as they began to tremble, then started moving towards him in jerky spurts. He peered at the undertaker, who still showed no signs of awareness, leaning silently on his staff. Antronos kicked at one of the mounds, then scurried away as the sand flowed upward into a curving pillar. All motion stopped. He crept forward again, reaching out for his mother's blue-ash hand, constantly glancing around for more signs of movement.

The sand of the pillar crumbled away, revealing a skeleton made of grey, cracked stone. It stood still for a second, then writhed and screamed, lurching towards Antronos. It fell over the ash-image of his mother, then rapidly sunk out of sight, taking her with it, leaving Antronos sobbing as he dug madly, trying to once again find the ashes that had submerged into the Desert's being.

The undertaker came to life and tottered into the embers, spewing ashes everywhere, flattening the sand mounds, destroying any chance of finding *Itya* again. Antronos tried to stop him, but was thumped aside impatiently.

This is over. She will not live, and you will not die.

"Then I will go mad."

As you wish. It hardly matters to me.

Antronos wondered how long it would take to lose all perception of reality. His gut twisted with uncertainty. Perhaps all he had ever been was some deluded wraith who only thought that he lived, but was denied the reality of both life and death for a crime he could not remember.

Little was left of the pyre. The sand creature gestured towards Antronos, wanting him to fetch the rakes. Another shove and the threat of a severe beating were needed to send him running back towards the cardboard hovel.

The wind picked up and began to fling sand into Antronos' face. He stopped, unable to breathe or see, and put out one hand to find the entrance to his mother's hut. His fingers finally scraped against the door, which he shoved aside and clambered past. He stood gasping for a few moments, trying to rub the sand from his eyes. They began to burn. The Desert shifted again. He felt it inside himself this time, pouring all of its intense heat and unmerciful drought into his eyes. The ground heaved under his feet, sending him tumbling as he felt the Desert reach more deeply into him to work its change.

Antronos screamed and dragged himself towards his mother's cot, and the bowl of water he had kept there for soothing her fever. Finding it, he tried to quench the fire in his eyes, and finally felt the pain melt into a subtle, aching burn. He gingerly pulled his hands away from his face. He could see his fingers, cast in a strange yellow glow. He could see the rugs and the walls of the hovel, even though there were no candles lit and it was the dead of night. When he looked down on himself, the outline of his body was covered with a silken atmosphere that pulsated over his heart and moved in flowing waves over his body. The other objects around him did not glow as he did, but had a paler, more diffuse light, with the exception of the brightly glistening beetle he saw busily digging its way into the food supply.

He got up, lit a candle and found his mother's old polished mirror. Raising it to his face, he felt his heart sink into his stomach. His face and the frizzy, yellow hair that framed it were the same, but his eyes had changed. No longer a natural, deep brown, the shift that had assaulted him had twisted them into the purple, diamond-slit eyes of a snake, sunk deep into their sockets. The skin around them looked dark red and bruised. Gasping, he tore at the rough shirt he wore, exposing the semi-hardened scales that now covered his skin in patches. Some were dark green, others white, still others a myriad of glistening colours.

The Desert's magic had touched him, as it had his mother. He remembered her saying that while he was untouched, he could go underground, to where water protected life. It was impossible now, even if he could have crept past the man wearing magic cloth, who had chased him away from the underground door. Why should he be changed like this? Was he dreaming?

Needing to feel connected to something definite, even if only the rotted sand-thing outside, Antronos grabbed the rakes from the corner of the hut and ventured back outside to find the undertaker. The wind was still blowing curtains of sand across the Plains, making it difficult for him to find his way back to the dimly glowing embers of the fire pit. After a moment he froze in his tracks, realizing that the distance between him and the sand creature had increased. Then the pyre was off to his left. Antronos began to run. The directions shifted again. And again. He ran faster, but still couldn't reach the pyre. He paused in disbelief as the creature turned from him and walked away.

"Wait!" Antronos screamed, but with the next wave of billowing sand the undertaker disappeared. The pyre was also gone. Had it ever been there? He screamed again, only succeeding in roughening his throat.

He stood in the near darkness of the sandstorm, still able to see by the hazy aura of the sand, recognizing belatedly that unlike the beetle and himself, the undertaker did not have more than a diffuse glow about him as he had walked away. How had the creature left him so easily? Had he walked right out of existence?

There had to be a way to make himself real.

2

Catalyst

ANTRONOS SPREAD HIS FINGERS and held them over the
sand, willing the dusty grains to move until a small pile collected
in front of him. Nothing else responded; no water or stone skulls
came to the surface, and never would, no matter how hard he tried. He
could still see living auras, but that hardly constituted magic, not the
kind his mother had been able to conjure.

The stone marker he had built, inscribed with his name and a short
message, had rested here for seven years, but was now inexplicably
gone. It was just as well, as he no longer really believed that his mother
still roamed the Desert, and that someday she might see the monument
he had left her and know where to find him.

After a few moments the small mound of sand he had just made
shifted sideways until it had completely flattened out. The elongated
magnets he had placed in a semicircle in front of him spun in random
directions, none of them aligning towards the world poles. They had
pointed steadily south for over three months when he had initially
selected this place, but now the Desert had mysteriously changed again.

He sat for a while longer, ignoring the prickling sensation of sand
blowing against his face, his scholar's robes wrapped tightly against
the wind. The hazy presence of the sun slowly rose from the horizon,
illuminating the dust in the air with shimmering waves of pink and
green. When he had been younger, the underground had seemed like a
marvellous wonder, and finding a place there had seemed so necessary.

239

In the tunnels, things were constant, unaffected by the random changes on the surface. He had thought that living there would end his terror of the Desert. He knew now that the world was much larger and more diverse than he had ever imagined, and that Temlocht was only one out of five States, the only place where most of the people lived underground, and were considered socially backward by the surrounding regions. He supposed that made his kind the pinnacle of social lowliness, if even the Temlochti had difficulty accepting him.

Antronos stood, feeling the sand that had collected around his legs sluice from the folds of his robes, and sighed, rubbing his fingers. They still ached from being broken during one of his early ventures into the tunnel dwellers' domain. Even though the dock hands, who worked along the river in the lowest tier of the Market Caverns, had eventually accepted him as a dung shoveller or cargo loader, they had never shown interest in protecting a surface creature from the idle sons of rich merchants.

For a moment, Antronos considered staying in the Desert, then rejected the idea. Although he didn't belong underground, living on the surface now would just be re-suspending himself in limbo, and his dung shovelling had lessened ever since he had rescued an academic administrator from drowning in the underground river. That had earned him a spot in the university. His mother had taught him to read, but he had to work twice as hard as the other students to make up for his lack of formal education, and ten times as hard to impress his teachers and earn a grade that would have been handed to another student not considered the local freak. It had been and still was his best and only chance to understand life, and perhaps what he was, so he turned and began the long trek back the way he had come. His class would be graduating tomorrow, and even though there was talk among his classmates that the university wouldn't really allow him to have a degree, there was the remote chance that someone might mistakenly fill out the parchment anyway, and he might be able to pick it up from the Chancellor's office after the ceremony—when there weren't many people around to laugh at him for even asking. He supposed he could continue studying at the university without a degree, but that would bar him from entering a higher level of research with access to better lab equipment, interfering with his still intense desire to analyze what made a human being live, what made it die, and what the Desert did to interfere with that natural process.

At this time of day, the back tunnels would still be completely dark, making it possible for Antronos to slip into the underground unnoticed. A series of stone markers sat along the edge of the Plains, outside of which magnets behaved as they should. These had been placed two years ago by the University Department of Physics, which had been made responsible for periodically testing the Desert's magnetic sphere of influence and moving the markers as needed.

He found the metal surface of the door he had come through, and had to tug sharply on the ring handle to force the steel slab upwards against its rusted edges. The lock that had been placed on the other side had long since disintegrated, and no one had bothered to check if it needed to be replaced. In general, the contempt of the tunnel dwellers, along with their bewildering array of noises and colours, were enough to keep most surface creatures out.

In the dark of the underground, Antronos found his way easily by the glinting auras of the innumerable busy insects and meandering tree roots that lined the tunnel. The ground and east wall were slick from water oozing out of the river that ran alongside this passage, bringing life to the underground as it could not be on the surface. It was also why this tunnel was not regularly used, as the risk of a cave-in was high.

He heard a rustling sound somewhere deep in the cored-out mud behind him and froze, listening intently. It came again. He moved ahead to where a thick bundle of roots protruded from the wall and pressed himself behind them, looking back the way he had come. Last week he had been followed by a pack of student would-be tormentors down one of his favourite back tunnels, abandoned only because of a disease which had died out long ago. He was now afraid to use it, in case his classmates had set up an ambush there. It would be damned inconvenient if he had to abandon this one as well. At least his Desert-changed eyes would give him an advantage in the dark.

Several bright, erratic auras were moving towards him, not taking on any shapes he could recognize. They would remain stationary for a few moments, then tremble until they seemed to muster enough energy to finally move forward in rapid, jerky spurts. What were they? Cautiously, Antronos leaned past the tree roots to get a better look, and saw something like crumpled-up dwarves who were stuck to the walls and ceiling.

Did something follow me down from the Desert? Antronos' heart sped up with anticipation. If these dwarves had followed him because of his monument, perhaps they knew something about his mother, or maybe had some message. From past encounters he knew that any contact with Desert creatures was best done on solid ground where he couldn't be suffocated in mud or sand, so he began to edge back towards the university.

As he drew closer to tunnels that were more frequently used, the walls were cut in deliberately straight angles, and bricks lined the floors. No one had bothered to tend to the lighting in this tunnel, and the bioluminescent moss, overgrown and dying, shone weakly from tanks embedded in the walls. With a final look back, he hoped the strangers would not be intimidated by the tunnel dwellers' structured territory and follow him at least that far.

The library foyer opened before him in a vast expanse of diamond-shaped tiles, stretching past administrative offices and blue stone pillars that reached up twenty metres to support an enormous glass ceiling. The early morning light was stunning, catching on polished marble desks, as well as metal accents that lined the railings, door handles and chairs. At this time of day, the foyer was completely empty, with silence to match.

He paused at the mouth of the tunnel to give his eyes a few seconds to adjust. Something tickled at his foot, and looking down, he saw a flash of jerky aura next to his sandal. He jumped away from it and it flipped out of sight. The creatures in the back tunnels seemed to be moving towards him steadily now, writhing past roots and outcroppings of rock with ease. It was still too dark in the tunnel for him to see them by natural vision. Backing away, he waited to see if they would come out into the open. The creatures paused at the edge of the tiles, then somehow burrowed underground, moving forward through solid rock.

Antronos could barely see their dimmed auras through the stone. He had never encountered this type of creature before, and realized that without Desert vision similar to his, the tunnel dwellers would also be unaware of these visitors. *Perhaps they are unable to break through the tile,* thought Antronos.

The dimmed bubbles of aura wiggled past him and disappeared under a door leading into the library archives. In the lower levels, not all areas were covered in tile, and the creatures might be able to emerge. Antronos chased after them and found that the side entry was locked. Determined to at least find out where the creatures were going, if not speak to them, he squatted and scratched at a section of the wall where the lacquer had cracked. The dusty stone crumbled under his nails, allowing him to gently pull a small blue beetle from its intended home. The little creature struggled briefly, then tapped the tips of Antronos' fingers with its antennae, seeming confused and curious as to where it had ended up.

Taking a pinch of Desert sand from a vial in his belt, he blew the grains into the lock, then held the beetle up to the keyhole. Thinking it had found a new lair, the little beast obligingly crawled inside. Antronos whispered to it, using the Desert's whimsy carried in the sand to influence the beetle to push the lock pins out of the way. *Such things were cluttering up its home.* The lock snapped open; the door swung inward.

Antronos quietly stepped inside and softly closed the door. The bubbles of aura were clustered together a few metres away, as if waiting for him. Without a sound, the tiles crumbled upward, and an intensely bright light seemed to peek at him before sinking back under the rock. Surprised, he ran forward and tried to jam his fingers into the spot where the thing had surfaced. It was completely solid, the tiles undamaged. The bubbles began to move again.

Antronos chased them past rows of aging filing cupboards and to the left, then got stuck as he realized that he'd wedged himself between a leaning rack of scrolls and an old chalk slate board. He froze, hearing voices approaching. Looking around, he noticed that he had left the archives and was now in a white and red tiled hallway, with alternating white pillars and multi-coloured tapestries displaying academic motifs that lined the walls. Teaching props littered the passageway like abandoned debris. He must be somewhere near the professors' offices. The aura bubbles swirled in a frenzied dance before coming to a stop, occasionally trembling but otherwise staying put. Antronos pulled back behind the slate and crouched down.

Several figures in black scholar's robes were coming towards him in a clumsy huddle. Laughing and talking loudly, half of them were holding hands, and the other half were kicking, slapping or punching each other as they strode down the hall. Antronos began to breathe again in relief. He could tell from the sloppy way they wore their robes and their long hair that these were priests from the Yrati Clan; healers known for their kindness and the only people in the underground who had not gone out of their way to make him miserable. If they caught him here, it was unlikely he'd be beaten. As they came closer, he could make out the red and blue patterns embroidered on their neckbands. They seemed completely oblivious to the aura bubbles, which jiggled excitedly as the priests stepped over them, then vanished, apparently sinking deeper into the Earth.

Antronos peered furtively at the approaching priests, feeling his heart speed up. He felt a strange mixture of resentment that his quarry had disappeared, and anxiety over his torn wish to remain hidden yet talk to the Yrati. Now might be as good a chance as any. Should he reveal himself? After he graduated, if he graduated, they might be the only group tolerant enough to accept him for higher study, and they had associated themselves with the river, which his mother had told him could halt the Desert's madness. He crept forward slowly and followed them, keeping far enough back that he might at least be able to hide behind something if they were to turn around. When they entered the office that must have belonged to My Lord Maxal, the Yrati High Priest, Antronos wedged himself behind a cracked podium opposite the opened office door, and peeked out from behind it. The room was much too small for so many people, but the Yrati seemed content to sit in a ring on the floor with some of their fellows perched on benches and bookshelves around them. They were still jabbering loudly as they passed books and parchments to each other, apparently planning lessons. Antronos had been taught about pharmaceuticals by a few of them, however, most of their postings were in the Faculty of Arts, as their medical approach was regarded as folklore rather than science.

One of the Yrati screamed as she was hit in the face by something that exploded in a great splash of water. She blinked indignantly at someone across the room, then stood up and dragged a red-haired boy over to where she had been sitting. The other Yrati laughed and pinned the youth down, as the soggy priest began to rub her wet hair in his face.

"Teach you to throw things at me," she was grumbling.

"It was a blessing!" screeched the boy. "Water is Life. So Dagnaum says! I was merely trying to bless you!"

"Old Dagnaum isn't here. Don't bring him into this." She picked up a tankard of something and poured it over his head before finally letting him go.

The boy jumped up and skipped into the hallway, rubbing his face. "Augh! Was that berry juice? Leelan, you sully the name of Dagnaum, founder of Yrati Water Magic."

"Dagnaum who now writes books for babies," said the wet priest.

"You who scoff at his wisdom shall surely be cursed."

"Go get buried, Tibeau."

"But I'm all sticky."

"Good. Maybe the ants will eat you."

Smiling at the exchange, Antronos shifted uncomfortably behind the podium. He liked the Yrati, but after all the abuse he'd suffered from other students, he wasn't sure he could cope with their rough brand of teasing if he joined them. He held his breath and pulled back as Tibeau came dangerously close to where he was hiding and rummaged through a box half-covered in the detritus of the hall. Pulling out something that looked like a wad of red and blue paper that had been dampened and squashed together, Tibeau struck a match and began trying to light the end of it.

"Earth, don't light that thing in here!" A stocky Yrati with a bushy, black beard and a glistening bald-patch erupting from a ring of long, dark hair, stepped into view from somewhere down the hall and slapped the paper-thing out of Tibeau's hands. Antronos recognized him as Ferril, who taught an alternative medicine course about brewing herbal tea.

"Why not?" Tibeau asked. "It would be funny, and I need to exact revenge."

"Exact revenge on this." Ferril put the boy in a headlock and dragged him back into the office.

Maybe I shouldn't ask to join them, thought Antronos. Despite that, and unable to resist, he wiggled to the other side of the podium and picked up Tibeau's discarded wad of paper from the floor. It smelled like firecracker powder. Starting to feel anxious that he had lingered too long, Antronos sidled a bit farther from behind the podium, painfully aware that the Yrati might see him walking away if any of them should step out of the office again. He swore silently as more footsteps echoed from the other end of the hall, and tried to make his lanky frame as small as possible, since he couldn't wriggle back behind the podium quickly enough.

The Chancellor of the Temlochti State University marched past energetically, his heavy ceremonial robes sweeping the tiles as he moved. His brown beard and shoulder-length hair made him look like some kind of aging warrior from a tavern song. The others who followed were all Sens, or professors declared as full medical scholars. None looked in Antronos' direction: all of them wearing grim expressions. A few were arguing as they walked, heading towards the Yrati office. Antronos could pick out his pharmacology and surgery professors, as well as the Yrati High Priest. My Lord Maxal wore a straight-cut black robe, was clean shaven, and his black hair was close cropped, in stark contrast to all other Yrati, who seemed not to know what a barber was.

The Chancellor paused at the door of the office, unable to enter because of the crowd of Yrati sitting on the floor, and abruptly turned towards Maxal in the hallway.

"By the *Earth!*" he exploded. "Am I being so unrealistic? All I'm hoping for is a day where interdepartmental politics are shoved aside and the faculty sits as a united front, tolerating each other for the sake of our shared achievement!"

"Yes, Amphetam. Shared," Maxal replied, "as in shared input into the format of the ceremonies."

The Chancellor took a deep breath, then put a hand on the High

Priest's shoulder. "I am not trying to insult you—"

"Well, you have," said Maxal.

"You insist on taking things the wrong way!"

"I fail to see how the format of the graduation ceremony has anything to do with external funding."

"Maxal, it's the whole attitude of this university. We have to change."

"Fine. Change. Change whatever you like. There is still no reason to exclude the Yrati blessing of the graduates."

"The representative from Raulen State refused to come because of your 'mystical hokum,' as she called it."

"Who cares? It's our ceremony, not Raulen's. And my mysticism is not 'hokum,' so she is quite clearly uneducated and incorrect. Why should you listen to her anyway?"

"Earth, Maxal! Nobody believes in magic anymore—"

"That's not true."

"Nobody *sensible* believes in magic anymore. We have to raise our heads out of the sand. Even if there are phenomena we can't always explain, none of them is going to generate us any money *or* international respect. We cannot compete internationally without Raulen's funding. Our resources have emptied. Gone! There is *nothing* left."

"And I keep telling you, if Raulen is truly judging us on our academic merit, then a simple ceremony should have absolutely no impact on their decisions."

"But it does! And we as scholars who should know better, should not be subscribing to these children's tales about—"

"They just want to control you, Amphetam. They want to see how far you'll go for money. If you accept their terms now, the next year they'll push for something else. Perhaps they'll insist you perform your functions naked."

"Don't be absurd."

"I'm not. I can quite clearly see that they are trying to humiliate and dominate you. And you are willing to let them for the sake of money."

"None of the other States take us seriously because of these traditions—"

"I can see this conversation is pointless."

The Yrati turned and walked back down the hallway, leaving the

Chancellor with his arm still raised. Sen Amphetam let his hand drop after a moment, then just stood there, watching Maxal push his way into the office. He released a shaky breath before turning away and striding off, looking absolutely miserable. The other Sens lingered for a few moments, some of them muttering vague apologies in the direction of the Yrati before following after the Chancellor.

Antronos let his lungs empty, wondering if his ties to the surface with all its implied mysticism would make his fears real. *Mystical hokum*? Children's tales? His Desert eyes were real and there was nothing he could do about it. If Sen Amphetam found the opinion of Rauleners so important and was so against belief in magic, he probably wouldn't want an obvious reminder of the Temlochti State's tainted history, like a snake-eyed surface creature, showing up at his office to claim a parchment.

Cautiously, Antronos stood up and began to sneak away from the office, not breathing until he had turned a corner and found the hallway empty. He hurried back towards the archives and ran into yet another Yrati as he rounded the last corner. The sandy-haired priest caught him in surprise, stopping his fall.

"Oh, it's you," he said, letting go and giving Antronos a once over. "What's that? Some Desert thing?" He poked at the paper wad still clutched in Antronos' hand. Feeling the heat rise in his face, and not wanting to be accused of stealing, Antronos moved his fist behind his back, looked down and didn't answer. He was also becoming angry. Why should everyone assume that he always ran around with only "Desert things" anyway? Even the Yrati, reputedly kind or not, seemed to be so ready to think he was some surface idiot, that this one didn't even recognize something made by his own clan.

"Right. Well, don't let me hold you up." The priest brushed past him and strode away, leaving Antronos feeling empty. It wasn't fair. He had worked harder than any other student, and he was due some kind of serious recognition. He would just have to find a way of confronting the Chancellor and insisting on his degree. If he dared.

Convocation Day. Several metres overhead, the glass panes of the convocation hall ceiling were covered in sand. A clear spot was slowly growing in the middle, and coloured panels were emerging as workmen briskly swept away the grit. The light from outside glittered as it spilled into the cavern and puddled dimly in the corners, lifting the shadows to reveal the blue cast of the pillars and hints of the academic motifs embossed in the stone walls.

A few early graduands were trickling into the hall. Even though the end of the hall where they were seated was still dark, Antronos could pick them out easily by their auras, and backed himself even farther behind a pillar next to the stage. He had chosen this spot because not only would it remain shadowed once the skylight was cleared, it was also near a door if he had to make a hasty exit. Pulling the hood of his formal robe over his hair, he hoped that no one would notice him, at least for a while. He wouldn't be able to hide his eyes from the Chancellor when it was his turn to receive his parchment, assuming they would even call his name, but he hoped by then it would be too late, and that Sen Amphetam would be too embarrassed to say anything—just hand him his degree as quickly as possible and get him off the stage.

The Chancellor appeared on the front dais, signalling for the parchments to be rolled out from the offices at the back of the hall, moving towards the spot where he wanted them. Not watching where he was going, he walked right into the oversized and over-decorated ceremonial font of the old Yrati gods. Antronos winced as he watched the other man bite his lip and lift his foot in pain. The Chancellor leaned against the basin of the font, stared into it for a few minutes, then shoved it as if he wanted to push it off the dais.

The waist-deep stone basin rocked back towards the Chancellor, almost defiantly. A sound like a stream burbling came from it, and Sen Amphetam took a step back. Antronos gasped as his Desert sight showed him several bright spots of living aura emerge from the stone floor around the dais, moving in the same jerky fashion as the creatures he had seen in the back tunnel yesterday. *Will I be able to catch them later?*

The spots grew in intensity until they were painful to look at, then converged at the base of the font and trembled at the Chancellor's feet. After a moment, the auras disappeared under the basin, which suddenly overflowed with water that was caught in a trough around the bottom, and somehow recycled so that it didn't spill onto the stage. The Chancellor stared at the font for a few seconds, then shrugged his robe into a more comfortable position and turned his back on it. The bright auras of the creatures did not reappear, and did not seem to harm the Chancellor, so after a moment, Antronos allowed himself to look away.

The Chair of Hekka, another relic of the old religion, had been brought from the Royal House and was being hefted onto the dais by some of the university clerks and the Yrati. Hekka was the Goddess of Sight, and therefore symbolically important in the search for knowledge. The great hewn Eye of Hekka was positioned within the wooden back of the chair such that anyone sitting there would have it pressing against the back of the neck. Antronos' worry doubled when he saw the look on the Chancellor's face. All of these mystical symbols would probably drain Sen Amphetam's patience to the point where he would not hesitate to make a scene when Antronos attempted to get his degree.

"Sen Amphetam?" The administrative secretary was tugging at the Chancellor's elbow.

"Yes, what is it?"

"The Lady Alain is here, Sen."

"'Lady' might be an exagger—" The Chancellor cut himself off as he turned around and ended up face to face with the head of the largest merchant house in Temlocht, who was grinning at his half-formed insult. Antronos caught his breath and stared at her, wondering how much trouble this unexpected presence was going to bring. The last two times he had worked at the docks for the House of Dra and their shipping partner, the House of Dan, they had cheated him on his pay. Alaindra had casually suggested to her oarsmen that no one would arrest them for pummelling him if he didn't stop complaining. However, she hadn't even looked up from her ledgers then. Perhaps she would not remember him now. The elegant diamond- and sapphire-studded linens she wore matched the pale hue of her skin and contrasted perfectly with her curling, dark hair. She daintily offered her fingertips to the Chancellor, who paused for a few seconds before lifting his own hand, although Antronos thought he did so reluctantly.

"Madam Dra," said the Chancellor. "Thank you for coming and funding the ceremonies. I hope you will excuse my obvious frustration at having to ask for your help."

There was a hard glint in the wide, violet eyes as Alaindra gave a faint knowing smile, and demurely dropped her dark lashes over satin-dusted cheeks.

"Of course, Sen Amphetam. Nobody enjoys financial difficulties. I'm only glad I could assist. I wish you had taken me up on some of my other offers."

"Oh, I think you've done enough, Lady." The Chancellor smiled tightly and moved away without greeting the head of the House of Dan. On that point, Antronos could not fault the Chancellor.

The hall had filled with excited, chattering graduands but now a hush fell over them as the great stone doors to the right of the dais were scraped open to the sound of a bass drum, making Antronos lean forward eagerly. *Were any more of the spasmodic ground creatures going to come through?* His interest faded as the Chancellor heaved a sigh and resignedly waved his hand, dropping into a deep genuflection as he did so. Whoever was coming had to be visible by natural sight, and probably completely human.

A few strange-looking people emerged from the doorway, remarkable only because they seemed insane in their clothing choice and the amount of powder they wore on their faces. Their postures and apparent need to fan themselves seemed completely artificial to Antronos. A few armoured soldiers followed, scanning the crowd and taking up positions around the dais. These looked genuine, and the one closest to him didn't miss his presence. She gave Antronos a hard stare, but said nothing. He closed his eyes and muttered a prayer just the same.

Everyone in the hall suddenly stood up, the echoes from their movement reverberating through the cavern like thunder. Antronos peered through the stone doors fearfully. After a moment, a very tall, pale, sick-looking man came through, reluctant in his movements. He wore a blue patterned gown with gold embroidered tippet sleeves. His long, dark hair looked rather unkempt, and he didn't seem to know where he was going. He got tangled up in his sleeves, and had to be hauled onto the dais by some of the preceding retinue and escorted to the Chair of Hekka. It took a few moments for Antronos to realize that he was looking at the High Prince: My Lord Jait, Purveyor of Wisdom, Bringer of Justice and Omniscient Consort to the Head of the Temlochti State. The High Prince hiccupped, fumbled for the chair arm, and had trouble sitting down. Jait looked like he was in pain, either mental or physical, Antronos couldn't decide which. He searched through Jait's entourage, looking for the Royal Physician. Shouldn't somebody be showing more concern for the High Prince, or forbidding his presence when he was obviously not doing well?

"Stand aside!" Someone had come through the side door and poked Antronos in the back, making him jump. "I am the Royal Treasurer. Let me through!"

Antronos looked down into the face of a small man, with huge yellow eyes and a very noticeable underbite, who was holding a tray of ledgers and several pots of coloured ink. Antronos quickly lowered his own eyes and bowed politely.

"Forgive me, sir," he said, and stepped out of the way, keeping the pillar between himself and the other graduands as much as he could. The Treasurer bustled past him and forced his way through the courtiers on the stage to offer the tray to Lord Jait. The High Prince belched and pushed dark hair out of his face with one unsteady hand, then shoved aside the Treasurer with the other. The small man managed to retain his grip on the ink and parchment he had been trying to present for Jait's signature, deftly raising it over the High Prince's arm at the second swipe. He wiggled his underbite at Jait and breathed heavily for a few seconds before discreetly forging the signature and pretending to thank the High Prince.

"The Royal Award in Science, Sen Amphetam," Antronos heard him mutter as he handed the certificate to the Chancellor. "I regret that there is only one this year, but it was the only way to keep the sum large enough to allow the financing of a complete research project."

The Chancellor sighed. "Yes, of course. Thank you, Guillian."

"As you can see, I had some difficulty obtaining the signature of My Lord Jait beforehand, and he has left the name of the recipient blank. It will have to be in your hand, as only the university can decide which of the two excellent intended recipients will be given the award."

"Actually we had hoped for three this year."

"Alas, and I had hoped for at least two. The resources cannot be found, I'm afraid."

"It will have to do, then."

The Chancellor pulled three parchments from the front of one of the document carts, thumbing through them with a frown on his face, as if unable to decide which one was most worthy. He suddenly slapped one parchment into the hands of his secretary, then carried the other two over to Alaindra. There was a quiet negotiation, in which Alaindra must have had the upper hand, as the Chancellor came away looking irritated, and Alaindra pleased. The two parchments were passed to the Dra secretaries, who began preparing a set of certificates. Antronos wondered how badly swindled the recipients of those awards would find themselves.

A group of Yrati priests had climbed onto the dais, and one of them bumped into the Chancellor from behind. He whirled around, looking furious, then rolled his eyes and stepped out of the way as another of the priests circled quite close to him, bent over at the waist, waving shrub branches and softly hooting something Antronos could not hear.

"There must always be balance!"

The sandy-haired Yrati that Antronos had collided with yesterday was now standing behind the ceremonial font, raising his arms to the graduands.

"The Earth will crumble when it leans. The water will flow to equilibrium. The air will move to fill a void. In all things, there must be balance, or balance will be made." The Yrati dipped some sort of pan into the font and raised some water over his head. Letting it splash back into the font, he intoned, "As long as there is balance, there will be life!"

Something was bobbing just past the surface of the water. Something red. Something alive. Antronos stood a little straighter, trying to see over the rim of the basin as he thought he recognized the pulsations of the aura. Were the movements rather jerky? The red object seemed to turn over in the water, started to look like a skull that leered at Antronos for a few seconds, then suddenly submerged and vanished. The Yrati merely nodded at the water as if it spoke to him.

"All ye who come here today, retain the balance of the Earth and the natural surroundings. Without dark, there is no light. Without silence, no sound. Without death, no life. Let each dipole end balance the other. Be at peace."

The priest bowed his head and lapsed into silence. The Chancellor, looking disgusted, stepped forward and conspicuously cleared his throat.

"All of you who are in the Medical Sciences, please stand and raise your hand," said the Chancellor. A section of the graduands rose.

"You are the healers of our State. I ask you to pledge yourselves to the service of My Lord Jait, and promise your teachers, the university, that you will undertake your solemn duty to help those who need you, and to do no harm."

The graduands shouted the oath in unison. For the first time, the Chancellor smiled, finally looking relaxed and genuinely pleased. Antronos didn't know if that was a good sign or a bad one. The Chancellor reached over to the document cart that had been trundled to his side and picked up the certificates that Alaindra's scribes had filled out. He called out the names and beamed at the two new medical scientists who stepped up onto the dais, smiling and elated, reaching to shake his hand and thank him profusely. He then picked up the document the Royal Treasurer had given him and hesitated.

"There's no family name here," he murmured to his secretary. "Is this correct? I don't want to offend someone."

"Yes, sir. This boy doesn't belong to any clan. Haven't you heard of him? He's quite the pariah."

The Chancellor looked at his secretary with an incredulous expression.

"No clan?" He flipped through the pages in his hand. "But it says here that he's also won the Gold Medal in Science. *And* the Creative Achievement Award. That's difficult to do without family support."

"I know, sir. I could make no mistakes with this one. He's the one who redesigned all the microscopes and modified our drug extraction techniques to make them three times as efficient. He's put us ahead about ten years."

Microscopes? thought Antronos. He suddenly couldn't breathe.

"I see. So just the one name, then?"

"Yes, sir."

The Chancellor turned back to the assembly and cleared his throat. The delay had started up some speculative discussion which was quickly hushed.

"This is the winner of the Royal Award in Science, special recipient of My Lord Jait's approval. This is the winner of the Gold Medal in Science, and the Creative Achievement Award.

"Antronos," called the Chancellor. "Come receive your degree. We hereby give you the right to practise medicine and bear the title 'Sen.'"

Caught between the urge to run out the door or just hide, Antronos felt dazed as he finally decided to move towards the dais stairs. The Chancellor looked around the dim hall expectantly, then took a step back, the expression of horror on his face growing as Antronos moved forward into the light. He imagined how he must seem as he towered over the Chancellor and pushed his hood back, progressively revealing his purple eyes, angular features and long, frizzy, yellow hair. He selfconsciously tugged the edge of his robe over the scales at the base of his neck.

Perhaps this was a mistake. Humiliating the Chancellor like this would probably ensure no Sen would ever give him a research position. The Chancellor pulled his mouth shut and forced a smile.

Antronos steepled his fingers and bowed to the Chancellor, who speechlessly handed over the parchment and accompanying awards. *Well, at least I'm holding my degree*, thought Antronos, while he waited for the command that he be arrested. *Itya, this is for you.*

"Congratulations, Sen Antronos!" cried the Chancellor. "Never in all my years as administrator of this university have I come across a graduate with such potential. The entire academic community will benefit from your contributions to microscopy and drug extraction. Well done."

"You honour me, Sen Amphetam," Antronos replied, startled.

The Chancellor shook a finger at him while turning to address the people around him. "You see this boy here? Here's a prime example of what I've been fighting for all week! You've chosen *real* science, haven't you, Antronos? You're not out in the Desert practising blood rituals, are you?"

"No, Sen!" *Earth, this is worse than refusal!* Antronos thought his face was going to burn off at any second.

"You see?" the Chancellor demanded. "This is a good step towards the changes we need to make. What will you do now, Antronos? Will you start a clinical practice? Can I offer you a professorship?"

Antronos swallowed hard, and took a second to force control over his wobbly legs and dizzy mind that were threatening to make him collapse.

"No, Sen. I thank you sincerely, but I, uh, wish to pursue a graduate degree."

"Very good! Very good!" The Chancellor, mesmerized, shook Antronos' hand enthusiastically and didn't let go. "What project are you planning to undertake?"

"I intend to control death," said Antronos, then grimaced. He realized how arrogant that sounded as the words came out of his mouth, and that there was a huge difference between what it was safe to think, and what it was safe to say. He hadn't meant to speak so plainly. The Chancellor merely stared at him and blinked a few times. "Or at least delay it." Antronos shrugged apologetically.

The Chancellor guffawed, and after a moment said, "Good luck to you, Sen. I will be watching your career with great interest."

Control death. Antronos had hated death ever since it had abandoned him in the Desert seven years ago. Perhaps it was an allegorical comparison, but he intended to be different in every way possible from the tattered skeleton of a man who had taken his mother from him. Medicine had seemed the perfect way to exact revenge on death.

Still shaken, still waiting for the Chancellor to come after him and explain that his praise on the dais had just been for show and the parchments would now have to be returned, Antronos left the convocation hall, avoiding the other graduates who were collecting outside for the requisite party, feeling like they watched his every stride as he moved past them.

"Not joining us, Sen?"

Antronos looked up to see one of the other graduates blocking his way, feet placed in a wide stance, fluted wine glass in one hand. He was unsettled to realize that most of the others *were* staring at him.

"You don't say much, do you? Did I hear correctly that you had taken a professorship? That would make you my superior then, wouldn't it?"

Antronos licked his lips and shifted uneasily, trying to hide his certificates under his arm. "No, I didn't take it."

"Didn't take it! That doesn't make any sense! What's the matter? It didn't pay enough? Didn't leave enough time for your *research*?"

Someone muttered, "He has a forked tongue. Did you see it just now?"

Antronos' head snapped around, but he couldn't tell who had spoken. That was one defect he did *not* have. The small group that had edged up to him snickered and backed off in mock alarm.

"I have work to do. Get out of my way." Antronos shouldered his way through. He was taller than any of them, and although slender, his years of manual labour and defending himself on the docks had made him more than a match for a group of spongy academics. Someone grabbed his elbow from behind, and he barely recovered from a motion that would have raised his fist as he recognized the Chancellor smiling up at him.

"Come, please, Sen! You must at least let me show you off a little." The Chancellor pulled Antronos back into the centre of the party, obviously trying to dispel any bad feelings the other graduates might have stirred up and show himself as being unprejudiced. "We're so pleased to have new blood at the university. Really. Are you certain you won't reconsider the professorship?"

"I'm certain, Sen Amphetam. I'm not finished with my studies. It's hardly right that I should teach." *Or that anyone would respect a surface creature as a teacher.*

The Chancellor clucked his tongue. "Nonsense. None of us is ever done studying. Will you at least consider holding a professorship after your graduate degree? I can arrange that right now. Perhaps set you up in an office just for starters?"

Antronos finally smiled and shook his head. "You are determined to give me more than I deserve, Sen."

"I think I know raw talent when I see it." The Chancellor was looking around for someone to make introductions with. He caught Alaindra's eye, hesitated, then pushed towards her. Antronos did his best not to resist, thinking that the Chancellor did not want to seem foolish by having the other faculty completely ignore his efforts, and so was heading for the first receptive person. Alaindra immediately put on her most glamorous posture and smiled engagingly. *She couldn't possibly remember me.*

"Lady Alain, I would like to present Sen Antronos to you," said the Chancellor.

Alaindra held out her fingertips again, which Antronos automatically took and brushed with his lips. She sidled close to him, and pressed against his arm, her raven curls curling over the curves of her . . . Antronos pulled his eyes upward, seeing that she hadn't missed the flush that rose from his neck. Or the scales.

"What a shame that you didn't win one of *my* awards. The Chancellor wouldn't let me choose. I think you would have made a very interesting recipient. Perhaps I can tempt you with an offer to be my personal physician instead?"

Antronos took a step backwards and tried to mask his irritation. There was more than one way to make fun of the local freak, and he resented Alaindra acting like he was not to be taken seriously. No woman of her status would stoop to dallying with a former surface dweller, and she obviously didn't realize he knew what a cheat she was.

"I'm afraid I've already made other commitments, Madam."

Antronos noted the subtle change in her face, and his eyes picked up the sudden organization of her aura into pulsating straight lines, betraying the iron control behind the relaxed façade.

"I'm quite serious," she said. "And I can be very persuasive."

"Persuasion by cheap, bawdy promises and money," somebody muttered. The Chancellor must have thought this was an opportunity to rescue Antronos, since he shoved an arm between him and Alaindra, bodily twisting Antronos away from her.

"May I present Sen Antronos," said the Chancellor to the mutterer. "This is Sen Vernus," he said to Antronos. "He's one of the Professor Emeriti."

"I am honoured to meet you, Sen Vernus." Antronos made a slight bow to what looked like a hooded pile of green and black rags shuffling past. *The colours of Desert magic!* His interest flared as he tried to peer into the Emeritus' face without seeming rude. A wrinkled hand reached out to poke him in the arm. The aura surrounding it was strange: nebulous and diffuse, yet too strong to be inanimate.

"This is the surface boy? Well, maybe he should be a geologist. Or an archaeologist. Since he knows so much about digging through sand." Vernus turned away and continued shuffling. With an appalled look on his face, the Chancellor cast about for someone else.

"This is Sen Opalena," he said, grabbing a woman by the arm and dragging her forward. "She is Vernus' research fellow, and was the last recipient of the Royal Award in Science."

Antronos smiled and bowed again. Sulky grey eyes stared back at him. Silvery-blonde hair fell straight down, perfectly complimented by the silver-gold gown. Skin so pale it was almost white. If he hadn't known better, he would have thought she was from the surface, judging from her pale colouring and the angles of her face.

"I'm honoured," he said.

"I'm not." Opalena ripped her arm free and walked off. As she moved towards an exit, she passed by the Chair of Hekka, where My Lord Jait sat. He tried to reach under the panels of her dress. She irritably smacked his hand away and kept going. Antronos gawped in disbelief. Jait did nothing but stare after her for a few seconds before returning his interest to his drink. *Would it be rude to ask after the High Prince's health?* Antronos wondered. He was about to open his mouth when the Yrati woman who had been doused with Tibeau's water trick yesterday, came forward and knelt before Jait, gently pulling at the glass in his hand and offering him something else. *At least someone seems to care.*

"Uh . . ." The Chancellor was looking around again. The light surrounding him swirled in agitation and uncertainty.

"Thank you for your efforts, Sen Amphetam. I do appreciate your acceptance of me," said Antronos. "But I think most people are tired, as I am. I would really like to rest."

The Chancellor sighed and smiled apologetically. "Things will change," he said. "I do hope you will not take offence. We need new scholars and the more diverse their background, the more they have to offer to the university. I must insist that people see the necessity of change. Everyone suffers when one caste or another is excluded from an academic society. There are talents there that are left untapped because of these prejudices. Pushing you out just encourages you to return to belief in—well, that is, I didn't mean—" The Chancellor blushed.

"No offence taken. In fact, your friendship encourages me greatly."

That last statement saw the tension drain from the Chancellor's face, making his smile more apparent.

"I *will* find you an office," he said.